a
ir
f
r
v

g

l
h
t
a
a
"

t
c
p
t
c
to
th
de
Ya
whi
triu

So
salty
have
LA
p

JANUARY THAW

JANUARY THAW

BY
BELLAMY PARTRIDGE

WHITTLESEY HOUSE
MCGRAW-HILL BOOK COMPANY, INC.
New York   *London*

JANUARY THAW

Copyright, 1945, *by the* McGraw-Hill Book Company, Inc.

FOURTH PRINTING

PUBLISHED BY WHITTLESEY HOUSE
A division of the McGraw-Hill Book Company, Inc.
Printed in the United States of America

JANUARY THAW

ʟʟʟʟʟʟʟʟʟʟʟʟʟʟʟʟʟʟʟʟʟʟʟʟʟʟʟ

2070

✓✓

COMING up the hill from the creek, you don't see the old house all at once. You get a little bit at a time, so instead of being suddenly overwhelmed you succumb gradually. Most houses look smaller toward the top. This one doesn't. The second story looks larger than the first, and the third looks larger than the second. This is no illusion, for the old place is built with a double overhang.

The peculiar construction may have derived originally from the pre-Revolutionary blockhouse, and though in this instance the extension of the upper floors is not so arranged as to afford additional convenience in the matter of shooting hostile Indians, there were plenty of redskins in the surrounding woods during the time when the house was under construction.

In color the old house resembles the rich earth of the Connecticut countryside. A long time ago the shingled exterior was painted a dull red, but the redness is now gone, leaving a soft brown on the weathered wood that can be achieved only by years and years of sun and rain and sleet and wind, a bitter concoction identified and accepted by all good New Englanders as "this gol darn climate." The house is as much a part of Connecticut as the rocks which dot the hillsides. It is, indeed, more indigenous than the rocks, which are really outsiders, having come riding in on the ice sheet from someplace up north, whereas the old house belongs—it grew here.

Built for a tavern, it stands close by the roadside beneath the sprawling branches of a giant maple, planted no doubt to adorn the scene, but also to shelter travelers as they stepped in and out of the old stagecoaches stopping to change horses on the Southbury-Fairfield run, back in the days when Fairfield was a big onion center. Side by side, the house and the tree have grown old together. They have taken the buffetings of two full round centuries and considerably more.

To Herbert and Margie Gage, as they came laboring up the hill in the car of the real estate agent, the tree seemed as much a part of the house as the square stubby chimney squatting in the center of the roof. Even with half the windows broken, with frayed window-shades fluttering through the empty sash, with blinds dangling and doors sagging drunkenly on the hinges, there was an unquenchable dignity about the place that could not be disregarded.

"How lovely!" Margie exclaimed, leaning over to peer out the window. "What place is this?"

Watching the road from the corner of his eye and speaking from the corner of his mouth the agent replied, "Old Rockwood place. Used to be called Lazy Corners Tavern. It's a real old-timer."

"But aren't we going to stop?" she protested when she saw he was putting on more speed. "I want to go in and see it."

The agent reluctantly drew up. "You didn't tell me you're colonial-minded," he said. "I thought you wanted a place to live in."

"Oh, we do."

"But nobody can't live in this place—it's a ruin. Been vacant so long it's fallin' to pieces. The weather's got inside it, and when that happens it usually costs more than the house is worth to make it livable."

"But it's so beautiful," Margie said. "It has so much character. Why hasn't somebody bought it?"

"A body could buy it for very little money, but nobody will —the title ain't quiet."

Margie gave him a puzzled look. "Quiet?"

"'Tain't clear. Got a flaw in it."

[2]

"Oh!" she said. "I see what you mean. But I'd still like to go in. Do you suppose we can get in?"

The agent pursed his lips. "You can get in all right, but you'll prob'ly want to get right out again. Place was a clutter last time I was in there." He led the way through the weeds to the weather-beaten side door and gave it a push. Dust and cobwebs came showering down as the rickety door swung inward. But Margie did not even see the dust and cobwebs as she peered inside. Huge hand-hewn timbers caught her eye, magnificent uprights, stupendous summer beams, partially squared ceiling joists. Then she saw the fireplace, yawning and black, its massive crane crusted with soot and rust and festooned with cobwebs. Wide floor boards through the cracks of which she could look down into the cellar. Wrought-iron nails with heads as large as pennies. Hinges and latches that had been hammered out on the anvil of a local blacksmith. Doors and paneling corrugated with the marks of a hand plane.

"The place is full of furniture," Margie whispered to Herbert.

He nodded. "Such as it is."

She peered into a front room. "Look at that ghastly organ—and that horrible imitation spool bed. Do you think they go with the house?"

"I hope not."

She turned to the agent. "Does all this furniture go with the house?"

He shook his head. "That's some'pm I couldn't tell you."

"But what's it doing here if the place has been vacant so long?"

The agent indulged in a mirthless smile. "The former occupants left in a kind of a hurry," he said. "Guess they ain't had time to come back for it."

Margie looked all around. "This house doesn't look as if it had ever been tampered with or done over," she said.

The agent dodged a swaying cobweb. "I'm afraid not."

As the agent had said, the place was a clutter, but to Margie it was a thrilling and magnificent clutter. Some of the furniture was hideously recent, but other pieces seemed to her priceless, though broken and temporarily out of service. Not even the wallpaper dangling all the way from the ceiling to the floor could dampen her enthusiasm, for underneath she could see the bumpy homemade plaster reinforced with horsehair and put on with a wooden trowel. Wallpaper could be pulled down and replaced, but original plaster, cracked and sooty though it might be, could never be duplicated or successfully imitated. And one never could tell when, in pulling down old wallpaper, a secret cupboard or a bit of rare paneling was coming to light. She kept returning to the big fireplace as if drawn by a magnetic power.

"I suppose they did all their cooking here," she said.

The agent grunted. "Cooking, baking, bathing, washing—everything. But you can give me a good cookstove every time."

For a moment Margie thought she saw a little old woman in a dark corner of the fireplace bending over the hearth, but the apparition vanished almost immediately.

"They must have done some wonderful baking in that Dutch oven," Margie said. "I've heard there's nothing like it."

The agent peered inside. "It's big enough to roast an ox, but I'll take a little old kitchen stove every time. This central chimney construction is no good. Takes up half the floor space in the house. And they're top-heavy. Always get cracked. Look at the cracks in that one. And these open beams don't last; look how they're checked. Those checkmarks go halfway through. Must weaken them. See how these floors tilt. Know what that means?"

"That the house is very old?" Margie guessed.

He shook his head. "Means that the sills are shot. I'll bet there ain't a foot of good sill under the entire house."

Since there was no chance of making a sale here, the agent was anxious to be on his way, but Margie refused to be hurried. She had innumerable questions to ask, most of which the agent couldn't or wouldn't answer. About all they were able

[4]

to learn from him was that the place had been run as a tavern before George Washington was born, and that in the opinion of the agent the rooms were so laid out that they could never be well adapted to modern living. He glanced at his watch and said that they had better be getting along. But Margie appeared not to have heard this, for she took Herbert by the arm and led him upstairs for another look at the arrangement of the rooms.

The east front room with the little narrow door leading into the passage around the chimney would be the master's bedroom. And the west front room, the one with that lovely old blue on the walls, would be Richard's. They could put all his things in it and have it ready for him when he came home from the war, and in the meantime they could use it as a guest room. The other big room on the west side could be Barbara's. She was now old enough to have a room of her own. In fact, no girl in her late teens should have to share her room with a child of eight, especially a child like Sarah, who was noisy and disorderly and who had no sense whatever of either the privacy or the personal possessions of another. She would have separated the two children long ago had it not been for the limitations of the city apartment in which they lived, and the fact that Barbara spent so much of her time at the school. And anyway, the little room under the eaves was just made for Sarah.

That would take care of the members of the family, and the room off the big back hall would do for a maid—if they ever succeeded in getting one. Margie had just begun to plan where various pieces of bedroom furniture could be put when the agent called up from the bottom of the stairs to say that they really must be getting along if they were going to see any of the "available" places he had to show them. "After all," he said, "this place isn't really on the market. When people pay money for a property, they want a clear title."

The agent hung around the bottom of the stairs watching Margie as she came down. He thought her a mighty pretty woman and wanted to see how she'd make out with that steep flight of stairs. Stairs were a good test for a woman. Sort of showed her up for what she was. If a woman was young and full of ideas she'd come down with lots of spring and bounce, not afraid of takin' a tumble or bothered with any false modesty about makin' a show of herself to those who happened to be down below. He liked what he saw. She was nice in every way, he thought. Not the hollow-chested schoolgirl type—and still there wasn't any too much of her. The agent liked her dark hair which fluffed out under a tiny hat, and he liked her brown eyes. He had a theory that people with brown eyes were usually easy to get along with.

Margie took the steep flight with jaunty grace, not glancing at her feet to see where she was putting them, and, while she was well aware of the agent's scrutiny, she had no suspicion that he was assessing her age, and getting very close to the mark, which was not far from forty-two. He had already assessed Herbert. These blond fellows were hard to guess. You couldn't tell whether they had gray hair or not, especially when they wore it a little long, as Mr. Gage did. And not being especially interested in the age of this man, or any other, the agent had classified him roughly as being in the forties, a studious-lookin' fellow with big round glasses and almost exactly the same height as his wife, who must have been somewhere around five feet six.

"Another thing about these old houses," the agent said as they were reaching the bottom of the stairs, "is that you never can tell what you're running into. Costs more to restore an old one than it does to build a new one—and then look at what you've got when you get through. In the first place, they're impossible to heat. And then these old beams get rotted in places where you can't see 'em, and either the roof will spring a leak in a storm, or a floor will drop and dump you into the cellar."

All the time he was talking he was herding them over toward the door in the hope of getting them out of the house

[6]

and on the way to a property that he could really manipulate. They had almost reached the doorway when Margie stopped and faced him.

"But you haven't told us about the flaw," she said, "and we're dying of curiosity."

"Tell you all about it as we go along," the agent said, waving his hands as if to shoo them out of the door.

After he had slammed the door behind them he made quite a play of wiping the dust from his hands.

Herbert meanwhile was surveying the landscape. "Look, Margie," he said. "What a nice view there is from here."

"Nice enough," the agent hastily interposed, "but hardly what I'd call a commanding view." He glanced at his watch and quickened his pace. "We've got to be moving right along if we're goin' to see the elegant properties I want to show you good folks."

They were in the car and on their way when Margie again brought up the flaw in the title.

The agent nodded. "Sure," he said. "I'll tell you all about it. Guess I told you already it's the old Rockwood place."

"Oh, but you said it was called Lazy Corners," she reminded him.

"Uh-huh, that was the old name for it back in the days when it was a tavern. But most folks wouldn't know what you meant if you should call it that today. And the Power Company always calls it the Rockwood place."

"What's the Power Company got to do with it?" asked Herbert.

"They own it. Bought it off Rockwood, and folks around here think old Jonathan put some'pm over on them. All the Company wanted was the hunderd-odd acres of land he had, most of it spongy with springs and brooks and marshland. They had no use for anything but the water, but old Jonathan made 'em buy all or nothing. And that wasn't the worst of it—he got a clause in there reserving the life use of the homestead for himself and his wife. Sharp old feller when it come to makin' a deal."

Margie leaned forward in her seat. "But you haven't told us about the flaw."

The agent half turned. "That's it," he declared. "You put your finger right on it."

"I'm afraid I don't quite understand," she said.

"Why, the old folks have disappeared," the agent explained. "Don't nobody know where they've gone, or even if they're alive. Don't you see how that puts the Company on the spot? They can't fish and they can't cut bait. What they goin' to do?"

"That ought not to be too hard for a good detective agency," Herbert said with a smile.

The agent shook his head. "Well, there's two sides to that. If folks don't want to be found, they ain't always so easy to find. And supposin' the Company does follow 'em up and spends a lot of money gettin' 'em located. All the Company finds out is that one or both of 'em is still alive—so what? They've spent their money—and they've got nuthin' for it. They're right where they was before. See what I mean?"

"But won't they come back for their furniture?" Margie asked. "There are a few lovely old things in that house."

"Ain't come back yet, and it's been quite a while—four or five years—I don't remember exactly."

"But doesn't anybody know where they went or why they went?" Margie persisted.

The agent favored them with a wise look. "Well, there's some pretty good guesses. Of course, I don't claim to know the whole inside story, but I do know they had a wayward son. Matt, they called him. That boy was always in trouble from the time he was knee-high to a pint of cider. Malicious mischief mostly, when he was little at any rate. He couldn't see a window without wantin' to fling a stone through it. And when he was old enough to have a gun he was in trouble with the game warden all the time. He just couldn't take his game in season, and if a thing was against the law, that was the

[8]

one thing he wanted to do. Somehow or other he managed to keep the old folks in hot water most of the time, and he didn't improve much as he got older, neither. Nuthin' very criminal about him, you know, more the hell-raiser type. It was his goin's on that finally got under the skin of the old folks. They was respectable, God-fearing, God-serving folks. They was pillars of that little white church in the fork of the road, and it must have went against the grain for them to keep livin' down some of his exploits, and puttin' up the bail every little while to get him outa the clink.

"Matt was a great feller for guns. Most of the scrapes he got into had some'pm to do with shootin'. Get a few drinks under his belt and then he'd want to show folks what a wonderful shot he was. He'd shoot the hats off their heads and the cigars outa their mouths. Not a bad feller, you know. Had a lot of friends, but he was reckless. Well, the old folks finally got all they could stand and they sent him off out west someplace—Montana, I think it was. They thought he might get along all right out in that gun-slingin' country, but it turned out to be the worst thing they ever done. That boy hadn't been out there six months before they had him in jail on a serious charge. He was mixed up in a killin'.

"The news come in a telegram, and one of the neighbors fetched it to 'em on his way home. I don't know if it's so, but the way they tell the story, the old folks got right up outa bed in the middle of the night and started for Montana. They blamed themselves more than they did the boy; they said they shouldn't have sent him out to that gun-slingin' country.

"See that brick house on the top of the hill, where the windmill is? A big publisher lives there. And there's an artist lives just around the corner. Does covers for magazines. Professional people all around here. But to get back to our story—there'd been a big gun fight out there and the boy was in it. I don't know whether they claimed he'd actually killed anybody or not, but he was implicated and he had to stand trial. It was one of these big range feuds. There'd been a number of killin's, and the trials dragged on and on for a couple of years or so. Don't nobody seem to know exactly how long it was. But they got him off finally. Some say the old folks sent him to Australia, and some say they didn't have enough money left to send him nowheres after the lawyers got through with 'em. The only one to see 'em after his trial was the woman who run the roomin' house where the old folks stayed. She said the three of 'em come back there and had a long talk. The way she tells it, the old folks was tryin' to get the boy to go home with 'em, and he wouldn't do it. So they finally busted up. The boy went his way, and the old folks went their way. And that's the last time anybody ever heard of any one of 'em."

"And nobody knows what became of the old couple?" Margie asked.

The agent shook his head. "No, ma'am. The trail ended right there."

"But hasn't anybody tried to find them?"

"Plenty of people. The Power Company been tryin' for a long time, and there's others, but they never could find hide nor hair."

Margie sighed. "What a pity."

"Yes," said the agent, "but ain't that about the most perfect flaw you ever heard of?"

↑↑↑

THE next time Herbert and Margie went house hunting, they went in their own car. They had made up their minds that they did not care to be dragged around by some real estate agent to see a lot of places which had nothing to recommend them except the fact that they were for sale. This time they would go by themselves, and they would not even turn their heads to look at a house if it did not really interest them. They ran out from town on the Merritt Parkway and drifted off first to one side and then to the other, but somehow they could not seem to find anything to their liking. The houses were too far away from a main road, or perhaps they were too close to one. What they really wanted was a house on a little side road like the old Rockwood place—though they never called it that. To them it was always Lazy Corners. Anything larger than Lazy Corners seemed too large to them. And anything smaller than Lazy Corners seemed too small. Greenwich and Stamford were not far enough out. Guilford, even Stratford, was too far. Fairfield and Southport were too near the shore; Newtown and Redding Ridge not near enough. They stopped at one or two real estate agencies to inquire what was being asked for property in the neighborhood, but the prices staggered them.

"We couldn't buy the doghouse to most of the places we've been looking at," Herbert growled after they were again in the car.

Margie was not so easily discouraged. "Well, anyway, we've

seen the inside of the houses. I've always been curious to know what those big country places were like."

Herbert scowled. "But we've got to find something we can buy."

"The agent said Lazy Corners could be bought for a song, remember?"

"Well, why not? Title no good, and look at the condition it's in."

"Oh, it's not so bad. Just dirty and neglected, that's all."

Herbert shook his head. "That's not the half. We must have a place we can live in."

"We could do most of the work ourselves. I just know we could make that place livable in a very short time. Why don't we go and look at it again?"

"But what's the use?" Herbert argued. "We can't buy it."

"How do you know we can't? We have nothing but the word of that agent, and all he cared about was selling us a more expensive place. Anyway, I'd like to see it again. It can't be very far from here, can it?"

Herbert was not unwilling. He had a certain amount of curiosity to see if the condition was really as hopeless as he remembered. They had some trouble in finding the old house. But at last, after making inquiries a few times, they turned into the wooded road, crossed the bridge, and climbed the winding hill. They brought the car to a stop in the shade of the big maple tree, where they sat for a while without saying a word, but thoroughly enjoying every moment of the time they were sitting there.

"I wonder if you feel the way I do about this house," Margie said at last.

"I like it, if that's what you mean."

"I mean more than that. I have a feeling of belonging here."

"Sounds a little silly," Herbert said, "but I will admit I like the place. Shall we go in?"

They found everything inside just as they had left it. Dust, cobwebs, dirt, rubbish; but in spite of these minor blemishes the beauty and dignity of the old place came through quite unimpaired. They walked slowly around from room to room saying little, but taking their time about looking things over. They peered down into the musty cellar, and they poked their way up the crooked stairs into a stuffy attic filled with old trunks and broken furniture; the floor strewn with odd pieces of china, faded newspapers, a homemade hobbyhorse on a stick, and all the remnants and rubble of two centuries of living.

Margie's eyes were gleaming as they moved from one antique treasure to another—mostly damaged or broken; but Herbert's were twinkling humorously over the most magnificent collection of junk he had ever seen. Most useless of all, he thought, was the huge wire star hanging from one of the rafters, until Margie explained that it was a floral form that could be used either for a Christmas decoration or a funeral piece, by wrapping it with greenery or flowers.

Later, as they stood in one of the huge bedchambers, they heard a curious tapping sound that seemed to be coming from outside. Herbert ventured a guess that it was probably a woodpecker, but from the window they saw that it was a herd of cows belonging to a farmer down the road. An odd little man with short legs and a curious three-cornered head was striding along in front of them, standing very erect and stepping out smartly in a manner reminiscent of a drum major. He was not driving but leading them, and the cows were hurrying to keep up, their full bags swaying from side to side, their heads bobbing with a determination not to be left behind. Even after the cows had passed, the fragrance of fresh warm milk and masticated grass still hung in the air.

"Don't you think it would be fun to keep a cow?" asked Margie.

Herbert shook his head. "Not if I had to milk it. My folks used to keep one," he said in a tone of disillusionment. "Talk about the law being a jealous mistress—it isn't in it with a cow."

He turned and walked out of the room and down the stairs. A heavy plank door that they had not yet opened attracted his attention. It looked as if it must have been the original back door. He drew the iron bolt and kicked open the door, producing the usual shower of dust and cobwebs. Down one step he could see what had obviously been a summer kitchen in the ell on the back of the house. A rusted kitchen range stood at one end, a warped table at the other. Pails, buckets, and tubs littered the place, and at the left a half-open door swayed on bent and sagging hinges. Outside was a latticed well house slightly askew, beside which stood a rusted bucket and an equally rusted chain. A thicket of weeds surrounded the well stone, while a few paces off a neglected grapevine had escaped from a dilapidated arbor and climbed a tree. Now for the first time he saw the barns and outbuildings to the rear. The land sloped gently towards them and on to the woodland in the valley. Off to the west was a magnificent view of the heavily wooded hills and ridges beyond.

Herbert stepped outside for a better look. What a vista! How restful and quiet. Here was a place where he really could work. This old summer kitchen would have to come down. A suitable addition for comfortable living could go up in its place. A sheltered terrace could be put in the angle in the house. A bit of landscaping—grading and planting—would sweep away the dilapidation, and they'd have one of the sweetest places in the state of Connecticut. Of course all those improvements would have to wait. The important consideration at the moment was finding a place to live, and not only that, it must be a place they could afford to buy and own. There had to be something permanent about it—a sort of mental anchorage. Herbert did not want to leave the city. A man hates to be told that he must get out for his own good, especially if he has had a hard struggle to get in.

As far back as he could remember it had been his ambition to live in the city. This was no reflection on the little town in the Mohawk Valley where he was born. That was a good enough birthplace; but it wasn't the place where he wanted to live. Always he had been full of big ambitions. When the other boys were content with a day of hunting in the woods, he was planning a trip to the North Pole. When they were saving their money to buy a bicycle, he was talking expansively of the horseless carriage he was going to have when he grew up. And before he was even in high school he had made up his mind to go to one of the big universities, one so outstanding that a fellow would not have to keep his mouth shut when people began talking over their college days. "Mohawk University? Never heard of it. Where is it?" That was what he wanted to avoid.

The chances are that if some ingenious fellow had not happened to think of making mittens out of cotton duck Herbert would have gone to Harvard. At the time when he was ready to begin his college preparatory work his father, Charley Gage, was a fairly prosperous maker of leather mittens, with a small factory of his own. His mittens, made of sheepskin, were of a special design which had the index finger separate from the other three, thereby giving greater scope to a workman wearing them. This extra finger was a selling point, and for many years his father had found a ready market at fifty cents a pair for all he could make. Then suddenly the mitten market was flooded with cotton mittens which had not only the index finger but all four fingers separate, and which were priced at only ten cents. So the Gage mittens went out of business and Herbert went to Mohawk University.

It was while he was in Mohawk that he had met Margie. She had come on from Ypsilanti, Michigan, for "finishing" at the Misses Bridges Select School for Girls and Young Ladies. He had thought her, with her copious brown hair and her lustrous dark eyes, the prettiest girl in the entire "Annex," which was old Mohawk's nickname for the Misses Bridges Select School for Girls and Young Ladies. Neither of them had realized at the moment of meeting that anything of very great importance was in the making, and yet by the end of the year they had found themselves inextricably in love and engaged to be married.

Herbert had seen nothing incongruous about being engaged though he did not have a dollar in the world that he could call his own. No more had Margie. She had thought it beautiful and wonderful that he cared enough for her to go out and win a home for them in which they could live out their life together to the full. His ambition to become an author had, she told him, thrilled her and filled her with yearning to starve with him and do anything else in her power to help him on to success.

In June of 1920, Herbert in cap and gown had stepped forward on the rostrum to receive his diploma. He had caught a glimpse of Margie in the audience and was more stirred at the thought that she was watching him than at the fact that his student days were over. The following week he had begun work as a reporter on the Rome *Sentinel*.

He remembered with a smile that the first big news event after his induction into the publishing world was the Democratic National Convention in San Francisco where James Middleton Cox was nominated for president with a young New York lawyer named Franklin D. Roosevelt as a running mate. Not caring for politics, Herbert had been unable to generate much enthusiasm over the prospects of the candidates; he had been much more interested in seeing how his paper handled the news of the convention as it came in.

For a year he had pounded the pavements of Rome and the surrounding towns in quest of news. It had been good training for him, but he had not been getting ahead financially. He had been, in fact, just managing to pay his own way. Then he had heard of an impending resignation on a Utica paper and had gone over and applied for the job before the editor had learned that his paper was about to have a vacancy.

"Where do you find out about such things?" the editor had demanded gruffly.

Herbert chose to treat this as a compliment. "Oh, I get around," he said, "and I try to keep my ears open."

"Think it's wise to know about things ahead of your boss?"

"I don't think that would often be possible on this paper."

"Bill Barnes is a good newspaperman."

"That's why I want his job."

"Think you can hold it?"

"If I can't, you won't keep me."

Herbert started work for the Utica *Press* a week later. This time there was more headwork and less footwork. Here he began to do special articles as a sidelight on the news. He liked Utica, but ambition drove him on, and he began to angle for a job on the Syracuse *Herald*. The day he landed it, he wired Margie to begin work on her trousseau.

Margie had already begun. She had, in fact, finished it so far as such things can be finished in advance, and when Herbert asked her how soon she could be ready to get married she dazzled him with her speed. She was ready long before he could accumulate the money for a respectable honeymoon. So he pretended that he could not get any time off to take a honeymoon just then—and they were married on a shoestring, and began their housekeeping in a little apartment on Genessee Street.

As long as there were only the two of them they managed to get along and were very happy. But at the end of the year Richard came into the world, and they had another mouth to feed. A ten-dollar raise helped to ease the situation, but it was not many months before they became aware that the family was due to have another increase. The little blond girl—they named her Barbara—was only a month old when Herbert asked for a short leave.

It was, in a way, a move of desperation. If he was ever going to get to New York, he argued, he'd better go before the family became any larger. After a week of tramping around, he landed a job with one of the newspaper syndicates, several of which were starting at that time. He wired Margie to begin packing and caught the first train for home. The pay was not much better than he had been getting in Syracuse, but he felt that his career had gone a long step forward.

They found an apartment on Bank Street and began to eat their lunch instead of their dinner in the middle of the day. But in spite of all their economies and their good management, they were unable to keep their heads above water on their salary alone. Herbert tried hopefully to take up the slack by free-lancing, and occasionally he was able to sell a little piece to one of the papers or to a pulp magazine. But even this was not enough. Some other fairly steady income had to be found. He eventually found it in writing "sentiments" for a greeting-card concern. This was something that could be done whenever he could find a spare moment.

The fifty cents a line that he received spelled the difference between solvency and disaster. On a number of evenings he was able to turn out fifty salable lines. The only trouble was that such a pace as that could not be maintained. After a fifty-line evening he might not be able to do more than ten or twelve lines a day for the next week. He was like a well that could be pumped dry and had to have time to fill up again.

From greeting cards he went on to a well-paid job with an advertising company. This enabled him to get a little money in the bank, but the depression was just around the corner.

However, before the depression arrived Herbert had saved enough money to tempt him into quitting the advertising business and go into a publishing house at less pay. Though it was in a way an erratic move, it proved to be a sound one, for with the coming of the depression almost the first victim to fold up was the advertising firm for which he had been working. The publishing house cut salaries and moved him from the editorial to the city sales department, but long after the advertising experts were selling apples on the street corners Herbert was still going to his job every day.

The soles of his shoes wore thin, and the seat of his trousers became pretty shiny, but he still had a job. Not enough to live on, but still a job. Gradually the bank account was whittled away, the last few dollars being spent to pay for the arrival of little Sarah, who chose this unfortunate time to come into the world. That was when Herbert began writing "true confession" stories to make ends meet. Then quite unexpectedly he sold a story to *Harper's*.

With this acceptance by a member of the "quality group" Herbert thought that the invisible wall had been breached, that he was on his way. Now, he assured himself, the other magazines would begin storming his doors for copy. But this was not quite what happened, for, try as he would, he was unable to sell another short story for more than a year. Nor was this because of any lack of effort on his part. He was a prodigious worker, a steady producer, and he gave each story a fair trial, making it his regular practice not to shelf a story until it had been rejected at least ten times. But the steady stream of rejections was disheartening, and combined as it was with his demotion from the literary department to the commercial, it had set him to wondering whether he did after all have the stuff in him to make a successful writer. Never one to hold her tongue when she noticed things, Margie began asking him why he was not writing any more in the evening. Herbert said he was tired, that tramping the city all day and standing around for hours waiting for a buyer was too much for his feet.

Herbert could always remember very distinctly how Margie had picked up the notebook she always kept around, and made an entry. When he stole a look at it a little later he found that she had written:

Make Herbert more comfortable.

Just how she was going to make him any more comfortable did not appear, but the mere writing down of the memorandum seemed to have made her more cheerful. It was a start, he thought. The initial step had been taken. Other steps would undoubtedly follow. What these steps might be he had no idea.

But Herbert's career was not his only worry at the time. He was constantly faced with the inescapable fact that the children were growing up and becoming more expensive every day. Richard had passed his college boards and would be entering Columbia in the fall, and, though Barbara was going to help in the kindergarten at Ivy Hall and thus pay part of her way, Herbert realized that the outgo was going to take a sharp upward turn, whereas the income promised to remain the same. That they would go quite definitely into the red was inescapable unless something was done about it.

It never occurred to Herbert that Margie might herself get a job. She was not the job-getting kind. Anything that was done would have to be done through him. He was the bread-winner, and he must devise some way to win more bread. Any material increase or improvement in his output seemed impossible. And he kept telling Margie that his real problem was to find some way of selling the material he had already written. He did from time to time speak of the possibility of having a literary agent, though he always had to explain that the time was not yet. A writer, he said, was of no worth to a literary agent until he had begun to win his spurs. They had indeed been talking about this very subject one morning when the postman had arrived with an armful of returning manuscripts.

Margie looked at Herbert sympathetically, sighed, and then turned away. A moment later he saw her writing in her little notebook. She was holding her hand so he could not see what she was writing. It occurred to him that he had never seen her do that before, but he said nothing about it and put on his hat and started for the office. When he came home that night there was no answer to his ring at the doorbell, and he had to let himself in with his key. On reaching the apartment he found that Margie had gone out, taking little Sarah with her. He looked around for a note, but found nothing. He did, however, find Margie's notebook and was reminded of the rather furtive air with which he had seen her writing in it that morning. He turned to the last entry and read:

See about a literary agent.

It seemed incredible to him that she would attempt such a thing without consulting him. But that was before he had looked in his files and found half a dozen of his best stories missing. He was angrily pacing the floor when she came in, leading little Sarah by the hand. He knew from the animated expression on her face that he was too late. She readily admitted that she had taken the stories to Archie Pyne, one of the best of the younger literary agents, and told him eagerly that Archie had promised to read them and let her hear from him.

As Herbert looked back on that day he was still ashamed of the way he had acted. He had lost his temper completely. He had come ripping out with cuss words before the children, and had given Margie the most severe and most undeserved tongue-lashing of her entire life. He had accused her of everything he could think of except infidelity, and had brought on a crying spell which had lasted half the night. He was unmoved by her explanation that she was only trying to help, and he was still in a huff when he left the house in the morning after hardly speaking to her at the breakfast table.

When he heard her voice over the telephone shortly before noon, he hardened his heart and prepared to rebuff any overtures for peace. But she only wanted to tell him that Archie Pyne had called up and asked to have Herbert bring over everything he had ever written.

That was the day, Herbert reflected, that his career as a writing man had really begun.

Quite a little grist had gone to the mill since that day. From a young writer of promise he had developed into a story writer of some prominence, and already his work was falling off and he was worrying over the possibility that he had written himself out. Archie Pyne had laughed at his fears, but he had approved most heartily when Herbert had suggested moving to the country to get himself away from the many delightful distractions offered by city life.

"It's something that happens to the country-bred boy," Archie had said.

"But I was a town boy."

"Small town or farm, it's all the same thing. There's something about the grass roots that does not thrive in the city. I've seen it over and over again. You don't have to go far—just far enough so you can no longer hear the voice of the city calling you away from your work."

"You mean a hundred miles or so?"

"Fifty is plenty. But there can't be any fooling about it— you've got to go with the intention of staying. It's the mental anchorage that's important."

Herbert wondered what Archie Pyne would think of the old house—whether he would consider it a sufficient mental anchorage. He turned from his reveries and looked at the dark bulk of it towering above him. Surely it was large enough to be almost any kind of an anchorage. And it was old enough to command the respect of all and sundry. There was, however, one thing about it that bothered him. He wondered if it was far enough away from New York. On leaving home he had set the speedometer, and, although they had not come by the most direct route, the recorded mileage ought to give him some idea. Picking his way through the weeds and tall grass, he went out to the car. After a little mental arithmetic he decided that the old house was between fifty and sixty miles out of town.

The distance, he thought, was just about right.

ʌʌʌ

LEANING on a fender of the car and looking aimlessly around, Herbert enjoyed a wonderful feeling of peace and serenity. After a while he walked slowly toward the back of the house to continue the tour of inspection he had interrupted when he went to consult the speedometer. He soon found himself in a tangle of orchard grass under a neglected apple tree. Hidden beneath a bower of mingled poison ivy and rambler roses stood a battered privy, the door slightly ajar. The magnitude of the door latch caught his eye, and he walked over to examine it, finding it to be a piece of expert hand hammering in the lily pad design, somewhat larger than the front door latch of the main house.

As he turned toward the house, he noticed a dead tree standing nearby. A long time dead, but still imposing. Not a shred of the bark remained, and all limbs smaller than a man's arm had rotted and been torn away by the winds. The trunk was pitted with the borings of woodpeckers, and near the top it was well ventilated with holes as large and as round as the bunghole of a barrel. From the topmost of these holes the head of a large brownish bird was protruding. Herbert tapped on the tree, and the bird flew away. When Herbert stepped back a few steps to look over this arboreal apartment house, he noticed a piece of old metal embedded in a crotch, where the scythe of some ancient reaper had been hung so long neglected that the wood had grown around the blade and buried it. As he peered at it in amazement, he could see below the first blade the remains of still another blade grown even more securely into the tough old applewood. Another blade—another generation. Here, he thought, was permanence enough to satisfy even the exacting Mr. Pyne.

To the east, beside an aged pear tree, lay a sprawling stone wall marking the property line, and beyond was an expanse of rolling pasture land nibbled short by the cows which lived down the way. Across the street to the south he could see a network of stone walls enclosing velvety meadows and pasture lots blotchy with boulders. The ground in this direction rose gradually to a ridge, the sky line of which was defined by a growth of young woodland.

Herbert strolled down the road to see what had become of the cows and followed a well-beaten path into the open door of a large farm barn. Here the cows were lined up in rows like the pickets of a fence, their patient heads framed by the stanchions. They rolled their gentle eyes and kept chewing. The milking machines were making quite a clatter, and farm hands were walking around the big barn carrying milk pails or rolling ten-gallon cans on the lower flange with single-handed expertness.

He tried without much success to talk to the little fellow he had seen driving the cows. About all he could get out of him was hello and good-by, with a smiling expanse of teeth in between. "Foreigner of some kind," he explained to Margie after he had returned to the old house. "But I'm sure he means well."

"I'm sure he does," Margie said. They were standing by the big fireplace, though they were not looking at it. They were looking at each other. She came over and put her hands on his shoulders. "Everything around here means well."

He took her in his arms and kissed her, and not at all casually. He meant it. The feeling came surging up out of him just as it used to when they were a couple of kids in that little apartment in Syracuse.

Her eyes were shining when he released her. "That's just what I meant," she said.

He was feeling a little puzzled and a little sheepish. He wondered what had come over him.

"It's being here that does it," she said as if in answer to his question.

"Do you suppose that's it?" He looked around at the dirt, the dust, the cobwebs, the confusion. "How could it?"

She shook her head slowly. "I don't know how it could, but it does. We've simply got to have this place."

This was ridiculous. He knew it was ridiculous. They couldn't have the place and that was all there was to it. "Tell you what we might do," he said. "We might go and have a talk with the town clerk. There must be one somewhere around here. He'll have the records, and we'll soon find out whether that realtor was telling us the truth."

They had little trouble in finding the town clerk's office, which was in the parlor of the farmhouse where he lived. The office sign was on the front door, and they had to ring the doorbell to get in. It was the town clerk's wife who opened the door, but she was making currant jelly and had no time for the official welcome usually given to those having business at the clerk's office. When people took the trouble to go there, something was usually afoot. Nobody was any better aware of this than the town clerk's wife, but after all a batch of currant jelly was something that would bear watching, especially in a year when currants were so scarce.

When Herbert asked if the clerk's office was open she gave him the official smile. "It's always open," she said, "so long as there's anybody home." At that moment a whiff of the jelly was wafted out of the open door. "Heavens, my jelly!" She shooed them into the parlor with a wave of her hand and disappeared. After she had taken the time to remove the kettle from the stove she came back, looking severely neat in her two-piece house dress. "If it's the records you want to see, they're in the safe." She indicated a large metal receptacle standing between the piano and her grandmother's mahogany lounge. "If you have business with my husband, I'll have to call him; he's out in the hayfield."

"It's the town clerk that we came to see," said Herbert, rising from the rocker in which he had seated himself.

"Don't get up. He won't be here for some time. He's got to walk in after I call him. I'll go ring the bell."

They sat and looked around after the clerk's wife had gone. A Boston rocker in perfect repair, two Hitchcock chairs with slightly worn rush bottoms; a copy of the *New England Homestead*, the *Farm Journal*, and a *Country Gentleman* or two on a marble-top table containing also a bottle of ink and a pen standing on a blotter. Brussels carpet on the floor, dimity curtains fresh and clean at each of the windows. Suddenly they heard the tolling of a bell, a fairly large bell that could have been heard a mile away.

"Some bell," said Herbert. "That ought to bring him."

"Some poise," said Margie in a whisper. "You wouldn't expect a farmer's wife to be like that."

Herbert smiled. "You forget that she's the official hostess of the township. They don't have such things as this out in Michigan, where you come from. There the land records are kept by the county, and sometimes a single county is as big as the whole state of Connecticut. Here it's a case of each town for itself, and unless I miss my guess this town clerk will know a lot of things that aren't down in the records."

The clerk's wife came back and said that her husband was on the way. She did not sit down, but stood in the doorway and chatted with them until she felt that she had put them at their ease. Then she excused herself to go on with her jelly. When the town clerk came in he stopped in the kitchen and washed his face. He was a tall broad-shouldered fellow in overalls. His hair was gray and he had a complexion which resembled a well-weathered shingle.

Herbert stood up and introduced himself and his wife. Then they all sat down and talked about the weather and the agricultural probabilities of the country until they became a little more accustomed to looking at one another. "Well," the town clerk said finally, "is there some'pm I can do for you folks?"

"That's what we came to see you about," Herbert replied. "My wife has taken quite a fancy to the old Rockwood place, and we thought we'd like to find out what you can tell us about it."

"I can tell you it's one of the oldest places around here," said the clerk. "Been through the house?"

"Twice!" It was Margie who answered.

"Somebody show it to you? Or did you stumble acrost it yourselves?"

"We happened to go through that road with a real estate man, and he took us inside. Perhaps you know him; his name is George Whiting."

The clerk smiled. "I know him all right, and if he told you the story you know as much about it as I do."

"He told us everything up to the point where the old folks disappeared," Herbert said.

The town clerk looked out of the window and whistled a little snatch of what might have been music. "Guess you got it all," he said. "That's right where the story ends."

"But doesn't anybody have any idea at all where they've gone?" asked Margie.

"Sure," said the clerk. "Prob'ly everybody in this town has got plenty ideas about it, and prob'ly all of 'em might be wrong, for nobody knows a darn thing about it. The Power Company must have spent a sight of money tryin' to find those old folks, and I've wasted quite a lot of postage stamps on it myself. I wrote to police chiefs and county clerks; I even wrote to some of the postmasters." He shook his head. "Never got a trace."

Herbert stood up and took a turn about the room. "But you said people had ideas. Could you tell me what some of them are?"

The clerk whistled to himself for a moment. "I can tell you what mine is. You never knew these old folks, so you don't understand how pious they were. Old Jon would drive a sharp bargain, but he never missed a meetin' at church for a good many years. Matilda was the organist."

"Why, that accounts for the old organ in the house," Margie put in. "We wondered about it."

"Yes," the town clerk nodded, "some folks thought she was quite a musician. Never cared much for organ music myself, but sometimes when I'd be goin' through that road at night I'd hear the old organ come pealin' out with one hymn or another. She certainly could make it talk. But what I started out to tell you was this. Matilda never missed a Sunday at the church organ for years and years. It wasn't until that boy of theirs began to grow up and get himself into one scrape after another that they both quit comin' to church."

"Because they were ashamed?" asked Margie. "You mean they couldn't face it?"

The clerk shook his head. "No, my notion is that it was the other way around. They thought it wasn't fair to the church for them to be takin' a hand in religious affairs when their family name was being dragged through the mud by their reckless offspring."

"That doesn't make very good sense, does it?" asked Herbert.

"Maybe not, but you asked me for my idea about the disappearance of the old folks, and that's my answer."

Herbert shook his head. "I'm afraid I don't understand."

"Well, now look," said the clerk. "If real pious folks will give up their church just because of a lot of reckless nonsense on the part of their son, ain't it reasonable to suppose they'd give up a lot more if he got himself into serious trouble and was charged with a homicide or some other atrocious crime?"

"Don't ask me," said Herbert with a smile. "Remember I'm a stranger in these parts."

The clerk smiled. "Everybody is entitled to his theory, and that's mine."

"Then you—you don't think they'll come back?" Margie asked hesitantly.

The clerk smiled and whistled softly to himself. "That's the kind of a question that makes horse races," he said.

At Herbert's request the clerk nudged one of the big record books out of the safe and laid it on the table. He ran through the index and opened the book to the proper page. "I know the title as well as I know my own doorstone," he said. "I made an abstract for the Power Company when they bought it. Found it clear as a bell. The only blemish is this life estate of old Jon and Matilda. There's the record of the instrument; you can read it for yourself."

Herbert bent over the volume and read the record all the way through. Margie came and looked over his shoulder. She wanted to see what a life estate looked like, and whether an "instrument" was different from any other kind of writing. The beginning looked interesting—"THIS INDENTURE, made the 17th day of May. . . ." It was written with many flourishes, about the party of the first part and the party of the second part, and all that tract or parcel of land. But after that she found it dull going. For a paragraph or two she skipped here and there, catching only enough to convince herself that there was little sense to it so far as she was concerned. Then she went back to her seat by the window and wrote a few lines in her little notebook.

Meanwhile the town clerk sat. It was something he had done a great deal of, and he did it well. He considered it part of his job to sit while people read or copied from the records. He could have been worrying about his hay, but he wasn't. The hay wasn't on his mind at all. If anything was on his mind it was a mite of curiosity about what Mrs. Gage could be writing in her little notebook. Occasionally he whistled softly to him-self, but for the most part he was quiet.

When Herbert had finished reading he stood up and stretched his legs. "So that's the way it is," he said to the clerk

The clerk nodded. "That's the way."

"And this life estate is all that stands in the way of our buying the place?"

"It's all that shows on the record, at any rate."

Herbert reached up with both hands and settled his glasses on the bridge of his nose. "How do you get rid of a blemish like this?"

"Well, there's two ways. You can buy the old folks off, or you can wait for 'em to die."

"Do you think they'd sell?"

The clerk whistled thoughtfully before he answered. "If they don't aim to come back they'd sell cheap. If they're dead —that would be cheaper still."

"But what if I couldn't find them?"

"Oh, the law would take care of that. After waitin' a certain length of time, six or eight years, I forget how long, they become legally dead."

Herbert shook his head. "Not dead enough to suit us, I'm afraid." He spoke a little sadly.

The clerk closed the big book and returned it to the safe. "I know how you feel about it," he said, "but just the same there's a nice little speculation there for some feller with nerve enough to take a gamble. The Company don't want that house. Never did want it. And now that they've got it they don't quite know what to do with it. They can't lease it, because it's already under lease. They're not willing to spend the money to repair it. It's prob'ly the only cheap colonial house in the county—and yet nobody wants to buy it."

"Do you know—how much they—want for it?" asked Margie, hesitantly.

"They want plenty, but all they been askin' is four thousand, and they wouldn't expect to get all of it in cash—prob'ly not more than half."

Herbert stood like a man looking on at a roulette table. "Just one great big beautiful gamble," he said.

"Is there anything we do that ain't a gamble?" asked the

clerk. "I'm takin' chances every time I plant a crop. Mebbe it won't come up. If it does it might get spoiled by a rainy spell just when it's ready to harvest. The way I look at it, everything in life's a gamble, more or less."

"Yes," said Herbert. "More or less."

W HEN Herbert left the town clerk's office, he had no idea of buying what looked to him very much like a pig in a poke. A man will toss in a chip now and then just to test his luck. He will cheerfully throw away a few dollars on a sweepstakes ticket so he can enjoy a momentary feeling of having a chance, a very long chance, on a very large prize. But no man wants to take a gamble when he is buying a home. At least, that is the way he put it to Margie as they were rolling through the Connecticut countryside on their way back to the city.

Margie did not say whether she agreed or not. The truth of the matter was that she did not pay very much attention to what Herbert was saying. She heard enough to know that in a general way it was a negation of her own attitude, and since it was a negation she could see no reason for listening to it, as her mind was already made up anyway. So while appearing to be listening she was busy with her own thoughts, and they were really very fascinating thoughts, for in her mind's eye she was going over the old house room by room, furnishing, decorating, restoring, and arranging. By some strange alchemy of imagination the dust, the dirt, and the cobwebs dissolved into thin air; rubbish vanished, broken-down chairs reduced the fractures of their arms and legs, sprouted new spindles, straightened their backs. Wallpaper which had long dangled from the ceilings or hung peeling from the walls miraculously resumed its proper place, some of it changing color, and much of it changing even its pattern during the transformation.

The rooms were pretty well settled in Margie's mind before they had reached the Hendrik Hudson Bridge, and she heard Herbert muttering, as he always did when they slowed up to pay the toll, that Mr. Hudson was an Englishman named Henry and not a Dutchman named Hendrik and that it was a pity the Bridge people could not find out about such things before they settled on a name.

Margie showed no indications of having received this same information from the same source at least half a hundred times. It had been her long-established practice not to spoil Herbert's pleasure in saying certain favorite things by reminding him that he had said them before. If he enjoyed saying them, why not let him? She would not permit herself to be bored by harmless repetition. She would not permit her ego to feel put upon or slighted or belittled. She knew what was coming, she let it come, and that was that. If Herbert found the audience reaction a little faint, he thought nothing of it. He said these things not because he expected an audience response but because these thoughts came to him with an impulse to be spoken.

When Herbert had said the same thing as they were going out of the city, she had made a little sound as of surprise and interest. But this time she omitted the sound, for her mind was quite definitely on something else. She was thinking of the children. Margie had ambitions to be a good mother. She believed she was a good mother. She thought she was an even better mother than Aunt Fannie, who had given a hand in bringing up most of the children in the entire family. Aunt Fannie was noted for her discipline, and once when Margie was having trouble in handling her own tiny flock and had gone to Aunt Fannie for help she was a little shocked at Aunt Fannie's admission, "Of course I never had any trouble with discipline; I never asked them to do anything they didn't want to." Margie was too modest to say so, but from that time on she always thought of herself as being a little better as a mother than the widely appreciated Aunt Fannie.

They were opposite the big clock on the western bank, the advertising wonder which blinked out night and day the inexorable passage of time minute by minute, when Margie laid her hand on Herbert's arm.

"The children will be terribly disappointed," she said.

Herbert kept his eyes front. The driver ahead was showing signs of turning off, and Herbert wanted to be ready to take advantage of the break before somebody beat him to it. "They won't have a thing on me." It sounded a little brusque, but he did not mean it that way.

"Richard's especially interested. He's had a lot to say about it."

"What does he say?"

"Oh, a lot of things." Margie's voice quavered. "He hates moving around from one apartment to another; he wants us to have a home for him to come back to."

"Well. . . ." Herbert signaled with his hand as he swung towards the exit ramp. "He hasn't gone yet."

"But he will. He passed the physical with flying colors, remember."

A strained look came over Herbert's face. "Why is it that war has to drag in the young, the hope of the future? Why can't it take the old and the useless and the broken-down? Why not begin by taking the bums and jailbirds and gangsters? Now that would be a way of getting rid of them that is economically sound. Why not let two armies containing the scum of creation fight it out between them?" He went on developing the idea for several blocks. Then suddenly Margie interrupted him.

"I've thought of something," she said. "Listen, I'll tell you what we can do—we can take the children out to see Lazy Corners."

"What good would that do?"

"We'll know whether they're going to like it, just in case."

"But what could we tell them?"

"Just that it's old, historical, fine example of early colonial homestead."

Herbert smiled. "I see what you mean, educational stuff."

It was as simple as that. They packed a lunch and made a picnic out of it. Never for a moment did they mean to give the children reason to believe that they had any intention of buying the place, or that it was even for sale. Margie tried her best to create the atmosphere of a visit to the zoo, but somehow she missed the spirit of fun and levity with which our furred and feathered friends are to be approached, and managed to endow the journey with some of the serious aspects of a visit to the tombs of the late departed illustrious or a pilgrimage to a sacred shrine.

"Just think, my dears," she said, "this house we are going to visit was already old when George Washington was born, and some of the timbers in it were growing trees, saplings of course, when the Pilgrims landed on Plymouth Rock."

"My teacher says that's all a fairy tale about the Pilgrims landing on Plymouth Rock," Sarah shouted back from her seat beside her father. "He says they couldn't; there wasn't room! And he knows what he's talking about."

"Was he there?" asked Barbara, smiling, though not enough to disrupt the lipstick she had just freshly applied.

Richard said nothing. He usually said nothing unless he had something to say. And as it happened, he had hardly been aware that they were saying anything, so absorbed was he in his contemplation of the countryside which he dearly loved. He was a personable lad, blond like his father, but half a head taller. And he was built like Margie's side of the family, with a straight flat back and shoulders so broad they needed no assistance from the tailor to give him the military bearing current at the time.

It was Barbara who finally claimed his attention. "I'm going to like this place," she said, half aside. "We've already passed two country clubs and a riding academy, and there are yacht clubs all up and down the shore of the Sound."

Richard smiled. He thought his sister very pretty, but he also thought her a bit frivolous and hoped that in time she would get over it. "I wouldn't give a hoot for all the clubs in the deck, but I hate the thought of leaving this part of the world."

Barbara suddenly leaned against his shoulder. "We aren't in it yet."

"We will be," Richard said, hardly moving his lips. "You don't think they're drafting us just for fun, do you?"

Margie warned them to be on the lookout as the car ran into the woods and started up the winding hill. "You'll see it just as we come out of the woods," she said, "and I don't want any of you to miss the first glimpse."

The children staged a well-organized whoop as the house came into sight. But they were impressed, and after they had emerged from the car before the front door they stood and looked, and for a time they said nothing. As usual Barbara was the first to come forth with a comment. "It's like visiting Mt. Vernon," she said, "only you don't have to pay anything to see it."

"How old it looks," said Sarah, her eyes big with wonder. "Did one of the very first families to come to America really live here?"

They were still laughing when Richard started for the door. "Let's have a look at the inside."

"You may have to kick the door a bit to get it open," said his father, "but it isn't locked."

The reactions of the two girls were all that could have been expected. Both were articulate and enthusiastic, and despite the discrepancy of some ten years in their ages they acted much alike, squealing and exclaiming and dancing from one discovery to another. Richard said nothing until his mother drew him aside and asked him privately how he liked it.

"I love it," he said slowly. "This is the place I'll think of while I'm gone." He turned and walked out in the yard, where he stood by himself looking around.

[36]

Herbert shook his head when Margie told him what Richard had said. "That's the trouble," he said irritably. "They all think we've bought it, and are springing it on them as a surprise."

Margie laughed a little nervously. "Well, I haven't the heart to tell them. Have you?"

A look of relief came over Herbert's face. "What's the use of spoiling their fun today? We can tell them later."

So they did not tell the children that day. They did not tell them the next. A week passed and they had not told them. Before long it was two weeks. Richard was called up, and still they had not had the courage to tell him. On the day of his induction he let his father go with him as far as the entrance to the Pennsylvania Station. Herbert had promised Richard not to go inside, and he kept his word. Richard had tried to be cheerful as they rolled along in the taxi, but his father knew it was an act. As they stood shaking hands outside the station, each one fighting to keep back the tears and trying without much success to think of the right thing to say, Richard suddenly found his voice.

"You and Mother have been keeping pretty still about the old house. I know you did it to spare my feelings, but you needn't have done that. I'll think of all of you being there and having the fun of fixing it up. I didn't know that owning our own home would be like this, but it—well, it gives me the feeling of having a definite place to come back to." He turned and strode into the station, walking fast with long determined strides.

The day after Richard went away, Herbert and Margie drove out to Connecticut and bought the old place. Herbert said it was the least they could do. He said it was just a little gamble anyway. Nothing at all compared with the gamble Richard was taking. Margie agreed, quite forgetting that her mind had been made up from the first moment she had laid eyes on the place.

By the time the transaction had been concluded, a steady rain had begun to fall, but this did not prevent Herbert and

Margie from driving out for a look at their new home. With the rain beating down, the house was pretty well saturated by the time they had reached it, and, instead of being thrilled by the sight of the first home they had ever owned, they found the place looking desolate and melancholy. Herbert said it reminded him of a homeless dog caught out in the rain with no place to go. Margie said nothing, but she was shaken. They stopped the car in front of the house, and there they sat for quite a long time. Then Herbert remembered that he had brought a new lock for the door, and he suggested that he might as well go in and put it on. Margie reminded him that it had gone for several years without being locked, but by the time she had finished speaking he was halfway out of the car, and he kept going. As he pushed open the door, a piece of broken glass was dislodged from it and fell on the floor with a crash.

Margie heard the crash and wondered what it was. A little later she heard him hammering, and that brought her scurrying in through the raindrops. They found the floor awash in nearly every room from the rain which was beating in through the broken windows or coming from leaks in the roof; but in spite of all the wetness Margie's spirits began to revive as soon as she was inside. And as Herbert was installing the lock she brought dry wood from the woodshed and built a small fire in the huge fireplace. From time to time Herbert came over to warm his cold-stiffened fingers, but it was quite obvious to Margie that he was still feeling pretty blue. He was in a hurry to leave as soon as he had finished with the lock, and threw water on the fire to put it out.

After they were in the car he leaned over and took a last look. "If you want to know what I think," he said, "we're two of the biggest damn fools on earth. What we need is a house to live in—and see what we've got!" Then he straightened up, started the motor, and went sloshing off down the hill spattering muddy water all the way back to the stone fences on either side.

However, as soon as the weather had cleared, he came out of his gloom, and before the week was over he had a carpenter at work repairing the doors and windows of the old house and patching the leaks in the roof. The carpenter was perfectly willing to do any kind of woodworking, but he refused to put in new glass, and Herbert went over to the dairy farm to ask if a glazier was to be found anywhere in the neighborhood. Nobody seemed to be around but Joe, the cowman, and by the time Joe had said, "Hello," and, "Nice day," he had practically exhausted his linguistic abilities and was waiting only for an opportunity to say, "Good-by." A less persistent man might have given up at this point, but Herbert was not one who surrendered easily. And in addition to his persistence Herbert had a theory that mere difference in language was not enough to prevent people from communicating with each other. He had long argued that a real desire for understanding could always find a way, and he welcomed the opportunity of putting his theory to a test.

"Want man—fix window," he said in a strangely guttural tone often associated with the supposed talk of the caveman.

Joe gave him a puzzled look, shook his head and said, "No v'steh."

"What I want is glazier—you versteh glazier?"

Again Joe shook his head, smiling regretfully. "No v'steh."

Herbert went over to the window. "Here, Joe, here's what I want." He had dropped the guttural tone and was speaking naturally and very earnestly. "I want a man to putty in the windows, like this. . . ." He ran his thumb around the puttied edge of a pane.

Joe threw back his head and laughed heartily, showing a great array of teeth. With Joe comprehension was always good for a laugh. "Me v'steh. Me get." He went out and started down the road.

Herbert, watching from the barn door, saw him disappear round the bend, but he had no idea where Joe was going or why. It might be business for the dairy farm, and it might be something else. Herbert did not know whether to wait there at the barn or to go home. After a little he heard someone coming and decided to stay and see who it was. It turned out to be one of the other men he had seen around the barn, a bearded fellow with thick shoulders and bowlegs. He nodded to Herbert and began peering up and down the rows of stanchions.

"Did you see Joe around here?" he asked in a slightly foreign accent.

"He was here," Herbert replied, "but he went off down the road. Didn't say where he was going."

"I know where he gone all right. Uncle Walter's."

Herbert smiled and shook his head. "I didn't know he had an uncle."

"Say, listen—not Joe's uncle—everybody's uncle. You don't know deaf man—lives on cross road?"

"I'm afraid not," Herbert replied.

The bearded man smiled. "You will," he said. "Good carpenter, good any work, but deaf as hell."

His prediction was not long in being fulfilled, for Herbert had hardly reached the old house before Joe appeared followed by a shaggy little man with thick glasses and gray hair. Nothing foreign about this man. A typical Yankee.

Joe introduced him with a motion of his thumb. "You see!" he said. "Him fix." His errand accomplished, Joe lay down on the ground under the big tree and waited to see what would happen.

Uncle Walter cupped a hand over his ear. "Did you want to see me?" He thrust the cupped ear so close to Herbert as to make the bristles in it plainly visible. "You'll hafta speak up; I'm a little hard of hearin'," he shouted.

Herbert raised his voice. "I'm looking for a glazier. Somebody to put in glass."

The deaf man blinked at him. "Glass? Did you say glass?"

"That's right, glass." Herbert stepped over to a window and indicated a broken pane.

[40]

Uncle Walter watched him, but said nothing. So Herbert indicated several other broken panes. "There's a lot of broken glass here. I don't believe there's a whole window in the house." He motioned with his hands to indicate one window after another.

"I can see 'em," said Uncle Walter irritably. "I ain't blind." He went over and picked a fragment of putty from a window sash. "Putty ain't goin' to stick to that old wood—not without you paint it fu'st and mebbe not then." He dropped the putty on the ground and drew from his inside pocket a flexible black speaking tube, the larger end of which he held out to Herbert.

"Who you doin' this for?" he shouted as if Herbert were the deaf one.

"It's for me." Herbert spoke slowly into the mouthpiece.

"You ain't workin' for old Jon, be you?"

Herbert shook his head. "Hardly."

Uncle Walter squinted at him quizzically. "You don't mean you're workin' for the Power Company?"

Again Herbert shook his head. "No, just for myself."

"Then you ain't heared nuthin' from old Jon?" Uncle Walter watched Herbert's face closely.

"Not a word." Herbert drew back, then bent over the mouthpiece again. "Have you?"

Uncle Walter slowly shook his head. "No, but I will. He'll be back. How do you come into this? You ain't a relative or some'pm?"

"No relative. I own the property. Bought it from the Power Company."

A derisive chuckle escaped from the deaf man. "Well, you might get title some day, but not until old Jon and his wife is dead and gone."

Herbert leaned over and spoke earnestly into the tube. "Do you really think he'll be back?"

"Certainly I do!"

"What makes you think so?"

"Well, sir, in the first place he belongs here; this is his home. And besides, where else has he got to go?"

"Some of the neighbors think he's dead."

"Dead?" Uncle Walter cackled with laughter, a toneless hollow-sounding laughter. "He ain't dead! Don't you never believe it!"

"Why do you say that? Do you actually know anything about it?" Herbert demanded.

"Certainly I know some'pm about it. I know he ain't that kind of a feller."

"What kind is he?"

"Well, sir," Uncle Walter shouted, "he's as rugged as they come; he'll live to be a hunderd!"

Herbert glanced around to be sure that Margie was nowhere within hearing distance. "And you think he'll be back, do you?" he asked uncomfortably.

"Think?" Uncle Walter bellowed. "I know he will. When he's ready to come, he'll come. Let me tell you some'pm about him. Once when he was cuttin' timber down to Ezra Miller's a tree fell on Jon and pinned him down. When Ezra found he couldn't move it he run to the barn to get a team and a log chain. But before he could get there with the team he met Jon comin' along on foot. He was limpin' a little, but he wasn't hurt much. Well, sir, when Ezra come up to him he says, Jon, he says, how'd you get loose? he says, and when Jon told him he chopped himself out with his ax Ezra wanted to know why he didn't wait for the horses. Old Jon kinda rubbed his side and he says, I couldn't do that, he says, 'cause I remembered we was havin' wheatcakes and maple sirup for supper, he says, and I didn't want to miss 'em. Oh, he'll be back all right."

Uncle Walter coiled up the tube and was thrusting it into his pocket. "Got to be goin' now—time to do my chores."

Herbert caught hold of the tube and reestablished the connection with Uncle Walter's ear. "Do you want the job or don't you?" he demanded.

Uncle Walter pulled away the tube angrily. "Wouldn't touch it!" he said and went off down the road.

Herbert had some difficulty in explaining to Margie who Uncle Walter was, but he finally managed to convey the idea that the old fellow was not only deaf, but was feeble-minded and had refused to put new glass in the windows because he thought the putty would not hold to the old and dried-out wood. And the upshot of the matter was that Herbert bought putty and glass and tackled the job himself. He spent days and days puttying in scores of the little six-by-eight panes; and though most of the glass he put in was ready to fall out before a year had passed, he did succeed in making the house rain-repellent in the meantime.

While Herbert was tightening up the house for the winter, Margie brought from Harlem some strong-armed help who scrubbed the place from cellar to attic, carrying out enough rubbish to make a smudge like a small city dump. The furniture in the place was found to be a good deal of a problem, but it was finally dismantled and carried off to storage either in the attic or the barns. And having cleared the house they could not resist the temptation of "settling" one of the bedrooms so that it could be used in a pinch. Of course after the room was in order they could not resist the further temptation to spend a night there just to see what it was like. They realized that they could not tell the children what they were up to without precipitating a riot. So they pretended that they were spending the night with friends in Westchester.

They stopped for dinner on the way and lingered so long over the meal that night had already fallen before they reached their new home. They had candles in one of the suitcases and had laid a fire in preparation for the big event on their last visit to the house. Herbert made quite a game out of stabbing around for the keyhole in the dark, and when Margie came over to help him find it he pinned down her arms and kissed her soundly. After that he quickly found the keyhole.

Herbert stepped inside and struck a match. Margie had the

candle ready and between them they lighted it. She carried it over to the narrow mantel and put it in a candlestick she had previously brought down from the attic. A second candle was lighted from the first and was placed in a bottle on the other end of the mantel. Meanwhile Herbert was starting the fire and, as the kindling began to catch, the details of the room gradually emerged from the darkness: hearthstone, walls, doors, windows.

For a time they stood before the fire warming their hands and looking around the room. Then they drew up a bench to sit on, and, though they found it none too comfortable, it was better than standing.

"We should have brought more candles," Herbert said.

But Margie shook her head. "It's better as it is. This is the way it must have been the first night they lighted the candles in this house, more than two hundred and forty years ago."

"I hope they had more than two."

"How happy they must have been to move into their new home."

"They'd have been even happier if they'd had enough light to see what it looked like."

"I don't think so. I think they were perfectly happy to be by their own fireside in their own home, just as we are." Herbert started to put his arms around her but she stopped him. "Just a moment, dear; I forgot something. It's in the brown suitcase."

"What is it?"

"Something I bought especially for tonight. It's a surprise! It's something very, very old."

"Very, very old?" He licked his lips. "Brown suitcase?" He lost no time in getting the bag, and as he set it on the bench beside her he thought he heard a clink from inside.

"It's a real antique," she said. "Probably as old as the house." She reached inside and drew out a quaintly framed hand-worked sampler containing the motto *God Bless Our Home*. "How do you like it?" she asked as she held it where the firelight could fall upon it.

"Very commendable," he said, "for a motto, but absolutely useless for anybody who wants to drink a toast. Shows what imagination will do; I thought I heard the darn thing clink."

"Here is what clinked," she said, and brought out a bottle of port. She had even remembered to bring glasses.

They drank their toasts and sat sipping their wine until the fire had burned low. Then, since the bench had proved to be an uncommonly comfortless seat, they decided to go to bed. They each took a candle and started along, Herbert in the lead. Their footsteps echoed strangely as they walked across the bare floors and toward the winding stairs which went up from a little hall just inside the front door.

Mellowed by the wine, Margie was thinking of the untold generations of children who had trudged unwillingly up those stairs to bed. She saw them with tapers and tallow dips, with wax candles and kerosene lamps, and it came to her that before long her own children would be climbing the narrow stairs by electric light. She did not stop to think that the first children to climb those stairs would have been septuagenarians by the time of the Revolutionary War. In her imagination the children of some eight generations went trooping up the crooked stairway together as if they belonged to one big happy family.

Herbert saw no children on the stairs. He was not thinking of children just then. He was thinking of two old people he had never seen and wondering if they would ever climb those stairs again. But he said nothing about this. No use in spoiling Margie's fun, for he couldn't remember that he had ever before seen her quite so happy. He had not realized that a home was going to mean so much to her.

They found the room cold. They found the bed cold, and for a long time they clung close together for warmth. Why they should have been whispering to each other with the entire house to themselves—with the exception of an occasional mouse that scurried overhead in the attic—they did not stop to think; but far into the night they lay there whispering happily of their future plans. Sleep was still far off for them when they heard a peculiar drumming sound, such a sound as neither of them had ever heard before. Herbert rose up on his elbow to listen; but he had hardly succeeded in getting his ear properly adjusted when the sound came to an end. The noise was more mystifying than disturbing and was noticeable only because of the deep silence out of which it had come to them. However, they were not yet through talking about it when their ears were suddenly assailed by another sound, one that was quickly recognized by both. It was the klop kloping of a horse's hoofs.

They laughed in each other's ears. "Probably a milkman just getting home from the daily grind," whispered Herbert.

"Or just starting out."

Suddenly Herbert rose up on his elbow again. "I know what that drumming noise was; it was the pounding of the horse's hoofs crossing the bridge at the bottom of the hill."

"Of course," said Margie sleepily. "And what a lovely noise it was."

The next thing they heard was Joe calling the cows in the dim light of the early morning.

"Cay—cay—cay! Koo—mong—koo—mong—!" It was not a command, it was an invitation. Joe's voice was low, it was resonant, and it was a little sad.

Herbert slipped out of bed and went over to the window to watch the procession led by Joe as it marched solemnly past. Margie remained in bed, her eyes closed, listening to the tapping of the hoofs on the roadway. She loved it, but not enough to get up and look at it. She preferred to imagine it.

↑↑

HERBERT GAGE sank into an easy chair by the antique pine table and reached for his pipe. It was the chair where he usually sat—if he could get there ahead of little Sarah, who seemed to take a perverse delight in curling up in that particular spot whenever she saw him heading for it. Margie took some little pride in seeing to it that the big crystal ash tray he liked was emptied and washed every day and kept on the table near by. She often spoke about it—too often for Herbert—and she also reminded him frequently that she never failed to put a fresh paper of matches there for him every day.

He glanced at the ash tray. There they were. He wouldn't have minded if she would forget once in a while. At least that would give him a chance to speak about it instead of always being spoken to. Margie came in from the dining room as he was putting the tobacco into his pipe. Just inside the door she stopped and ran her eyes around the room.

"How do you think we look?" she asked.

Herbert struck a match and puffed a few times before he answered, "I think we look all right."

"Just all right?" Margie sounded a little disappointed. "Personally I think we look magnificent, and I don't think you're very appreciative of all the work I've done to get ready for your friends."

"I appreciate it all right." Herbert aimed the burned match at the fireplace. "But I wish you wouldn't take the attitude that you're doing it all for me."

Margie smiled with reservations. "And who else could it be?"

"Yourself mostly. You don't mind showing the local literati that we have friends who are tops in the publishing world."

By this time Margie was looking the other way. "Did you notice what I've done with the old wooden butter bowl?" She paused with her head on one side surveying it. "Don't you love it?"

Herbert pulled on his pipe in silence as he looked at the ancient receptacle banked to overflowing with yellow blooms. Then he asked, "Where did you get all the daffodils—certainly not on our place?"

"Certainly not," she said. Daffodils were something they had discussed before. "They came from the florist's. He's almost giving them away. But don't you think it was an inspiration to get just that shade of yellow for a butter bowl?"

"Couldn't you find anything to put them in but that lopsided old chunk of wood?"

"That's just the point. Isn't it quaint?"

Herbert slowly shook his head. "Margie, you don't have to strain yourself to get quaintness in an old place like this. The room itself is quainter than anything you can do to it. It isn't like Ypsilanti, Michigan, you know."

Margie knew this was Herbert's way of teasing her, but she was still loyal to the place of her birth, and though she hadn't even seen the town in years she was always ready to fly to its defence. "Ypsilanti is all right," she said, "only please pronounce it correctly. How many times have I told you it's 'Ip,' not 'Yip'?"

Herbert smiled with satisfaction. And he was wondering, though he did not say it, if there was anybody so colonial-minded as a person from the Middle West whose interest in early Americana had been only recently acquired. As for himself, a native New Yorker whose antecedents had come from New England, furniture and all, he liked old things if they were nice, but he could not work up enthusiasm over rubbish just because it happened to be old.

"It isn't that I'm straining for quaintness," Margie said. "It's just that I want things in keeping."

"Look at that mantel," said Herbert, further pressing his point. "It might have been whittled out of an old fence board. And what does the Dutch oven amount to really but a black hole in the chimney with a rusty tin cover over it?"

"Yes," Margie said slowly, "that's so; but please remember that the tin cover wasn't even there until I found it in the attic and recognized what it was for. It's just as I said, I only want things in keeping."

"I guess that's right," Herbert murmured automatically, his mind wandering to other things.

"I'll tell you something else that would look well hanging there beside the fireplace," Margie said, "an old bed warmer. We must hunt one up." She sank slowly on the couch. "This is the first time I've sat down today."

Herbert heard the sound of her voice, but he was not paying attention. He was looking through into what had been the tap-room back in the pre-Revolutionary days when the place was operated as a tavern. He could see the uneven place in the wall where the old side entrance used to be, and, though it had been closed and plastered over for more than a century, it was the door through which the lusty pioneers of his imagination always entered when they wanted a mug of ale or a tot of rum. Lazy Corners—Herbert loved the name; it gave the old joint such a ribald flavor, such a bawdy background, such a tradition of good times, good fun, pleasurable goings on.

He thought of the old stagecoach clattering up in front and coming to a stop with sparks flashing from the pounding of the steel-shod hoofs on the flinty rocks of the roadway—the same rocks that were right there today. In his imagination he could see the foaming tankards shoved across the bar, the dancing in the big ballroom upstairs, now rebuilt into two bedrooms and bath with a spacious hallway. His fancy carried him to the dueling tree a short distance down the road, a giant sycamore, the stump of which, solid as a rock, still marked the spot where men had died for honor. He seemed to see once more the flash of steel, and his mind leaped to the crossed swords he had hung over the fireplace in the taproom—old ones bought from a dealer who was an expert on weapons and armor.

A question from Margie brought him back to the present.

"Do you suppose that such typical New Yorkers as the Livingstones will have any appreciation of these old colonial relics?"

"I don't know why not." With his left hand Herbert reached for a match, but found the folder empty—and in almost no time at all Margie was hovering over him.

"I put a fresh folder there only a little while ago," she said.

"You needn't move everything on the table." Herbert hated to be hovered over. "I'll find it if you'll just keep out of my way."

"There, what did I tell you!" She found it behind the jar of tobacco and held it out for him to take from her hand. She never could set anything down on the table for him to pick up at his own convenience. Always he must take it out of her hand even if both his own were occupied. He knew that it was just her way of calling attention to her personal service, but it annoyed him.

"You needn't have gotten up." He was a little ashamed of himself for being short with her. "I would have found it. But to get back to Philip and Katharine—they're civilized people, they won't be hard to entertain. Park Avenue puts on a lot of dog. They live like a motion picture because that's what people expect of them; but they're real human beings under the skin."

Now it was Margie who was not paying attention. "You still haven't told me what you think of the churn. Don't you think the dogwood looks lovely in it?" she asked sweetly.

Herbert blew out a cloud of smoke. "Dogwood looks lovely in anything; it even looks well on the tree."

Margie moved over to the door and stood looking out

[50]

through the little six-by-eight panes, across the driveway, over the stone wall and into the pasture beyond. "How Richard loved the dogwood," she said slowly.

A moment passed before Herbert replied. "Yes, he'll like the ones we planted. They're the only dogwoods anywhere near the house, and heaven knows it cost enough money to move them."

Margie turned from the door and came slowly towards him. "Then you think we'll be here to see those trees grow up? You don't think we made a mistake in buying this place?"

"Loomis does, as any lawyer would, but I don't. I'm not afraid to take a little gamble—for a good stake."

"You don't think we'll ever hear anything from those old people, do you?"

"No," said Herbert sharply. "I do wish you wouldn't keep asking that. Look at the money we've spent trying to find them."

Margie sighed. "I know, but sometimes it seems to me we took an awfully long chance."

"Oh, not so long. You forget how old they are."

"Just how old are they?"

"Loomis says they're both in their seventies, and they can't live forever."

The outer door flew open and Sarah, large for her years, came galloping in on all fours. She swung at an easy lope through the living room and into the library. By the sound of her hoofs they could trace her course across the library and front hall, through the taproom, and back into the living room where she reared, then stopped with a snort and a whinny.

Herbert looked at her with an expression of extreme severity. "Sarah!" It was a cry of protest, of irritation, of disappointment.

Her only reply was a haughty toss of her bobbed hair which she handled with a remarkable imitation of a mane, and Herbert began to understand why she had so willingly parted with the once cherished pigtails.

"Aren't you getting a little old for that kind of nonsense?"

As Sarah gave an impatient stamp of a forefoot and another toss of the mane, Margie remarked indulgently, "Daddy forgets that horses can't talk."

"Well, he doesn't forget that horses belong outdoors," Herbert said stoutly. "If you're going on with that horse routine you can take it outside."

Sarah rose reluctantly from four feet to two, and came over and leaned on the arm of her father's chair. "Daddy," she said in a wheedling tone, "when can I have a horse?"

"Not before you're eighteen," he answered with some positiveness.

Sarah received this ruling with an outraged cry. "Why, Daddy! You told me seventeen the last time I asked you."

"The market has gone up a point," he said. "And it's likely to keep right on going up so long as you run about on all fours. Turn around. What's this thing on the back of your dress?" He pointed at a piece of frayed rope dangling from her belt.

Sarah drew herself away with dignity. "That's my tail," she said.

Herbert was amused, and at the same time he was annoyed. For some time past this equine preoccupation of Sarah's had been bothering him. He wondered what it meant and why it had persisted with such pertinacity over so long a period of time. He had been tempted to have the child psychoanalyzed, but Margie had ridiculed the idea. She insisted that all imaginative children identified themselves with animals at one time or another. Not all of them, she admitted, carry on their little make-believe quite so openly; it was just that Sarah was the kind of child who did everything openly. Margie's honest opinion was that the cause was just as likely to come from vitamin deficiency as from falling down on a horseshoe when she was a baby. So the psychoanalysis had been sidetracked, and Sarah went right on being a horse. If she wasn't being one she was drawing one, or perhaps she was only teasing for one.

Herbert's eyes followed Sarah as she flounced away from

him after her admission of the tail. He had an idea she was going to be a little ashamed of herself, though he saw nothing in her walk to support such a supposition. Quite the contrary, indeed, for after she had gone about halfway across the room she dropped on all fours and swung into a canter with the ease of a well-gaited saddle horse. Her rump was a bit too high and her withers a bit too low, but she was giving a mighty good imitation of a horse—too good, in fact; so good it made him a little uncomfortable. He glanced quickly at Margie to see how she was taking the demonstration, and from the eager expression of her face he got the impression that she would herself have loved to be doing exactly the same thing at exactly that moment.

As Sarah went loping through the door and out of sight, Margie turned and came over to the davenport, where she perched on an arm and sat looking into the empty fireplace for a few moments before she said:

"I had a strange dream last night; it was about a horse. It was a big black horse, black as coal, but with pink nostrils. It was tied to the tree out in front." She paused, searched her memory for a moment, and then went on. "The funny part of it was that the tree was very much smaller than it is now. It couldn't have been much larger than a telegraph pole, for the reins were tied right around it, and of course nobody could tie reins around the tree as it is now." She paused again to search her memory. "I don't remember exactly what it was that happened to frighten it, but suddenly the horse reared and gave a frightful snort. For a moment it stood pawing the air, and then the bridle snapped, and the horse went thundering down the hill toward the bridge, striking fire from the road at every leap."

Herbert looked at Margie with a newly discovered interest. He had never seen her dramatic before. "What happened?" he asked.

Margie smiled self-consciously. "Well, nothing, really. I woke up."

But Herbert suspected that there was something more. "What do you mean by 'nothing really'?"

"It seems silly now." Margie gave a little laugh. "I shouldn't have mentioned it; but it didn't seem silly to me last night. To tell you the truth I was scared stiff."

"What were you scared about?" asked Herbert.

"The sound of that horse's hoofs. I could hear them long after I was wide awake!"

Herbert smiled. "What makes you think you were wide awake?"

"I don't think anything about it, I *know!* I was sitting bolt upright in bed trying to look out of the window."

"That proves that you were more asleep than awake," said Herbert, "for you can't see the road from your bed, even in broad daylight."

"I didn't need to see anything, but I could certainly hear those hoofbeats. They went down the hill as plainly and distinctly as anything you ever heard, and I sat there and listened to see if they would cross the bridge."

"Well, did they?"

"That's the funny part of it," said Margie. "They didn't."

"You mean they just died away in the distance?"

"I don't mean anything of the sort. They went thundering along full tilt until they had gone far enough to get to the bridge, and then suddenly they stopped short. I just didn't hear them any more."

Herbert burst out laughing. "And then you woke up?"

"Make a joke of it if you will," said Margie, "but I was as wide awake when that happened as you are right now."

"Only one thing to do." Margie knew from the expression of Herbert's face that he was now poking fun at her. "Go out in the kitchen and consult Mrs. Flint's dream book. If you dream of Apples, you'll climb a tree. Dream of Mail Box— you'll get a letter. Dream of a Horse—then what? Will you go for a journey, or just be led to water?"

[54]

"That reminds me. . . ." Margie started for the kitchen. "I must ask Mrs. Flint about the salad."

Herbert gave no sign that he knew this was just another way of saying that she was going out to look at that dream book. He stood up and walked over to the door which had recently been cut through to the terrace from the far end of the big living room. He recalled all the trouble he had run into getting this simple job done. He had already had an old door, and he had had the old hardware to go with it, but to find a carpenter who could build the door frame and a mason who could do the little plastering that was necessary and could set the stone step had taken him days and weeks of running around. Even yet he could bridle over the cocky independence of those two workmen; their take-it-or-leave-it attitude; their insistence that their time began when they left home and ended when they were delivered back there.

However, he forgot all that as he stood in the doorway and looked out over his fifteen acres of land. There was something about owning land, he reflected, something steadying. He recalled what Mr. Loomis, the lawyer, had told him about the legal fiction that the rights of a landowner extended downwards, in theory, to the center of the earth, and upwards to the outer rim of the universe, standing precariously on the imaginary point of an inverted pyramid, and ending in a place called infinity. He was wondering how many stars were floating around in the upper reaches of his property, when his eyes chanced to fall on the big farm barn standing on the margin of a field in which he had planted some small trees and was now calling "the orchard."

This building was a substantial structure designed for the accommodation of horses and cattle and for the storage of hay for their subsistence throughout the winter months when the pasturage was buried under a blanket of ice and snow. Like most of the colonial buildings, the barn was built without eaves, crowding its carrying capacity to the very edges of the roof, and like so many of the old New England barns, it had, for all its roofspread and sprawling size, very gracious proportions. The big double doors designed to admit a load of hay faced hospitably towards the house. Covered stalls for the horses were on the left, with a haymow above, but the rest of the barn rose all the way to the rooftree like the nave of a timbered cathedral.

The possibilities of this huge space had appealed to Margie, and she had had it cleared and cleaned and made over into a studio barn, where the children could entertain their friends, when they were old enough. She had done a good job of it, and after a suitable dancing floor had been laid and indirect lighting had been installed up among the beams and rafters, she had had fresh hay brought in and tacked securely to all the places where hay would naturally have been expected to cling. And not only that, but she had arranged to have a few forkfuls of fresh hay brought over from the farm across the way and tossed up in the mow above the horse stall to give the place the "new-mown" flavor which city guests always expected to find in a country barn.

And having completed the project, Margie could think of nothing to do with it except to have a gigantic "barnwarming" which would serve as an excuse for showing their friends the entire establishment.

In doing over the big hay barn, the one box stall with an open front had, with a bit of whimsy on Margie's part, been turned into a bar, and where old Dobbin had once masticated his oats and munched his hay now stood an array of thin-stemmed glasses flanked on either side by tall dark bottles and square light bottles with familiar brands, while hidden underneath was a chromium sink and a capacious refrigerator with an unfailing supply of ice cubes.

Margie had given Herbert a pair of fancy red arm elastics with suspenders to match, both embroidered with revolting little Venuses who were chubby or slim according to the amount of stretch exerted on the elastic. Herbert hung the atrocities on a nail at one side of the bar, and, while he did not object to shaking up a drink for a few guests, he never put on either the arm elastics or the suspenders, preferring to dispense his hospitality merely as a host entertaining his guests. So the job of barkeep naturally fell to the young men who came to see Barbara. And since her budding beauty seemed to possess great charm for the younger members of the armed forces there was never any dearth of candidates for the position.

As Herbert stood looking out over the terrace he could see one of these young warriors, the tall rangy-looking Husted boy she called Georgie. At the moment Georgie was standing in the doorway of the big barn, holding in his hand a tall glass which looked to Herbert as if it might contain a Scotch highball, a delicacy to which Mr. Husted seemed to have no particular aversion.

The young man was raising his glass as if pledging a toast, doubtless, Herbert thought, to Barbara's eyebrow. Had Herbert been near enough to hear, he would have discovered that the youth was drowning his sorrow and wishing himself better luck next time, having just been rejected by the Air Corps— too much height for weight.

"How obnoxious," Barbara was saying. "Now you'll never fly—until you become an angel; and it is such a stunning uniform."

"That reminds me," said George. "I'll have to do something about the uniform I ordered. Perhaps I can get the tailor to switch it to still another service."

"Why not make it the Marines this time?" Barbara suggested quickly. "Their uniform is simply out of this world."

"Got a better idea," George said hopefully. "You marry me, and I'll have the tailor switch it to a morning coat with long tails."

Barbara smiled gratefully. "Thank you, Georgie, I appreciate the honor. Please keep on asking me, but I really prefer the Marine uniform."

George wondered gloomily just what she meant by that.

[57]

Back in the doorway of the house Herbert felt a hand on his arm. He knew from the perfume that it was Margie's. "Hello, dear," he said without looking—they were forever saying hello to each other. "I don't quite understand it—the lad with Barbara is not in uniform. You don't suppose the war is over?"

Margie smiled. "Give him time. Did they finish arranging the bar?"

"Seems to be working all right," Herbert said.

"They were polishing the glasses when I left."

"I hope George doesn't polish off too many. I want his help tonight."

Margie nodded reassuringly. "You needn't worry about him. He never takes any more than he can handle." She waved a hand towards the barn. "Here they come now."

"What a gorgeous specimen that girl's getting to be," Herbert observed.

Margie smiled appreciatively. "Everybody says she looks exactly as I did at her age."

Herbert ran his eye over his wife's figure appraisingly. "Do you mean to tell me that your waist was ever as small as that? I can almost put my thumbs and fingers around Barbara's middle."

Margie lowered her eyes becomingly. "And what was it you used to put around my waist at her age?"

"The best part of my arm."

"That isn't what you used to tell me."

"But, Margie," he protested, "do you imagine for a moment that your stomach was ever as flat as Barbara's? She almost bends in."

"Of course she does; that's the style."

"What's style got to do with it?" muttered Herbert. "God gives you a stomach, and there you are."

"Not at all, my dear. At Barbara's age my stomach was as thin as hers; but the style at that time was to bend the other way."

"And yours bent—shall we say—out?"

Margie nodded. "I wanted to be stylish."

"That's exactly the way I remember it," said Herbert. "So I don't see what we are arguing about."

"Herbert!" Margie shook his arm to give emphasis to what she was saying. "Did you take care of the organ?"

"What organ?"

"You know what I mean—that hideous old thing upstairs."

"I don't know what's hideous about it. There used to be one of those in every well-arranged home."

"You promised me you'd get it into the hall closet. What would the Livingstones think if they should ever see that in our house?"

"They'd probably think we have a sound religious background."

Margie glowered at him. "You're not fooling me; you haven't touched it."

"You didn't expect me to move it alone, did you? The thing must weigh a ton."

Margie stepped out on the terrace and called to the young people who were meandering across the lawn at the snail's pace that only youth can achieve without trying. "Hurry up! I have another job for you!"

George stopped in his tracks. "What is it?"

She motioned impatiently. "There's no time to waste. Philip and Katharine may come rolling up at any moment, and we are none of us dressed."

George grinned. "What do you expect me to do about that?"

Margie motioned even more impatiently. "I want you to help Herbert move the organ before they arrive. It's right outside the door of their room."

George allowed that he was the Atlas of organ movers; and with the help of Herbert, advice from Margie, and a few bright remarks from Barbara, the ponderous walnut monstrosity was beginning to gravitate into the hall closet when the telephone rang. Barbara, who answered, reported that it was long distance calling for Herbert. If it had been a local call Herbert would have gone through with the job and let the caller wait. But long distance was not to be denied, and they tugged the organ back out of the doorway so Herbert could answer the call.

Herbert was a long time at the telephone. First the operator lost the New York trunkline, and before she had been able to restore the connection the party calling had stepped down the hall. By the time he had been located and brought back, some local installation had cut in and was trying to put through a call. Meanwhile Margie had dropped wearily into a chair and Barbara was taking George back into the hallway to show him the curious passage around the big chimney.

Access was through a little door wide enough to admit a suitcase but not a trunk, and as George peered in he could see nothing but a wall of rough masonry and his own shadow. However, he proposed exploring it, and Barbara, though she had been through it hundreds of times and often used it as a short cut, was not unwilling. She knew from experience that as they went inside the little door would swing shut, but she was curious to know what George would do in the total dark-ness—at least she thought at the time that it was curiosity. They squeezed through the little doorway with George in the lead and Barbara not far behind. The door swung shut—and there they were.

"Are you there?" asked George.

"Close behind you."

"Let me feel where you are." He put back his hand. Some-how in the dark he missed her, and when he began to feel around to find out where she was he discovered to his delight, as well as his consternation, that he had her in his arms.

It was a tight squeeze. The narrow passage was pressing them close together. A wisp of hair touched his cheek. Then he could feel her breath on his face. It was warm and sweet and coming rather fast. By lowering his head just a little he could reach her lips with his. He lowered it. Their lips met, but only for a moment.

She quickly turned her head away. "Aren't you taking an unfair advantage?" she demanded, but in a whisper.

"What's unfair about it?"

"There isn't room enough for me to slap your face."

"But why would you want to do that?"

"I'm supposed to; you kissed me."

"Then you haven't changed your mind about the long tails?"

"Hardly," she said. "But listen, Father's through telephoning; I just heard him hang up." She reached back with her hand and pushed open the door. "We must hurry; Father's bellowing for us."

George and Herbert had returned to the task of moving the organ and were balancing the cumbersome instrument in a precarious position in the doorway when Sarah came clattering up the stairs at an excited gallop.

"Mother!" she cried. "Oh, Mother!" She could hardly get out the words. "There's the most be-e-e-utiful horse coming up the hill!"

′′

THE democrat wagon creaked and rattled as it went slowly along the dirt road, and the old couple occupying the seat looked as if they might creak and rattle, too; but this was only because they had come a long way and were tired. Considering their years, they were both, as they said, pretty spry and full of ginger. The man sat hunched under a broad-brimmed hat that was obviously not of New England origin. This hat, together with the brand on the horse, was enough to give the impression that the caravan had come out of the west.

He was a tall man, though he did not look it as he sat slumping slightly forward, swaying easily with the motion of the vehicle. Slumping he may have been, but he was not missing anything. His gray eyes, looking very pale and washed out in contrast to the bronzed complexion, were sharp and watchful.

Suddenly he hauled up on the sagging reins, brandished them menacingly and brought them down with a slap on the well-toughened rump of the horse, accompanying the blow with a sharp warning that he'd better be gettin' along there. But the horse recognized this gesture as a bluff and treated it accordingly. He switched his tail, tossed his head, flicked his ears back and forth as if on the alert, but he did not go any faster than before.

At this point the woman intervened. "Don't force him," she said. "Shadrach's doin' all right."

"I ain't aimin' to force him." The man was always annoyed

by any advice as to his driving. "But I got to keep him awake, ain't I?"

At the sound of their voices the horse immediately relaxed. It was as if he understood that as soon as they began to argue, he would be forgotten. The fact was, however, that they did not argue much—nowhere near enough to suit the horse. People who have lived together for nearly half a century are usually through with arguing. Not so much because they realize the futility of it as that they each know the other's answers. And most certainly not, in the present instance, because of any desire to create the appearance of amiability.

Amiability for its own sake was something of which they sternly disapproved. Being by nature mirthless and a little grim, they regarded amiability as a weakness of character, and easy laughter as something that like as not would lead to deception and therefore sin.

They were nearly of an age, though they did not look it. The man was wizened; his hair was as gray as a badger. The woman was not wizened at all; she had hardly a wrinkle in her wide shiny face, and scarce a silver thread was to be found in the earthen-colored hair which she wore drawn primly back above her flat ears, and twisted into a tidy but unbeautiful knot on the back of her head. Topping all this was a practical hat of her own contrivance. She never sagged; she never slumped; she never slopped over. She had come as far as any of them, and she was tired, and yet she was sitting as bolt upright on the seat as the day they had set out on the journey many, many months before. The truth was that with her bad hip she was more comfortable sitting straight up. Seated, she had the appearance of being taller than the man, an illusion which quickly vanished when the two stood side by side, for the man came a full half-head above her.

"You needn't worry about Shadrach," he said after a long silence. "The nag's goin' to make it all right. It's that loose felly that's worryin' me."

"Is that loose again?"

The man nodded. "Can't you hear it rattlin'?"

Without moving her body she turned her head to look. "A-yuh—funny I didn't hear it before."

"Guess we'll have to drive in a brook and let it soak awhile."

She sighed. "I was hopin' we'd get through without any more of that."

Brooks being numerous along the wagon roads of the Connecticut countryside, they had no trouble finding a place to soak up the felly, but the man was impatient to be on his way.

"Hope that thing swells up in a hurry," he said. "We got no time to be settin' around in a brook."

"Quiet yourself, Jonathan," said the woman. "Frettin' won't fix it no faster."

"I know that, but we got to be movin' right along if we're goin' to get there before nightfall. Shadrach can't travel only so fast, you know."

"Now you just set awhile and enjoy yourself, Jonathan. We're back in Connecticut, and this is the first chance we've had to take a good look at it. All I needed was one glance to tell me it's still the prettiest state in the Union, if I do say so myself, who was born here."

Jonathan ran his eyes over the shaded dell in which they had stopped. Nowhere had he ever seen the flags at the edge of a brook so blue, the bloodroot so waxy, the dogwood so white, the trees so upstanding and distinguished-looking. "Guess you're right, Matilda," he said after a little, "and we ought to know what we're talkin' about, we been in enough of them other states. Look at that rock maple there. Ain't that a beauty? Remind you of anything?"

Matilda nodded. "Of course it does. Reminds me of the big tree in front of the house."

He straightened up and looked at her. "Matilda, do you suppose the tree is still there?"

"I don't know why not," she answered stoutly. "It had been right there for more'n a couple of centuries the last time I saw it."

[64]

"So it had, but I wouldn't know what to do if I should find that some'pm's happened to it. A lot of things could happen in five years, you know."

"A lot of things could happen in two hunderd years," said Matilda. "But they didn't. How is the felly comin'?"

Jonathan moved the horse a short distance ahead to bring the affected part of the wheel above the surface of the water. He looked it over and tried it with his hand. "Nope. 'Tain't ready yet. Got to go back under water."

When he had again immersed it, Matilda bowed her head and folded her hands in her lap. "Take off your hat," she said to Jonathan in an undertone such as she would have used at a funeral. "We're going to pray."

It so happened that Jonathan was in the act of consulting his watch. He had taken it from the pocket of his vest to which it was attached by a piece of an old porpoise-hide shoestring, and had opened the hunting case of the ancient silver time-piece. Having gone this far he did not propose to abandon the project, so even at the risk of keeping the Lord waiting he opened the watch and stole a quick look at the dial.

With the case open he could distinctly hear the ticking. He hadn't realized that it was so quiet there by the brook, and not wishing to have Matilda know what he was up to, he quickly closed the case, but did not snap it. He held the watch in one hand, and with the other he took off his wide-brimmed hat and laid it on his knees. For the next few moments the old couple sat there side by side composing themselves for a talk with God. Minnows in the brook rose to the surface and snapped at flies. Shadrach mouthed his bit and switched his tail. An irreverent robin tugged at an angleworm to wrench it from its home in the mud of the bank. Little patches of sunlight danced silently on the ripples. Then Matilda spoke. She began in a voice that, though nasal, was low and reverent. Matilda had little patience with the "thee" and "thou" school which she regarded as just so much "puttin' on." She talked with God as she would have talked with a next-door neighbor.

"Our Heavenly Father, you know all things, so you must know much better than I can tell you, that on this nice spring day, our hearts are full of gratitude. We're mighty glad to be back in Connecticut. I don't know why you ever let us go away from here, for trial and tribulation have followed us every step of the way. For five straight years I've been prayin' to you two or three times every day to bring us back to Connecticut, and at last you've heard my prayer and you've answered it, but you've certainly took your time.

"Now, Lord, I don't want you to get the idee that we don't appreciate all you've done for us, because we do. But what I want to tell you is that it ain't human to forget all we been through the minute we cross the state line into Connecticut. We thank you for bringin' us back to the home state, but we want to remind you that we got quite a little ways to go yet. We know we're goin' in the right direction because we keep seein' the Sound off there to the south. You needn't bother about guidin' us from here on; Jonathan knows the way without any help, but we're worried about that felly. If that gives way, we can't possibly make it before nightfall, and you know as well as we do that Connecticut is no state for campers. So I ask you in all earnestness to make that felly strong, press it down hard, make it fit, mold it, clamp it, hammer it with the anvil of your might. . . ."

At that moment Jonathan's hand gave a convulsive movement which shut the watch case with a snap. He had not intended to do it, and had not known that he was doing it. The first intimation that the thing had been done was when he heard the snap. Matilda brought her prayer to a speedy termination and turned on him.

"Do you think that is showing proper respect for the Lord?" she demanded. "Snappin' your watch on him?"

"Nuthin' disrespectful about it—just a accident."

"Do you expect me to believe that?"

"Whether you believe it or not is something I got no control over. I said it was a accident and it was, but I'd had plenty of reason for stoppin' you if I'd done it apurpose. If the Lord's any kind of a blacksmith he knows you didn't understand what you're talkin' about. You don't mold a felly, and you don't clamp it, and you certainly don't hammer it with no anvil of any kind. What we're settin' here in the water for is to make the wood of that felly swell so it will fit tight up under the iron tire. And if there's any more prayin' to do about blacksmithin', I wish you'd leave it to me."

Jonathan bent over and disengaged the reins from the whip-socket. "Get along there, Shadrach, we're startin' for home."

As the rickety wagon rolled out on the road Jonathan stopped and again examined the felly. He whacked it with his fist and kicked it with the toe of his boot. Then he took hold of the wheel with both hands and shook it.

"It's the best it's been in a couple of days," he said.

Matilda smiled complacently. Her praying was not so bad.

Jonathan swung back into the democrat and again took up the reins. "Come on, Shadrach," he said, "this time we're really starting for home."

Shadrach kept up a steady jog trot on the level stretches and the easy down grades, but the rest of the time he walked. What a plains horse might have been thinking of a country with so many ups and downs can only be conjectured. He must have approved of the long shady stretches, something he had never encountered in all his life on the plains; and he must have relished the lush grasses he munched during the noon hour and the cooling waters of the innumerable little streams they crossed from time to time.

As the day went on, Shadrach's spirits seemed to be rising. Finally he broke all precedent and started to trot without being urged. After he had done this a second time Jonathan spoke of it. He wondered if he and Matilda could have communicated to the horse some of the suppressed excitement that they could not help feeling.

With every mile they traveled their eagerness grew. A thousand miles from home, it had never occurred to them that they

[67]

would not find things exactly as they had left them, but after they were in the home county a strange feeling of uncertainty and apprehension began to settle upon them. Finally Matilda came out with it.

"I keep kinda wonderin' if everything's all right," she said.

"Why wouldn't it be?" Jonathan asked brusquely, as if he had not been thinking the same thing himself.

"Well, after all, we been away a long time, you remember."

"Uh-huh, so you told me once before today," Jonathan muttered. "And I heared you tellin' the Lord about it, too. Anything else a-frettin' you?"

"Yes, considerable. There's all my family things that we didn't have time to put away. Have you forgot about my risin' sun quilt that Aunt Emily pieced; and there's Mother's log cabin comfortable. I been worryin' about the blankets, too. What if the moths got in 'em, especially my old Quaker homespun from Buck Hills Falls? That was Aunt Annie's weddin' blanket, and if the moths have been worryin' it—well, I'll feel like dyin'."

"Tck-tck!" Jonathan chirped at Shadrach. "No amount of frettin' ever mended a hole in a blanket. 'Twon't be long now before we get there. Quit your stewin'."

"But there's one thing I can't help frettin' over," Matilda insisted. "Don't you think we oughta locked up the house when we come away?"

"No!" Jonathan declared with gruff positiveness. "Why should we? Never locked 'em when we was home. What's the diff'rence?"

"Somebody might come in."

"Who, for instance?"

"Some stranger."

"How many strangers come to the door when we was home?"

"Not many, I'll admit. But they might."

"Well, hold your stewin' till they do."

For the next few minutes there was no sound save the klop-

klop of Shadrach's hoofs and the clatter of the iron tires against the stones of the road.

"Don't seem like I remember much about this road," Matilda said uneasily. "You sure we been over it before?"

Jonathan ran his eye over the prospect spread out before them, the black shiny road, four giant maples standing in front of the crumbling ruins of what had once been a house.

"I have," he said. "More'n once."

"I suppose you recollect who used to live there?"

"Nope. From the looks of things there ain't nobody lived there in forty or fifty years. Takes them old hand-hewn houses a long time to die. There's a couple of 'em up on Rockhouse, been empty ever since I can remember and that's quite a while, but they're still standin'. Long as there's a roof over 'em, they can hold their own with the elements pretty good. But after the roof falls in they go fast; first thing to weaken is the stairway, then the floors, but those old wood-pegged frames can certainly take it. They'll stand there a long time."

"Jonathan," said Matilda in a hushed tone, "how was the roof on our place when we left?"

"Well . . ." Jonathan clucked to the horse, "as I recollect, it wasn't any too good. If we hadn't sold I'd prob'ly had it reshingled before this. But you don't exactly feel like shinglin' a house that belongs to somebody else. It's the owner's place to do that."

"Mebbe the Company's done it?" she suggested.

He slowly shook his head. "It ain't likely, not when it ain't down in the papers. I can't make 'em drive a nail if they don't want to."

"But wouldn't they want to keep their own property from fallin' to pieces?"

"Not if you ain't got it in writin'. When I spoke to 'em about it they turned me down. They said that so long's we stayed there we'd have to keep the place livable for ourselves."

Matilda turned on her husband indignantly. "Why, Jonathan, I didn't know you'd ever spoke to 'em about it."

"Well, I did. I told 'em the house hadn't been shingled in twenty-five years."

"Twenty-five? Is it as long as that?"

"Certainly is, and more, too. And while you're worryin' I'll tell you another thing to worry about, and that's the windows. There was a sight of broken glass around that place. On the back of the house there was a gunny sack or an old straw hat stuffed into just about every sash, and there was glass missin' from most of the other windows, too."

"But they was small panes," Matilda reminded him, trying to take an optimistic view.

"Small, but numerous. Just remember there's twenty-four of 'em in one of those twelve-over-twelve sashes. Try puttyin' one of 'em and you'll know what I'm talkin' about."

"But you told me you had mended a good many of 'em."

"I did mend some of 'em, but most of the glass was just held in with tacks. I never got around to puttyin'."

"Well, Jonathan," Matilda said sternly, "I won't thank you for that if all our things are spoiled."

Jonathan thought that over for a while before he said, "I don't reckon there's anything that would be hurt by a few drops of water."

"What about my spool bed? I been dreamin' about that bedstead for the last two or three nights. And I never could forget that feather bed. There ain't another one like it in the state of Connecticut, such goose feathers; I plucked every one of 'em myself. If there's any better sleepin' than that bed, well, I ain't never found it."

"Think it's better'n sleepin' in the back of a democrat wagon, do you?"

"I certainly do," said Matilda. "Once I'm in that spool bed, I'll never want to see another democrat wagon as long as I live."

"After all, Matilda, the wagon was better'n sleepin' on the ground."

Suddenly she reached out and caught him by the arm.

"Jonathan, my Estey organ—do you suppose anything has happened to that?"

Jonathan could feel her hand trembling on his arm, and he could see her mouth working with agitation. "Now, let's see," he said, "the Estey stood in the little room against the inside wall. No windows close by and no patches up above on the roof. As a matter of recollection, the best shinglin' on the house was right up over that room."

"I've missed my organ more than anything else. Sometimes I've wondered if the Lord ain't missed it, too. I used to sing him a lot of hymns when I had that organ right to hand."

"Yes, Matilda, you used to be a powerful singer."

"Used to? What do you mean by that?" Matilda spoke a little sharply.

"Just that we're both gettin' along in years, and I kinda expect your singin' voice ain't been improvin' with age. Some things don't, you know."

"We'll leave that up to the Lord," said Matilda.

The words had hardly been spoken when a yank on the reins by Jonathan brought Shadrach to a sudden and indignant stop.

"What happened?" asked Matilda, a look of puzzlement on her face. "What's the matter?"

Jonathan pointed down the road. "That tree, there in the fork of the road, don't you see it?"

"Of course I see it, but what of it?"

"Don't you know where you are?"

"No, do you?"

"Matilda, where's your brains? That's the Lyons Plains road. We're only a few miles from home. The old Redding road goes right over the top of the hill."

Shadrach tugged them up the hill, resting often. He walked along the ridge recovering his breath, and just as he had recovered it Jonathan started him down on the other side. Soon after reaching the bottom of the hill they entered the little patch of woods and came to the bridge. Until reaching the

[71]

bridge Matilda had not quite known where she was, though she was sure they were not far from home.

"Why, if that ain't our bridge!" she exclaimed. "We're on our own road."

"It's our road all right," said Jonathan, "and it's our bridge—and look at the guardrail. I complained about that before we went away, and the selectmen ain't done a dern thing about it. Well, I can tell 'em one thing, they'll hear from me at their next meetin'."

Shadrach's hoofs made a pleasant clumping sound as he crossed the bridge. It was a sound that aroused old familiar memories for Jonathan. He wondered how many times as he lay in bed in the stillness of the night he had heard the pounding of a horse's hoofs on the planking of that bridge. Matilda had no such memories; she was a better sleeper.

Jonathan felt his breathing quicken as they wound through the trees and approached the last turn of the road ahead. When they reached that turn they would be able to see the peak of the house above the trees, if the house was still there.

If it was still there? Why wouldn't it be there? The thought of fire, windstorm, and lightning passed quickly through Jonathan's mind. Fire—that was something the old houses couldn't withstand. Windstorm and lightning they could in all probability weather. But fire, that was enemy number one to those dried and seasoned timbers. Jonathan could feel himself sweating under the band of his broad-brimmed hat. He shoved it back and wiped away the moisture with his hand, telling himself that the house had been there a good many years without any considerable damage by the elements. Then suddenly he thought of something else, something that the elements would have nothing to do with. Perhaps the Company had decided that the old place had been abandoned and wasn't worth repairing and had torn it down.

Meanwhile Matilda was doing a bit of worrying about her belongings which passed before her eyes like a procession. But Shadrach, troubled by no rights of property and having a grade to climb, went right ahead and climbed it. Step by step the patient animal hauled the battered wagon nearer the top. As the peak of the weathered house top rose above the shrubbery like the prow of a stranded ship, Jonathan lifted from the seat, then caught himself and dropped back, but he could not entirely exclude from his voice a note of exaltation.

"It's there! Did you see it!"

"Certainly I saw it. Where'd you expect it was going to be?"

"And did you see the big tree? So they ain't cut it up into imitation mahogany table tops and dressers after all." His eyes were shining and his breath a little short.

A few paces farther on, the whole west side of the house came into view. "Look at it, Matilda," he said. "Ain't that a sight for sore eyes? And don't it remind you of the old Pilgrim Fathers, the way it stands up there so firm and reliable?"

"Don't remind me of no Pilgrim Father." Matilda did not hold with extravagant language. "But," she added, "it does remind me that I never had that kind of curtains in them side windows."

Jonathan was taken by surprise. "You didn't?"

"I certainly didn't, and if you want to know what I think, there's somebody livin' there."

It was then that Jonathan noticed that the old woodshed which had leaned wearily against the back of the big house had been swept away and its place taken by a modern wing that copied the style of the old house so faithfully that the new seemed to have grown out of the ribs of the old. The fence had been mended, the missing pickets replaced, the shutters on the house repaired and repainted. The grass was cut, and there were trees and flower beds that he couldn't seem to remember. Something fluttered out back—clothes on the line. There was no longer any doubt about it.

"It's so, I tell you," Matilda declared testily. "I saw a child go round the far corner of the house. Guess that settles it."

"Guess it does—but cracky! It's some'pm I didn't expect. Guess I thought of ever'thing else."

[73]

"But, Jonathan, what'll we do? Where'll we go?"

"We're goin' in. We got our rights."

"What if they won't let us in? What then?"

"We'll get in."

This sounded vaguely threatening, and Matilda laid a restraining hand on his arm. "Jonathan, we don't want no violence. I think we better go straight to the Company and find out what's what."

"Too late. They'll be shut up long before we could get there, and Shadrach never could make it anyway."

"But what about takin' counsel; there's Uncle Walter? 'Tain't fur to his place."

"If he was our own kin I'd go to him, but we got no claim on him, and we don't know how he's goin' to take things."

"He ain't no kin, but he was always our friend."

"There's times when friendship don't count for much, and this might be one of 'em."

"I'd trust Uncle Walter any time."

"No, Matilda, this time we got to go it alone."

ꜰꜰꜰ

I F HERBERT had not happened to squeeze his finger between the organ and the doorjamb he might have paid some attention to what Sarah was saying. But with that finger to think about, the horse was completely forgotten. Even Sarah was forgotten until Herbert began to stamp around the floor shaking his fingers and snorting words which, like cocktails, were supposed to be less harmful to adults than to children. Meanwhile Margie remembered the child and quickly herded her out of the room.

Barbara said hot water was best. But Margie disagreed with her; she had learned in her first-aid course that hot water would draw the blood to a bruise, increasing the pain; but that cold water would have just the opposite effect.

"I can show you in my book, if you'll wait while I get it."

"Never mind," said Barbara, "all I know is what I see in the movies; you remember how Raymond Massey comes rushing in as the young doctor and calls for hot water and plenty of it. I've seen it in slews of pictures and so have you. And just the other night Dr. Watson called for hot water in one of the Sherlock Holmes stories that was on the air."

"But wasn't that a pregnancy?" asked Margie.

"So what?" said Barbara. "Can you think of any better example of pain?"

At this point George came out of the closet. "The organ is properly concealed," he said. "Our mission is performed."

Herbert held up his hand. "Damn our mission!" he cried. "Look at that finger. I won't be able to type another word in a week, and I've got a dead line swooping down on me like a nose dive."

George nodded sagely. "And while Rome burns the women stand around and argue about which is better, hot water or cold."

This brought an immediate protest from Margie. "I only want to do the right thing; I don't want Herbert to be laid up with a bad finger."

"All right," said George, "then give him brandy, a good stiff jolt of it—and you might as well bring highballs for the rest of us."

With all the argument and confusion, nobody upstairs heard the knock on the living-room door. But Sarah, who on her expulsion from the organ-moving scene had gone downstairs and was now on her way to watch the horse go by, both heard and answered it. She could hardly believe her eyes when she saw the beautiful horse standing on the gravel driveway in her own yard. Indeed, she hardly noticed the rather seedy-looking old man who was blocking the doorway, otherwise than to resent the fact that he was obstructing her view.

"Anybody home, youngster?" he asked in a subdued voice.

"Sure, everybody. Is that your horse? I think he's beautiful."

"Who's here?"

"My father and mother and a lot of other people. What's his name?"

"Name's Shadrach. Where are they?"

"Who?"

"Your ma and pa and the rest of 'em."

"Oh! They're upstairs. Mind if I go out and pat him?"

"Not if you don't mind our comin' inside."

"Of course not; come right in. They'll be down in a minute. You sit anywhere you want to, and I'll go out and pat—what did you say his name was?"

The man turned and motioned to the woman on the seat. "Come on, Matilda, we been invited in." He bent over and picked up a large black satchel, banged and battered, and reinforced with a section of rubber blanket which had been tied around it with a piece of rope; but before he could manipulate it through the door Sarah had darted out and was raising a gingerly hand to pat the nose of the exhausted but not unfriendly Shadrach.

Matilda came down off the wagon with surprising agility for a woman of her size and age, snatched a smaller bag from the seat, and followed her husband into the house. Inside the door the old couple paused. The interior was so changed they could hardly recognize it. What had been three small rooms across the back of the house had now become one large room, and where patched and sagging plaster had hung precariously from the ceiling great oaken beams now lay exposed to view. Only the big fireplace remained the same, even to the smoke-stained masonry and the charred cracks in the brickwork.

"Don't look much the way it used to," he said.

She shook her head. "If it hadn't been for the fireplace I wouldn't knowed where we was." She cocked an ear and listened. "They're comin', Jonathan. What'll we do now?"

"We'll make ourselves to home; that's what we'll do." He put the bags to one side near the wall. "Set down there on that bench. It ain't very comfortable, but it belongs to us—even if they have put a new seat in it."

She sat down and looked up at him. "Ain't you goin' to take off your hat?"

"I'm comin' to that," he said. He ran his eye along a row of pegs in the wall just inside the door. "I always used to hang my hat on that first peg there, but it's got things on it. It's mine just the same, and this might be a good time to claim it." He stepped over and moved a sweatshirt and a raincoat to a peg farther down the line and hung up his hat, the broad brim of which reached most of the way to the adjacent peg. "Guess it would be better to do this when there's somebody else around," he said, and he recovered the hat from the peg and stood holding it in his hand.

"Goin' to set down?" asked Matilda.

"No, guess not. A man's got more authority on his feet."

"But what about me? Want me to stand up, too?"

Jonathan shook his head. "Stay where you be. A woman's better settin'." For a few moments he stood looking all about the room. Then he turned to Matilda. "They got a lot of our stuff around. You reco'nize that old ox yoke up there?"

"Looks fermilliar enough, but what's a ox yoke doin' in the house?"

"It's the one I used years ago when I was showin' oxen at the Danbury Fair. That old hunk of wood hung useless in the barn for forty years—and now they set it up on the mantelshelf in the house—just to look at."

"And look at that lamp on the little table," Matilda said. "Know what that is? It's my old coffee grinder."

"What about the other one over there?" Jonathan pointed.

"Well, of all things!" Matilda could hardly believe it. "That's the old spice box that used to be in the attic!"

"Hush, not so loud!" Jonathan cocked an ear to listen.

The sound of voices which they had been hearing intermittently since entering the house came nearer. Footsteps were now distinguishable, and there was feminine laughter interrupted from time to time by masculine voices.

"They're comin' down the other stairs," said Jonathan in a guarded tone. "Now you just stay where you be, and don't do nuthin' unless I tell you to."

"I wisht we'd seen Uncle Walter," she whispered nervously.

At that moment they could hear Margie's clear voice in the next room. "You all wait here in the study. I don't want a lot of dirty glasses around the living room when guests arrive, which may be any minute now."

She had walked halfway across the living room before she discovered the visitors, and at the sight of them she stopped short with a gasp. Later she told Herbert that she knew instantly who they were, but Herbert always felt sure that her recognition was an afterthought. In either event, after the initial surprise was over she went slowly towards them.

[78]

"I beg your pardon," she said, "I didn't know anyone was here, and I was startled when I saw you. Is there something I can do for you?"

"No, ma'am, I think not." With a practiced motion Jonathan stepped over and hung his hat on the first peg without even looking at it. "We live here."

"I *beg* your pardon!" Margie drew back, her eyes large, her body tilted slightly to the rearward. She was a handsome sight as she stood there in her red silk slack suit which was not exactly new and was becoming a little tight; her dark eyes snapping, her lips slightly parted, her brown hair in very becoming disorder. "I think you must be in the wrong house," she finally managed to say.

"No, ma'am, I guess not," said Jonathan. "My name's Rockwood. This is my wife. You must know who we are; we used to own this place, and we still have a right to live here."

By this time Margie was wilting somewhat. "There must be a mistake," she said weakly. "I'll call my husband."

There was, however, no need to call her husband, for at that moment Herbert emerged from the library, with Barbara and George following after him. "What's going on here? What is all this?" Herbert asked.

Jonathan moved forward. "I was just telling this lady that my name is Rockwood and this is my wife. Does the name mean anything to you?"

Herbert stopped short, swaying slightly. The breath went out of him. Caught unawares, he was not the master of the situation as he had dreamed he would be should this occasion arise. "Rockwood?" he said hoarsely. "I'm afraid not."

Jonathan's gray eyes narrowed. "I've got an idee we'd come a little closer to understandin' each other if you'd be accommodatin' enough to explain how you happen to be occupyin' this property."

"That's very simple," said Herbert. "I happen to be the owner."

"Who'd you buy from?"

"The Connecticut Power Company."

Jonathan ran his eyes over the room. "And you mean to tell me they sold you this property free and clear?"

"Of course our attorney had a proper search made of the title."

"Couldn't been very proper if it didn't show our life lease. That's on the records—I've seen it there myself—and I've got the original papers here in my satchel." Jonathan pointed. "Want to see it?"

At the sight of the baggage a troubled look came over Herbert's face, but he tried to hide it behind a smile. "To tell you the truth, Mr. Rockwood, I know very little about such things myself. I have to leave them to my attorney. And this isn't a convenient time for us to be discussing such matters. If you will drop in at Mr. Loomis's office tomorrow and bring the papers with you, we'll go over the whole situation and see what's to be done."

Again Jonathan glanced around the room. "That would be nice for you, but it wouldn't be so good for us."

Herbert looked puzzled. "I'm afraid I don't quite understand."

"Didn't you ever hear the old proverb that possession is nine points in the law?" Jonathan eyed him closely as he asked the question.

With increasing uneasiness, Herbert slowly nodded his head. He did not want to make any admissions that might cause trouble afterwards, but this seemed harmless enough. "Why, I believe I have heard the saying," he confessed, "but I never thought a great deal about it."

"Even if you ain't, your lawyer has," said Jonathan. "The man in possession has got odds of nine to one over the man who ain't. Up to today you've had a nine-to-one margin over us, but from now on your margin's gone; we're in peaceable possession here same as you are, and we're goin' to stay that way."

Margie's cheeks were flaming. "Oh, but you can't stay!" she

cried. "It isn't possible. We have house guests coming, and there's no place for you."

Jonathan shook his head. "We'll be sorry to discommode your guests, but after all, legal rights is somethin' you can't tamper with just because they ain't handy for the other party."

"But, Mr. Rockwood, there's just no place for you. Every bed in the house will be occupied."

"Don't let that bother you at all." Jonathan raised both hands with a gesture of dismissal. "We left enough beds and bedding around here to take care of ourselves all right."

"Why, yes," Matilda put in hastily. "There's my spool bed." She turned to Margie. "You found it here, didn't you?"

"We found a number of beds."

"But my *spool* bed!" Matilda insisted. "We left it in that room right there." She pointed with her finger towards Herbert's study. "We was usin' that room as a downstairs bedroom. Do you mean to tell me you didn't find it?"

"All the beds we found were put in the attic," Margie replied.

At this point Herbert skillfully imagined a telephone call and excused himself to answer it. Once he had his hands on the instrument he put in a hurry call for Mr. Loomis's law office. Meanwhile the discussion about beds was proceeding.

"And my feather bed?" Matilda demanded. "Where'd you put that?"

"It's in the attic," Margie replied. "With the exception of an occasional article that seemed to belong right here everything's in the attic."

"We could set up one of our own beds most anywheres— just for tonight," Jonathan conceded.

Margie was shaken, but she pulled herself together and decided to make an appeal to the better nature of the two old people. "It's too bad," she said slowly, "but we simply can't make room for you until after the week end. You'll understand our situation, I'm sure, when I tell you that we're all ready for house guests; and tonight we're giving a large party for them. So you can see for yourselves how impossible it is for us to take in anybody else. You'll just have to make other arrangements, that's all. I'm terribly sorry and I hope you'll understand the situation."

Jonathan, to whom most of this had been directed, stroked his chin. "We'd like to accommodate you, but the law ain't built that way; it don't accommodate."

"I don't know why not," said Margie. "All I'm asking you to do is to put off your arrival here until after the week end. Surely you ought to be willing to do that."

The corners of Jonathan's mouth drew firmly down. "No, ma'am, we can't do it—and that's that."

"But why not?" asked Margie, plainly surprised at the refusal.

Jonathan looked her up and down in what Margie thought was a very disrespectful manner before he replied, "I don't know whether you're as innocent as you sound, or if you're just a very slick article, but I want you to get it straight that we got legal rights same as you have, and we don't mean to be outsmarted or thimblerigged or run around the stump. Here we are; here we stay."

"But," said Margie with great earnestness, "all I'm asking you to do is go away and come back Monday, just as if you had never been here at all, and take everything up right where you left off. That certainly doesn't seem like asking very much, not when you stop to consider that you've already let this place go for several years without lifting your finger to do a thing about it."

Jonathan blinked at her. "Lady, you don't understand what you're talking about."

"Oh, yes, I do," Margie answered him quickly, "and I think you're trying to take an unreasonable advantage, coming in on Saturday afternoon and expecting us to change all our plans."

Jonathan looked around helplessly, hoping that the woman's husband would soon return, for by this time the old man was pretty well convinced that nothing he could say was going to make any impression on this woman, and still he couldn't just stand there and listen to her.

"We've got nuthin' at all to do with your plans." He was struggling to hold his temper. "Whether you change 'em or not is entirely up to you. But we're here; we come in peaceable; we was invited in that door; and we've got just as much right to be here as you have, and we're goin' to stay. You seem to forget that this is our home. We got no other place to go to."

Margie brightened at once. "Oh, well, why didn't you say so?" she asked with a display of good humor. "There's a tourist rest down on the Post Road not ten miles from here. Comfortable little cabins, and I'm sure they'll have a place for the horse, too. We'll put you up there as our guests until Monday, and then you can begin right where we are now."

"No, ma'am." Jonathan shook his head. "We won't do that. Couldn't if we wanted to; our horse is tuckered out. He couldn't go another mile if it was to save our lives."

Margie had an answer for that. "We'll send you down in our car." She stopped short. "Oh, no, we can't do that—we're short of gas. We have only an A card, you know, though Herbert thinks he'll be able to get a B. But perhaps I can find somebody who's going down that way."

"You needn't trouble," said Jonathan scornfully. "We've got no idee of leaving this place, in a car or any other way. We ain't hankerin' to upset your plans, but I'd like to get it through your head that we're here to stay."

It was at this point that Herbert rejoined them. As he came up, Margie caught him by the arm.

"Well, it's about time," she said irritably. "Where have you been?"

Herbert firmly disengaged her hand. "I was at the telephone."

Margie understood, but she was still a little annoyed. "You picked a rather unfortunate moment, I should say, leaving me. . . ."

Herbert cut her short. "I'm afraid we're not doing our duty

[83]

by the former occupants of the old place. Mr. and Mrs. Rockwood must have noticed the changes since they were here last, and I think it would be nice if we should take them around on a little tour of inspection."

"But, Herbert. . . ." Margie tugged at his sleeve.

"How about that, Mrs. Rockwood?" Herbert continued heartily. "Wouldn't you like to look around the place and see what we've been doing here?"

Matilda very promptly came to her feet. This was the thing she particularly wanted to do. And as they started along Herbert hung back long enough to whisper to Margie that Loomis was on his way. The lawyer, he said, had urged him to keep the visitors occupied until his arrival.

↑↑

NOTHING around a house, with the possible exception of a bedroom, is such a catchall for memories as a fireplace—a big old-fashioned wood-burning fireplace. This was the thought that passed through Jonathan's mind as he stood looking into the hearth at which he had warmed his shins through the winters of a fairly long lifetime.

He had gone there as a lad of eighteen. Hired hand doing general farm work. What cords and cords of wood he had cut for that old fireplace. A four-foot stick was what used to go best. Oak was all right, and there was more of it than anything else, but it wasn't in the same class with hickory. Hickory was easier to split, and was a freer burning wood. He'd cut plenty of ash and some chestnut and now the chestnut was gone. Time was takin' its toll out of nature same as it was out of man.

Jonathan bent over and peered into the Dutch oven when Herbert removed the cover and lighted the inside with a gleam from a flashlight. The rest of them saw only dingy bricks, but Jonathan noticed something else, a white patch at the far end. He took the flashlight in his hand and poked his head into the aperture. So the patch had stuck. How well he remembered the time when he had helped to put it there, considerable over fifty years ago. It came to him how easily the flimsy patch had outlasted the mason who made it after the lightning had come down the chimney and knocked a hole in the old oven. No need of bricking the hole up, the mason had said. Nobody ever used a Dutch oven no more, and brickwork cost money.

Little patchin' plaster would do the trick—cover up the hole so nobody'd ever know the difference, and wouldn't cost hardly anything at all. Just another little intimacy between himself and the old house. Nobody knew the secrets of that house as he did.

With a sly twist of his toe as he was turning away from the fireplace, Jonathan shoved back the rug and stole a glance at the floor. Yes, the marks were still there that were left by the shoe of a horse once when he had hauled in an extra large hickory log for the Christmas fire. He could still blush when he thought of the dressing down he had received for that bit of carelessness.

It was at this point that Margie broke in upon his reflections. "I suppose," she said, "that you keep seeing the old familiar things."

Jonathan nodded. "Yes, ma'am, I see plenty of 'em all around here. How'd you come to hang that old ox yoke up there on the mantel? I don't see nothin' very beautiful about that."

Margie smiled. She was determined to be agreeable. "But don't you think it's quaint?"

"It's funny lookin', if that's what you mean."

"And the old churn, don't you think it looks lovely with the dogwood in it?"

"Always looked good to me with butter in it."

"Oh," said Margie, "but it's such a darling. It's too quaint to leave in the cellar. And it holds the dogwood branches so beautifully."

Jonathan turned away. "I see you put a new piece of carpet on the Connecticut bench."

Margie couldn't help wincing a little. "The other seat fell to pieces," she said. "We had to have it done over. But that isn't carpet. It's a piece of hand-woven material brought over from Sweden. Don't you like it?"

"It looks all right to me so long as it ain't quaint."

That Connecticut bench could never look quaint to Jonathan. It was the seat on which he and Matilda had done most of their courting, and it had been one of his favorite jests through the years that if they'd only had a little more comfortable place to set on their courtship might have lasted longer. It had been a whirlwind affair—only three years of Sunday night callin', and they was ready to face the parson. If they could have took a couple of years more they wouldn't been so pinched for money when they first set up for themselves. He remembered how disappointed he was when Matilda chose the bench as a wedding present. Her folks had given her the choice of several things, some of which would have come in very handy. But she never made no choice at all; she just took the bench. She might at least have took that walnut table; then they would have had something to eat from.

Margie's voice broke into his ruminations. "It was the red that appealed to me. Red belongs in this room. It goes with the beams; it goes with the floors and with the lovely old featheredge paneling on the stairway, now that we've got the paint off."

"Jehoshaphat! Is that the natural wood?" Jonathan went over and ran his thumb along the surface. "I thought it was just a good job of stainin' on top of the paint. How'd you get the paint off? Must been eight or ten different colors on there, one right on top of another."

Margie smiled with a little touch of pride. "There were. I took them all off myself, with paint remover, and what you see is what we found underneath, the natural patina."

Again Jonathan ran his thumb over the surface. "Wouldn't it look better if you put a coat of stain on it?"

Margie gasped. "I hardly think so," she finally managed to say.

Meanwhile Herbert, who was exerting himself to be nice to Matilda, had taken her on a trip through his study. She had shaken her head at the number of books on the shelves and had asked if he wrote them all.

"This is really a downstairs bedroom," she said. "You can't

heat those upstairs rooms in the winter, you know. The heat from these fireplaces will go just so far and no farther."

"But the steam heat is different," Herbert explained tactfully. "You can pipe that wherever you want it. Of course, with the rationing of oil I have to be careful about it now, but up to this time heating hasn't been a very serious problem for us."

"You're wasting space when you make this nice downstairs bedroom into a office; you could just as well have all them books tucked off upstairs where a body wouldn't have to see 'em all the time."

Herbert had suffered another slight setback in the barroom when he had been on the point of calling Matilda's attention to the mellowed scent of musty ale which still clung to the old walls and timbers. At the door she had seized her nose between thumb and forefinger.

"This is a room I always hurry through," she explained. "After all these years it still has a stench like an ordinary beer saloon."

Followed by Herbert, Matilda had gone through into the living room, where she now caught up with her husband. "You been in the front room?" she asked.

Jonathan shook his head. "Ain't got that far yet."

"Well, you'll never know our old bedroom. . . ." She stopped and touched his arm. "Look what they got the daffodils in."

Herbert pretended not to be listening, but he could not help hearing Jonathan say to Matilda in a not too subdued voice, "Reckon it must be quaint."

The old couple looked through the open door into the new wing and said it was nice, though Matilda was enjoying a quiet laugh at some of the old ironstone china from her kitchen displayed in the corner cupboard along with a collection of Sandwich glass. At the same time Jonathan was deriving some amusement from the old back door of the house, which was now being used as the door into the dining room. The lower corner of the door was grooved with the scratches of a succes-

[88]

sion of farm dogs, and Jonathan remembered how his own dog, Major, had caught his toenail in a crack of the door and had stood yelping for half an hour before a member of the family had gone to his rescue.

"Pretty long table you got there," Jonathan said.

Herbert nodded. "That's an old refectory table from the Hudson Valley. It was made by the patroons a long time ago. Notice where the borers have gone through it."

Jonathan squinted at the holes. "You could fill 'em with putty."

"Mrs. Gage wouldn't like that," Herbert explained. "She paid extra for those wormholes. Genuine ones are rather hard to get."

Margie had expected some surprise and perhaps a few suppressed exclamations of delight when she showed the old folks the very elegant bathroom on the second floor. But they received in silence the glittering display of chromium, the recessed porcelain, the floor-length mirrors. Somewhat annoyed at the lack of appreciation, Margie finally asked them what they thought of it.

Jonathan shook his head. "Couldn't you find no other place for it?" he asked. "Where you got it now it shuts off the only window on this hall."

Margie touched a switch. "But the hall is very adequately lighted," she said.

"Oh, you can see all right," Jonathan conceded, "but who wants to keep turnin' lights on and off every time you go through the hall?"

With that they moved on. In the first bedroom they visited, Matilda discovered an antique hand-woven wool bedspread of authentic colonial origin. This was something that she could and did understand, and she went to scrutinizing it by both feel and appearance. She held it up to the light and peered through, she put it up to her nose, sniffing like a hound on the scent, and finally she touched her tongue to the wool, tasting and savoring it.

Herbert had strolled over to the window and was looking out, and thus he missed the fine details of this examination. He followed along as they crossed the hall and opened the door of the guest room where he again posted himself at the window to keep a lookout up the road for the appearance of Loomis's car.

"Except for the furniture, we've left this room exactly as it was when we came," Margie said to the visitors as if they had never before seen the room. "We haven't touched the walls or the woodwork. Of course we've polished the floor, and put up new curtains, but otherwise it's just the same."

The old couple looked around the room, then at each other with understanding. "Yes," said Jonathan slowly, "I guess it's about the same."

"Certainly looks like it," Matilda admitted. "Does that blue still come off when you rub against it?"

With a regretful smile Margie admitted that it did, and voiced the pessimistic view that it would probably all be rubbed off in time.

Jonathan shook his head over this. "I don't know about that —wouldn't be too sure. We slept in this room ourselves for quite a while—even before we owned the place and was just workin' here—and I used to go around with that blue stuff on me most of the time."

"What a nuisance," said Margie.

The old man declined to go quite that far. "Well, no, not partic'lar," he said.

"You didn't mind having that blue powder on your clothes?" Margie raised her eyebrows in the characteristic manner that Herbert called her fraudulent expression of intelligent interest. "It's terribly hard to get off."

"I didn't want to get it off, not in partic'lar."

Now Margie was really interested. "You didn't?"

Jonathan gave his wife a sly look. "No, ma'am, I didn't. The fact is I used to enjoy lookin' at it. Sometimes I'd see it on my shirtsleeve when I was out in the field, and it would make me feel pretty good."

Matilda stepped between them. "We had our bed turned the other way. Looked better with the head over there. It was my spool bed, the one you put in the attic. We had two lovely beds."

"But we only used one of 'em then," Jonathan put in.

Brushing this interruption aside Matilda pointed at the dimity-covered dressing table. "We had my mother's mahogany bureau there. And over here we had Aunt Alice's commode, with an eight-piece set of rosebud china." She paused, wrinkling her brow. "I ain't noticed any of that china around—is it still here?"

"Oh, yes, I found that set," said Margie. "I'm using the soap dish as an ash tray in my bedroom. And the water pitcher is in Barbara's room. It's filled with iris and looks perfectly heavenly. The rest of it is in the attic."

As they started along Matilda suddenly stopped, staring hard at a little daguerreotype case lying on the bureau. Her mother's picture was gone from it, and it was full of cigarettes. She was on the point of asking what had become of the picture when Herbert turned quickly from the window.

"Here's Mr. Loomis now," Herbert said. "He's just turning in the driveway. Hadn't we better go to my study where we can all sit down and talk things over?"

"Loomis?" asked Jonathan warily. "Who is he and what's he got to do with it?"

"He's our lawyer," Herbert explained.

"Um-m-m—yes, I see." Jonathan stroked his chin thoughtfully. "I expect you'd like to talk with him private. Why don't you folks go down and have your talk, and Matilda and me, we'll set down here and rest a mite? We'd kinda like to look at the old room a little longer."

"Not a bad idea," said Herbert. "We won't be long. Come on, Margie."

After he was sure they were out of hearing Jonathan turned

to Matilda. "There you are," he said. "That's what the stallin' was for. I suspected as much. But it don't make a great deal of diff'rence one way or another. Here we are, and here we stay."

"Did you have to tell 'em we spent our honeymoon in this room?" Matilda asked irritably. "Have we got to share our private life with every Tom, Dick, and Harry?"

"I don't recollect tellin' 'em no such thing as that," Jonathan said firmly.

"You would have if I hadn't shouted you down and choked you off."

Jonathan's eyes twinkled. "Well, mebbe I would. The sight of this room brought back some pretty good recollections."

Matilda softened. "Yes, I guess it did. I recollect I was just fillin' the feather bed at that time." She had a dreamy look in her eyes, but suddenly it gave way to a more militant expression. "What I want to know is, what's become of the organ? I ain't seen it anywhere around, and it ain't easy to overlook."

ʍʍʍ

WITH the stage carefully set, Herbert stood aside to let Matilda go into the study ahead of him. Opposite the door and on the further side of Herbert's desk sat Mr. Loomis looking more than a little like an owl. He was a small man with his head set well down between his shoulders, and though he was only in his thirties he had acquired a legal asset in the form of a sizable bald spot the color of fine old parchment. He blinked behind his thick glasses as the newcomers were introduced, and bobbed his head as if it were on a swivel.

Margie was already seated on the davenport at the extreme right, and between the desk and the davenport was a large easy chair which Herbert had placed for Matilda. With a motion of the hand he indicated that it was for her, and though she started in that general direction she passed the easy chair and seated herself in a sturdy slat-back chair which she drew out from the wall. Taking one's ease in an overstuffed chair was something that Matilda did not hold with. She may not have gone quite so far as to regard it as wrong, though she did feel that there was a certain danger of having one's strength of character undermined by too much comfort. Partly that, and partly the fact that with her lame hip a straight-back chair was more comfortable.

Jonathan sat down in the chair that had been placed for him across the desk from Mr. Loomis, and Herbert sat at Jonathan's right in a Philadelphia stick chair he had moved over from the wall.

It was Mr. Loomis who opened proceedings. "We're faced here today by a rather peculiar situation. Mr. Gage is in peaceable possession of this property by virtue of a deed from the Power Company. Would you care to tell us, Mr. Rockwood, by what authority you claim right to come in here and make yourself at home?"

"I can tell you that in a hurry; I got a life lease of this property. My wife and I reserved the right to stay here as long as we live."

"And your claim is that you retained this right when you deeded the property to the Company?"

"I most certainly did," said Jonathan with a positive nod of the head. "This farm didn't come all in one piece like some do. It was sort of collected, one parcel at a time. But when I sold to the Power Company I reserved the right to live on this one parcel where the buildin's stood. I got the papers if you want to see 'em."

Mr. Loomis shook his head. "No," he said, "I'm quite familiar with the record. I'm just wondering if you are."

Jonathan gave the lawyer a scornful look. "I guess I know what's in my own papers."

"Then," said the lawyer, "you may remember the part where it says that the tenant shall not waste or destroy the freehold."

Thoroughly outraged, Jonathan leaned across the desk. "I never wasted or destroyed a thing in all my life!" he declared angrily.

"What do you call it when you abandon a place and leave it to the ravages of wind and weather for a term of years?" asked the lawyer.

"Somebody's been tellin' you things," said Jonathan. "We never abandoned this place; we never moved out at all. When we went we expected to be back in a month or two, but we was delayed by what we considered good and sufficient reasons. All we took with us was what you could carry in a satchel. We left all our household goods and furniture right here—and it's still here, except what's been removed by meddlers."

For a few moments the lawyer sat in silence blinking his eyes. Then he said slowly, "The question of abandonment is an issue to be decided by the court."

"The court won't have no trouble decidin' that," Jonathan said emphatically. "If we'd abandoned the place we wouldn't be here now."

"I'm not entirely sure that you *are* here," said Mr. Loomis. "Not in a legal sense, at any rate. This property is in the possession of Mr. Gage under recorded papers which make him the legal owner."

Jonathan nodded his head sagely. "I know all about that possession business," he said. "You're tellin' me that he's got his nine points—all right, so have I. My papers went onto the record ahead of his, don't forget that. And don't forget that I'm in possession same as he is. I didn't break in. I didn't force my way in. I was invited in. I've got just as good a right to live here as he has, and by cracky, I'm gonna stay!"

"You understand, of course," said the lawyer, "that your alleged life lease here is not by its terms exclusive."

"What do you mean it's not exclusive?" Jonathan glared at him.

"Your papers merely say that you have a right to make your home here as long as you live. But it's not an exclusive right. The word *exclusive* does not anywhere appear in the papers. If you'd gone to a lawyer to have your papers drawn he would have taken care of that for you. But when you let the buyer draw his own papers he's going to take care of himself."

Now for the first time Matilda projected herself into the discussion. "Jonathan, I told you that you ought to gone to see Uncle Walter about them papers—but you wouldn't do it!" she declared bitterly.

Jonathan motioned to her to quiet down. "That's all in the past," he said. "There's a question I want to ask the lawyer. If my life lease ain't exclusive, what do you claim it is?"

"Let me explain it this way," said the lawyer. "Mr. Gage owns the property, subject to your alleged life lease. Upon the death of you and your wife the property will belong to him free and clear. Until that time, unless you sell your interest or the court invalidates your lease, you and Mr. Gage will be regarded in the eyes of the law as tenants in common."

"Tenants in common," Jonathan slowly repeated. "Does that mean we both got a right to live here?"

"I'd prefer not to answer that question," the lawyer replied. "In fact, I'd prefer not to discuss this question any further until I've had a few moments of private conversation with Mr. and Mrs. Gage." He stood up. "If you'll excuse us, we'll just step into the adjoining room. We won't be long."

They went across the hall and into the taproom, and as soon as the door had closed behind them Margie began waving her hands in protest.

"It can't be left like this!" she wailed. "We can't have two strangers dumped into our midst, people we don't know, never even saw before!"

Herbert pushed in front of her, his face red, his eyes blazing with anger. "What the hell, Loomis!" He bent over and shoved his face belligerently close to that of the lawyer. "What's the matter with you? You've told us all along that if these old buzzards ever showed up you could throw the case into court and stall them off for years, and now that they're here you cave in and tell them that their rights are as good as ours." He caught Loomis by the shoulder and gave him a shake. "What's the matter with you? Have you lost your nerve, or what?" He glared steadily into the lawyer's face as if he expected to see his answer there.

All he saw was a surprised and disconcerted look. Clearly Loomis was taken aback, but he was not afraid. "I told you I could *keep* them out, not *put* them out," he replied indignantly.

Herbert straightened up his shoulders. "For God's sake don't quibble. Get in there and play ball!" he pleaded.

"But, my dear fellow, I'm not quibbling!" Loomis was clearly annoyed.

"I don't know what you'd call it—you can 'keep' but you can't 'put.' What kind of talk is that?"

Loomis shook his finger at Herbert, but at a safe distance. "That's exactly the situation, and you have nobody but yourself to thank for it."

"Oh, so it's all my fault, is it?" Herbert demanded gruffly.

"It certainly is. When you admitted them to the house, you sacrificed all the legal advantages and presumptions that your possession had given you. You threw your law suit right out of the window!" Loomis punctuated the statement with graphic gestures.

Herbert was instantly on the defensive. "I didn't let him in," he protested. Then he slowly turned on Margie. "Did you?"

"I most certainly didn't!" she replied indignantly. "I wonder who did."

"Forget it," said Herbert. "It doesn't particularly matter. He got in, and he's still in, and you say our law suit's gone out of the window. All right, you're our lawyer; what do we do now?"

Mr. Loomis passed his hand reflectively over the parchment-colored bald spot. "That's a tough question," he said slowly. "The peculiar manner in which these events have happened changes the situation completely. Yesterday you had things right where you wanted them; today, legally, you're no better off than he is."

Margie grew very red in the face. "You mean that we must always have those two impossible people hanging around our necks like a dead albatross?" she demanded.

"All I mean is that they have what appears to be an unbeatable right to live here for life," said Mr. Loomis.

Herbert took a turn across the room. "Why, damn it, man, they might live on for years and years."

"That's the risk you took when you bought the place," said Loomis. "I told you that you couldn't come back on the Company for restitution, since they had given you nothing but a quitclaim deed. Remember that?" asked the lawyer.

Herbert glowered.

"I warned you at the time that some such thing as this might happen," Loomis went on; "but you were bullheaded. You said you had a good reason for buying this particular place even if the title was clouded."

"We had a perfectly good reason," said Herbert, "and still have. What we want right now is some guidance from you. Where do we go from here?"

"The answer to that," said Loomis, "depends largely on you. You've got quite a little money tied up here. Your improvements must have cost you more than double the purchase price. But you must know that with this flaw in your title you can't sell and you can't borrow. The only way you can possibly win is to sit it out."

Herbert reached up with both hands and resettled his glasses on his nose. "You mean wait for them to die?"

"I mean that only in a limited sense." Mr. Loomis blinked his eyes rapidly. "That's the impression you must give them. Of course we don't forget the saying that every man has his price. It's probably true. But you can't make a deal with these old folks the way they're feeling. You'll have to take your time and work around to it."

"But we can't have them here now," wailed Margie. "We simply can't. It would spoil everything."

The lawyer shook his head. "I'm afraid, Mrs. Gage, there isn't any choice about it. I'll admit that it's a difficult situation, but you and Herbert are intelligent people. You're capable of coping with anything that comes along. You aren't going to turn this place into a battleground; you're going to take these old people on, and you're going to handle them with tact and understanding. You're going to lick this situation. You're going to find some space for them; you're going to fit up quarters where they can sleep and live and carry on, and you're going to get along without any unnecessary friction until you can come to terms with them."

Herbert listened with misgivings. He knew, or thought he

knew, how Margie was going to take this. He felt sure she was not going to have her week end ruined if she could help it, and as the lawyer finished speaking Herbert braced himself for an explosion. But no explosion came. Instead Margie's eyes opened wide. Her lips parted.

"I've just thought of something," she said brightly. "The relaxation room!"

Loomis looked puzzled. "I'm afraid I don't understand."

"She means the big room above the garage," Herbert explained. "I refuse to call it any such silly name as that." He was tempted to resume the argument, which had been one of long standing, and was diverted only by the pressure of the present events. "But I see what she means," he added. "The idea is possible, though not very practical at the moment. The place was laid out for servants' quarters and never finished off."

"What's impractical about it?" Margie demanded. "It's down on the blueprint as sitting room, bedroom, and bath."

"But, my dear," Herbert insisted, "it takes time to remodel, and what about tonight? There isn't even a bed in that loft."

Margie brushed these objections aside with characteristic enthusiasm. "We can have a bed set up there in fifteen minutes, and if they have a bed to sleep in what more can they ask? Naturally they'll have to put up with some inconveniences while we're getting our household readjusted to take in—roomers." She paused, then went slowly on. "But after all, they'll have to eat; that's another complication." Suddenly her face lighted again. "I know what we can do; we can send their meals up to them for the present, and that will take care of their dinner tonight and get them out of the way while we're having our party!"

"Have you seen that room lately?" Herbert asked with a dubious smile. "Sarah has been playing there, and she's got it converted into a horse stable."

Margie disposed of that with a wave of the hand. "All they'll need is a bed, and perhaps a table and two chairs. I'll get

George and Barbara to help. They're wonderful in an emergency." She came over to Herbert with the air of one who had things all settled and said as she patted him on the arm, "You can go in, dear, and tell the old persons to make themselves comfortable in the study, and we'll have temporary quarters ready before they even know what's going on."

Herbert grunted an unwilling affirmative. "We will if the Livingstones don't come crashing in on us."

"Oh, I don't think they will," Margie said cheerfully.

"You haven't forgotten that Archie telephoned they're on their way," Herbert reminded her.

"I know, but they'll get lost. Everybody gets lost the first time, that's what you always say." She kept patting Herbert on the arm, to his great annoyance. "Go ahead, dear, go in and talk to them, and I'll gather up George and Barbara and start right in on the relaxation room."

Herbert pulled away from her. "All right," he said, "only don't let them hear you call it that."

For some time after Herbert had finished being tactful with the old folks in the library and had left the room, they sat without moving or speaking. They were both in the chairs where they had been during the conference with the lawyer. They could hear people talking and moving around. Doors opened and doors closed, and occasionally the house shook a little, as if pieces of furniture were being moved.

Matilda was the first to speak. "What do you make of it?" she asked.

Jonathan shook his head. "Don't know. He didn't tell us much. We'll have to wait and find out. But here we are, and here we'll stay."

She folded and unfolded her hands. "He did say they'd get a place ready for us."

"That's what he said." Jonathan stood up. "But he didn't say where."

"And he didn't say nuthin' about Shadrach," Matilda reminded him.

"Nope. Must have forgot about him. Forgot about him myself. Guess I better go out and see how he's gettin' along."

Matilda saw him leave the room. She heard the outer door of the living room close behind him. Papers and magazines lay within reach on a small table. Matilda could have read them, but she didn't. She did not even glance at them. Instead she sat and looked around her, taking a very definite satisfaction from the fulfillment of the homing instinct. She noted that the room had been done over, that rugs all but covered the floor, but she was glad to see that the wide oak flooring was still there. The bookshelves annoyed her; seemed like such a useless waste of space. But they were mostly behind her, so she did not have to look at them.

On the mantelpiece she saw an old pewter candlestick which had been brought down from the attic. Wasn't much good when she had put it up there, all battered and dented, and it never would hold a candle very good. Then she discovered another old thing from the attic, a china matchbox with a blue cat curled up on the cover. The tail was broken off before she had put it up there and was still gone. A door slammed in the distance, and a moment later Jonathan came in tugging their hand baggage. She could see that he was excited.

"You know what's goin' on?" he asked in a low tone.

Matilda shook her head. "Don't know nuthin' new since you went out."

"They're cleanin' out a place for us in the new part—up over the *garage!*"

"Over the garage!" She bristled with indignation.

"Think I'd sleep in the same buildin' with a stinkin' car—gasoline and what-not poisonin' the air?"

"Not with me you wouldn't!" she assured him.

"We got just as much right around this place as they have," Jonathan said with a contentious shaking of the head. "And if we start out lettin' them tell us what to do, they'll keep right on tellin' us."

"How'd you find out about it?" she asked.

"From the little girl, Sarah, the one who wanted to pet the horse. I could hear 'em bangin' around up there, and I asked her what was goin' on and she told me."

Matilda snorted angrily. "I been feelin' in my bones that some'pm was up!"

With the baggage still in his arms Jonathan stood shaking his head. "It's a trick. We got no rights in that new part; they're just tryin' to get us out of possession of the old part. We'll show 'em their new tricks ain't goin' to work on the old dog!"

Matilda folded and unfolded her hands. She was worried. It was not that she did not have a certain amount of relish for a good smart disagreement; but she was always uneasy when Jonathan lost his temper; he never knew when to stop. "What do you calculate you'll do?"

"Come along with me and I'll show you," he said with spirit. "Ain't nobody usin' this blue walled room overhead, and we're goin' to move right in."

The old lady's face lighted. "The honeymoon room?"

"I don't mean nuthin' else."

"But they got that room all ready for their company."

"Well, the company ain't here yet, and from now on it's goin' to be first come, first served around here."

"Go ahead," she said. "I'll foller."

They quietly climbed the twisted stairs, and Jonathan put down the luggage at the foot of the bed in the honeymoon room.

"Now, Matilda," he said, "I'll tell you what to do. Get unpacked as fast as you can. Put stuff in the drawers, hang clothes in the closet, get things spread around so they'll know we're in possession."

Matilda sighed. "Now if I only had my spool bed."

"Listen, this is no time for nonsense," Jonathan warned her. "We want to get settled in this room before anybody can stop us. And while you're doin' that I'll go down and find a place for Shadrach. Poor old feller was asleep on his feet when I was out there. I got to get his harness off and find a place for him to bed down."

"You don't aim to leave me here alone?" Matilda asked nervously. "What if they should come in and tell me I got to get out?"

Jonathan considered for a moment. " 'Tain't likely that'll happen, but we might as well be ready. I'll tell you what to do—just open up the bags and scatter things around a little, and if you hear anybody comin', get into bed."

"At this time of day?"

"Certainly. You're tired enough, ain't you? You must be done in. You could worry yourself into bein' a little sick."

"Wouldn't take a heap of worryin'," Matilda said. "Right this minute I got a pain in my hip. Too much goin' up and down stairs, I guess."

"Better get on your nightgown before you unpack. Then you'll be all ready for 'em." He gave her a knowing nod and started for the door. "Now I'll see if I can do as well by Shadrach."

↗↗↗

WHILE these interesting preparations were being made for their reception at Lazy Corners, the house guests were approaching over the Merritt Parkway in Philip's rather flashy roadster. This was a custom-built job with Philip's own monogram on the hubcaps. It was equipped with an eight-day clock which not only struck the hours, but which showed the day of the month. Philip had an idea that a man's car should be as personalized as his stationery or his golf clubs. When his car went past he wanted people to say, "There goes Philip Livingstone, the big publisher." Some did, but not as many as Philip thought.

Philip Livingstone had built up his publishing business from scratch. True, he had built it up with the very comfortable inheritance he had received from his father, but he had done it all himself, and he took a justifiable pride in his achievement. Not enough pride to make him objectionable among the book trade, but still enough to keep him on the alert for new ideas and new talent. He was the first and only publisher who had seen the manuscript of Herbert Gage's novel, *The Mitten*. He had accepted it with enthusiasm—accepted is hardly the word, for he had practically confiscated it after having read only the first ten chapters.

And the success of the book had demonstrated beyond per-adventure that Philip had known what he was about.

Herbert and Margie had gone through a wonderful summer the year the book was published. They were spending their first season in the old house, camping out there, as they used to say, without any of the modern facilities or improvements. They drew their water from the well with an old oaken bucket, they did their cooking on a kerosene stove, and lighted the house with oil lamps and they were very, very happy. Salesmen had gone out with the book soon after the Gages had moved into their Connecticut home, and it was not long before Archie Pyne began calling up in the evening after he had reached his home in Westport to tell them how the orders were coming in. Telephone tolls were less that way.

He reported that they were approaching five thousand before the salesmen had been out a week. A day or two later he brought the exciting news that they were well above seventy-five hundred.

"If it goes to ten thousand we'll have electricity this summer," Herbert declared a little breathlessly as he came away from the telephone. A few days later he was promising Margie that if it reached fifteen thousand they would put in a bathroom. A week after publication the book was on the best seller list. Within a month it was at the top and there it hung week after week and month after month.

By midsummer Herbert decided not to wait any longer before starting improvements on the place, and soon architects were swarming over it with their tape measures and sketching pads. The well driller had set up his rig outside the door and began a thumping and thudding that went on continuously day after day for a full two months. Wreckers came in with their crowbars and tore off the back of the house. A power shovel spent a noisy day excavating for a cellar under the new addition. Stone masons moved in, then rough carpenters, plumbers, and electricians. Plasterers came in with their white caps and lime-spattered shoes. Painters, glaziers, roofers, cabinetmakers, stair builders, floor layers. Big trucks rumbled up with supplies and lumber, unloaded, and rumbled off again. For months the highway was lined with workmen's cars, and the sound of hammering could be heard for miles around.

The snow had already begun to fly before they were finished, but after the last workman had gone there was a comfortable feeling of quiet and accomplishment. The old house had been spared as a sort of museum piece, with the addition of unobtrusive heat and plumbing, of course, and a service wing had been added on the back with all the most recent equipment and gadgets, electrical throughout, with servants' quarters and garage attached. The new wing had been expertly planned, with visible timbers here and there and low ceilings. It followed the pattern of the old house so faithfully that there was no shock in going from the old to the new. And the outside matched so well that no passer-by would ever suspect that the main part was two hundred and forty years older than the wing.

The Livingstones knew little of all this. They had heard plenty about the remarkable old house where the Gages lived and knew in a general way that restorations and improvements were being made. Philip Livingstone had smiled over this. Herbert was running true to form. It had been his experience that about the first expenditure of an author who had hit the jackpot was to buy or improve a house in the country. Katharine was rather patronizing towards old houses. They were amusing and all that, but for the comfort and convenience of living you could give her the newest thing there was. And as for Margie Gage's preoccupation with the ways and things of an earlier day, Katharine had remarked to her husband more than once that Margie had gone antique in a big way and was showing signs of developing into a pre-Revolutionary bore.

She was, in fact, thinking about Margie as the car went spinning along the Parkway through the rolling hills of western Connecticut. Paying money for wormholes in wood and cracks in the wall was something Katharine could not understand. Suddenly the remarkable clock on the dashboard chimed out the hour of seven, thereby bringing Katharine to the edge of her seat.

"Is that clock anywhere near right?" she asked.

Philip was quickly on the defensive. He resented criticism of any part of that car. "It's on the dot," he replied.

"In twenty minutes all will be ruined."

"What are you talking about?"

"The dinner."

Philip smiled. "It's my bet that we won't get any dinner at a 'barnwarming.'"

"No dinner? What will we get?"

"Probably a handout in a horse stall."

"We'll get another kind of handout if you don't keep your foot up off the floor board. This Parkway is infested with motor police."

Philip glanced ahead. Then in the mirror. After that she saw the pin slowly rise from sixty to seventy on the dial.

"They love to pick up a New York number," she said. "About all we need to make us stylishly late is a little visit to the police station. What's the hurry if there's no dinner to spoil?"

"After all, we're house guests."

"I know, but if the dinner isn't spoiling? What's a barnwarming anyway?"

"You know what a barn is," Philip said patiently.

"Oh, yes, I know that, though I never was in one."

Philip chuckled. "I won't spoil your fun by telling you what it's like, but you'll be amused to see how the other half lives."

"I don't care how the other half lives, and I certainly don't look forward to being entertained in a barn."

"Don't be ridiculous," said Philip. "The Gages are swell people, and you know it."

Katharine smiled ironically. "Herbert must have passed the hundred thousand mark."

"As a matter of fact he has," Philip admitted. "But why do you say that?"

"When authors reach twenty-five thousand, they're *good* people—we invite them to cocktails. When they reach fifty thousand, they're *nice* people, and we have them to dinner. It's not until they pass one hundred thousand that they become *swell*, and we have to accept any invitation they send, even if it's no more than a handout in a horse stall, as you so elegantly put it."

For a few moments Philip made no answer. Then he said slowly, "It's all right for you to make these wisecracks to me, but for heaven's sake don't say such things to anybody else."

"Never fear," she said. "All my best friends are authors." She felt the brakes go on and added, "So sanity has returned? You've decided not to visit the police station?"

"This is where we leave the Parkway—at least I hope it is." He made the turn on two wheels with squealing tires, swung through the underpass and started in a northerly direction. Philip was a driver who hated to ask directions and seldom stooped to such a practice. Whenever he was on strange roads he was habitually lost, and this occasion was no exception. He was completely at sea as soon as he had left the Parkway. Being lost never worried Philip; he had a supreme confidence that keeping in motion would somehow bring him to his destination, and it eventually did. He was not visibly surprised when half an hour after leaving the Parkway he saw the name HERBERT GAGE on a mailbox.

"This must be the place," he said casually.

"It can't be," Katharine groaned. "Ever since we left the Parkway we've been going in the wrong direction."

"Then what's Herbert doing out there in the garage?" Philip insisted. He had already brought the car to a stop, and now he gave a little toot on the horn.

At the sound Herbert, who was holding a large basket of trash in his hands, quickly turned and peered anxiously towards the street. When he saw who it was he threw the trash, basket and all, into a corner, and turning his face upward shouted, "Hi, Margie! Come on down—the Livingstones are here!"

The situation was a little annoying to Herbert, who was inclined to be a careful dresser. Whenever he was in town he kept himself looking like a fashion plate, and now to be caught

[108]

in dirty slacks, runover sandals, and a faded sport shirt visibly saturated with his sweat was, to say the least, embarrassing. It was an unfortunate beginning for a visit which, he had hoped, would prove to be somewhat overwhelming even to Park Avenue. But he shouted a hearty greeting and hurried out to welcome the guests and direct them into the parking space by the side of the house.

He took particular pains not to dust off his hands as he went along. That gesture, he felt, was a flagrant notice to guests that their arrival had been somehow untimely and that the fault lay with the visitor rather than the visited. Tracks dug in the gravel by the turning of iron wagon tires caught his eye, and he was relieved to note that the horse-drawn vehicle had disappeared, though he hadn't the time just then to find out where it had gone.

The Livingstones were stepping down from the car in all their sartorial perfection when Margie came dashing out of the house squealing what was intended as a thoroughly hospitable welcome.

Philip was wide at the top like Joe Palooka or Li'l Abner, and tapered down to a pair of exotic sport shoes. He had on a heather-colored jacket of Shetland with off-white flannel slacks, and was so tall he could look over the top of his car. Katharine was wearing a sharkskin suit of dandelion yellow which went particularly well with her shining black hair. A perky little hat was cocked over one ear, but her face had no more expression than the plastic countenance of a window display dummy.

Barbara and George remained discreetly out of sight, though from their hidden lookout in the playroom they were missing none of the details of the arrival and the reception. Little Sarah, however, exercised no such restraint. She had never before seen a publisher in the flesh, and she meant to miss none of the details. She loved the color of Katharine's suit, she loved the way it fitted, and she especially loved the Nuit d'Amour perfume of which Katharine reeked. Sarah noted instantly Philip's resemblance to Li'l Abner, and was on her way to tell him that if he would stop parting his hair in the middle and slicking it down on both sides he'd look more like her favorite hero of the comics.

Margie put an end to this project, temporarily at least, by capturing Sarah and dispatching her as a messenger to see that the doors of the study were closed. To Sarah this seemed like an unnecessary errand as she had just come from the study, and she knew from her own observation that the room was devoid of all human occupation. She tried to pass this information on to her mother, but Margie was in no mood to have Sarah telling her things at a moment when she was being dispatched on an important errand. She cut Sarah short without comprehending a word of what the child was trying to say, and propelled her into the house by a firm grip on the shoulder. "And then go straight upstairs and take a bath—in Mother's bathroom. Understand? Mother's bathroom, not the usual place."

Sarah went murmuring, but she went. While she was gone some very elegant airplane luggage had come out of the rear compartment of the wonderful-looking car, and Herbert had carefully set each piece inside the house, remarking that it could be taken upstairs later.

The visitors had been in old houses before and they promptly responded with admiring allusions to the hand-hewn timbers and the authentic cracks in the plaster. They knew without being told that the ox yoke above the mantel was quaint, though Katharine, having little acquaintance with the ox, had no idea what such an article was used for. The quaintness of the churn and the lovely old butter bowl were acknowledged immediately and Philip ingratiated himself with Margie by asking to see the inside of the Dutch oven.

The old taproom enchanted the visitors. They would have loved to linger there in the mellowed scent of musty ale to which Herbert called their attention, had not Margie very definitely vetoed the idea. They all had some freshening up to do, she said, and no doubt the visitors would like to be shown to their room and have an opportunity to get at their luggage. She went with them to the foot of the stairs, noting with satisfaction that the door of the study was still closed.

"You're going to love your room," she said, her expression full of promised surprises. "It's like a breath of the old colonial days. We haven't changed a thing about it. It's exactly as we found it. Same walls, same ceiling, same woodwork; everything's the same except the furniture, and that looks the same. Of course everything has been freshened, but what I'm trying to tell you is that the room hasn't been. . . ." She hesitated.

"Renovated?" Philip suggested.

"The very word," Margie said gratefully. "I couldn't think of it. It's the door at the head of the stairs. I won't go up, but Herbert will be right along with the bags."

As Katharine started up the stairs Philip called back to Herbert, "How about giving you a hand with those bags? Can't I take one of them?"

"Oh, no," Herbert replied. "One balances the other."

"Okay," said Philip. "Just as you say." And he followed Katharine up the winding stairs.

At the top Katharine paused with her hand on the latch. "In here?" she asked.

"That's right," Margie called. "Go right in!"

Margie waiting at the foot of the stairs for "Ohs" and "Ahs" heard something quite different.

"Oh, I beg your pardon!" It was Katharine's voice, followed immediately by Philip's, "Sorry! We must be in the wrong room!"

As Margie reached the head of the stairs the Livingstones, angrily embarrassed, came backing into the hall. A glance into the guest room was enough to tell her what had happened. In her treasured maple bed lay the bulky form of Matilda Rockwood, clad in a flannelette nightgown. Raised on one elbow, Matilda was glaring angrily at the intruders; while sprawled in a dainty slipper chair, in shirtsleeves and stocking feet, sat old Jonathan smoking a corncob pipe.

As Margie collapsed against the doorjamb, out on her feet and unable even to say a word, Herbert had a brilliant idea for saving the day.

"Wrong door—wrong door!" he called. "It's the room on the other side of the hall!"

Margie knew full well this was a blunder, but before she could pull herself together enough to stop them they had pushed open the door and gone into her own bedroom. The place was a shambles. The unmade bed had been thrown wide open for airing. Margie's nightgown lay in a ring by the side of the bed where she had stepped out of it in the morning. Herbert's pajamas and slippers were scattered all the way from the window where he had looked out at the weather to the bathroom in which he had taken a shower. A jumble of open magazines topped by a notebook and pencil lay on the floor by Margie's side of the bed, and on Herbert's side the various pages of a daily newspaper were scattered in magnificent array.

And this was the agonizing moment that Sarah chose to come galloping through the room on her way to the bath, clad only in the piece of frayed rope that she was still using for a tail.

Herbert went around kicking things under the bed as he removed his glasses to wipe away the tears of laughter that had been streaming down his face. "I can—explain—everything . . ." he coughed, still unable to control his voice.

By this time Katharine, who really did not enjoy laughing, had recovered her composure. "You might begin by explaining what you and Margie are going to do if we take your room," she said.

"Katharine is absolutely right," Philip put in. "If it's not convenient for you to have us overnight, we can drive back to the city after the party is over and come another time."

"Forget it!" cried Herbert hospitably. "We have all kinds of room in the house. We intended the other room for you, but somehow the wires got crossed. So we'll just switch you over and put you in here. Margie is a whizz at straightening up a room. I'll guarantee she'll have it in perfect order by the time I can take you down to the taproom and show you how the old Pilgrim Fathers used to go about shaking up a drink."

As they were going down the stairs they could hear Margie calling to Sarah through the bathroom door, "Now don't forget the ring in the bathtub, dear!"

JONATHAN sat in the slipper chair and puffed content-
edly on his pipe. It had been quite a few years since he
had slept in that room. Yes, a good many years. He was
quite a man in those days. Quite a man. A regular he-man. As
he searched his recollection, it seemed to him that they had
never slept in that room after Matilda had her fall. That was
it; the stairs bothered her, so they slept downstairs in summer
same as in winter. And if she'd had her say this time she'd
have took a downstairs room. But the time to take a thing was
when you could get it, and here this room was all ready for
somebody to step right into. Some better than a stinkin' loft
over the garage. Quite some better. And the best part was that
they had a real toehold. They were where they had a right to
be, and they were there to stay.

He ran his finger into the bowl of the old corncob, gently
tapping down the ash, and then for a moment he puffed
briskly to brighten the coal. Funny how this blue finish had
stuck on the wall. It struck him that he must have wiped off
enough of it one time or another to color two or three rooms,
and still the walls were as blue as ever. Prob'ly nothin' but blue
chalk mixed up with skim milk, but how it did last.

Matilda, still stretched out in the bed and making a very
considerable mound under the bedclothes, raised her head.
"What'd you do with Shadrach?"

"He's out back of the barn. He can get inside if he wants to.
Door's open."

"Did you water him?"

"I dropped the bars into the pasture so he can go through to the brook."

"Think he'll know enough to go?"

"If he's thirsty he'll get to water."

"Where's the wagon?"

"That's out back, too. Guess it's safe enough. Who'd want our stuff?"

"What do you think they're doin' now?"

He shook his head. "I wouldn't know. But I guess we give 'em a pretty considerable surprise. They wasn't lookin' to find us in here."

"I guess they wasn't! Did you see her eyes when she first come in that door? They're big anyhow, but they looked as big as tea saucers. And when she got a glimpse of me layin' in this bed, she wilted like a lettuce leaf on a hot stove."

"Well, who wouldn't? That's the time we give 'em a punch where they could feel it. 'Tain't goin' to be long before they begin to realize that we got rights and ain't afraid to stand up for 'em."

"Oh, there's some'pm I didn't tell you." Matilda raised up on her elbow again so she could see how he would take it. "I found the organ."

Jonathan snatched his pipe out of his mouth. With his teeth, he couldn't hold it and talk the way he used to. "Where is it?"

"Right there in the clothes closet." She pointed to the small door leading into it. "They musta put it in through the big door out in the hall."

Jonathan stood up and peered into the closet. "That's it, sure enough. Wonder what kind of shape it's in."

"Looks all right."

"You ain't tried it yet?"

She shook her head. "Nope, not yet, but I'm itchin' to."

He closed the door and went back to his chair. "Well, take your time, there's no hurry. 'Tain't music that's worryin' me right now half as much as supper. I keep smellin' the cookin' that's goin' on down there, and we ain't got a blessed thing to eat."

She sank back on the pillow. "There's stuff in the wagon. Why didn't you bring some of it in?"

"Didn't think of it. Guess I had too many other things to think about."

"What'll we do?"

"Well, I don't know. Mebbe I can go out and fetch in a snack."

Matilda thought about it for a while. "But ain't they gettin' ready for a party?" she asked.

"Well, what if they are? We ain't invited."

"Mebbe not invited, exactly, but there's goin' to be a lot of food left over, I'll betcha."

"Well, what of it? You ain't proposin' to steal their vittles, be you?"

She struggled up to a sitting position. "No, I ain't proposin' nuthin' of the sort, but I'd like to ask you a question. I got to go somewhere, and I want to know where to go."

Jonathan glanced around the room. "That's the first time I noticed they ain't got a commode in here." Then he bent over and peered under the bed. "They ain't got nuthin' else neither."

A troubled look came over her face. "How far is it to go outside?"

"That's some'pm I couldn't tell you. I didn't see no reg'lar place outside."

"But what'll I do?"

For a few moments Jonathan drew on his pipe in silence. "Afraid I can't tell you that," he said finally.

"But, Jonathan, I've got to make up my mind to something."

He drew a long breath. "Well, there's that fancy toilet bathroom she was showin' us across the hall. I wouldn't kill pigs in it myself, but if you want to go it ain't far away."

As Matilda lay there considering he became impatient. "Well, are you goin' or ain't you?"

"I aim to."

[116]

"All right, what's keepin' you?"

"Hand me my wrapper. It's hangin' over the chair."

Jonathan still sat smoking when Matilda came back. He waited for some comment from her on the modern improvements, but she volunteered nothing. Finally he asked her. "How'd you like the facilities?"

"Want I should get back into bed?" she asked.

He nodded. "You better, until we find out what's what around here; it's safer. Get along all right in yonder?"

"I think it's real nice," she said with a slight implication of defiance. "I like everything about it except the lookin' glasses, and they're all over the place. I don't know why they got so many of 'em; there's times when a lookin' glass ain't exactly welcome."

She went back to bed, and as she was pulling up the covers a knock came at the door. Jonathan stepped over to open it, alert for emergencies and ready for action. "Who is it?" he demanded curtly.

"It's your supper," came an equally curt answer.

He opened the door a crack and peered out to see a grim middle-aged maid in white apron and cap holding a large tray of covered dishes. "Who you lookin' for?" he asked.

"The Missus told me to bring supper up to the two of you."

"She did?" Jonathan threw open the door. "Come right in."

It was a peculiar tray which opened out into a table top, and there were folding legs for it to stand on.

As Mrs. Flint was setting the table she glanced at the occupant of the bed. "You feelin' sick?" she asked.

Matilda shook her head. "Just restin'."

"You look poorly to me," Mrs. Flint insisted.

"Oh, I'm all right."

"You certainly don't look it." Mrs. Flint drew her lips firmly together with an expression which implied that somebody was either lying or badly mistaken, and went on arranging the plates and silverware.

"You're Connecticut," said Jonathan. "I'd know that talk anywhere."

"I certainly am," she replied.

"Where'd you come from?"

"I was born and raised in the Naugatuck Valley."

"What part?"

"Born in Seymour, but I've lived all up and down the valley—Derby, Ansonia, Beacon Falls, Naugatuck, Waterbury."

"Over in the brass towns, hey?" This sounded a little scornful.

"That's what some folks call 'em."

Jonathan grunted. "Well, why wouldn't they? It's about all they make. Nuthin' but foreigners in them brass towns mostly. Can't talk our language. I never could figger out why folks call that part of the country Connecticut."

"Oh, you don't?" Mrs. Flint spoke disdainfully. "That's too bad. I don't know who you are, nor where you come from, but I want to tell you one thing, you can't insult the part of Connecticut where I was born, and not hear from me. We've got the finest brass factories in the world, but I'm sorry to say that they're no match for some people." She bowed stiffly. "Supper is served." Then she walked out of the door closing it behind her with an insulting gentleness.

From the window of the room above the garage, Herbert could see the parking space below, and the crunching of gravel told him that another car was arriving. He recognized the maroon sedan as belonging to the Archie Pynes and realized that it must really be getting late for Archie always came out to Westport on that malingering, meandering, uncivilized five thirty-one local instead of the far more convenient five-three express used by practically everybody else. He sometimes wondered if Archie was quite as busy as he pretended to be, if perhaps his hanging around the office, day after day until everybody else had left, was not calculated to create the impression of omnipresence.

[118]

Herbert reached for his socks. Only one was there. That was the trouble of moving out of your own room and camping somewhere else. You were practically certain to overlook something.

"Who's that driving in?" asked Margie, looking up from her little notebook in which she was making an entry.

"Looks like Archie's car."

"We are late. I thought you never were coming up from that taproom. I must have called you half a dozen times."

"Yes, it was a little embarrassing, but I couldn't tell Phil and Kathy to bolt their drinks and get up there and change."

"What I heard didn't sound like bolting drinks; it sounded much more like shaking up another." Margie spoke with a trace of irritation.

"Seemed to me you were a long time in getting that room in order," said Herbert, mildly on the defensive.

Margie kicked off her sandals and worried her feet into a pair of open-toed slippers with altitudinous heels. "Well, don't stand there gazing out of the window; get into your clothes. It doesn't look very well for the host and hostess to be the last persons to appear at their own party. People will think it's very funny."

Herbert shook the cardboard out of a clean shirt. "They wouldn't if they understood the circumstances. Do you suppose those old folks will have sense enough to stay in that room they're in?"

A deep sigh escaped from Margie. "If I only knew," she said with feeling.

As Herbert was drawing on his slacks he grunted out, "Well, you always wanted a good ghost for the house and now you've got two of them—in our best room."

"But why," asked Margie, "should they take that particular room?"

"We won't worry about that right now. Let's just try to keep them isolated there. Did you send up their supper?"

"Mrs. Flint is taking care of it. I wish we had a mirror in

here." Margie was patting down her hair and giving it little shoves here and there.

"Did they take it?"

"Heaven knows. Did you bring a comb? She just sniffed when I asked about them. I don't think she likes them. Do hurry, will you? I'm all dressed and you're nowhere near ready. We can't leave Barbara there alone to receive *all* the guests."

Herbert straightened up. "Now, just a minute: to begin with I have no comb. I'm all dressed but my socks, and since you brought me only one I'll have to wear the pair I've been wearing all day. And as for Barbara, you needn't worry; when she asks a man into the taproom to have a cocktail, he'll go."

"Are you sure George has plenty of liquor?" asked Margie.

This brought a chuckle from Herbert. "There's enough stuff down there to reopen Lazy Corners as a tavern."

Margie looked skeptical. "Then why is everybody talking about the shortage?"

"Oh, there's a shortage all right, but the fellow down in the Depot Liquor Store warned me that it was coming, and I got ready for it."

With a puzzled shake of her head Margie asked, "But what is there about the war to make a liquor shortage?"

Even yet Herbert was a little mad about it. "The government needs the alcohol," he replied in the tone of a man who was carefully holding himself in check.

Margie looked even more puzzled. "For the soldiers?"

"No, for the ammunition," said Herbert with a laugh. "Praise the Lord and pass it."

"Herbert." Margie looked at him closely. "You didn't have too much, did you, while you were down there shaking up that drink?"

An expression closely akin to outrage came over Herbert's face. "Most certainly not."

Instantly Margie was apologetic. "Of course not," she said. "I shouldn't have asked that. But wouldn't it be awful if the host at a party did have too much before the guests arrived?"

To this Herbert disdained an answer. Margie, however, had resumed worrying about her hair and so missed his masterly look of disdain. "What I really want is a comb," she said. "And I'll tell you something else I'm worried about. How is Mrs. Flint going to get the steam wagon down to the barn in the dark, unless you and George can help her?"

"Well, George and I can't help her," Herbert answered promptly. "George is going to be very busy taking care of the drinks. Fortunately the punch is made and it's down there. All it needs is the ice, and that's in the freezer ready to put in. As for myself, I'm going to be very much engaged with the Livingstones. I want everybody to meet them—and to know just who they are and how very important they are. By the way, we must be very particular to see that when they get to the barn they are seated with the right people. . . ."

By this time Margie was waving both her hands before his face. "But, my *dear!* What about the steam table?"

"Don't give it another thought," said Herbert as he slipped into a white sport jacket with blue buttons. "I've taken care of that. Old Joe from the dairy is coming over to move it down for her, and he can see in the dark like a cow."

"But how did you arrange all this, and when?" asked Margie skeptically.

"I caught him when he was putting the cows back in the pasture," Herbert explained. "I told him what I wanted and he said he'd be there."

"But, darling," Margie protested. "He wouldn't understand a word you said!"

Herbert smiled. "Never had a bit of trouble. That old boy's not so dumb."

"What language did you use?" Margie was smiling dubiously. "He doesn't speak English."

"He may not speak it," said Herbert, "but I had no trouble at all in making him understand every word I said to him. Remember how I used to get on with that Lithuanian janitor— the one who couldn't understand a word you said?"

She nodded but was still unconvinced.

"Well, there's a little trick to it, that's all," Herbert elucidated. "You speak very slowly, and you leave out every unnecessary word. You drop all the articles and particles and adjectives and keep only the nouns and verbs."

Margie was fussing with her hair again. "Well, I hope he understands."

"It's as clear to him as a cow," Herbert assured her. "Are you ready?"

"All but my hair—I still wish I had a comb."

Herbert caught her with her arms high and swept her into his embrace. He was a little surprised to find her there. Didn't know quite how he happened to do it, but he went on and kissed her with a flourish, and not a little relish.

"Why, darling!" she gasped as he released her. "You haven't kissed me like that in ages—but you must have had a tremendous Martini—I can fairly taste it!" She began licking her lips.

"Pretty good one, don't you think?" he asked.

"I prefer mine firsthand—but I'm afraid you've ruined my lips. Now I *will* have to go where there's a mirror." As she started along she called back over her shoulder, "Be sure to latch that door. Perhaps you'd better turn the key and take it with you."

ꞪꞪꞪ

HERBERT could see before he had reached the bottom of the stairs that the enterprising drinkers had already begun to gather in the taproom. This was as it should be. It was, he thought, a room for loud laughter, roistering, and big talk. The living room, on the other hand, was the haven of those who thought more of being socially adequate than of getting pleasantly tipsy.

He found Barbara waiting for him at the bottom of the front stairs. "Everything under control?" he asked, rolling his eyes towards the room occupied by the interlopers.

Barbara smiled reassuringly. "Haven't heard a peep out of them," she said, and turned back to the handsome captain of marines hovering nearby.

"What about Philip and Katharine? Not down yet?" Herbert asked.

She shook her head. "I've been right here watching for them."

Margie, who had come down the other stairs and had already greeted the guests in the living room, was now filtering through the taproom calling out gay greetings and trying to make everybody welcome. She was just starting to ask Barbara if she had seen anything of the Livingstones when she heard them coming down the stairs.

Katharine, sheathed in yellow satin, was moving carefully to avoid catching her high heels on the crooked steps of the silly little stairway, and Philip, for all his double-breasted puissance, was wondering if his perfect-fitting slacks had been

[123]

zipped in all the places where they ought to have been zipped, though he realized that coming down the stairs was not the place to go into such matters.

Margie smiled up at them. "Oh, my dear," she said to Katharine, "you're simply divine in yellow!"

Katharine's impulse was to spoil the compliment by saying that it was just because literary people always looked so dowdy, but she remembered where she was and compromised with herself by saying that the dress was "just an old rag." Even this was wasted, for Margie, preoccupied with the matter of introductions, did not hear it. The bookshelves in the library had caught her eye, and she was thinking they would make a wonderful background for so distinguished a publishing couple. The only trouble was that Philip already had his eye on the taproom and was showing signs of interest in that direction. It was at this moment that Archie Pyne joined the group.

"Hello, everybody," he said. He tried to pat them all on the shoulder at once. Then he leveled a finger at Philip. "Were you able to follow my directions?"

Philip nodded. "Perfectly."

"We're here, aren't we?" Katharine said in her usual expressionless tone.

"Then you didn't get lost?" Archie asked.

"We were never anything but lost," she retorted, "after leaving the Parkway."

Philip indulged in a smile of disagreement. "Being lost is only a state of mind," he said. "Some people manage to keep themselves that way most of the time."

"He was more surprised than I was when he saw Herbert's name on the mailbox," Katharine declared.

"Well, anyway, you're here," Archie said heartily, "and fortunately Margie hasn't got you in a receiving line. Of all the senseless inventions of a bewildered world I think the receiving line is the most ridiculous. I'm glad to see that you agree with me, Margie."

Margie's eyebrows went up. She swallowed hastily. "Well," she stammered, "I suppose there are times. . . ."

"Exactly," said Archie. "But this is not one of them. Just imagine, if you can, a receiving line at a barnwarming!"

"Imagine a barnwarming!" Katharine put in.

Archie quickly glossed this over. "Yes, there's nothing like a barnwarming," he said. "These informal parties are so much more fun. You can just drift around and mingle." He caught Katharine on one arm and Margie on the other. "Shall we mingle a bit?" Starting them in the direction of the study and the big living room, he added, "We'll leave the men to their own devices."

Herbert smiled as he watched them go. "Very capable fellow," he said. "That clears the decks for us and leaves us to do a little mingling on our own. How would it be if we should begin in the taproom?"

"That idea might bear investigating."

"You think it's sound from a publishing angle?"

"It's sound from any angle," said Philip. He laid his hand on Herbert's arm. "Isn't that the rear elevation of our eminent historian over there in the corner?"

"That's Fayrbanks all right," Herbert replied. "I'm glad you spoke about it—we'll get our drink at the other end of the bar."

George saw them coming and set up a pair of Martinis from a row he was holding in reserve behind the bar. He watched Herbert's fingers close on the slender stem of a glass and heard him murmur, "What is spring without a swallow!"

But George's real attention was directed elsewhere. He was, as a matter of fact, trying to keep tabs on Barbara and that dashing-looking captain of marines who had come in with some people from Westport. He hadn't caught the fellow's name when introduced, but it had seemed to him that Barbara was flustered when she saw him. Not flustered exactly, but just a little too glad to see him—and George suddenly remembered what she had said about the marines and their handsome uniforms. So this was the picture she had in her mind; there was more to this than met the eye. That was one point against him—and another was that the handsome young visitor had taken a highball at the cocktail hour. These two items and the further fact that he was too good-looking had put George on his guard. He picked up a tray full of drinks and hovered around near enough to hear what Barbara and the handsome marine were talking about.

"Sweet old house, don't you think?" he heard her say.

"Swell."

"The taproom's nice."

"Swell."

"The bar's not old, but it's authentic."

"Who's the youngster over there?"

"That's little sister Sarah."

"What's she doing in here with all these hooch absorbers?" he asked.

"Just standing around in the way and listening with her big ears."

"But she can't understand what that old boy's saying—he's talking about Einstein. And look at the way she's gazing up at him. You'd think she was spellbound."

He heard Barbara laugh softly. "She is."

"But why?" demanded the Marine.

"Simply because she thinks he looks like a horse—and he does."

George lost the thread of their conversation for a time, and when he caught it again they were talking about something else.

"So it's the South Pacific," he heard Barbara say a little sadly. "Dick's out there somewhere; my brother, you know. It's a tough assignment. Better reserve a good foxhole."

"That I will—hot and cold water—with insects to match."

"You'll find life rugged there."

"It's rugged right here—you never even give me a tumble."

Barbara laughed softly. "Silly boy," she said. "I've known you only a few days."

"But I've got only a few days left, and you aren't being kind to the armed forces."

"Listen, goon, when you're gone I'll be alone; I mean actually." George turned and looked at her, but she appeared not to be aware of his presence. "Every man I know is now in the care of the Postmaster at New York or San Francisco. Even my girl friends are all gone. They're in the Wacs, the Waves, the Marines. . . ."

"There's a tip for you, my ravishing pin-up—why don't you join the Marines?"

"And see the world?"

"Just the South Pacific area. I'll make it a double foxhole."

Barbara slowly shook her head. "My job is in the Motor Corps. I'll see the world some other time, thank you very much."

"All the more reason you should give me an occasional smile before I start for the jungle."

"I'll do better than that—I'll ride with you tomorrow."

"Swell, but what about tonight? That's part of my furlough, too."

"Tonight? Why—I'll show you around the house," she said gaily.

George pricked up his ears.

"We haven't found any underground tunnels," she said regretfully, "or secret staircases, but we have the cutest little passage around the big chimney! Want to see it?"

The glasses rattled on George's tray, but he did not turn around.

"Is it dark?" asked the marine.

"Like a pocket."

"Has it ever been explored?"

"It's been looked into."

"And you think I might find something nice there? Something to make me remember the occasion?"

[127]

"You might."

"What are we waiting for?" he asked.

Over his shoulder George saw them disappearing up the stairs.

The thing had happened. Fayrbanks had captured Livingstone and had involved him in one of the interminable discussions with which he loved to smother the gaiety of a social occasion. The truth was that eminent and able as the fellow was as a historian, he had won for himself an unenviable reputation as a bore. Herbert was taking no part in the discussion. He was standing by, blaming himself for not having prevented it, and trying to think of a way of bringing it to an end. He was listening to the sound of their voices rather than to their words. Fayrbanks was doing most of the talking, and when Fayrbanks talked Herbert usually found it hard to listen. However, his attention was attracted by a very positive assertion on the part of the historian.

"There," he said, "is a man whose name will go down in history."

Herbert wondered who the man was, and he listened with some interest to find out what, if anything, Livingstone was going to say about him. But it was not Livingstone who spoke next, it was Sarah.

"Professor Fayrbanks," she piped up in her clear voice, "I want to ask you something . . ."

She had been able to get no further than this before her father had her by the hand and was leading her away more firmly than gently. "You mustn't interrupt when other people are talking," Herbert said to her. "And the taproom isn't quite the place for a little girl to be hanging around."

"Why not?" asked Sarah, her eyes opening wide.

"It's too crowded, for one thing," her father replied rather unconvincingly. "Too many men there."

"But Barbara's hanging around in there," said Sarah.

"Barbara's quite another matter—but we won't go into that.

The place for you is right over by your mother. I'm sure you'll like it there much better."

"Okay, Daddy," Sarah said cheerfully and started towards the farther end of the big living room where her mother and Mrs. Livingstone were occupying the center of an animated circle.

Herbert looked over this part of the gathering with satisfaction. Archie was doing a good job—a much better job than he was himself. His conscience told him that he ought to go back to the taproom and do his duty, but he compromised by going the long way around through the study. This took time, for there were a number of guests here to whom he had not yet spoken, and he felt that he must stop for a few words with each of them. But eventually he extricated himself and pushed on to the taproom. He could see as he entered the door that Livingstone had not yet managed to escape. Herbert hated to be rude, but he had no other choice—he'd have to break up the discussion. To his astonishment he met with very little resistance in getting the two apart. Not only did Philip go along readily enough, but the historian made no effort to detain him. There was no outstretched hand to stay the departure for the finish of a sentence. Herbert was not one to question why, so long as he was getting what he wanted, and he guided Philip out of the taproom by the most direct route. They were already in the doorway of the living room when Herbert heard Sarah's voice behind him. She had come in by the other door and was speaking to Professor Fayrbanks.

"I wanted to ask you something, Professor," she was saying. "Do you think my father will go down in history?"

"Your father?" Fayrbanks let out a great guffaw of laughter.

Herbert was instantly furious. Punching the historian's face would have been a pleasure to him. And even more he would have enjoyed taking Sarah over his knee. But his instinct told him to get away from the scene as quickly as possible, not to delay even long enough to see who—if anybody—might have overheard.

[129]

"Wasn't that Fayrbanks who let out the big laugh?" Philip asked over his shoulder.

Herbert began to stammer but finally managed to say, "Sounded like him."

"Stuffy old boy," said Philip. "I didn't know he could laugh. He's obsessed with the idea that the Germans are coming over to bomb us."

"What with?"

"Blockbusters, poison gas, death rays, or something of that sort—where are you taking me?"

Herbert motioned toward the farther end of the room. "Over there to join the ladies. I want to sell them the idea it's time to eat."

WITH his new black-out switch in the cellarway Herbert winked all the lights in the house. Almost instantly the hum of conversation ceased, and people began to look around and ask each other what was going on.

After he had announced that the party was now moving to the barn, he turned to Katharine and said, "It's shaking their confidence that does the trick. As long as they're sure of the lights you can't do a thing with them. But the truth is that human beings are afraid of the dark."

"Some, perhaps," Katharine replied. "Won't I need a wrap— for the barn?"

He smiled. Not for this barn; it's heated. We have a fireplace down there that will take six-foot logs."

"Are there any in it?"

Her pessimistic smirk annoyed Herbert, but he tried not to show it. "Plenty," he said pleasantly. "It's ready to light. All it needs is a single spark from a match."

"I'm afraid I don't understand about a barnwarming," she said as they walked across the lawn, with the rest of the party trailing out behind them. "Surely we can't be going to a real barn where animals are kept. It must be a glorified studio or something of the sort."

Herbert laughed softly. "It may be glorified," he said, "but don't get the idea that the old barn isn't real. It served as a farm barn for a good many years, but that was a long time ago, and you'll find it as sweet as a new-mown hayfield."

[131]

Katharine sniffed the air audibly. "I haven't been in a new-mown hayfield since I was a child, but it certainly didn't smell like this."

"I know what you mean," Herbert said quickly. "The farmer down the road has a sizable herd of cows, and sometimes we get a little whiff from his barns when the wind comes from that way. Just one of those nice country smells."

"Then you like it?"

"Love it. Margie and I both do. Nature has a lot of good healthy smells—not at all like the carbon dioxide from your city smokestacks, or the smell of tar from your torn up streets."

Mrs. Livingstone exhaled disapprovingly. "I'm afraid I can't appreciate the subtle country odors."

"They aren't so subtle," Herbert said. "Margie had some fresh hay put in only today, and you'll notice the difference the minute you get inside the barn. The fragrance of that hay fairly blankets the place."

"How far is it to the barn?"

"It's right in front of us—we're practically there; but we'll have to wait where we are until the rest get here—we're supposed to be dazzled when the lights come on. Kind of a World's Fair arrangement, you know."

While waiting, Herbert heard sounds from inside the barn, but he did not take the trouble to investigate. He assumed that Mrs. Flint or some other attaché of the household was probably there attending to necessary matters of detail and was having difficulty in getting around in the dark. It was not until he had started for the light switch that the noises from inside took an alarming turn. As he stepped in the doorway he was greeted by loud and disparaging snorts and sniffs followed by an indescribable clatter. Herbert was startled, but though he drew back he did not run away. He kept fumbling for the switch, and he found it just in time to see the last of Joe's inquisitive cows careening out the rear door and into the dark of the night.

Only Shadrach was left. He was standing quietly in the stall built for a horse, though recently converted into an imitation bar. Framed by the rows of glasses and bottles, only the long placid countenance of the horse was visible to the guests now crowding about the doorway. Shadrach had dined well on two gallons of potato salad and half a hundred sandwiches. He had also dipped liberally into the big punch bowl and had about him the look of mellow content that comes with refreshment after a day's work well done.

Sarah, arriving on the run, was on the point of going inside to pet Shadrach when her father captured her. He had to restrain her by force.

"But Shadrach wouldn't hurt me," she argued irritably.

"Probably not, but you can't go in there."

"But he's a kindly horse."

"No doubt."

"He's kinder than most parents I know anything about."

"That's enough," said Herbert in a stern undertone. "Pipe down and behave yourself or you'll be sent to bed."

Sarah sighed heavily. "If I hadn't stayed back there to work on my poll I wouldn't have missed any of it. And this is all the thanks I get." She turned from the door and pulled away just as her mother arrived, breathing hard.

At the doorway Margie stopped short and drew back, raising her hand to her face as if she had been slapped. "Dear God!" she gasped. "What ever happened? Herbert! What has been going on?"

"Gate-crashers," said Herbert. "Joe's cows. The whole herd was in here. They've wrecked the place—turned it into a regular stable."

"Cows in our barn?" She peered inside. "The place is ruined for years to come!"

She had backed away and was starting a wild mirthless laugh when Herbert caught hold of her.

"Margie!" He gave her a rough shake. "Come out of it! Everything's going to be all right." He tried to lead her away, but she resisted, laughing hysterically.

Guests were already crowding around and necks were being craned by the time Barbara came hurrying to the rescue. She had heard the hysterical laugh and had recognized the symptoms, and, though she felt that slapping her mother's face would have been the quickest way to straighten her out, she forebore and caught Margie by the arms.

"Never mind about Joe's four-legged pets," she said with an attempt at gaiety. "You're needed at the house. You must go right back there to receive the guests—we'll serve the supper in the dining room. Help her, Daddy. She's a little weak in the knees. And I'll turn the party around and start it the other way."

Herbert and Margie came in by the terrace door followed by a number of the guests, and led the way to the dining room. Margie had by this time recovered a measure of control over herself and was feeling somewhat ashamed of having gone to pieces at the barn. But as she reached the door of the dining room another unnerving surprise was awaiting her.

Just inside the door stood Jonathan and Matilda, looking around like visitors at the Zoo. Jonathan was still in his shirtsleeves and smoking his corncob pipe, and Matilda was wearing a calico wrapper which came all the way down to the floor.

Margie stiffened like a ramrod and would probably have relapsed into her hysterics had not Mrs. Flint at that moment appeared in the kitchen door. At the sight of her Herbert caught Margie by the arm and propelled her across the room.

"Mrs. Flint is motioning for you," he said. "She needs you in the kitchen." And before Margie had time to demur he had forcibly delivered her into the hands of the woman from the brass towns.

Mrs. Flint would have liked to stay, but she had no choice, for as Herbert handed Margie into her care he grasped the knob and firmly closed the door behind her.

Matilda made a hasty exit, but Jonathan disdainfully took his time, puffing on his pipe and shuffling slowly around. He spoke to nobody, and after he had eyed all that he wanted to eye he ambled out of the room and made his way upstairs. Herbert could see the guests raising a surreptitious eyebrow or suppressing a knowing smirk, but before he could think of anything fitting to do or say Barbara came breezily in, and with her the rest of the party. As soon as he could, Herbert made his way into the taproom in quest of a drink. He thought he needed one.

Under the calming influence of Mrs. Flint, Margie quickly returned to her normal state of efficiency and once more took up the management of the party. It was only in the department of logistics that confusion resulted from the change of plans—Joe insisted upon going through with his original orders. That the cows had been in the barn meant nothing to Joe. What was a barn for? That they had eaten the ornamental hay was unimportant; there was plenty more where that came from. That they had tipped over the furniture was to be expected; they had no more use for furniture than he had. Herbert smiled when Barbara came to him and told of the trouble they were having in handling Joe. All the hot food for the party was on the steam table, and, though she now had the dining room ready for it, Joe was insisting upon taking it to the barn. Mrs. Flint couldn't stop him. Margie couldn't stop him. They couldn't make him understand. And if Herbert was as good as he thought he was about making people understand, here was a wonderful opportunity for him to show it, for Joe already had the vehicle halfway to the barn.

Herbert strode out of the house, the picture of a man full of authority. He intercepted Joe and told him in his simplified language what he wanted. Joe said okay and resumed his journey to the barn. Again Herbert stopped him. He simplified his universal language even further. He had previously discarded everything but the nouns and verbs, and now he discarded the verbs and put the entire burden of explanation on the nouns. Herbert felt sure that if he could have added a little sign language everything would have been all right, but in the darkness the use of sign language was futile.

[135]

From the dining-room door Margie could hear the sound of muffled nouns coming out of the darkness. Occasionally she would hear the words, "No, no, Joe! Not that way—*this* way!" Then more nouns. At first the nouns were mostly common, but after a little they became proper. Strictly proper, though perhaps improperly used, but they did the business. For eventually she heard grunts and the rattling of the pans in the steam table, which shortly afterwards came rolling up on the terrace and stopped outside the dining-room door.

It wasn't where she wanted it—outside the kitchen door would have been much better, but after all it would do and she did not feel that she could risk the time to make the change.

"You're wonderful!" she said to Herbert. "Did you do it by simplified language?"

Herbert wiped the perspiration from his brow. "Simplified and amplified," he replied. "But I'll have to go up and put on a clean shirt."

She laid her hand on his arm. "Don't forget that we're rooming up over the garage," she said in an undertone.

Herbert pulled away. "But I've got to go into the front room —that's where my clean shirts are."

"All right, dear," she said, "but don't disturb anything." She came up close to him and whispered, "And while you're there you might just—glance towards the other front room."

Herbert scowled. "You don't think they'll be coming down again?"

She shook her head. "I hope not. People are saying enough things already." Margie paused, searching her memory. "There's something else I want to tell you but I can't think what it is— wait till I look at my notebook." She opened a drawer of the side table and consulted the little leather covered book. "Oh, yes, now I remember! It was to have Mrs. Flint see what she can find out when she goes for the tray—but of course she can't go until after the supper's over."

Herbert slipped upstairs and into his own room, where he

dug out a clean shirt from his drawer. He was just leaving the room when he heard peculiar noises coming through the wall. He stopped and listened. Subdued voices. Arms brushing against the plaster. Somebody was in there. His mind leaped to the old folks—what could they be doing in that passage around the chimney? They had no business in there. He strode over to the little door and threw it open—to find Barbara and a handsome young soldier feeling their way through the dark passage. Herbert was surprised, more surprised than if he had found the old folks there.

Barbara was even more indignant than astonished. "What's the big idea of scaring a person to death?" she demanded. "Can't I show anybody around the house without being jumped at?"

Herbert began to laugh. "I guess we were both surprised," he said.

Barbara ran her hands over her hair to smooth down any stray locks. "I guess we were," she said.

Feeling considerably refreshed in his clean shirt, Herbert glanced in the mirror, gave his tie a pat, and started to go down to rejoin the party. As he paused at the top of the stairs to listen for a moment at the door of the guest room now occupied by the old couple, he heard voices. But they were not coming from the guest room; they were coming up from the lower hall.

"But Herbert told us they were distant relatives," he heard Katharine Livingstone say in a guarded voice.

"Rubbish!" This was the voice of Mrs. Fayrbanks, wife of the eminent historian.

"But he was explicit," Katharine insisted.

"Must have been drunk."

"Not at all. He was quite sober, though he was mixing us a cocktail at the time. Philip and I both thought that Herbert and Margie were as surprised as we were to find the old creatures in that room."

[137]

"You say the Gages were surprised?"

"Definitely. They sent us up to the guest room. And when we opened the door—there the old couple were!"

"You don't say!" Mrs. Fayrbanks exclaimed delightedly.

"The old man was in his stocking feet, and the old woman in bed."

"You don't tell me! How preposterous! But what happened?"

"Herbert pretended we'd gone into the wrong room, and sent us across the hall into their own bedroom."

"Yes, yes—then what?"

"Nothing really. It simply wasn't ready for guests."

"How embarrassing. And they made no apology or explanation?"

"None whatever, though Herbert did tell us later that they are eccentric relatives who have a way of dropping in on them unexpectedly."

"They're no more relatives than you are," exclaimed Mrs. Fayrbanks.

"They must be," Mrs. Livingstone protested. "Who'd ever claim such people as relatives if they weren't?"

"Well, let me tell you who they are—they're the old folks who used to own this place. They've got some sort of a claim to the title. This house was empty for years. Nobody around here would take it as a gift with that kind of a title, until Herbert and Margie came along. They fell into the trap like a couple of innocent lambs."

"You mean they were cheated?"

"Nobody seems to know. They suddenly turned up and began to do the place over. My husband always said they were playing with fire. And now see what's happened. Just a couple of ninnies."

Herbert stepped quietly back and slammed the door of the bedroom. Then he walked noisily to the stairs and started down. He found the women gone; but a glance into the library showed him that they were still talking together with an air of secretiveness. On a sudden impulse he started towards them, just to see what they would do. Mrs. Fayrbanks was considerably flustered at his sudden appearance; Katharine, however, was equal to the occasion.

"We've been talking about you," she said, her face expressionless, her lips scarcely moving.

Mrs. Fayrbanks colored furiously, but Katharine went on quite unperturbed.

"We were wondering about you."

"What were you wondering?"

"How you could manage to give a big party—with food rationing staring us all in the face."

"Oh, we just happened to have some food in the house," Herbert said. "Margie would have filled the cellar with groceries, but I wouldn't let her."

"Not a patriotic writer?" Katharine murmured. "Aren't all writers radicals?"

"Nothing patriotic about it," Herbert replied, trying not to show his irritation. "I simply didn't want to go to jail."

"Jail!" The word came from both women at once.

"Haven't you read the *first* paragraph of War Ration Book One?" Herbert demanded. "Punishments as high as ten years' imprisonment and a fine of $10,000 may be imposed for a violation of the law."

"That's about what you'd expect of any country which has the same man as President for three terms," said Mrs. Fayrbanks. She had started to say more but stopped short when an airliner passed over the house, making, because of the low ceiling, more noise than usual. The talk immediately veered to the danger of being bombed by long range Axis planes. Others joined in the conversation, and during the flurry Herbert withdrew and drifted around through the other rooms to see how things were going.

As he went along he noticed more than once that people who had been talking in low tones with heads close together would at his approach straighten up and begin to talk loudly about practically nothing, or possibly about the danger of air raids. He suspected, of course, that they were speculating about the presence of the old couple in his household. This was annoying, and still there was nothing to be done about it since he was not ready to discuss the matter in public.

And as for the talk of air raids, it seemed to him that Americans had a positive gift for worrying about the wrong things. Here they were getting all wrought up over the remote possibility of nuisance bombing at home, when the fate of the whole Mediterranean Basin and perhaps the entire globe was hanging in the balance. It pained him to think that even our military men had been won over to the idea that Axis psychology would demand the dropping of a handful of incendiaries on the Empire State Building or a time bomb on the grounds of the White House. Personally, Herbert thought the idea ridiculous. A stirrup pump in every home struck him as downright silly; and though he had yielded to the local black-out authorities in the matter of the main switch in the cellarway, it was only because he thought such a cutout would be useful during the severe electric storms to which the neighborhood was subject.

Once the guests had finished with supper, the party settled down into the familiar pattern, the young people in the semi-darkness of the terrace, the merrymakers in the taproom, and the others in congenial groups wherever they could find a place to sit down. Herbert was pleased with the number of notables they had managed to produce. Several writers, a well-known columnist, and quite a collection of associate editors and reviewers. He smiled as he caught a glimpse of the two returned war correspondents still shaking a finger at each other in a distant corner of the room. They had, he thought, added more color than distinction to the occasion, for they had been politely disagreeing all the evening. However, he hoped the Livingstones had been properly impressed with the literary background of the place.

Stopping for a moment in the doorway of the taproom, Herbert happened to notice Sarah questioning people and writing down their answers with a stub of a pencil. He remembered her poll and thought this might be a good time to look into it. But she saw him coming and quickly moved on. He made no attempt to follow her, feeling quite sure that whatever she was up to was harmless, and without a doubt connected with her present all-absorbing preoccupation with the horse. Herbert did not find out how wrong he was until the party was breaking up and guests were beginning to go home; and it was the eminent historian who took no slight pleasure in breaking the news.

"Well, Gage, you seem to be pretty anxious to find out what history's going to think of you," Fayrbanks said with a taunting grin as he stepped up to take his leave. "Your little daughter has already polled me on it three times, although I told her. . . ." He stopped short, cocking an ear. "Listen to that plane! Sounds mighty low to me. . . ."

While he was still speaking a peculiar piercing shriek began. At first it sounded far off—but it was coming! The volume swiftly increased with the terrifying crescendo they had all heard at the newsreels showing the air raid films. Instantly the place was in an uproar. Those who had just gone out the door rushed to get back in for shelter, and those who were inside rushed for outdoors to escape the danger from falling timbers and debris. In the midst of the confusion every light in the house went suddenly out.

Men called in fear and anguish upon their Maker. Some of the more timid women screamed, some prayed, and a few fought to get their arms around something or somebody. All braced themselves for the great blasting concussion that seemed inevitable. But the concussion never came.

The terrifying sound wavered, fumbled from one tone to another, and eventually fell into a slow and mournful rendition of "Nearer, My God, to Thee." To some of the listeners this was even more terrifying, for they thought it must indeed be The End.

To Herbert, however, it gave a clue to the right answer.

When the lights went out he had caught Margie by the shoulders and backed her into the nearest corner, determined to keep her out of the expected rush for the doorway. Well braced against the wall he was standing guard over her when suddenly he relaxed and gave her a delighted squeeze.

"I know what that is!" he said. "The old folks have found the organ. . . . !"

"But the lights?" Margie still clung to the idea of disaster. "How could that put out the lights?"

"I have a hunch about that, too," he said through clenched teeth. "Stay where you are—don't move—and I'll find out."

He felt his way over to the cellar door. It was partly open. When he reached for the switch he found a hand already on the lever, but it was snatched away. He made a grab, caught an arm, turned on the current, and hauled his captive out into the light. It was Sarah.

"I thought so," he said.

"Daddy—you scared me 'most to death!" she protested. "I didn't know who it was. But wasn't I quick on the black-out?"

Herbert drew a long breath. "Yes," he said, "you certainly were."

JONATHAN watched with satisfaction as the last car swung out of the driveway and went down the hill, its headlights brightening the ribbon of roadway and picking out the stalking shadows hiding in the shrubbery on either side. By turnin' night into day a man could make his going easier and faster, but Jonathan wondered if he was making it any better. This seemed at the moment pretty doubtful to him.

He hadn't been much of a hand to go ramblin' around at night. He had found bed to be the best place after a hard day's work. Of course, once in a while he had to go when there was sickness or some other emergency. Never would he forget that night the baby was born. It was the last week in March. Frost comin' out of the ground, and rain ridin' in on an east wind that a man could lean against without fallin' over.

What a night. Black as the inside of a jug, and ruts in the road halfway up to the hubs. It wouldn't have been so bad if he could have tied the lantern under the buggy axle, but the ruts were too deep for that, and the best he could do was to hang it on the dash. Lighted up the back end of the horse fine; the only trouble was he couldn't see nuthin' else.

He remembered how he untied the lantern and walked ahead before he reached the bridge. No handrails at that time, and he thought he better show the horse where to go across. The water was high—didn't miss the plankin' by more'n a foot, and he wasn't any too sure the bridge would be there when he come back.

But it was, and with the doctor along it didn't seem like quite so much of a job to get across. Things had happened fast after the doctor got in the house. It wasn't long before little Matt let out his first squawk, and after that he made more noise than a mess of kittens. That was a night of thanksgiving and hope. Hope for the baby and thanksgiving for Matilda. She had come through all right; but the baby—that was different.

The Lord had a mysterious way of handlin' these matters, but Jonathan was sure that his life would have been happier if little Matt had never seen the light of day which came filterin' through the south window soon after he was born. Of course Jonathan had no wish to run the Lord's business for him. As a general thing the Lord was able to handle matters pretty well himself, but that boy had proved to be the greatest tribulation of what was turnin' out to be a pretty long and tangled life.

Jonathan turned from the window and looked through the narrow door into the closet where Matilda was still seated at the organ, her feet on the pedals slowly rising and falling with just enough force to keep air in the bellows. A quavering hymn tune was droning out of the reeds. It was a tune that through the years had helped them to keep up courage—"There's a Land that Is Fairer than Day"—the words floated through Jonathan's mind. Pretty good words. Sung 'em along the roads many a time. Sorta give you courage and guts.

He walked slowly over to the closet door. "Guess we can go to bed now. The last one's just gone down the hill, so their noise won't be keepin' us awake much longer."

Matilda struck a chord and closed the organ. "Ain't those hymn tunes pretty though? Made me feel good to hear 'em again."

"Sounded nice," he said. "Hymns on a organ are some'pm to listen to—but let me tell you I'm about ready for bed. Last night at this time we was sleepin' under a tree. Tonight, by cracky, we'll sleep in a bed."

[144]

Matilda came out of the closet. "I wisht it was one of my spool beds."

"Time enough for that," he said. "We'll get around to it—but I still keep wonderin' about some'pm. Why do you s'pose all them folks come back from the barn in such a hurry, after gettin' it all set up for a party?"

Matilda shook her head. "Don't ask me. I got outa there in a hurry when they all come crowdin' in. I felt kinda funny bein' there."

"Well, I didn't," Jonathan declared. "We got some rights around here. We can go anywhere we feel like it. Say—did I tell you about the horse stall—all set up like a saloon with bottles and glasses? I don't know whether Shadrach's gonna like it or not." Jonathan put on his shoes, which he had taken off during the latter part of the hymn tune playing.

"Yes, you told me," Matilda said. "I hope he don't get cut on no broken glass. What you puttin' on your shoes for?"

"I'm goin' outside for a little."

"Well, don't fall into no holes or nuthin'," she said. "Must be pretty dark out there."

Jonathan stood up. "There ain't no holes around this place any more. I might fall over a birdbath or stumble into a outdoor fireplace, but I couldn't find a hole to fall in if I tried." He paused with his hand on the door latch. "Think you'll be goin' outside a little later, mebbe?"

"I'll not be goin' outside tonight," she said severely. "I'm too tired to be climbin' up and down stairs."

"You needn't take my head off. I just asked you."

Jonathan was feeling his way cautiously down the stairs. At the bottom he paused and listened. He could hear the refrigerator running in the kitchen, and the sound of water being drawn somewhere upstairs. Otherwise the house was still. The smell of liquor was heavy in the air, and there was the staleness that comes from an overabundance of cigarette smoke.

[145]

He moved across the hall and drew the big hand-wrought bolt. He would have known that bolt anywhere, in the dark as in the light. He opened the door and stepped outside, closing it softly behind him. For a few moments he stood on the old stone doorstep, breathing in the night air. Then he walked across to the maple tree and laid his hands on it.

"Here we are together again," he thought. "The tree, the house, and the old man."

He raised his hand and gave the rugged bark a pat. "I'm glad to get back," he said in a low tone. "Shouldn't never gone away in the first place." And he walked slowly around the corner of the house and started in the direction of the barn. Occasionally he stepped into a flower bed or stumbled over some unexpected shrubbery. As he neared the back of the house he could see a light shining through the uncurtained windows of the loft over the garage.

He stopped and looked up at it. "That's where they wanted to stow us," he thought, "but it didn't work, and somebody else had to take it."

As he stood there in the dark, he could hear people talking in a low tone but could not understand what they were saying until suddenly the voice of Herbert Gage came out quite plainly.

"Zipper trouble, hey? Back over this way and I'll fix it for you."

Margie walked past the window. "It's stuck," she was saying. "I can't move it up or down."

So they had to take it themselves! Jonathan could hardly restrain a chuckle as he walked on towards the barn. He found the big barn door wide open, but did not go in. Standing just outside, he could hear old Shadrach snoring. Jonathan sniffed the air. Even the barn smelled of liquor. He wondered how Shadrach could stand it. Aside from the alcoholic flavor it was a pretty good smellin' barn, though he couldn't see why anybody would want to give a party in a barn when they had a good house.

He circled around the barn and walked over to the pasture just to be sure that Shadrach could get through to the brook if he wanted water. He was a little surprised to find the bars up and was on the point of taking them down again when he discovered the presence of the cows on the other side. So they were using that field for a night pasture. He had, he reasoned, given Shadrach a good chance to get to the brook, and if the nag hadn't done it—that was his own lookout. That was the way Jonathan would have treated himself, and what was good enough for him was good enough for Shadrach.

On returning to the house he found Matilda in bed. "Did you go in there?" he asked, motioning with his head towards the bathroom.

Matilda avoided the question. "How'd you find Shadrach?" she asked.

"Shadrach's all right," he answered. "Snorin' like a baby when I was there."

"Everything all right outside?"

"As far as I could see in the dark—yes. But you ain't answered my question—have you been in this indoors—place?"

"Yes, I have."

"What's the idea of makin' an excuse of the stairs—why don't you say right out that you like indoor plumbin'?"

"I couldn't see no reason for talkin' about it, that's why."

As Jonathan was getting into his nightshirt he remarked that the old-timers certainly made their beds high enough.

"Guess that was to make room for the trundle beds they kept underneath."

"Mebbe so, but they might have furnished 'em with a pair of stairs."

"My spool bed ain't too high."

"Nope," Jonathan grunted as he slid down under the covers. "It ain't as soft as this neither—and good glory! Got my head against one end and my feet against t'other, and I'm doubled up like a jackknife. I can't sleep like this."

"My spool bed ain't too short, neither. It's plenty long, if you'll recollect."

"I recollect all right," muttered Jonathan, "but I don't know what good recollectin' is goin' to do. Take more'n recollectin' to get the kinks out of my legs in the mornin'."

"Now you wait a minute till I get my feet way over on my side, and then you try layin' kitty-corner."

"Might as well try it." Jonathan shifted himself around.

"Well," Matilda said, "is that any better?"

Jonathan grunted. "Could be worse. But I'm still a mite cramped."

"You could stick your feet out through the slats at the bottom," suggested Matilda.

"Could, but I ain't aimin' to. I got to have my feet warm when I sleep."

"We'd be all right if we only had my spool bed down here."

"Keep still about that spool bed, will you? I'm tryin' to get myself used to this one, so I'll forget I'm in it." He rolled partway over. "These folks eat pretty good here, if that was a fair sample we got tonight."

"Well, it wasn't," Matilda replied with emphasis. "That was party vittles. And besides, you needn't think they're gonna feed us right along."

"I don't think so," the old man mumbled. "Never did think of such a thing for a minute. I knew all along they was just tryin' to keep us out of sight—but it didn't work."

"No, but I'd have been ashamed to be invited to such a party as that—all that liquor drinkin' and carousin'. What do you reckon will happen next?"

Jonathan drew a long breath. "Your guess is as good as mine."

"Think they'll try to put us out of this room?"

"How can they?"

"Well," said Matilda in a whisper, "the furniture don't belong to us."

"Part of it does," said Jonathan, "that box with cigarettes

in it. And that lampshade in the hall has got some of your old music on it."

Matilda raised her head up from the pillow. "I know, I know, but do you reckon our furniture's all right?"

"Right as it ever was." Jonathan was twisting his feet and trying to get his legs straightened out a little farther.

"What do you mean by that?" asked Matilda sharply. "It was always good furniture, and you know it."

"Oh, I suppose it was all right."

"All right? My Connecticut bench is the best-lookin' piece of furniture in that livin' room, and you know it."

"Yes," he muttered begrudgingly, "and right this minute I wisht I was sleepin' on it. It ain't any too soft, but, by cracky, it's long enough. But let's forget about it and go to sleep."

"I don't see how you can lay there and go to sleep, when you don't know what's gonna happen to us in the mornin'. These folks got money for lawyers, and they've got the Power Company on their side. They may go to law and put us right out on the street—and here you are yawnin' and droppin' off to sleep just as if you didn't have nuthin' to worry about."

"Listen, Matilda, we ain't got no more to worry about than what they have. We've got back every nickel we ever put into this place. It's gone, of course, but you can't deny that we had it."

"We won't talk about that. I don't even like to think about it."

"Well, neither do I, but I just want to show you they ain't in the same boat with us. They got a lot of money tied up here, and they ain't goin' to like it to have us livin' in the same house with 'em. I don't like it any too well myself. But it's our home and we're goin' to stay here."

"They're prob'ly sayin' the same thing."

"I don't claim to know what they're sayin'. They can stay if they want to. But I reckon there ain't no harm in hopin' that they won't find it as pleasant around here as what they expected."

"You better not go tryin' any of your smart tricks until you're sure our papers'll hold."

"They held all right today, didn't they?"

"We're still here, if that's what you mean. But I'd feel a lot better if you'd go over everything with Uncle Walter. He's got more brains than he knows what to do with, and if he says it's all right, I'll quit worryin'."

"Think he'll be friendly, do you?"

"I don't know why not."

"Well, you know how folks are."

"But he ain't. Uncle Walter's got sense."

"Don't forget all we been through."

"But Uncle Walter wasn't uppish none of them other times."

"Nope."

"He's always been your friend. Remember how he come around to see you whenever Matt got in trouble and folks begun talkin'?"

"Uh-huh."

"You always thought he stopped in just to show that he was loyal."

"Still think so."

"He knows more law than most lawyers."

"I know that."

"Then why don't you go to see him tomorrow?"

"By cracky, I will."

Matilda sighed. "I feel better already."

JONATHAN scorned the idea of lowering the window shades, and the light of dawn filtering through the young woods on the ridge had found his wrinkled eyelids and gently parted them long before the first rays of the sun had come over the rim of the world.

For a time the old man lay motionless on his back, staring up at the faded ceiling. The plaster was cracked and uneven, just as it had been the first morning he ever woke up in that room. It didn't look as if it had been done over in all that time, and he couldn't recollect that it had. He could still see where the ceiling timbers went across; white paths along the dusky plaster, some wide as a barn rafter and others no wider than a good fence rail.

Expert axman that he was, Jonathan had never learned to use the adz, which long before his day had been displaced by the speed and accuracy of the saw. As a boy he had spent many an hour watching the screaming blade of steel in the old sawmill on the creek. He had been fascinated, but a little frightened, at the swift destructiveness of a machine which could, in a matter of seconds, make a lumber pile out of a tree which had taken God a century to grow.

Hand hewing had always seemed to him much more respectful to nature, and he had grown up in the belief that no sawed beam could ever be anything but cheap and shoddy. He lay and looked at the exposed plate beams as he had looked at them many years before. This was the place where he and Matilda had started their life together. A lot of years had gone by, and there they were lying side by side in that same room. They had both growed some older. You couldn't dodge the years. In spite of anything they'd keep pilin' up on you, and though Jonathan would admit it to nobody else, he couldn't deny to himself that he was no longer quite the man he had been.

For a few moments he lay and listened to Matilda's breathing, then he slid quietly out of bed and put on his clothes. Carrying his shoes in his hand so as not to waken her, he let himself out the door and went softly down the stairs, his stockinged feet clinging a little too tenaciously to the heavily padded carpet on the stair treads.

At the bottom of the stairs he turned and glared at the carpet. He could not see why they wanted to cover those good straight-grained oak boards with any such stuff as carpet—and pink at that. He couldn't imagine anything that would be easier to trip on. He wouldn't even sit on it to put on his shoes, but seated himself on a sturdy seaman's chest at one side. As he sat there he realized how still the house was, and it came to him that he must be the only one stirring. The temptation to look over the remains of the party was too great to resist. He hated a snooper, but after all he had a right to be there and to know what was going on if he wanted to.

With a righteous air he stepped over to the door of the taproom. This room had always annoyed him. He thoroughly disapproved of its past, and though no liquor had been sold there since the days when George Washington was President, Jonathan had never been able to forgive and forget. He regarded the room as he would have regarded a fallen woman; she could repent and reform—she could adopt a life of the utmost purity and piety—but once defiled she could never recover her reputation.

At no time had he liked that room or respected it, and as he stood there looking around the day after the party he liked it less than ever. Thick oaken chairs were drawn in a cluster about a low table standing before a wooden bench. An array of empty glasses cluttered the table top. A corkless bottle stood on the floor beside it, and under the table was an empty glass lying on its side. An ash tray on the table was so rounded up with cigarette butts and burned matches that it reminded him of a load of hay, and a circle of cigarette ashes on the bare floor surrounded the group of chairs like a garden path.

Jonathan sniffed with disgust; he hated the smell of stale liquor. He hated having even the imitation bar reestablished there and wished for a moment that he could have called in Carrie Nation. He marveled at the full bottles still lining the wall back of the bar, not realizing that they were a collection and were, for the most part, filled with water. His indignation having been sated, he turned and walked across the hall to the door of the study.

Here the empty glasses were parked all over the place. They were on the window sills and the mantel, the bookshelves and the floor. Cigarette stubs and ashes were plentiful, but they were mostly in the ash trays. A pencil-drawn diagram lying on the desk showed how Tokyo could be taken by a joint attack from Kamchatka, China, and the Aleutians. Another diagram indicated Dakar with a number of radial lines projecting in all directions. Several warped sandwiches lay on a silver tray, beside which were a stalk of wilted celery and two shrunken sausages impaled on toothpicks.

A few strides brought him to the door of the living room. Here he found better order than in either of the rooms he had previously visited. Fewer glasses were around, and he noted with surprise that some of them still contained liquor, one or two filled to the top. Must have been some'pm wrong with the drinks, he thought, and he began to wonder what it could have been.

He had lifted one of the full glasses in his hand and was looking at it before the light from the window when he heard a slight noise from the direction of the dining room. On turning his head to look over that way, he saw Mrs. Flint standing in the doorway watching him with an expression of scornful amusement.

"Ain't it a little early for that kind of business?" she asked.

Deeply chagrined, Jonathan snapped back at her, "I was just lookin' at it."

"So I noticed."

"There was a couple of full glasses left here, and I was wonderin' what was the matter with 'em."

"And what did you expect to find out just by lookin'?" she asked.

He set the glass down on the table, carefully replacing it in the ring on the varnished top from which he had taken it, and turned away with a show of indifference which he certainly did not feel. "I don't know's there's any great call for me to be tellin' you my business."

"If I'd known you made a business of it I wouldn't have said nuthin'. I expected it would be you when I heard somebody prowlin' around in here."

"I wasn't prowlin'. I don't have to prowl. This house is my home and I've got a right to walk around in it."

"You think that gives you the right to snoop—and to let cows through into the barn whenever you feel like it?"

Jonathan glared at her. "Who said I let the cows into the barn?"

"Nobody said so. Who else could've done it?"

Still glaring at her Jonathan said slowly, "Did it ever come to you them bars might been put down so's the horse could get through to water?"

"There's a water tap in the barn."

"That may all be, but my horse ain't never learned to handle a tap. And besides, there wasn't a cow in that pasture when them bars was let down."

"Then you don't deny you let 'em down?" she asked as if she had trapped him.

"Certainly I don't deny it," he said testily. "You can't seem to get it through what you're usin' for a head, that this is my home and I've got some rights around here."

"I don't know nuthin' about your rights, and care less," she said impassively, "but I do know that if you don't get that old nag of yours out of the barn they won't be able to have another party there for the next five years."

Jonathan made a clucking sound. "Now wouldn't that be too bad! That's the only horse stall on the place, and Shadrach's gonna stay in it."

"So the horse has got rights, too!" she said sourly.

"Never you mind about that horse," said Jonathan. "He'll come in mighty handy around here."

She moved as if to go, then paused and pointed with a finger towards the mantel. "There's another full glass up there, in case you hadn't noticed it," she said.

Without deigning to answer, Jonathan turned his back and walked slowly into the study. Then he heard her coming and turned to face her, wondering what she was up to. But she was no longer acting in her individual capacity of a woman facing a prowler. Now she was the well-trained servant speaking on behalf of her mistress.

"One thing more, sir," she said. "Is the lady awake?"

"What lady?"

"The one who was in your bed last night, in the room above."

He shook his head. "Who wants to know?" he asked. "And what for?"

"I wanted to ask about breakfast, sir."

"Well, what about it?"

"Does she like it early on Sunday? Or later, sir?"

The news of the return of the old folks was all over town in a very short time. Uncle Walter knew about it the night of their arrival. He was tempted to go over to see Jon that same night, but he did not want to appear to be rushing matters. He had all along kept an uneasy eye on the changes and alterations, and knowing the importance of possession in the eyes of the law he was fearful that Jon might have run into serious trouble. Of course he couldn't go over there and offer his services; that might be humiliating to his friend. But he could go on the pretext of needing help himself. That would give Jonathan a good opening if he wanted one.

For some time Uncle Walter had been puzzling over the weight of a beef critter. He had a buyer for it, but he did not like to let it go until he had made a fairly accurate estimate of the animal's live weight. No tellin' what kind of tricky scales these cattle buyers might have. Jonathan, he knew, had a formula for estimating the live weight of cattle, and Uncle Walter figured that if he should stop by to ask for that formula, it might be a good way to break the ice. So Uncle Walter drove over the next day.

He saw Jonathan standing in front of the barn as he came up the road, and with a wave of the hand he turned in and brought his one-horse lumber wagon to a stop in front of the big barn door.

"Hello, neighbor!" he shouted loud enough to have been heard on the farther side of a forty-acre lot. "You're quite a stranger!"

"Y'ain't none too fermilliar yourself!" Jonathan bellowed in return.

"How you been?"

"Fair to middlin'."

"How's Matildy?" Uncle Walter was still putting on plenty of power.

"Tol'able."

By this time Sarah, attracted by the shouting, had come down from the house. "What makes him holler so loud?" she asked Jonathan.

"Because he's deef as a post," he answered. "Now you run back to the house—I got some bus'ness with him and don't want to be bothered."

"Can't I go in and pet Shadrach?" she teased.

"Not now, Sarah. You get right back up there to the house, and don't come down here again until he's gone."

Sarah went reluctantly, looking back over her shoulder as she crossed the lawn.

Meanwhile, Uncle Walter was clambering down from his wagon. "I come over to get your receipt for figgerin' live weight of a beef critter." He still spoke as if Jonathan were somewhere out behind the barn.

Jonathan bent over his ear and shouted. "Ain't you got your trumpet along?"

"My what?"

"Your tube—your long black talkin' tube." Jonathan measured with his outstretched hands, then poked a finger in his own ear. "Your tube!"

"My tube? Oh—that. Don't need it no more. Don't use it hardly at all with my lip readin'."

Jonathan knew all about that lip readin'. It was just about sixty per cent wrong. He bent down and bellowed into Uncle Walter's ear. "Better get out that tube. My lips ain't workin' good today!"

"What's the matter with 'em?"

"Kinda stiff." Jonathan ran his fingers across them. "Don't work good. Get your tube!"

Uncle Walter, muttering protests, drew it out from under the seat of the wagon and went into the barn with the speaking tube squirming in his hands like a newly caught eel. Inside the barn Jonathan picked up a piece of cord and proceeded to give a demonstration on Shadrach, talking into the open end of the speaking tube, which Uncle Walter held up to him like a little black funnel.

"First you measure the girth around the breast just behind the shoulder blade." He did so. "Then you measure the length of back from tail to fore part of shoulder blade." This, too, he demonstrated. "Now you multiply length by girth and divide by 144." He took the pencil out of Uncle Walter's hand and made the computation. "When it's less than three feet you

[157]

multiply by eleven. If it's between three and five feet you multiply by sixteen. Between five and seven you multiply by twenty-three—and if it's over nine feet. . . ."

"Wait a minute!" bellowed Uncle Walter. "What do you think I'm measurin'—a elephant?"

"If you ever do you'll know how," replied Jonathan. "Now watch. If your animal is lean, subtract one-twentieth, and you get the live weight—pretty close. Or if you want the net weight, you multiply the live weight by point 605. Understand?"

Uncle Walter nodded. "Sure." He put the pencil and paper in his pocket, but the truth was that he knew little more about the computation of cattle weight than he did when he came. However, he had broken the ice, and it was not long before he found himself in a position where he could ask, "Who is this feller that's livin' in the house?"

"Just set down there," Jonathan said, pointing to an overturned pail. "Make yourself comfortable while I fetch a box to set on. I want to go over this whole thing with you."

"You been gone a long while," Uncle Walter said as Jonathan sat down and took hold of the conversational end of the flexible black tube.

"Quite a spell."

"I saw in the paper that Matt come out innocent, but that was some time ago. Where you been all this time?"

Jonathan scratched his head. "Well, we stayed around to see how we liked the West. Mighty pretty country out there. If we coulda made a go of it—we'da stayed. I tried just about everything—but it's a young man's land. An old-timer ain't got much of a chance there. We mighta stuck at that if it hadn't been for Matilda. She wanted to stay all right, but the climate didn't agree with her, and she was poorly all the time we was there. She had a couple of long sick spells, and we finally decided we'd hafta come back after all. Tell you the whole story sometime, but right now there's other matters kinda pressin'. We're in kind of a muddle up to the house."

Uncle Walter got out his pipe. There was nothing he liked better than being in a position where he could help a friend— by giving advice. "Well, get agoin'," he said.

He was a picture of contentment as he leaned back against an upright and crossed his legs. His hair on this day was more shaggy than usual, but this was more than offset by the fact that he was cleanly shaved, having attended to that matter only the day before. He rarely missed shaving once a week, usually on Sunday morning. That was how it happened that all day Sunday he seemed pale; by Tuesday his appearance was that of a convalescent, and it was not until the latter part of the week that Uncle Walter really looked himself.

The Sunday shaving would usually be interrupted by a call from Joe. The caller would remove his hat and come into the kitchen to say hello. Uncle Walter would answer through the coating of lather on his face. He would wave the razor in greeting—an old sway-backed, bone-handled Wade & Butcher. Joe would stand around for a while watching the barbering, and then he would go outside and take a nap on the ground under the elm tree.

When the shaving was done, Uncle Walter would join Joe under the elm tree. Joe never would sleep while Uncle Walter was there. That was not good manners. He would rise up on one elbow, or he would sit cross-legged. And there the two friends would stay sometimes for an entire afternoon. They never talked. What was the use? Uncle Walter couldn't hear, and Joe couldn't understand. Still, they were great friends.

On weekdays, whenever things happened to be dull at the dairy, Joe would stroll down to Uncle Walter's and pay a little call. If Uncle Walter was there, the two would sit for a while, of course saying nothing, but still enjoying each other's company. If Uncle Walter happened to be away, Joe would drop down under the elm tree for a little nap. It was his favorite napping place, except when the elm beetles or caterpillars were in season, and then he would do his napping under the maple on the other side of the house.

As a matter of course Joe appeared on the day when Uncle Walter came over to get the weighing formula from Jonathan. The cowman was lying in the shade outside the barn door while Jonathan was talking with Uncle Walter. Jonathan recognized the relationship between the two much as he accepted the attachment between a man and a dog. He knew that if Uncle Walter came Joe could not be far behind—and he never was.

This was the first of the meetings between the three old men, but it was by no means the last. Questions had a way of coming up that were puzzling or perplexing to Jonathan, and if he wanted to have a meeting all that was necessary was to tell Joe.

"Get Uncle Walter," he would say. "Me want." Joe would grin and nod and go away, and in about half an hour Uncle Walter would come driving up the road.

Herbert saw Uncle Walter from the window the first day the old fellow came to see Jonathan. It was the shouting that had attracted his attention. He recognized the shaggy little deaf man at a glance, and immediately remembered his peremptory refusal to do the glazing job for which Herbert had called him in. It was impossible for anyone in the house to be unaware of one of Uncle Walter's visits, though he came no nearer than the barn. That Jonathan and Uncle Walter were close friends was now obvious to Herbert. He wondered why he hadn't thought of it before.

ꜰꜰ

BARBARA was lying flat on her back on the floor of the study with the telephone resting on her stomach. She was talking, largely in monosyllables, to the marine captain who was back in town after a brief visit at his post. She had her knees drawn up high, and as she talked she occasionally kicked one foot towards the ceiling, for emphasis, or perhaps just from the joy of living.

Herbert, sitting at his typewriter, looked at her from time to time and wondered if he hadn't been born about one generation too soon. These young things of today were certainly a glorious and glamorous lot.

"Barbara!" This was from Margie, who had suddenly appeared in the doorway. "Get up! That's undignified. It's almost indecent to talk over the telephone in such an outrageous posture. What if some outsider should come into the house and find you that way?"

"Just a minute, captain," said Barbara sweetly. "Somebody's at the door. Call me back in half an hour—will you, dear?" With an effortless motion she came to her feet and restored the telephone to its accustomed place on the top of the desk.

"I won't argue with you about it," Margie said, trying to be reasonable. "I know it isn't your fault. It's just that you belong to the age of slacks. The minute a girl gets on slacks all her sense of propriety vanishes." She turned and went away just before Sarah came galloping into the study and stopped beside Herbert's desk with a whinny and a toss of her mane.

[161]

"Daddums," she panted, "may I go for a ride with Gramp Rockwood and Shadrach?"

Her father motioned sternly with his hand. "Stand up," he said. "Two legs, please." And as she rose to the standing posture of a human being he added, "Don't call me Daddums, and that old man is definitely not your grandfather. Now, what is it you want?"

"May I go for a ride in the wagon with Shadrach and Mr. Rockwood?"

Herbert scowled. "Sarah, you know perfectly well that I don't want you to have anything to do with either of them."

Sarah looked at him brightly. "He said I could drive part of the way. Please, Daddy, please—if you please."

"Where is he going?" His tone implied no promises, merely curiosity.

"Just over to Uncle Walter's," she answered, still clinging to a shred of hope.

He shook his head. "It's too far to go with that old nag. What's he going for?"

"To get a cow and fifty chickens. That's why he wants me to go along and drive, so he can sit in the back and lead the cow."

Herbert looked helplessly at Barbara, who stood by the bookshelves hunting for something to read, then back at Sarah. He had seen the old deaf man out there but he never dreamed anything like this was in the wind.

"Please, Daddy, make up your mind!" Sarah was becoming impatient. "Please—please—please."

"I don't understand about the cow or the chickens," Herbert said. "Is he moving them for somebody?"

"Oh, he's bringing them here for himself. He wants to beat milk rationing, and he says no home is fit to live in unless you keep chickens."

Herbert had a very good idea what would happen to his Victory garden with a cow eating off the tops of plants and fifty chickens scratching up the roots. "I don't suppose he told you where he is going to keep all this livestock?"

[162]

"Oh, yes, he has," said Sarah, fidgeting to be on her way. "There's a stall in the barn for the cow, and he has built a cute little house for the chickens. It's back of the barn."

Herbert looked at her searchingly. "You're telling me that he's already built a hennery back of the barn—and I don't even know about it?"

"It isn't a hennery exactly." Sarah was squirming towards the door. "It's more of a coop."

As Herbert turned and reached for the telephone, Barbara made an unobtrusive sign to Sarah that this was a good time for her to be on her way. And Sarah, with a quick glance at the back of her father's head, left the room swiftly and silently, traveling on two feet instead of four. A short time later, while her father was still discussing the cow and chicken situation with Mr. Loomis over the telephone, Barbara stood by the window and watched Sarah drive out of the yard and off down the hill with her father's elderly tenant in common.

Downhearted and disgusted, Herbert turned from the telephone and slammed on the receiver. "Score the round for Rockwood," he said with a scowl.

Barbara came over from the window and perched on the corner of the desk. "Then the old man keeps his cow and his chicks?"

"Absolutely!"

"Nothing to be done—I mean actually?"

Herbert struck the desk with his hand. "Not a thing—not a damn thing. He's entirely within the law. He has just as much right to keep a cow and chickens as we have to keep a cat or a canary bird." He glanced around the room, looking behind chairs and eventually under the couch. "Where's Sarah?"

Barbara waved farewell with her hand. "She faded while you were on the 'phone. Do you want her?"

"No—no!" Herbert replied distractedly. "I simply didn't want her to hear what we are saying. There's no telling what she passes on to that old man."

"Plenty, I imagine," said Barbara. "But what does Winnie

Loomis say about all this? Doesn't he give you any good cheer at all?"

Herbert shook his head. "Just keeps telling me to get the working agreement he suggested."

"Well, why don't you?"

"How can I make an agreement with a man who disagrees with everything I say?" Herbert demanded.

Barbara smiled with a quick flash of white teeth between carmine lips. "Sounds like the neatest trick of the week," she said.

"Loomis tried it himself a while back."

"Any luck?"

"None whatever." Herbert spread out his hands. "The old man knows his rights—why should he dicker them away?"

"I suppose you could tangle him up in a law suit."

"What good would that do? His legal position is just as sound as ours."

"There's always a possibility that you could wear him down," said Barbara.

Herbert snorted at this. "I'd just wear myself down," he declared. "He'd like nothing better than a good mean law suit. He's never so happy as when he's being obnoxious."

"But did you ever try agreeing with him?"

"It can't be done," said Herbert with a disgruntled smile.

"What makes you think so?"

"I've tried it."

"What happened?"

"He switched right over to the other side."

This did not strike Barbara as being such a tough situation. "But can't you switch with him?"

"No, I can't," said Herbert. "I can't hold my temper long enough."

Barbara reached over and patted the top of his head. "I'm afraid my old dad was never cut out for a diplomat," she said. And then she went off and left him.

She was talking about it later with George, who had dropped

in to report that the Marines would have no part of him. "It doesn't seem like such a difficult situation to me," she said. "If it were worth my while I could switch from one side to the other just as many times as he could."

"Why bother?" said George. "I've got real troubles to worry about."

"Oh, this is real enough," Barbara insisted. "That old couple are running wild all over the place. Dad and Mother can't do a thing with them. Dad isn't getting any work done at all."

"But if you do tame the old nipper—what then?"

Barbara smiled. "Ah, then they can make an agreement as to just what part each family is to use."

"But how is it now?" asked George with a puzzled look.

"As it stands now," said Barbara who was herself not entirely unperplexed, "they are tenants in common."

"What does that mean?"

"Well," said Barbara, "as Winnie Loomis explains it, that means each one has the right to all of it."

"I see," said George. "And what you propose to do is to get each one to give up the whole for only a part?"

"Roughly speaking, yes. But the part they get will be exclusive."

George shook his head vigorously. "It won't work."

"I think it will," said Barbara. "And anyway I'm going to try."

The conference in the library had been long and tiresome, but it was getting nowhere. Herbert had known this for the last hour, but Mr. Loomis could not seem to take the same view. Jonathan had made it plain early in the discussion that his interest in the place was not for sale. He had put it very briefly and clearly, not once but a number of times. "I just ain't sellin', that's all."

From the first Herbert felt that Jonathan really meant what he said. He had a strong instinct about it. Mr. Loomis had no such instinct. He had been brought up to believe that in making a bargain only one thing was really essential, and that was keeping the discussion open. It must never be brought to a definite end. If you could keep it going long enough there was always a chance you might bring the other party around.

It was in following out this theory of barter that Mr. Loomis suggested that Matilda be invited to join the discussion, thinking that in addition to keeping talk going he might arouse her interest by the possibility of having some money to spend.

Jonathan shook his head. "Nope, she ain't comin' down," he said.

Mr. Loomis gave one of his most owlish looks. "It seems to me that in all fairness your wife's interests should be consulted as well as your own."

"Her interests will be consulted all right," Jonathan assured him. "Don't worry about that. But ever since she got that fall on them stairs she's been a little partial about goin' up and down."

Mr. Loomis peered at Jonathan over the tops of his glasses. "Do I understand that your wife got a fall on these stairs?" He motioned vaguely towards the front hall.

Jonathan nodded. "Certainly did. Them stairs right there. Catched her heel on the top step, and down she come, all the way to the bottom."

With an accusing stare at Herbert Mr. Loomis said sharply, "You told me nothing about this."

"For a very good reason," said Herbert. "I never heard of it until this moment."

The lawyer turned slowly around and stared at Jonathan. "How did it happen you didn't report this to Mr. Gage?"

Jonathan was amused. He knew what was going on—they were worried over a damage suit. He had neglected to tell them that the accident had happened some years ago—even before he had sold the place to the Power Company—but if they wanted to worry he'd let them worry. He was in a contrary mood and did not feel like explaining.

"Come near fallin' there myself this mornin'," he said. "I

tell you them stairs is dangerous the way you got 'em fixed."

"What's dangerous about them?" Mr. Loomis asked quickly.

"That tarnation pink carpet that's on 'em. It's too soft, too deep. Catches my heels every time I try to come down."

"I hope your wife isn't severely hurt—you've had a doctor, of course?"

Jonathan grunted. "Nope. Don't hold with doctors."

"You haven't even called a doctor?" Mr. Loomis demanded, his eyes round with surprise.

"I tell you we don't hold with 'em. About all they do is feel your pulse and take your money. You got to do your own gettin' well anyhow. Break a leg or have a baby—then you got to have a doctor. But the rest of the time we do our own doctorin'."

The lawyer shifted uneasily in his chair. "But under the peculiar circumstances don't you think you'd feel a little easier if a first-class physician should give your wife a thorough check-up just to be sure you haven't overlooked something?"

"Nope. Don't want a physician or a doctor neither."

"Not if Mr. Gage is willing to pay the bill?"

"Not even if the doc would come free. I'm a good enough doctor for this case. I give her black cohosh tea for her inside, and I rubbed magnetic ointment on her outside. No doctor couldn't do more'n that."

"But isn't there something we can do?" Herbert asked anxiously.

"Yes, isn't there something?" Mr. Loomis echoed.

Jonathan had not intended to take advantage of the situation, but the anxiety and the solicitation of the other two were beginning to annoy him. "Why, yes," he blurted out, "I'll tell you somethin' you can do—you can take that tarnation pink carpet off the stairs before somebody else gets a fall there."

He said it more to shut them up than anything else, but to his astonishment they readily assented. Herbert promised that the carpet would be out of the way before night. But this was not all, for they both began to urge that they be allowed to do

[167]

something to make Matilda more comfortable. Jonathan shook his head. He did not know quite what to say. He had not, he was sure, made any misrepresentation whatever. They had jumped to their own conclusion, and it was through no fault of his that the conclusion was wrong. He had not tricked them—they had tricked themselves, and they had certainly given him a wonderful trading advantage. It was just too good to be thrown away, and eventually the temptation proved to be too much for him.

"You been wantin' to do somethin' to make her more comfortable—I'll tell you a little somethin' you can do. She's always set great store by her patent rocker. Since her accident she ain't been able to set in no ordinary rockin' chair, not with comfort. And this mornin' she asked me to fetch her patent rocker down from the attic. I was willin' enough, but when I went up to get it I found that somehow it had got broke. Now understand, I ain't sayin' who broke it—I'm just tellin' you I found the chair broke."

Herbert waved the question aside. "Never mind who broke it. I know the chair you mean and I'll have it fixed right away—probably by tonight. Small matter anyway. Now isn't there something else?"

Jonathan reflected for a moment. "Well, she's had a lot to say about her spool bed. The one we got in there now is a good enough bed, but she thinks that spool bed of hers would suit her better."

"Where is her spool bed?" asked Loomis.

"It's in the attic," Jonathan said. "Saw it there when I was lookin' for the rocker."

"Oh, well," said Loomis, "if it's right there of course we'll have it brought down."

Jonathan rubbed the back of his head. "But there's more to it than just the bedstead," he said. "It's got special hickory slats and a horsehair mattress that sets on a Indian splint pad—I guess you'd call it. Then her own homemade feather bed goes on top of all that."

[168]

Herbert nodded. "If they're up there we'll have them brought down."

Jonathan was still rubbing his head a little dubiously. "They're up there all right, but there's somethin' else—what about her commode and the chinaware that goes with it?"

"Commode?" asked Herbert with a puzzled look. "What's that?"

"You'd call it a washstand," Jonathan explained.

"But what would she want of a washstand?" Herbert protested. "The bathroom is just across the hall."

"That bathroom is yours," said Jonathan, "but the china belongs to her."

Loomis dismissed all objections with a wave of the hand. "Let her have her commode if it will make her any more comfortable—and her china, too. Now then, is there anything else?"

Jonathan stroked his chin thoughtfully but said nothing.

For a time the lawyer sat watching him and waiting. Then he said, "I can see you've got something on your mind, Mr. Rockwood. Why don't you tell us what it is—if we don't know about it how can we discuss it?"

"I'll tell you what's on my mind," Jonathan said with an aggressive shake of the head; "when I went away I left some good outside plumbin' on this place, but since I come back I can't find it, and I want to know what's become of it."

The lawyer turned to Herbert. "What about that?" he asked.

Herbert shook his head. "When I came there was no plumbing at all, inside or out."

"Then where did you get that lily-pad latch that's on the side door?" Jonathan asked quietly.

"Oh, that! I see what you mean." Herbert was covered with confusion. "You mean the little house that was out back, covered with rambler roses and poison ivy."

Jonathan nodded. "That's just what I mean. What become of it?"

"Well," said Herbert, "we had no use for it, so we burned it."

"Burned it, hey?" Jonathan said as if hardly able to believe it. "And every stick of it straight-grained chestnut!"

"I didn't notice what kind of wood it was. Is chestnut so valuable?"

"Is it valuable?" Jonathan blurted out irritably. "It's extinct! The blight killed off all the trees, and we won't have another stick of chestnut wood in this country for at least fifty years."

Mr. Loomis straightened up in his chair. "Aren't we getting off the track? We've got some business to settle; now let's see if we can't settle it. As I understand the situation is this: with modern improvements in the house there was no further use for your outside plumbing—it was merely an eyesore and was destroyed."

Jonathan raised his hand with an objection. "Just a minute! Who said there was no use for outside plumbin'?"

The lawyer blinked at him. "Well, is there?"

"You better believe there is." Jonathan glared at him. "I don't hold with inside plumbin'—never used it and don't intend to begin—not at my age."

"But what do you want us to do?" asked Mr. Loomis helplessly. "Build you another?"

Jonathan shook his head. "Well, no, I wouldn't ask you to do that. There's plenty of lumber right there in the barn, and if you ain't got no objections I'll take some of that and build one for myself."

Herbert was obviously relieved. "Can you do that?" he asked.

"I ain't never built one," Jonathan replied, "but I reckon I can. Guess I'm enough of a carpenter for that."

"And is this the extent of your demands in connection with your wife's accidental injury?" asked the lawyer.

"I'll settle for what we said, if that's what you mean," Jonathan replied.

The lawyer reached for a sheet of paper. "Just a minute and I'll get this down in writing."

"Never mind about that." Jonathan stood up and started

slowly for the door. "You do all these things you said, and when they're done it'll be time enough to sign papers."

Loomis left soon afterward, and when he had gone Herbert picked up a letter recently received from Richard. It had been written in Australia more than a month before, so there was no telling where the boy was now. Somewhere in the South Seas. Over yonder. Over There. That was as near as they could come. When Richard had smuggled a brief note into the mail at San Francisco saying that he was shipping out, they were sure he was going either to Pearl Harbor or to the Aleutians. The papers had been full of Kiska and Attu, and the northern sector had not seemed at all unlikely. Still, here the boy was on the other side of the world. Down under.

But it did seem to Herbert that things had begun to look better in the Pacific. The Navy had certainly given the Jap task forces a couple of bad maulings, and the way MacArthur was working up through the islands had undoubtedly stalled any chance that the Japs would ever get to Australia. He fingered the letter and wished that Richard could write them a little more about what he was doing.

Herbert was a little surprised to find that his interest in the war had suddenly gone over to the other side of the world, and to discover that he was becoming impatient with the newspapers for giving all their front page space to the European war. However, the thing that made Herbert the most impatient was the way the news from the Pacific front was being held back by the Army and Navy. A big carrier could be sunk, or a whole flock of warships, and the news would not leak out to America for weeks or months or possibly a year. This might be a good way to fool the Japs, but it also fooled the Americans at home. It made them ripe for rumors. You would hear of somebody who had received a letter in a secret code telling of a big American massacre in the jungles of New Guinea, or that our boys had been driven from this island or that with a terrific loss of life. And Herbert found himself giving unmerited

[171]

credence to sweeping claims of Japanese victories broadcast by the Vichy radio, which our government would not even take the trouble to deny for fear the Japs would find out how badly they themselves had been beaten.

He found himself combing through the inside pages of the papers in quest of items, however brief, which were even remotely connected with the war in the Pacific. Then he did something that he had never supposed he would do—he bought a big map and hung it on the wall of his study.

H ERBERT didn't like the way things were going. His career was falling to pieces. Here he was in the ideal place to work, and he was getting nothing done. This legal dispute was ruining him and still he was getting nowhere with it. Loomis was too static, too cautious. He did not seem to understand what a terrific inconvenience it was to have an old couple plumped down into your household. That the lawyer's primary intention and objective was to protect the interests of his client Herbert did not doubt, but he still felt, as he had felt from the beginning, that Loomis was not the best man for the job.

What Herbert craved was action, and only a glance at Loomis was necessary to convince the most casual observer that the probability of getting any considerable activity from that quarter was remote indeed. That Loomis might be a very able office lawyer was something that Herbert would readily have conceded. That he was an expert on titles and the law of real estate was another admission that Herbert would have made without a question. But mere legal accuracy wasn't what Herbert either wanted or needed. The shrewdest quibbler in the world, the smartest *i*-dotter, the most correct *t*-crosser, would have had little appeal to Herbert at this particular moment, when, as it seemed to him, action was of the essence.

That he was facing a tough adversary was a fact that had become more and more evident to Herbert with each passing day. He had come to know that in spite of the old fellow's psalm singing and praying, and his habitual quotation of the Bible, he was a man to watch when making a bargain.

This was not the first time that Herbert had encountered that curious blend of rascality and religion. In his business dealings in the locality he had found it quite common. He remembered very distinctly the time that one of his neighbors had stopped in to invite his affiliation with the Methodist Church and had sold him, at a stiff price, a basket that had appeared to be full of apples, but which turned out to have been stuffed half full of newspapers before the first layer of apples had been put in.

Never for a moment did Herbert doubt that the legal advice he received from Loomis was sound. But he had a growing feeling that legal advice was not enough. What he wanted was action.

The days had been slipping by. Quite a lot of them, and still the old couple were firmly squatted in the best room in the house, and with the passage of time were becoming more confident of their position and more cocky and presuming.

It seemed to Herbert that Loomis paid altogether too much attention to the legal rights of the opposition. Herbert's idea of a good lawyer was one who looked out for the interests of his own client and let the devil take those of the other fellow. He did not give a hoot for the scholarly dissertations that Loomis was given to pronouncing on the theory of life estates and easements, covenants running with the land, suspension of the power of alienation, and other kindred topics.

Herbert wanted somebody to take his side, to stand up for him, to shout and call names for him if necessary. He wanted an advocate, a partisan, a champion—somebody to meet old Jonathan on his own terms—to outyell, outtrick, outtrade him.

He remembered so well his original instructions to Loomis— Throw him out if you can; and if you can't, buy him out. At the time he had visions of square-toed minions of the law who would come tramping in, bulging at the hip, flashing bright shields from underneath their coats and serving imposing-looking writs and mandates. When this course was suggested to Loomis, the little fellow actually laughed.

"Herbert," he said, "things aren't handled like that in real life—you've been seeing too many mystery thrillers."

"I want to throw a big bluff," said Herbert. "I want to make them think I mean business. Why do you suppose a dog barks and bristles all over his back?"

"Dogs are out of my domain," said Loomis. "You'll have to go to your veterinarian for that. All I can tell you are the legal aspects of this case, and they don't look any too good. You threw your advantages out of the window and since then you've been on a catch-as-catch-can basis."

Never in the world, Herbert told himself, would he have chosen Loomis as the lawyer to represent his side. That was Margie's idea, and she had put it through in spite of quite a little objection on his part. She had seized upon it as a wonderful chance to establish relations with the Loomis family, who were without doubt one of the most socially prominent and distinguished families anywhere in the neighborhood. Not that it would mean much to her or to Herbert either, but it would be important to the children to have such lovely friends as the young Loomises.

Herbert had hesitated to ask a big law firm like Loomis & Loomis to handle the picayune job of clearing the title to a house and lot. He had heard, he told Margie, that old Judge Loomis, the most distinguished lawyer in the county, would not consider anything less than a thousand-dollar retainer.

Margie had inquired around until she was satisfied that there was no truth in the story about the thousand-dollar retainer, and then one day she went into the office herself and asked if the firm would care to handle the matter. It so happened that Barbara was with her, and they had not been inside the office for more than a minute or two before every Loomis in the place was offering his services.

Unfortunately the job had fallen to Winthrop, the least attractive of them all, who happened to be the land expert, instead of Alden, the youngest member of the firm, a youth fresh from Harvard Law School, then in charge of the collection department. Margie had sighed over this on more than one occasion, and Herbert had derived a peculiar satisfaction by reminding her that the Loomis office was a law firm and not a matrimonial bureau.

About the only advantage in having the law firm chosen by Margie was the perquisite of being able to refer to them as "her" lawyers. Herbert had found this especially effective in the past, and he was counting on it to cover the disagreeable concessions made in settling Matilda's supposed claim for damages. Margie, being of the resilient type who prefer to prove their point by repetition rather than logic, had in the past won many an argument by pertinacity alone, but that was before she had placed this inelegant but effective weapon in the hands of her husband.

And now, with the weapon up his sleeve, Herbert was to face her again, for Margie had not been present when the damage suit had so unexpectedly come up for discussion. It was her day with the Red Cross, and she did not return home until long after Mr. Loomis had left, which shifted to Herbert's shoulders the burden of explaining the necessity for such peculiar and annoying terms.

Herbert had intended to begin his explanation with a full account of the danger and uncertainty of defending a suit for damages, and the very clever strategy by which he and Mr. Loomis had circumvented and settled the matter before it had really had time to come to a head. If he could have done this, it would have been much easier to elucidate and explain some of the concessions, which, when come upon suddenly, were a little hard to account for.

There was, for example, the pink carpet on the stairs. When Margie came in and found Herbert ripping it up with a claw hammer and a small wrecking bar, her first thought was that he had been suddenly bereft of his reason. And it was at almost the identical moment that she heard noises in the hallway above and looked up just in time to see Jonathan, assisted by Joe the cowman, in the act of moving Matilda's atrocious and unspeakable furniture into the guest room to replace Margie's priceless antiques, which they had already taken to the attic.

Herbert hurled himself into his exculpation with all the power and persuasiveness at his command. He told how desperately he had fought off the demands of the opposition until at last Loomis had advised capitulation.

Braced against the newel for support, Margie gazed at him with eyes wide and glassy. She made no attempt at response until he had finished. Then she said in a voice that was strained with anguish:

"But that hideous spool bed in our lovely guest room! The thought of it nauseates me—it's not only hideous, it's a counterfeit—and it isn't even maple!"

"It isn't? What's it made of?"

"Elm or poplar—some worthless wood that's used only for kindling. Oh, why didn't I burn it when I had the chance!"

"Because your lawyer advised you not to burn or destroy anything," Herbert said more gently than generously.

She turned and walked slowly into the taproom, with Herbert following. Suddenly she turned on him. "But I thought Mr. Loomis was coming here to buy off those insufferable old parasites, and he only gets us in deeper than ever. Didn't he even try to buy them off?"

"He tried," Herbert assured her, "but he didn't get to first base."

"Why not?" she demanded irritably.

"Simply because old Jonathan wouldn't sell."

"Wouldn't sell," she repeated. "Jonathan wouldn't sell. It's more like offering them a present. What have they got to sell? They don't own anything—there isn't one square inch of this property that belongs to them. Do you realize that?"

Herbert nodded. "But as Loomis says, you can't measure an intangible right with tangible instruments."

Margie sighed. "I suppose not. But it does make you sick when you think that all they own is the flaw in our title!"

"And even that is not for sale."

For a time they stood and looked at each other, saying nothing. Then Margie asked dejectedly, "Didn't Mr. Loomis have anything to suggest?"

Very slowly Herbert nodded his head. "Yes, one thing more. Now that we know we can't buy the old folks off, he insists that we must reach a working agreement with them. He says the way we're living now we have nothing but an armed truce with them. He thinks we should have a very definite arrangement as to just what part of the house they are to use and what we'll keep for ourselves. He says that if we don't have an understanding as to who gets what, we'll be in hot water with them all the time."

Margie looked troubled. "But can we ever get them to agree to anything?"

Herbert doubted it. "We're not in a good trading position," he said. "They're the ones who are sitting pretty. Occupying the best room in the house with first-class room service and free meals."

"And this damage settlement," said Margie despondently. "It has completely ruined any chance we may have had of getting them into the garage." Suddenly she drew herself up. "But the room service and free meals are quite another matter."

"You might have something there," Herbert said with a smile.

"I think I have." Margie's spirits were quite definitely reviving. "Mrs. Flint hates them. She says that old man insults her every chance he gets, and she has asked me not to insist on her taking any more meals to their room."

"Then somebody else will have to carry up their meals?"

Margie pursed her lips. "If we give them any meals."

Herbert's face lighted. "You're suggesting we might starve them out?"

"It wasn't what I meant, but it's an idea. The trouble is, they haven't any ration books, and with only our own books I can't get enough food for ourselves and for them, too."

Herbert shook his head. Just one damn thing after another. Only the day before he had been refused a tube of shaving cream just because he did not have the empty tube to turn in, and he'd have to go without shaving cream until the next time they had enough gas to drive into town. And now this ration book thing had to come up—he knew what it meant—gas to take them to the ration board. It never occurred to him that the Rockwoods might refuse to go.

But when Margie intercepted Jonathan in the yard the next day and undertook to explain the situation, he simply shook his head and said, "I'm sorry, ma'am, but I can't do it."

"I'm afraid I haven't made myself clear," she said, and then she proceeded to go all through her explanation again.

Jonathan nodded. "Ayuh—ayuh, that's just the way I heard it before."

Margie took this as an indication that he was now agreeable to her suggestion and went on to explain that Herbert would take him down in the car, and that it would not be necessary for Mrs. Rockwood to go since he could make the application for her.

Jonathan stood and stared into her face. "It's dirty politics."

Margie felt uncomfortable at his scrutiny. "I don't know anything about politics."

"Well, I do. I was mixed up in 'em for years, and they're as crooked as a cow's hind leg. I don't know who's gettin' the money out of this ration business, but somebody is, and you can be pretty sure it's the politicians."

"Oh, nobody's getting any money out of it," Margie explained. "The books are free."

Jonathan drew down the corners of his mouth. "Don't you believe it. Nothin's free—except salvation, of course—and you'll find that costs you some'pm before you get through."

"What I'm trying to tell you is that we don't have to pay

anything for these ration books, but we must have them. If we don't have the books we can't get anything to eat."

"You don't want to believe everything you hear," said Jonathan. "You think there's a food shortage because that's what you read in the paper. Well, it ain't so—there's just as much food in this country as there ever was."

Margie was beginning to become a little flustered. She certainly had not expected Jonathan to give her an argument on the question of applying for ration books solely for the benefit of himself and his wife. She began to wonder if he was really in earnest or if perhaps he was indulging in the masculine prerogative of telling her what it was all about. In either case she felt that the discussion had been going on long enough and should be brought to an end. "We all want our soldiers to have enough to eat, and the only way we can be sure of that is to have rationing. And that is why I can't buy the food for you and your wife to eat unless I have ration cards."

Jonathan gave her a sour look. "Oh, so you're goin' to be stubborn about it, hey?"

"I have no idea of being stubborn," said Margie. "But you don't seem to understand that a ration card will supply the food for only one person, and we can't possibly stretch our points to include you and your wife."

"If that ain't bein' stubborn I don't know what is." Jonathan drew back and looked her up and down. "And I can be just as stubborn as you can—I'll have nuthin' to do with this crooked business of rationin' food in a land of plenty."

"But why?" asked Margie, her eyes large with amazement.

"Matter of principle," he answered promptly. "You can't mix in with wickedness and not get smirched. It's never goin' to be said of me that I sided in with the political blacklegs in stealin' the food out of the mouths of the poor and needy."

By this time the problem was presenting a very practical side to Margie, so practical, in fact, that she paid no attention to what he was saying. Instead she began counting on her fingers. He stopped his tirade and watched her.

"What you figurin'?" he asked.

"Just the things that I won't be able to serve to you any more," said Margie with a solicitous inflection. "First there's coffee, then sugar, then butter, and cheese—and bacon or meat of any kind—canned fruits, canned vegetables. . . ." She ran out of fingers. "There are so many things I can't count them all."

"I didn't hear you say nuthin' about eggs and fresh vegetables and milk," said Jonathan.

Margie smiled a little uncertainly. "Well, those things aren't exactly rationed—not yet, that is, though I understand milk is going to be—but they're all very scarce; we can't always get them. And not only are the fresh vegetables scarce, but they are so expensive that we refuse to buy them."

Jonathan stroked his chin. "Looks like poor pickin' for an honest man."

It seemed to Margie that the old man's determination was wobbling a bit. "There are still plenty of things to eat," she said. "You can have all the cornmeal you want, and the other cereals. And there is spaghetti and cornstarch, and for dessert you can still have a nice rice pudding, or arrowroot. But I'm afraid there'll be no more 'stalled ox' and no more canned vegetables."

He turned and was looking away, his eyes sweeping slowly over the ground. "You folks certainly have changed things around here. All this where you got the lawn and the flower beds and bushes—this used to be our vegetable garden."

"Yes, I know," said Margie, "but we moved the vegetable garden out back where it doesn't show."

"But this is the best land on the place. It's been cultivated and fertilized for a couple of centuries."

"Oh, but the land out there is good, too. You never saw such vegetables as Herbert had in his Victory garden last year. Of course he used the best fertilizer that money could buy—Victory fertilizer."

"If he's goin' to have a garden this year, he better be gettin' it in—the ground's about ready to plow."

Margie nodded. "He's already sent off his seed order. You're—sure you don't want to change your mind about the ration book?"

"No, ma'am. I still refuse to compromise with rascality and sin. We may not get that 'stalled ox' you was talkin' about, but I reckon that in time we'll have plenty of the fine herbs that goes with 'em." And he turned and walked away.

That night Margie provided for Jonathan and Matilda the first meal consisting entirely of unrationed foods. The next morning she was awakened by Herbert who stood by the side of her bed shaking her arm and demanding urgently that she "come out of it."

"Why, Herbert," she said sleepily. "What's the matter?"

"Plenty!" he growled. "When you're awake enough I'll tell you all about it."

She sat up in bed rubbing her eyes. "What is it, dear? Are you sick? You look terrible—you're all hollow-eyed—what's the matter?"

"I'm not sick." He ran his fingers through his hair. "But there's plenty the matter."

"It isn't Richard?"

"No—but so much has happened I hardly know where to begin."

"But don't keep me waiting," she begged. "What is it?"

"To begin with—there was that blasted horse. . . ."

"Shadrach?"

"No, no—the one you dreamed about. It haunted my dreams all night."

"It ran down the hill?"

"With a noise like thunder."

Margie's eyes lighted with eager satisfaction. "What did I tell you!"

"You were right," he admitted. "It was just as you said—he

ran to the bridge but never crossed it. But listen, Margie, do you remember what happened after you had that dream?"

She nodded. "*They* came."

"Right—and the minute I woke up I knew something terrible was hanging over us—and it was!"

"What was it—what happened—tell me, Herbert?"

"That old fiend has plowed up all our lawn and flower beds, and is making a vegetable garden right here beside the house, where it used to be years ago!"

Mumbling half-uttered exclamations, Margie rose up out of the bed and ran to a window which looked down on the side yard.

"Oh, my poor flower beds," she was moaning. "My King Arthur delphiniums and my Haarlem tulips—and there'll be no more bulbs until after the war." Suddenly she stopped and gasped. "My roses—what's become of my roses?"

Herbert, who had followed and was standing behind her, said angrily, "Still there but badly trampled."

Margie could not believe in such sacrilege. "Not my magnificent President Hoover!" she wailed. "Not my Mary Margaret McBride rose—and my General MacArthur!"

"They will never bloom again," Herbert muttered.

"But my English wallflowers—and my precious regal lilies. . . ."

"Those might be all right, but I'll bet they've been walked on. The flowers can be replaced, but it's taken an awful lot of work to grow that lawn."

"But how can he do that?" Margie burst out angrily. "In Michigan we'd have him in jail for such a thing."

"This isn't Michigan. And Loomis says the old devil has got just as much right to raise potatoes there as I had to grow a lawn."

"When did he say that?"

"Just a few minutes ago when I got him out of bed to tell him what was going on."

"Have we just got to take it?" Margie demanded.

[183]

"You must remember that his rights are coequal with ours."

"You're getting so you talk like Loomis yourself."

Herbert gave her a wry smile. "Don't forget he's your lawyer."

As Margie turned away from the window her eyes were snapping angrily. "Just watch the hand that feeds him from now on." She lifted the hem of her pink nightgown and walked slowly back to her own room.

↗↗↗

JONATHAN hadn't really intended to put those chickens in the greenhouse, but the night had turned cold and he had to put them somewhere, especially the little ones. Of course if the Gages hadn't torn down the old hennery he probably wouldn't have been so uppish about it; but since they had, he felt it was no more than right that they should furnish a warm place for his little chicks.

He had not meant to leave the chickens in there more than the one cold night, but their presence in the greenhouse had created such havoc in the Gage family that he was tempted into leaving them there for a few days just to show his mettle. It was little Sarah who had discovered them, and she had gone galloping into the house with delight to invite the family to come out and see all the cute little things. The family had responded as if they were going to a fire. Even that sourpuss from the brass towns, wearing her apron and her silly little white cap, had gone out to look over the situation.

"Why didn't Gage come to me like a gentleman?" Jonathan said in explaining the matter to Matilda. "If he'd asked me to take those chickens out of there, I'd a done it. But what'd he do? He run off to the telephone and called that little owl-eyed lawyer of his and had him come tearin' out in his car. Even then I'd have moved 'em if he'd asked me like a gentleman."

"Don't try to tell me that," Matilda said. "I don't believe you'd have moved 'em at all. I ain't forgot how you come in here that night and told me what a snug place it was for chicks. You said it was better'n any brooder you ever see."

"It was a good place all right," Jonathan admitted, "and still is. But I'm tellin' you that if either of them fellers had come to me like a gentleman and requested me to move 'em, I'd a done it."

Matilda nodded. "I understand," she said. "They'd had to *request* you, just *askin'* wouldn't have been enough."

"I wouldn't been no stickler about that," Jonathan insisted, "but when that little hair-splitter come out there and ordered me to remove them chickens 'forthwith or suffer the consequences,' well, natchally I had to stand up for myself, didn't I?"

"You ain't never been much troubled with givin' in, I guess."

"A man can't give in," Jonathan declared. "The minute you give in, then they begin to push you around. Now you take that ration business—if I'd give in on that and went down there and got books for both of us, we'd have had to run all over this county to get enough to eat. The folks here do their food shoppin' in a dozen diff'rent towns. One week they try Bridgeport, and the next week it's Danbury, and then probably after that they'll go down and see what they can get in Fairfield. And the big trouble is that all the runnin' around takes gas, and if you don't have tickets you can't get gas."

"From what I hear there ain't much gas. Little Sarah says her folks had to stay home from a party the other night 'cause they didn't have the gas to get there and back."

"Sarah's worried about her pa—she wants to know if I think he's gonna go down in history."

"Well, what do you think?" asked Matilda.

"I think he's goin' down in some'pm all right, but I don't know if it's history or not."

Through the crack of the door Jonathan could hear the sound of the typewriter coming up from the study. Herbert was just swinging into his stride. The sound annoyed Jonathan, and, not wanting to have Herbert go down in history too fast, he reminded Matilda that he hadn't heard her at the organ lately and asked if she wouldn't like to play a few hymns.

Matilda took her hymnal from the table. "What'll I play today?" she asked, fingering through the pages.

"How about a couple of verses of 'Rock of Ages,'" said Jonathan, "and mebbe a little 'Lead, Kindly Light.'"

For a few moments Matilda pumped with her feet at the pedals filling the bellows. Then she struck the opening chord for her first selection. Jonathan softly pushed open the door into the hall, and the hymn tunes began. At the end of the first stanza Jonathan listened at the door, but the typewriter was rattling along like a cornsheller. Then after a little it began to go by fits and starts.

He went over to Matilda. "Why don't we have a little of that 'Lead, Kindly Light'?" he suggested.

Matilda nodded and opened the book to the page which she had previously marked with a bit of yarn. Once more she struck the opening chord, forgetting that it was in two flats instead of one. She was only halfway through the first stanza when Jonathan heard a door slam in the distance. From the window he could see Herbert striding across the yard. At the end of the stanza Jonathan called to Matilda:

"That was fine," he said. "I'm feelin' better." Then he sat down and lighted his pipe.

"How's the peas comin'?" Matilda asked as she emerged from the closet.

"Those cold nights slowed 'em up a little, but they're comin' fine now. Ought to have a mess of 'em in another day or two."

Matilda resumed her patent rocker in which she had been taking great comfort ever since it had come back from the repairman. "I'm gettin' mighty sick of this unrationed stuff. Tastes like what they feed cattle. I'll be glad to get a mess of new peas."

"Think old sourpuss down there in the kitchen'll cook 'em for us?"

"Why wouldn't she?"

"Burn 'em, prob'ly."

Matilda did not think so. "Whatever else is the matter with her there ain't nuthin' wrong with her cookin'."

"You don't reckon she'd spoil 'em just to spite us?" Jonathan suggested.

"No, sir. She's too good a cook to spoil any vittles apurpose."

"That stuff she serves for coffee ain't much good."

"Don't pretend to be coffee. She says you can't get coffee without them tickets. That stuff is called 'cereal beverage.'"

"Well, the cereal beverage is pretty bitter. Couldn't drink it if it wasn't for the maple sugar Uncle Walter give us."

"What I miss is a little fresh meat now and then."

"I'm glad eggs ain't rationed," said Jonathan.

"It's meat I'm hankerin' for. I'd like to stand beside the range and fry us a couple of chickens."

"You wouldn't know what to do with the range they got in this house—runs by electricity."

Matilda sighed. "Wisht I had my old wood range set up."

Jonathan rubbed his chin. "Where could we set it up? No place in this room. Be some job to cut through into the chimney."

"Ain't we got as much right to have a stove as they have?"

"Sounds reasonable," he said.

Jonathan laid aside his pipe and put on his broad-brimmed hat, while Matilda sat rocking back and forth as she sewed a patch on the elbow of a faded workshirt.

"What you goin' to do now?" she asked.

Jonathan paused with his hand on the doorknob. "Thought I'd get to work on my outdoor plumbin'."

"Did you find the tools you was huntin' for?"

Jonathan nodded. "Found practically all of 'em. Pretty rusty, and the saws is a mite dull, but I'll get along. Only thing I need is a compass saw. Never had one myself, but I guess I can borrow one from Uncle Walter."

Matilda looked up from her sewing. "Ain't never heared of a compass saw," she said. "What is it?"

"It's what you use when you want to saw two or three big

round holes in a board. "Don't need that kind of a saw more'n about once in a lifetime."

He gave his hat a hitch and went out. On the doorstep he stood and looked at the big tree. There it was, sturdy as ever. In passing, he gave the tree a pat with his hand. It was hard for him to go near it without touching it. His garden, too, drew him like a magnet. He couldn't walk past it without stooping here and there to examine a plant or pull a weed.

As he left the garden and went on towards the barn he was feeling the satisfaction which comes to the tiller of the soil when his crops are growing well. New peas tomorrow, and new spinach in about three days. He thought of the story of creation and how God looked over everything he had made, and saw that it was good. Jonathan thought that he knew a little mite about how the Lord God had felt when he quit work at the end of the sixth day on the job of creating and getting the crops planted in a world.

Jonathan had expected to see Herbert working in his garden, but he was nowhere in sight. Herbert never failed to call it his Victory garden in speaking of it. This annoyed Jonathan, who regarded it as an attempt on Herbert's part to make out of his puny little plot a great contribution to the war effort. And another thing that never failed to irritate Jonathan was to have passing neighbors compliment Herbert on his fine garden, meaning Jonathan's garden, and have Herbert calmly accept the compliment and say that yes, it was looking pretty well. One of these days, Jonathan used to promise himself, he'd step over to the fence and put that young man in his place.

Tucked away in the upper part of the barn Jonathan found two of his old sawhorses. He moved them outside and stood them on a level piece of ground back of the barn. Across them he laid the old chestnut scantling which he was using for framework, and marked it for cutting. His carpenter's square was rusty, but it was still true enough for the job at hand. The frame pieces were cut and fitted and had been partly nailed

[189]

together when Barbara came around the corner of the barn.

"So you're the one who's doing all the hammering?" she said.

Jonathan went right on with the nail he was driving. "Who'd you think it was?" he muttered without looking up. He continued with his pounding until the nail was in and more than in, for he gave it a couple of final blows that severely dented the wood—the usual hallmark of the home carpenter.

"I might have known it was you," she said in a friendly way. "You seem to be able to do everything."

It was at this point that Jonathan turned and looked at her. When he saw her clad only in yellow shorts and halter, and with rope sandals on her feet, his jaw fell, his eyes popped open, and his hammer almost slipped from his grasp. In her hand she was carrying a large straw hat with yellow ribbons dangling from it. His first thought was that she must have accidentally left something off, and it came to him that the hat was big enough to afford some cover if she would just hold it in front of her. But she did not hold the hat in front of her. In fact, she swung it around behind her and let it dangle over her shoulder by one of the yellow ribbons.

Jonathan had seen such things as this on magazine covers and even in the mail order catalogues, but never had he been anywhere near such a vision of loveliness in the flesh. He had not realized how overpowering the nearness to feminine beauty could be. For a moment he stood staring, his jaw trembling, the hammer dangling from a limp and powerless hand.

Then he pulled himself together and looked away. He turned his back and fumbled in his pocket for a nail—found one and tried to drive it; but aside from the initial taps used to start it he was unable to strike it squarely again, and after a number of near misses he struck it a glancing blow which bent it double. With that he lost his temper and hammered down the distorted piece of metal until it was embedded in the wood.

He had hoped that turning his back would show her that she was not wanted, but it had just the opposite effect. Barbara came nearer and stepped around to one side so as to get a better view.

"Driving a nail always looks so easy," she said, "but I've found from experience that it's not as easy as it looks."

"Not in this hard wood it ain't." He moved around so as to turn his back on her again and started another nail. This time he did better; he got it almost in before it bent over.

Barbara did not like the idea of talking to the old man's back, and moved around to the farther side of the project where he would be facing her. "What is it you're making?" she asked.

His hammer paused in mid-air. "Don't you know?"

"I haven't the slightest idea."

"You'll know when it's finished," he said, and he resumed his hammering with a great flurry of industry. He came around to the side where she was standing so as to get her once more at his back, but by the time he had made the move she was around on the opposite side of the job. Jonathan wouldn't look at her. He wouldn't even turn his eyes in her general direction, and he was driving home most of his nails without bending them over.

It was a new experience for Barbara to find a man who would not look at her and who went so far as to turn his back on her as much of the time as he could. She was not so much piqued as intrigued. It was a problem with which she had never had occasion to cope and one that challenged her closest attention. She had not realized that it was going to be so difficult to make friends with the old man, but in spite of his gruff answers she was not at all discouraged.

"I came out for a sunning," she said, "and this is as good a place to sun as any."

He made no reply, but went on with his hammering.

After a few moments Barbara tried again. "I've been tanned so many years that I don't seem to sunburn any more."

Jonathan kept right on hammering. He was nailing on some longer pieces, and the framework began to look like a large crate.

"That isn't something for the horse, is it?" she guessed.

"Hardly." Jonathan went on with his hammering.

Barbara stepped back when the old man dropped his hammer and reached for two pieces which had been sawed on the diagonal. She had wondered why they were cut this way, but when Jonathan had joined them together and put them in place they immediately suggested to her the roof angle of a small building. Other pieces cut the same way seemed to confirm the supposition, but she was mystified to know why he was making it so small—it was no bigger than a playhouse. The thought of a playhouse reminded her of Sarah, and she recalled that, in spite of all that the family had said, Sarah still spent all the time she dared in the company of Shadrach and the old man.

The more Barbara thought about the playhouse idea, the more certain she became that she had hit upon the right answer, but Jonathan was hammering so lustily that she had to wait a bit before making known her discovery. It was not until he had again dropped his hammer and reached for a second pair of the diagonal pieces that she tried it out on him.

"I think I know what you are making," she said.

"You ought to," he replied without so much as a glance at her.

"Is it—something for Sarah?" she asked, her eyes shining brightly.

With a diagonal piece clasped under each arm ready to put together the old man glanced at her. "She could use it," he said. "Anybody could." Then without another word he dropped the two pieces on the ground and went into the house.

⚡⚡

HERBERT hated pigs. He hated the sight of them, he hated the smell of them, he hated the very thought of them—and here he was, faced with the necessity of having them on the place. Jonathan's cow he did not particularly mind. In fact, he thought she looked rather picturesque in the orchard. But the two nasty little black and white pigs, grunting, quarreling, squealing, and stinking, were just too much for him. One day he had seen old Jonathan building an enclosure in a fence corner back of the barn, and the next day he had found the two pigs in it.

He had not inquired what the enclosure was for. Loomis was still hopeful of reaching a working agreement that would define and confine the rights of the parties, and was constantly warning him against crossing the old man or wrangling with him.

"There are some hairline questions here," Loomis said one day. "Just what the equities are as to the rights of the parties in the improvements which have been added since the *status quo* was established by the conveyance of the fee to the Power Company presents not one question but many questions closely interrelated and at the same time separable and distinguishable, not only because of the lapse of time, but because of the peculiar circumstances under which the changes and improvements were made."

Herbert was tired of "hairline questions" and "*status quo.*" What he craved was action. And he had just about reached the conclusion that what he needed was a new lawyer. One who wouldn't know a *status quo* if he should see it but who knew how to fight and snarl and hit in the clinches.

"Had the *status quo* remained the same," Loomis went on, "the situation would be simple. Of course you understand that any improvements attached to the freehold become part of the fee simple, and even though prior to attachment they may have been of a chattel or personal nature, subsequent to attachment they are considered by the law to have changed their nature completely and to have been transformed from personal property into real property."

A lawyer who knew just one thing—how to fight.

"I have been studying this question with close scrutiny, and while I find a great mass of authorities applicable to the *status quo ante,* I have been able to find very few decisions touching the *status quo post;* and absolutely nothing that is on all fours."

Herbert brightened perceptibly. "Speaking of all fours," he said, "there's a question I would like to ask—has that old fellow got any right to keep pigs?"

Mr. Loomis blinked at him. "Did you say *pigs?*" he asked incredulously.

"Well, hogs, swine, whatever the legal usage is." Herbert was determined not to be held up by any technicality. "What I want to know is, has he got a right to keep them on the place?"

"Now that raises another interesting question," said Mr. Loomis. "It all depends upon the situs."

Herbert glared at him. "Is that any part of a pig?"

"Hardly," replied Loomis. "It refers to the place, the location, the particular portion of the premises where he proposes to keep them. For example, he could not keep them in the house, nor in any place contiguous thereto; that would be a violation of the sanitary code. I hope the old fellow hasn't proposed anything of that sort."

"He hasn't proposed anything," said Herbert. "He has simply

bought a couple of pigs and put them in a disreputable little shanty he has built back of the barn."

Mr. Loomis cocked his head. "How far from the house, would you say?"

"Two or three hundred feet."

The lawyer cocked his head the other way. "I should say that was plenty far enough away to comply with the code."

"But they stink," Herbert insisted.

Again Mr. Loomis could not restrain a discreet laugh. "Well, after all," he said, "what do you expect of swine?"

"I don't expect anything of them or want anything of them," Herbert said, unable to keep from showing some irritation. "But I would like to know if there isn't anything I can do to stop him."

Mr. Loomis looked wise. "Well," he said slowly, "I suppose you've heard the old saying that the best defense is offense. There's nothing to keep you from stepping out and buying a few swine for yourself—if you want to pay him in his own coin."

"In other words, there's nothing I can do about it?" said Herbert, feeling helpless and resentful.

The lawyer shook his round head. "Not a thing. But what about the chickens?" asked the lawyer. "Has he still got the little ones in the greenhouse?"

"Not any more," Herbert said. "They're running all over the place."

"Don't they get in your garden?"

"They did, but I fenced it."

"What about his garden?"

Herbert glowered. "That was fenced before he let them out."

"Any progress on the working agreement?"

Herbert glowered. "No."

"But you must keep trying. That looks like the only way out."

"How can I make any progress when he won't even speak to me?"

"I'll admit the need of tact and diplomacy." Mr. Loomis took off his glasses. "By the bye," he added as he sat polishing the lenses with his handkerchief, "he'll be slaughtering those pigs as soon as they're big enough. Had you thought of that?"

Herbert smiled sadly. "And meanwhile I can do nothing but sit and wait for the day of execution?"

Holding up his glasses with both hands and peering through them, Mr. Loomis shook his head slowly. "Your cotenant is strictly within his rights," he said. "The pig is no more than a domestic animal, *domitae naturae,* such as any reasonable man engaged in farming is accustomed to keep on his property. If the old fellow wanted to keep a python or a polar bear, something dangerous to the public, that would bring us into the purview of the wild animal, *ferae naturae,* and would raise quite a different question."

He settled the glasses on the bridge of his nose and hooked the bows behind his pointed ears. "The old folks still refuse to get a ration card, do they?"

"Still stubborn about it," Herbert said. "That old fellow doesn't believe even yet that there's a food shortage. He says if each man will raise it for himself there'll be enough and to spare."

"Then a diet of unrationed food hasn't unconvinced him?"

Herbert made a sour face. "He's living better than we are. Gets all sorts of fresh vegetables from his garden—far more than we do. You never saw such a productive garden; and whenever he wants a little meat he goes out and kills a chicken. We cook it for him in our kitchen, but we don't get any of it."

Mr. Loomis rolled a pencil back and forth in his fingers. "I suppose you could buy one from him occasionally."

Herbert's jaw tightened perceptibly. "We wouldn't think of such a thing. Before we'd ask him to sell us any food, we'd starve."

"Perhaps you're able to get chickens somewhere else around the neighborhood," Mr. Loomis suggested hopefully.

"For a while we could," Herbert said; "but no more. Who wants to sell chickens when eggs are worth their weight in gold?"

"But what do you do for meat?" asked the lawyer. "I hear it's almost impossible to buy it in the markets."

Herbert let out an indignant snort. "I'll tell you what we do—we go without. We've gone as long as three weeks without a taste of fresh meat."

"But what do you eat?"

"California sardines and ham. Those are the two stand-bys. Of course we've reached the point where we can't stand the sight of either one of them, but they have been lifesavers." Herbert rose to go. "Do you know the California sardine?"

The lawyer shook his head. "Never been introduced."

"Personally, I don't think it's a sardine at all," Herbert said. "I think it's a herring or a shiner—something of that sort. The first time I ever tasted it I thought it was wonderful. Perhaps it was, but I've eaten so much of it I've lost my point of view. And as for ham—the less said the better. It's strange how your viewpoint changes. When meat first began to be scarce, I used to dream of thick juicy steaks, and I often spoke about them to Margie. We thought the shortage only temporary, you know—that in a little while the markets would be flooded with meat again, that a buyer's only limit would be the amount of money in his pocket. For a while we had a lot to say about steaks, but soon we began to think that just an ordinary slice of roast beef would taste pretty good. Then we stopped talking about the unattainable and began to develop stratagems to enable us to get a lamb chop apiece for each member of the family. Before long the objective had dropped to a veal chop, and finally to a pork chop. Eventually the day came when Margie would have pawned her jewels to get a couple of pounds of ground beef. Good old ground beef—that has become our company dish, and if there is ever a time when Margie can get five pounds of it all at once, enough to make a sizable meat loaf —then we will call in our friends and have a party. In the circles in which we move the meat loaf has almost completely superseded the turkey and the squab." He glanced at his watch. "Margie's out trying to get some ground beef for a meat loaf now."

Loomis blinked sympathetically. "I wish her luck."

"What do you do for meat?" Herbert asked, hoping that Mr. Loomis might have some confidential connections with a secret source of supply.

"Meat?" Mr. Loomis smiled. "I don't do anything about it. I'm a vegetarian."

Herbert bit his lip and said nothing.

"By the bye," Mr. Loomis said, rising from his chair, "there's something I think we'd better be considering. I wonder if we haven't been trying to kill those old folks with kindness."

"But," Herbert said with a puzzled look, "you've told me all along that I ought to humor them until we get that working agreement."

"I know—I know." Mr. Loomis waved an index finger in the air. "But it's occurred to me that perhaps we've been just a little too lenient with them. You know how some people are, the more they get the more they want. I've just been wondering what the effect would be if we should tighten up a little bit in some place where it hurts."

"I'm in favor of it," said Herbert, "but I wouldn't know quite where to begin."

The lawyer blinked, looking very wise. "I can think of several places," he said, "but perhaps the most advantageous from our point of view would be to attack his supply line. I had hoped that restricting him to unrationed food would bring him around; but he seems to have solved that problem very nicely. However, I still think his supply line is vulnerable."

"I'm afraid you're overoptimistic," Herbert said slowly. "He has his own garden, he has his own chickens and eggs, and in a few weeks he's going to have his own ham and bacon and pork. In a military sense he sounds impregnable to me."

"I know—I know," said Mr. Loomis, "but don't forget that these are all raw materials, and no obligation rests on you to furnish him with the means of cooking them. See what I mean?"

Herbert began to laugh, though there was not much mirth in his laughter. "Funny that you should bring that up," he said. "Margie and I have talked about that several times. Feeding them seemed to be the easiest way when we started out, but it has turned into a real headache. Margie was saying only this morning that if something isn't done about it we'll probably lose Mrs. Flint, and, as you know, we're the only people in the township who have a maid. All the rest of them have been lured off by the defense factories. Mrs. Flint would be in defense work herself if she were only a little younger."

"But wouldn't she get higher pay in a factory?"

"She would if she could hold the job. But she worked in a factory when she was younger, and she knows just what it takes. If she thought she could deliver the goods she'd be spot welding today. No, Loomis, if we lose her she'll go into a household where she'll have to cook for only one family."

Mr. Loomis caught Herbert by the arm. "Well, now, Herbert, if she does leave you I beg of you to let me know ahead of time."

Herbert shook himself loose and backed away laughing.

"Don't misunderstand me!" cried Mr. Loomis. "It's not for myself—I don't keep house, I'm single—it's for my brother Robert. They have that big house, and a little new baby. . . ."

"It's no use," Herbert protested. "Mrs. Flint isn't leaving. But I'm going to adopt your suggestion and tell our cotenants that we're finding their light housekeeping a little too heavy, and they'll have to make other arrangements about their meals."

The lawyer raised a cautionary hand. "Now, Herbert," he said, "don't go into this thing rashly—don't rush in where an-

gels fear to tread. In other words, don't pronounce an ulti-
matum—don't do anything you'll have to undo later on, and
don't say anything you'll have to take back."

"I won't," said Herbert. "But I'm just beginning to realize
what a soft snap they've had of it. All they've had to do is pro-
vide the raw materials they raise on the place—and these have
come on the table all cooked and prepared. It was like the fairy
story.

> Little goat, bleat,
> Little table, appear.

And there it was. When they were through eating, they would
call the goat again, and the little table would disappear—and
not even a dish to wash."

"Very nice," said Mr. Loomis, "very nice. For the first time
we really have them at a disadvantage—perhaps it would be a
little more accurate to say, on the hip. No matter how much
food they have, if we can deprive them of the means of cooking and serving it they're going to be in a bad way."

Herbert grinned. "Why, I believe we've got the old son of
a gun in a position where he'll have to say uncle."

Mr. Loomis rubbed his hands together with great satisfaction. "My idea exactly. This time we've got him in a position
where *he's* the one to make the concessions."

"It's about time," Herbert said.

"Now, Herbert, if we handle this thing right we ought to get
that working agreement out of him—that is, you ought to get
it."

Herbert wilted slightly. Always he was the one to do the
dirty work.

"You handle him, and I'll handle the terms of the agreement," Loomis said. "I'll get down in black and white just what
space each cotenant is going to occupy, and what rights and
privileges each will agree to accept for himself, and to respect
for his cotenant."

By this time Herbert was licking his lips. "Sounds like quite
a job," he said.

[200]

"It's more than a job," the lawyer said, rubbing his hands together as if in anticipation of getting hold of it. "It's a wonderful opportunity."

Herbert was scowling. Ah, if he only had another lawyer, a go-getter.

"I can't understand why we never happened to think of it before—starving them into submission is a splendid idea," Loomis said. "Not a legal remedy so much as a tactical one."

"Margie and I have thought of it a good many times," Herbert said.

Mr. Loomis shrugged elaborately. "Why didn't you speak to me about it?"

When Herbert stopped to think about it, the reason was that they had always been expecting Mr. Loomis to find some loophole in the law that would relieve them of their cotenants, and Mr. Loomis had never succeeded in finding any such loophole.

Herbert glanced at his watch. "Margie will slay me if I don't return to the car pretty soon. I'll talk it over with her, and we'll try to decide on the best way to handle it."

"Good idea," Mr. Loomis said. "And if there are any more questions, give me a ring. I hope Margie won't be cross with you for being late."

"I hope not," said Herbert, and with a wave of the hand he hurried out the door and down the stairs to the street. He found Margie waiting in the car, but she was not cross at all. She was flushed and glowing over her success with the shopping, for she had been able to get five whole pounds of top round, which had been ground right before her very eyes.

"Now we can pay back some of our indebtedness," she said. "We can have two couples in for dinner. How about the Pynes? Archie and Rose haven't been over in a long time."

"Fine," he said. "I always like to see them. Maybe Archie can suggest some way for me to get a little more writing done."

"And shall we ask the John Preston Fayrbanks? We're indebted to them, you know."

Herbert scowled. "She's all right, but I can't stand her husband. Why should we spoil an evening by having that eminent ass around?"

"I don't know why you say that," Margie protested. "He's not eminent."

ꞏꞏꞏ

JONATHAN stood at the window and looked down at his garden. The sight of the growing things brought peace to his soul. The thought of the Lord God Almighty looking out of the cloud-curtained windows of Heaven came back to him. He knew just how the Lord felt as He was walking in the Garden of Eden in the cool of the day. And he wondered, without any hint of irreverence, if the Lord's tomatoes in the Garden of Eden could hold a candle to his. In all the years that he had been making a garden he had never seen such a year for tomatoes.

Of course he realized that the Lord was entirely inexperienced when he did his planting there in Eden, and that it really takes time to become a first-class gardener. He wondered if the Lord knew that little trick of using a piece of pasteboard to keep out the cutworms. As for himself, he had been making a garden for many years before he caught onto it. But it was worth waiting for; it really did the business.

His snap beans also were in the championship class—six inches long if they were an inch, meaty and round but tender as a kitten's ear; and if anybody, in Eden or elsewhere, had ever raised a finer row of limas he would like to see them.

Matilda came over and joined him by the window. "What you lookin' at?" she asked.

"Tomaters mostly."

"They'll bear lookin' at."

"Guess they will—ain't no better ones in the township."

"Oughta be picked."

"Mebbe so."

"They're ready to go into the cans right now. Has old Brass Towns been doin' any cannin'?"

"Nope. They ain't got much to can. They eat it all fast as it grows."

"Ain't we got some Mason jars in the cellar?" Matilda asked.

Jonathan yawned. "Plenty of 'em. Guess there's two or three hunderd of 'em down there on the shelves right where we left 'em."

"The beans is ready to go in the jars, too. And the chard and beets is just perfect for puttin' up. Jonathan, what about my range?"

"Range is all right if we only had a place to put it."

"I can even remember the name of it—Happy Thought— made in Pittston, Pennsylvany. It was a wonderful stove."

"Ain't nuthin' the matter with it now that I can see, except you can't turn it on and off with a button," Jonathan said.

"Who wants to turn a kitchen range on and off with a button?" she asked with a contemptuous sniff, and went back to her rocker.

"A lot of folks, I guess."

"What's the matter with tossin' in a couple of pieces of good split stovewood? Know any better way of cookin' than that?"

"Reckon I don't. Wood's the best cookin' heat there is. But let me tell you some'pm—the whole world's gone crazy about pushin' a button. You know what they got on the door of the new wing? Nuthin' but a little round pearl button no bigger than the end of your thumb. You press it in, and if nobody comes you press it again. That's all you can do—just press that button. If it rings, all right—if it don't, all right. You never know."

"That ain't much like the old knocker," Matilda said as she settled back into her chair. "If folks don't answer that they ain't nobody to home."

"I should say not," Jonathan agreed. "You could hear that clear over to the neighbors'."

"I wouldn't be so sure about the neighbors." Matilda did not hold with exaggeration. "But you certainly could hear it all over the house."

Jonathan sat down and filled his pipe. "Nobody wants to work any more—they want machinery to do it all. They push a button to cook their vittles, and another right beside it to freeze ice for their drinks."

Matilda shook her head disparagingly.

"Folks used to earn a livin' on a farm," he went on. "Now it costs 'em money to run one. They're spoilin this place—if it ain't spoiled already. You can't move without fallin' over their pipes and wires. Why, they got a thing down there that beats their eggs and another that chops their meat for hash. They can't even stir up a batch of biscuits without pushin' a button."

Matilda straightened up in her chair and looked sternly at her husband. "Jonathan," she said, "how do you happen to know so much about what's goin' on in the kitchen of this house?"

Jonathan turned and watched her closely as he replied. He did not want to miss any of her discomfiture. "The truth is that I ain't never been inside the kitchen."

"Then how do you know all this?"

"Sarah told me."

"Oh!" Matilda dropped back into her chair. For a little time she rocked slowly to and fro. Then she asked, "I don't guess she told you nuthin' about their cannin'?"

"Yes," Jonathan said, "as a matter of fact she did."

"I'll bet they don't do that by pushin' no button."

"Well, it appears they do." Jonathan nodded his head several times. "They got a thing they call a pressure cooker."

Matilda snorted. "I heared of that, but I wouldn't trust it."

"You wouldn't? Why not?"

"I'll tell you why—because that don't half cook the stuff. Who ever heared of such a thing?"

"The folks downstairs. That's just the way they do it. Sarah told me all about it. You put the stuff in the jars, and you put the jars in the cooker, and then you screw on the top and push a button."

"I'd never trust that. The stuff wouldn't keep while you was gettin' the lid on."

"Steam cookin' don't take so long as the reg'lar way."

"I wouldn't trust it."

"It's the pressure what does it—three or four hunderd pounds."

"Listen to me, Jonathan, don't believe all you hear. If they put a lot of pressure on vegetables it wouldn't cook 'em, it would only smash 'em." Matilda sat rocking slowly. "When garden stuff is ready for the can, it won't wait," she said.

Jonathan nodded. "I know."

"A lot of it's ready now."

"I know."

"Be a lot more ready next week."

"I know all about that, too. And I know there's a long hard winter ahead."

Jonathan took his pipe from his mouth and looked at her. "Recollect where we was last winter?"

She did not meet his eyes. "I guess we won't talk about that. We couldn't help ourselves. I was sick and I had to have care and doctorin'. This year is different. We're in our own home and we got some'pm to do with."

He stood up and walked over to the window. "We got plenty of stuff growin' in the garden, if that's what you mean."

"I could use my big copper boiler."

"You mean the one they're usin' for a scrap basket?"

"And I could use the two brass kettles."

"Then she'll have to get her flowers out of 'em."

"Now then, what about that stove?"

"I'll figger out some'pm. It'll take lookin' into. Well! See who's comin' up the hill! If it ain't the Mister and Missus."

Matilda straightened up and peered out. "Wonder where they been?"

"Out tryin' to buy theirselves some food, prob'ly. Can't get chickens or even eggs any more; but they must have got some'-pm, for they're lookin' pretty chipper. Don't you think we might have a little music goin' when they come in, just to remind 'em that we're here and enjoyin' life?"

Mildly complimented, Matilda sat down at the organ. According to Jonathan's calculation Herbert and Margie must have been entering the door of the house at about the moment when Matilda was striking her opening chord. With Matilda the opening chord was a matter of some importance. It was not unlike the stroke of the gavel at a public meeting or the salute of the brasses at the circus. It warned all and sundry that something of great moment was about to occur.

There had been a time when Matilda was almost as good with her closing chord as with her opening, but of late years her footwork had deteriorated, and there was not always enough wind left in the bellows for a diapason finish with all stops out and the sharps and flats running wild. Into her opening chord, however, she still put plenty of style, imagining herself in a church on the bench of a hand-pumped organ with real pipes as big around as a teacup. And on this occasion she gave everything she had. She had played twice through her opening number, improvised for a while, and was just closing the cover of the organ when a knock was heard on the door leading into the hall.

The fact was that Herbert had been sitting on the stairs waiting for the musical devotions to come to an end. But he delayed no longer after the sound of the organ had ceased. At his knock, Jonathan called to him to come in. As Herbert pushed open the door he saw Jonathan standing at the window. Matilda was a snug fit in the small doorway leading from the closet.

"Good morning," Herbert said.

Jonathan looked at him warily. He was always on his guard when people began to talk about the weather. He knew they were not really interested in it and were merely using it as a cover for something else they wished to say when they could catch him at a disadvantage. Appreciation of the amenities was not in Jonathan. Anything said merely for the sake of being agreeable was to be regarded with suspicion.

"Think so?" he said.

"Yes, I do," said Herbert, not at all perturbed. "This is the kind of day I like, but I can see that you're too busy to waste any time on the weather, so I'll tell you what I came for. There was quite a little confusion, you will remember, when you folks first arrived. I'm afraid we didn't any of us know just where we stood."

"Know any better now?" Jonathan asked.

Herbert's collar began to feel a little hot, but he held himself in check. "I know more than I did," he said not unpleasantly. "But what I started to say was that when you came the place was not arranged for double occupancy, and my wife and I concluded that it would be more convenient for all concerned if we should temporarily furnish you with meals. That turned out to be all right as an emergency measure, and we were willing enough to do it."

Matilda crossed the room and sat down in her rocker.

"I suppose," Herbert went on, "we could have stopped when we ran into the rationing trouble and the food shortage, but we kept hoping that if we would carry on a little longer we might be able to reach some kind of friendly understanding." He paused and looked from one of the old folks to the other to see if either had anything to suggest, but both remained silent. After what he thought was a reasonable pause he continued.

"The time has come when we can't wait any longer. We've run into something more powerful than the United States Government, the OPA, or even the law of supply and demand —we've run head-on into the servant question."

"I don't see what that's got to do with it," muttered Jonathan.

"Just that Mrs. Flint is threatening to leave," said Herbert with a suspicion of a smile.

[208]

Jonathan shrugged. "Wouldn't be no great loss. I never did think too high of her. What's her complaint?"

"I'm afraid," said Herbert, "that she has a curious antipathy to doing the cooking for two families in one house."

Jonathan snorted. "All right, let her go!"

Herbert shook his head. "No," he said firmly, "we're not going to let her go. She's a good servant and we're going to keep her, but I'm afraid you'll have to make some other arrangements. Up to this time you've been treated more or less like guests in the household, and I'm sorry to have to tell you that after this week we'll be able to furnish you with no more meals, either from your materials or ours. You'll be on your own—strictly on your own."

"You mean she won't do no more cookin' for us, hey?" Jonathan asked sourly. "That what you mean?"

Herbert nodded. "Exactly."

"All right, why didn't you say so?" Jonathan exclaimed brusquely. "Twitterin' about the weather. What's the weather got to do with it?"

"Quite a little." Herbert turned towards the door. "I still feel that it's a nice day, and I hope you won't think I'm twittering when I wish you both a very good morning."

Herbert's footfalls on the now uncarpeted stairway were still reverberating in the little front hallway when Matilda turned on her husband.

"Well, there you are," she said with a note of challenge in her voice. "What'll we do now?"

Jonathan stroked his chin thoughtfully. "You needn't try to hurry me," he said. "We got till the end of the week, ain't we? And as I told you a while back, this'll take a little lookin' into."

↑↑

JONATHAN'S "looking into" was characteristic. His first move was to call a meeting of the three old men, and they came together out behind the barn. Joe, as usual, was seated on the ground. He preferred the ground. It was his belief that time spent in sitting on the ground was not entirely wasted, since the earth possessed certain mysterious qualities which it imparted only to those who came in close contact. Joe was convinced that the animals obtain their strength, greater strength than that of any man, largely from the long periods they spend lying on the ground. The truth was that Joe not only admired the animals, he envied them, and if he had had it to do over again he would have liked to be born an animal, a well-built Holstein, perhaps. As to sex, that did not particularly matter, and his preference was about evenly divided between being a premium bull or a fourteen-quart milker.

Uncle Walter, seated on an upturned wooden pail, was paring his nails with his jackknife. He kept wondering what it was that Jonathan had on his mind. Must be something, or Jon never would have sent for him; usually some kind of trouble brewin' when he brung the three of 'em together. At frequent intervals Uncle Walter would glance at Jonathan to see if he had started talkin'. Had to listen with his eyes, as the feller said, and his eyes was none too good. Be needin' new glasses one of these days if he was goin' to do any considerable lip-readin'. Uncle Walter was waiting to see how the pain in his side turned out. If it was serious he wouldn't need glasses; but if it turned out to be a little lameness or a touch of rheumatiz, then he s'posed he'd have to put the money into some new glass. The frame was still good. Prob'ly last as long as he did.

Uncle Walter had just finished with the nails on his left hand when Jonathan drew up an inverted crate and sat down directly in front of him. Holding his hand as a sound amplifier, Uncle Walter presented his left ear.

Jonathan shoved it aside with his hand. "Get out your speakin' tube!" he bellowed.

Uncle Walter gave in and drew the tube from an inner pocket. "Well, sir, what's up?" he asked.

Jonathan put his lips close to the tube. "Cookin'!"

Uncle Walter drew back and squinted an eye at him. "Cookin'? What's cookin'?"

"Nothin'! That's the trouble—where we goin' to do it?"

With a judicial expression Uncle Walter asked, "What's the matter with the kitchen?"

Jonathan's head shook with an emphatic negative. "It's all electric!"

"Some folks claim that's the best there is. All you gotta do is push a button."

"Matilda don't hold with pushin' buttons."

Uncle Walter nodded understandingly. "Some don't. But what's the matter with your wood range? You got one."

"We got one all right," Jonathan admitted. "But where to put it?"

"Where do you want it?"

"Best place is downstairs, front room on this side."

"They's a stovepipe thimble in that room, ain't they?" asked Uncle Walter.

"Sure." Jonathan nodded. "A good one. But I can't use that room—it's his office and it's full of his furniture."

"We'll move that out."

"Have I got a right to?"

"You bet! You're tenants in common, ain't you?"

"So Loomis says."

"That settles it. He can't keep you out of no place. You both got a right to occupy it all."

"He won't want us cookin' in his office," Jonathan said.

"And you won't want him writin' in your kitchen. But there can't nobody stand in the way of your right to cook. Cookin' your vittles is one of the fundamental rights—like freedom of speech or freedom to keep your mouth shut. You just go ahead and set up your stove, build a good hot fire into it, and then go and tell him he can come in and use it if he wants to."

"But," asked Jonathan, "is it legal to move his things out?"

"Just as legal for you to move 'em out as for him to move 'em in. You moved his stuff outa the bedroom, didn't you?"

"That was a little diff'rent," Jonathan explained. "He agreed to that."

Uncle Walter pondered a moment. "All right," he said, "you could put the stove in the upstairs bedroom."

"But I don't want to," Jonathan protested. "Think I want to carry wood and water up and down stairs? It wouldn't be so bad just for cookin', but when cold weather comes on I wouldn't have time to do nuthin' else, and besides, the stove won't go up the stairwell. There ain't room. I measured."

Uncle Walter shook his head disparagingly. "Why didn't you say so in the first place?"

"You wouldn't give me no chance."

"No what?"

"No chance."

"No what?"

"Oh, never mind. Let's get to work and move that stove."

"Any hurry about it?" asked Uncle Walter.

"Not in partic'lar," Jonathan replied. "Only thing is, he ain't to home right now."

Uncle Walter smiled. "Well, I guess there's no use waitin' for him. Got a stunboat?"

Jonathan motioned for Uncle Walter to follow him and led the way to the furnished portion of the big barn, where he lifted the corner of a Navajo rug spread over what appeared to be a table. Underneath lay the polished bottom of his stoneboat.

Uncle Walter howled with laughter. "Well, I'll be larruped! What won't they be usin' next!"

Jonathan pointed underneath to show that the stoneboat was merely resting on two sawhorses and could easily be removed, but Uncle Walter shook his head.

"We'll use my hickory pung," he insisted. "Better'n any stunboat you ever seen."

"This'll do," Jonathan said, not wishing to take either the time or the bother to go to Uncle Walter's for the pung.

"Ever see that pung of mine?" Uncle Walter demanded, as he coiled the speaking tube and put it in his pocket.

Jonathan nodded elaborately. "Lots of times."

"There ain't a better hickory pung in the county. Did I ever tell you how I come to get it?"

"Not more than fifty times," said Jonathan.

"That's funny." Uncle Walter smiled as if a little reluctant to go on with it. It's a pretty good story—I'll tell you how it happened."

Jonathan looked helplessly at Joe. "I can tell that story just as good as he can, but all hell couldn't stop him now."

"It was some years ago, when I still had my hearin'," Uncle Walter began. "I was cuttin' wood one winter down to Ezra Miller's—a lot of oak and hickory in the wood lot back there on the hill. . . ."

Jonathan made one final effort. He looked Uncle Walter straight in the face from a distance of about ten inches. "I've heard that story," he said very distinctly. "It's a good one, but. . . ."

"You're tootin' it's a good story, and I know how to tell it. You listen. We'd been cuttin' there for about a week when we come to a tall straight hickory, and I says to Ezra, Ezra, I says, this tree's too nice to cut up into firewood, I says. Yes, he says, it's a nice tree all right, he says, but if we don't cut it up into firewood what'll we cut it up into? he says. Well, I says, you could cut it up into plank, I says. It'd make a couple of pretty fine pungs, I says.

"Well, sir, he walked up and down that log and looked it over, and, he says, by George, he says, I'll do it, he says. And one day he loaded it up and took it off to the sawmill, and the next time I saw that log it was made up into two of the nicest hickory pungs you ever laid your eyes on. One for him and one for me. Made me an entire present of it.

"Well, sir, that night when I started for home I loaded the pung onto my wagon, and, as I was passin' Preston Dilly's house, Preston come out. He says hello, Walter, and I says hello, Preston, and he says what you got there, he says. And I says it's a pung. And he says where'd you get it, he says. Why, I'll tell you, I says, I been cuttin' wood down to Ezra Miller's, I says, a lot of oak and hickory in the wood lot back there on the hill, I says. We'd been cuttin' there for about a week, I says, and we come to a big tall straight hickory, and I says to Ezra, Ezra, I says, this tree's too nice to cut up into firewood, I says. Yes, he says, it's a nice tree, he says, but if we don't cut it up into firewood what will we cut it up into? he says. Well, I says, you could cut it up into plank, I says, it'd make a couple of pretty fine pungs.

"Well, sir, I says to Preston, I says, Ezra walked up and down that log and looked it over, and he says, by George I'll do it, he says. And one day Ezra loaded it up, I says to Preston, and took it off to the sawmill, and the next time I saw that log it was made up into two of the nicest hickory pungs you ever laid your eyes on. One for Ezra and one for me, I says to Preston. Made me an entire present of it.

"Well, sir, I hadn't gone half a mile from Preston's when I met Jake Dadson on the road. He says hello, Walter, and I says hello, Jake, and he says what you got there, and I says it's a hickory pung, I says. And he says, where'd you get it, he says, and I says, well, I'll tell you, I says. I been cuttin' wood down to Ezra Miller's, I says, a lot of oak and hickory, I says, in the wood lot back there on the hill. . . ."

Jonathan turned his back so that Uncle Walter could not see that his lips were moving, and said to Joe, as if Joe could understand what he was saying, "He's got two more stops before he gets that pung home, but I'm afraid we ain't got time to wait for him."

Joe smiled as if he understood and said, "Too much."

Uncle Walter's voice was droning along in the background. ". . . and I says to Ezra, Ezra, I says, this tree's too nice to cut up into firewood, I says. . . ."

Sarah came galloping around the corner of the barn and brought up in front of Jonathan with a great show of prancing and snorting and tossing of the mane.

"Whoa, girl, whoa—quiet now, quiet," Jonathan said. "Better get up on two legs so's you can talk. I'm thinkin' of takin' Shadrach out for a little exercise, and I don't like to have too many folks around."

Sarah stood up with alacrity. "Will you let me drive?"

"That depends a little on who there is to see you. Your family don't specially like to have you drivin' Shadrach. I know your pa and ma's away, but there's others. And who knows how long your pa and ma will be gone."

Sarah laughed gaily. "Why, Grampa Rockwood, my father and mother won't be back until dinnertime. They've gone to the end of the bus line in our car, and then they take the bus into town to save gasoline."

"You don't think your sister would tell on you?"

"Barbara? She'd never tell on me—and besides she's not home. She's gone horseback riding with a Marine. Didn't you see his car stop in front of the house? He took her down to the Riding Club. I think Barbara's kinda sweet on him. . . ."

"You think she's gone for the afternoon, hey?"

"Oh, I'm sure of it."

Jonathan lost no time in summoning Joe and Uncle Walter with a combination of pidgin English and a sign language that bordered on personal violence. Uncle Walter resented being interrupted in the telling of one of his best stories, but he came, leaving his pung still half a mile from home, but hopeful that he would be able to get it the rest of the way a little later. Inside the barn, Jonathan removed the *objet d'art* from the table, snatched off the Navajo blanket, and lifted one end of the stoneboat.

After a futile protest that the pung would be better, Uncle Walter lent a hand, and the three together carried the heavy vehicle to the door of the barn. Here they loaded the stove on board, and it was only a matter of minutes before Shadrach had hauled it to the front door of the house. A few minutes more and they had carried it inside, set it up before the fireplace in Herbert's study, and wired the stovepipe into the thimble. Then, working fast, they carried Herbert's desk through into the taproom. They moved the davenport into the big living room, thrust the remainder of the study furniture wherever they could find room for it, and deposited the room-size rug, neatly folded, behind the bar in the taproom. Because of their great profusion the books were left temporarily undisturbed, their removal to the attic being postponed until a later day. And after the study had been otherwise cleared, they brought down from the attic and up from the barn the usable remnants of the kitchen equipment that Matilda had collected in half a century of housekeeping.

There was, of course, no running water in the room, but neither had there been running water in any kitchen Matilda had ever had; at no time in her life had she asked for anything better than a rain barrel just outside the door, and a well within easy walking distance. Shadrach with the stoneboat made several trips from the barn hauling up dilapidated pieces of furniture that the Gages had not deemed worthy of attic room, but which they hesitated to destroy. On the last trip he brought an old cider barrel on which Jonathan had been coopering for some time, tightening the chimes and soaking the staves to make them watertight.

Jonathan set the barrel at the corner of the house, and by disconnecting a section of the new copper conductor pipe, he provided a convenient if not very handsome rain barrel. Drinking water was already available at a sill tap a few steps from the front door. Only the sink was missing, an old portable wooden dugout that stood on four legs and emptied its contents, when released, into a bucket standing on the floor underneath. It was of course the one thing that Matilda insisted upon having. However, a thorough ransacking of the premises brought no trace of the sink, and then belatedly Sarah remembered that her father had once taken away an old sink in the station wagon. Jonathan said it was unimportant at the moment, and that he would speak to her father about it later.

It felt like old times to Jonathan to come walking into the house with an armful of wood, and he had a fire going and the teakettle singing on the stove long before Matilda was ready to wash the hayseed and cobwebs from her utensils and start the dinner. He caught hold of the old kitchen chair in which he used to sit and gave it a shake. He found it, as always, elastic in the joints, but it held together, and he sat down on it.

At the creaking of the joints Matilda turned. "Looks kinda natural to see you settin' in that chair," she said. "How does it feel?"

"Same as always," Jonathan replied. "You have to be careful in this chair or you get pinched."

"Where?"

"Same place where it always pinched me. If I should tell you, you wouldn't like it."

Matilda looked at him down her nose. "I wasn't talkin' about you—I was askin' about the chair, what part of it to look out for."

"You never set in it anyhow," Jonathan said. "I ain't too sure it would hold you."

"Better not hold you too long." She turned back to the rusty utensils she was sorting in the old cracked cutlery box. "If we're goin' to cook our own dinner we'll want some vegetables fetched in. And if you was to kill one of them cockerels I guess it wouldn't be missed from the flock. I don't know how you ever got so many roosters out of fifty chicks."

Jonathan made no reply. That kind of talk was senseless. He had no more responsibility for the sex of those chicks than the hen who laid the eggs. Without a word he picked up his broad-brimmed hat and went out of the door, wondering why it was that Matilda could never see him settling down to take a little comfort without she'd think up a job for him. It wasn't one of the things you could argue with a woman. Every woman he ever saw thought she spent her whole life doing little things to make some man comfortable.

As he came out of the barn, ax in hand, he saw the smoke rising from the chimney and paused to watch it. There it was, their own smoke coming out of their old chimney at last. Up to this time they'd been no more than boarders. Now they were really beginning to live there again. Up above the roof top he could see the branches of the old tree swaying against the sky. He wondered if those branches couldn't see that the smoke was different. This was no foul-smelling odor from the sooty smokestack of an oil burner. This was sweet-smelling smoke from birch wood raised on the place—and there was plenty more where that came from.

Both Jonathan and Matilda were in a mellow mood as they sat in the squeaky chairs eating, from a battered table with a short leg, the best meal of victuals they had tasted during the five years since they had left the old house. The fried chicken browned to perfection, seemed to have a special flavor; the sour-milk biscuits were light as thistledown; the string beans were golden with fresh-churned butter; and the cucumbers and tomatoes sliced in vinegar and Uncle Walter's maple sugar were something to melt in the mouth. Then on top of all this was a hot berry pie, fresh out of the oven and still bubbling.

The old couple felt almost as thrilled as when they had set up housekeeping together under that same sturdy rooftree half a century before. But of course neither one spoke of such a thing. Complacency was something that was not to any great extent in the nature of either. Matilda, however, could not help gloating over their best china, which they had found intact in the attic. She was tempted to smile every time she thought of the old pieces of kitchen ironstone displayed in the Gages' corner cupboard while all that lovely Larkin premium with the pink flower pattern was gathering dust in the attic, all except a saucer that the Gages used for feeding the cat.

Sarah tapped on the door and came inside sniffing like a hungry puppy. Jonathan pulled up a chair for her. Without leaving the table he took down an extra plate from a stack on a bookshelf lately relieved of a set of Anatole France, now piled on the floor waiting to be carried to the attic. He didn't know what the child's mother might say if she ever found out that they were stuffing the youngster with fried chicken and other homely delicacies she was no longer accustomed to, but he did not particularly care. The look of hungry longing was a little too much for a fellow who was himself rapidly reaching the point where he couldn't hold any more.

"What do you like?" he asked. "A drumstick?"

"That would be fine," Sarah said enthusiastically.

ERBERT had smelled fried chicken before they entered the house. At least he thought it was fried
chicken. He did not speak of it. Margie had been
moaning and groaning all the way home about the food situation, and especially the meat shortage. She had had so much to
say about the impossibility of getting chickens that he would
hardly have expected her to turn up a platter of fried chicken
for dinner—unless, of course, all that talk about scarcity had
been a big build-up so that she could give him a surprise.

Margie's predilection for surprises had long been a puzzle
and often an irritation to Herbert. That they were vestigial, a
leftover from childhood, was obvious to him; but the part he
could not understand was Margie's viewpoint. Why should she
derive a particular pleasure from inducing a state of unexpect-
edness on the part of another person, and then suddenly bringing him up short with a surprise?

She had always done it. Probably she always would. But
she had given him fair warning. Indeed, the very act of meeting her had been a surprise—she had been a blind date while
he was in Mohawk. From that time on she had been treating
him to a series of unexpected pleasures. He couldn't deny that
he had found the boy and girl attentions pleasant and amusing.
Probably at the time he had thought them cute and even ador-
able. But, after all, it had been more than twenty years, and
the novelty had worn thin. Herbert still couldn't see why it
would not have been just as well for her to say that she wanted

to make him a present of a necktie and would he please come and help her pick it out.

But that just wasn't Margie's way. She would slip off by herself and pay for a tie four times what he would have thought excessive—usually a tie that was freakish or hideous—and then could she just come in and give it to him? No! She must wrap it in gold paper tied with a silver ribbon and hide it under his pillow. Once at a cocktail party he had found a silver-handled penknife in his pocket and had tried to give it back to every man in the house until finally Margie discovered what he was doing and explained to him that she had put it there as a surprise.

Earlier in his life Herbert had thought that she might outgrow the habit, or possibly confine her surprises to the children. Now he knew that she never would; for, although she had always given the children plenty of unexpected pleasures, she had saved the best of them for him. And after two decades of married life a man begins to learn that even the most inconsistent wife may be steadfastly consistent about her inconsistencies.

Had Herbert been a little more boorish he might have told Margie what he really thought about some of her surprises. Many times he had been tempted to, but had managed to check himself with the realization that she meant well; and he hated to deprive her of what was, after all, an innocent pleasure. It was for these reasons that he had said nothing about the supposed smell of fried chicken. He had schooled himself in the expectation of surprises until he was, as he thought, practically foolproof.

However, the aroma of fried chicken became so pronounced as they were entering the door that an unguarded exclamation did slip out.

"Sniff, sniff! What's cooking?" he heard himself saying.

But Margie paid no attention to him. She was so engrossed in another matter that she did not even hear him as she stood pointing vaguely at the fireplace.

"The brass kettles," she finally murmured.

"What's the matter with them?"

"That's what I want to know," she said. "They're gone."

It didn't seem very important to Herbert. He felt sure that they would be found somewhere around. "Perhaps Mrs. Flint," he began, then stopped short. "Well, of all things," he went on after a brief pause. "How did my desk get in there?" He pointed through the doorway into the taproom.

Margie glanced over that way. "Why, so it has," she said. "But, Herbert—do you see?" She pointed to the further end of the living room. "The davenport out of your study—what's been going on here?"

He shook his head and stepped through into the taproom. "Look—chairs from the study." He went a few steps further. 'And there's my filing cabinet in the hallway."

For a time Margie stood motionless, her eyes wide, her lips slightly parted. "You don't suppose there's been an emergency —perhaps a fire?"

Herbert slowly shook his head. "Doesn't smell like a fire to me. Smells a lot more like—something cooking. We could ask Mrs. Flint, you know."

"I'm afraid Mrs. Flint has nothing to do with this." Margie stepped softly over and listened at the doorway leading into the hall. "Somebody's in your study—I can hear talking in there—and I'm going in." She did not knock, but suddenly threw open the door and stopped in the doorway.

It was the wood range which first caught her eye, jutting its austere iron form out into the room, with an angular stretch of stovepipe going up and over to the chimney. Then she saw the group gathered around the table, Matilda on the right, Jonathan on the left, and on the farther side the astonished visage of Sarah, well decorated with gravy and minor particles of equally adhesive food, and half hidden behind a drumstick held in her two hands.

Margie leveled a gloved finger at her child. "*What* are you doing here?" she demanded.

[222]

"I smelled some'pm good and came in to see what it was." Warned by some animal instinct that she was in danger of being robbed of her food, Sarah broke off suddenly and began devouring her drumstick in great savage bites, gulping down the meat to save all she possibly could before the blow should fall. The blow, however, was upon her.

"Sarah! You know such a thing as this is not allowed!"

Still stuffing herself, Sarah mumbled what might have been meant as an explanation. Whatever it was, it was designed primarily for purposes of delay.

Sensing this, her mother cut her short. "You may go to your room instantly," Margie said with the voice of authority. "But first. . . ." She was going to order the child to put down the drumstick, had not Herbert, foreseeing what was coming, and speaking from the goodness of his heart, cut her off by saying, "Stop at the bathroom and wash your hands and face."

Margie let it go at that and stood rigid until Sarah had wriggled out of her chair and left the room, making greedy attacks on the drumstick as she went along. Assuring herself by a backward glance that Sarah was gone, Margie delivered a sweeping gesture covering the entire room and all it contained.

"What is the meaning of this?" she demanded.

Jonathan rolled his head around and looked at her over his shoulder. "I was goin' to ask you the same thing—bustin' in on folks without even a knock on the door. It's gettin' so there ain't much privacy around here."

"Privacy?" said Margie. "Is there such a thing when people feel at liberty to scatter our furniture around the house without so much as mentioning the matter to us? Don't you think it would have been more considerate to discuss the situation with us before taking matters into your own hands quite so ruthlessly?"

A look of amusement came over Jonathan's face. "How much did you discuss it with us before you grabbed the whole house and built it over to suit yourselves?"

"If we didn't," Herbert said firmly, "it wasn't because we didn't try. We spent a lot of our time and our money trying to find you."

"Indeed we did!" Margie put in. "It was just as if you were in hiding."

Jonathan stood up, sucking at his teeth after the manner of one who has enjoyed a good meal, and picking at them with his fingernails to dislodge stubborn particles of fried chicken wedged in between. "You didn't look in the right place, that's all." He drew a long breath and straightened up to ease his clothes which were feeling a little snug. "About shovin' your furniture around—I guess you'll find we didn't harm it none. But there's one thing you don't want to forget—you was the one who come around and said we'd have to make a change. Well, we made it, and I'm mighty glad we did. We ain't had such a meal of vittles since we went away from here quite a spell ago. And let me tell you some'pm else—if you'll go and talk to that owl-eyed lawyer of yours you'll find out we ain't done nuthin' except what's within our rights. You know this tenant-in-common business works both ways."

"Of course it does," Herbert said, wondering if this was not perhaps an opening for a discussion that might lead to the beginnings of a working agreement. This capture by strong-arm methods of another room was something that he felt should be stopped before it had gone any further. No telling where it would end. Jonathan had seized the guest room; he had plowed up the best part of the lawn and turned it into an unbeautiful if productive vegetable garden; he had excluded them from the barn—probably for years to come—by housing his animals there; and now he had appropriated the finest room in the house and turned it into a kitchen. In his mind's eye Herbert could see little globules of dust-covered oil gathering on his first editions, yellowing the pages and disfiguring the leather bindings of the few old and rare items he possessed. Yes, something certainly must be done. He must not let this opportunity get away.

[224]

"Old Judge Loomis says a tenancy in common is worse than a bad case of hives," he ventured, "likely to break out in a dozen places at once."

"He oughta know—scratchin' backs is his business," Jonathan muttered.

"But he thinks people ought to settle their differences out of court."

"Wants the lawyers to starve?"

"Hardly that," Herbert said with a smile. "But he insists that there never was a case in court that couldn't have been better settled on the outside. He's a great believer in the peace table; thinks the pen is mightier than the sword."

"Let's ship a few boatloads of pens to Eisenhower and Mac-Arthur."

Herbert could see that he was rapidly getting nowhere. Generalities were falling on barren ground and he felt that his one chance of success would be to come to the point without further incubation. "Lawyer Loomis thinks that you and I ought to sit down by ourselves and talk things over, and see if we can't make an agreement that will satisfy both of us."

The corners of Jonathan's mouth drew firmly down. "When I got anything to say to you, I'll say it."

Herbert turned away with the feeling that the opportunity —if there ever had been one—had passed. But Margie, entertaining no such feeling, faced Jonathan.

"There's one thing I'd like to say to you," she said. "This room was originally built for the ladies' parlor of an inn, and it will never be anything but a mere makeshift as a kitchen. If you had let us finish off an apartment for you in the relaxation room you would have had one of the most complete and convenient little kitchens you ever saw—running water, a sink, and all the conveniences."

"Glad you spoke about that," said Jonathan. "Reminds me about some'pm. When we went west we left a fine old dugout sink in the summer kitchen you tore down when you was remodelin' the house. I ain't seen that sink nowheres around. Recollect what you done with it?"

"A dugout sink?" Herbert and Margie looked at each other with a blank expression.

Matilda began to shake her head reminiscently. "I just couldn't keep house without that sink. About the most convenient thing we had."

"Dugout sink—a dugout sink. . . ." Herbert kept repeating. "What did it look like?"

"Big long contraption." Jonathan stretched out his arms to indicate the length. "Hollowed out like a sink, with a drainpipe near one end. You'd catch the water in a bucket underneath—real handy for emptyin'. Then you turn it upside down and you could use it for a table when you didn't need a sink."

"Oh-h-h—" drawled Margie. "Seems to me I do remember something like that."

Herbert nodded a little uncertainly. "I think I do, too."

"You *think?*" Jonathan demanded, recalling what Sarah had told him. "Don't you know?"

"It's just that I don't want to be too positive." Herbert smiled weakly. "There was a lot of confusion when that old summer kitchen was torn down. It wouldn't be safe to say off-hand just what was done with anything."

"But we need our sink," Matilda insisted. "You can't keep house without a sink, you know."

"Oh, we'll find it all right," Herbert said reassuringly. "We took care of everything. Nothing was destroyed. It's just a question of being able to put your finger on it."

"That's the trouble exactly," Margie agreed. "We remember it, but we're not quite sure where it is."

Jonathan looked very skeptical. "There's only about so many places around here where you could put anything as big as that."

"Isn't that the truth," said Herbert, backing towards the door. "I'll tell you what we'll do—Mrs. Gage and I will look around a bit and see if we can find it. Oh, I'm sure we'll locate your sink for you. By the way, what would the money value be in case we couldn't find it?"

"Money value?" Jonathan demanded stridently. "We ain't interested in the money value. That dugout sink's a heirloom. Been in the family a good many years, more or less. We don't want money—all we want is the *sink!*"

As the door closed behind them, Herbert and Margie looked at each other with deep understanding and equally deep dismay. Both remembered very clearly what had been done with the dugout sink. It had passed into the hands of an antique dealer in a transaction involving a four-poster bed and an ancient roll-top tea canister for Barbara's room. Up to the present time they had all been a bit jubilant over the transaction, feeling that for once they had bested the antique dealer, who was noted for tying a twenty-dollar price tag on anything that had cost him as much as a dollar. An added reason for their delight was that the old sink had spent some weeks incognito on a lumber pile in the back yard, during which time it could have been bought for fifty cents, or even a quarter.

To Herbert and Margie this particular antique had looked like a homemade workbench with a hole through one end. Everything about it seemed wrong to them. Wrong height, wrong length, wrong width. The legs were so crudely made and so poorly placed in the frame as to allow no overhang. It had stood in the woodshed a long time before they had taken any notice of it, and the only reason they had noticed it then was because the shed was being torn down and the contents had to be removed. The wood looked old enough, but the nailheads had rusted away to such an extent that all semblance of hand-forging had long since been lost, and after prodding at them with an ice pick Herbert had concluded that they were modern anyway. It was, however, the unsavory smell of the wood that led Herbert to suggest the lumber pile. He couldn't believe that anything with such a vile and musty odor could be of value to anybody—which shows what a novice he was in the matter of antiques.

The only wonder was that the lumber pile, which was composed almost entirely of rubbish, had not been burned while the old sink was still one of its most prominent features. The match was spared however, and Alice Dunbar, the interior decorator, identified the old dugout for what it was and had insisted that Herbert must put it in the barn for safekeeping. Herbert pretended that he had known all the time what it was, and explained that he had put it outside in the hope that it might lose some of its noisome odor. This was a bad giveaway, and after a proper amount of swooning and gesticulating Miss Dunbar explained that the aroma was usually the determining factor in arriving at the real value of an antique dugout. It was, she explained, like the wormholes in a piece of ancient furniture.

Herbert examined the piece after she had gone and found that by lifting off the upper part and inverting it a hollow receptacle was disclosed which could have been and undoubtedly was, in some dim and unsanitary past, used as a sink. Not knowing what to do with the monstrosity, he moved it into the barn, where it was soon covered with a protective film of dust and hayseed. And that was where the antique dealer had seen it. Herbert had taken him there to show him an old hinge that had been plowed up in the garden, but it was quite obvious that the dealer was much more interested in the dugout than in the hinge. He wanted the top taken off so that he could look at it, and Herbert noted with some amusement how carefully the old fellow sniffed at the dugout part. After he had taken a good look at it, he apparently lost all interest, saying that though it was quite an old relic, it was useless, and passing on to something else. Nothing was said at the time about the probable value of the piece. That was to come a little later, when Barbara and her mother were showing an interest in a four-poster bed that they had seen among the dealer's antiques.

They had gasped at the price he had put upon it, and he had suggested that if they wanted to make a trade he would consider taking the old dugout in part payment. Herbert had a good laugh when they came to him with the proposition. He said they could have the four-poster bed if the dealer wanted to make an even exchange. They weren't able to do quite as well as that, but the cash differential was slight, and the day when Herbert had driven away with the dugout in the back of the station wagon he had brought home the four-poster bed.

That was why Herbert and Margie had looked at each other with understanding and dismay. They knew where the four-poster bed was, but they had no idea in the world what might have become of the old dugout sink.

ᚱᚱ

ERBERT'S first step looking to the return of the sink was to send Margie and Barbara over to the antique dealer's on a spying expedition. This cost him the price of an old student lamp, but he felt that the money had been well spent. He had succeeded in acquiring the information he needed, and he had acquired it without giving the antique dealer any hint as to the real state of affairs. There was very little doubt in Herbert's mind as to what would happen to him if the crafty old antique dealer should find out how badly he really needed the dugout sink. The spies reported that the dugout was still in stock and was not too prominently displayed. They also brought back the encouraging news that the dealer was getting ready to hold one of his periodical auction sales at which customers could select the articles on which they desired to bid.

The sale, however, was a full week away, and Herbert spent much of the intervening time dodging his cotenant, who with each passing day was becoming more and more impatient, and who by the arrival of auction day was beginning to sound somewhat insistent. Herbert had decided that it would be unwise to do the bidding for himself. He did not want the dealer to know that he had any interest whatever in getting back the sink. He would have been glad to have a native do the bidding for him, but he did not know any native well enough to ask such a favor. Then Barbara suggested George Husted. George had never even seen the antique dealer. And he was equally sure the dealer wouldn't know him from Adam. George rather fancied the idea of being in on a family secret. He liked to feel that Herbert trusted him and counted on him to come through in a personal and confidential matter of this kind. It was a great relief to George to have been chosen for the job in preference to that blooming captain of marines, who had been very much in his way lately and who had seemed to have the inside track with Barbara. George didn't like the way the marine had been using his furlough as an excuse for monopolizing all of Barbara's time, and he especially didn't like the way his rival had managed to keep getting his furlough extended. He began to wonder if it was a furlough—or something else.

Off and on, George considered abandoning his effort to get into the Marine Corps. The thought of belonging to the same branch of the service as the captain was distasteful to him, but he kept reminding himself that the marines were a mighty big outfit and were scattered all over the face of the globe, and he argued that if Barbara was so fond of the marine uniform he'd do his best to get himself into one. The day of the auction, however, found George in a very cheerful and optimistic mood. Barbara had rejected him twice that day, but she had done it very sweetly and was still treating him like a human being, and the family was displaying great confidence in him. What more could a prospective son-in-law ask, he wondered.

The party drove away from the house like a gang of gay conspirators. George could have gone in his own car to carry out the illusion that he was a stranger to the Gages, but they all thought this an unnecessary precaution. They could let him out by the side of the road as if they had just given him a lift, and he could go in alone and shift for himself until the bidding on the dugout was finished; after that it would not matter. Herbert's instructions to George were brief and simple. He was to have the old dugout put up, and was to keep bidding until he had bought it. George was proud of the simplicity and breadth of those instructions. Showed faith in him and confidence in his ability. Also showed what he chose to regard as the budding of a future family solidarity. He was being taken into the family councils and given a position of trust. Enough to lighten the heart of any young man who was as much in love as George Husted.

It was a perfect day, with little puffs of white cloud dotting the blue of a summer sky. The hills and valleys of Connecticut had, George thought, never looked lovelier. The air seemed like wine to him. He became more exhilarated with every breath he drew. He saw birds and butterflies wherever he looked, without stopping to think that the one was interested only in eating the other. George was, however, in no state for dreams. His nerves were keen, his eye quick, his mind alert. He was in form—he was on the trigger—he was ready to go to bat for the family.

At the first corner they came upon a red flag and a directional arrow, universal insignia of the auction sale. They saw other red flags at intervals as they went along, and they began to feel the excitement of the vendue even before they had come near enough to see the long lines of cars parked by the roadside, in the fields, and even in the dooryard among the old farm buildings where the antique dealer maintained his establishment. When they were still some distance away, George clambered out and went ahead alone while Barbara, who was driving, took her time about parking the car.

The Gages, and Margie especially, were old hands at attending auctions. They understood very well that in the country an auction is regarded by the public as eighty per cent entertainment and not over twenty per cent business, and they were quite familiar with the custom of coming early and installing oneself in a comfortable place from which to see and hear all that is going on. If there was furniture to be sold, they knew that somebody would be sitting on it until the moment when it was to be put up for sale. People were still wandering around looking over the place when they arrived, and they had no trouble in finding seats on the funeral chairs ranged in a semicircle in front of the auctioneer's stand.

Margie and Barbara sat down where they could watch the fun, but Herbert, not wishing to be within sight of the auctioneer's stand, found a secluded spot for himself around by the side of the house. He had just seated himself when the ringing of the auctioneer's big bell announced that the bidding was about to begin. The funeral chairs were quickly filled, and many rows of standees gathered in the back. The auction started with the offering of some trinkets of little value, odd pieces of china and glass, a picture frame or two, and a pewter pitcher. This was just to break the ice and get acquainted, and, after the people had begun to enter into the spirit of bidding, articles of greater value were handed up: a pine bedside stand, a bird-cage chair, a tip-top table with a damaged leg.

In asking to have the sink offered for bidding, George had made it very plain that he had only a limited time at his disposal, and the auctioneer had put the item near the top of his list of requests. While waiting, George took a position at one side well toward the front, and when finally the old dugout was offered—with what he considered a very considerable fanfare—he started the bidding with a modest, though he hoped not too modest, offer of five dollars. He would not have been overwhelmed had the old relic been struck down to him at that price; but after a great storm of whooping and shouting by the auctioneer a rather timid raise of one dollar came out of the crowd over at the left.

More from surprise than from any planned strategy, George quickly jumped to ten. And having made the bid, he waited expectantly to have the dugout struck down to him. The price was a little high, he thought, but his instructions had been explicit. Herbert wanted the old thing and now he was going to get it. No use in sparring with an opponent at an auction sale. The sooner the knockout punch was delivered, the lower the price would be. George was glad of this opportunity to prove his stuff to his future father-in-law, to show that he was a fellow who could be relied on—and he didn't mind having Barbara there to see how steady he was under fire. After all, the marines weren't the only good soldiers in the world.

Meanwhile the auctioneer, who could not seem to understand that the bidding was all over, continued his exhortations. He shouted and whooped, he gesticulated and pleaded, he ridiculed and fulminated, while George stood smiling with confidence and waiting for the hammer to come down. But the hammer did not come down. Something quite different happened. Another bid came from the crowd. It was a raise of one dollar.

"Eleven I am offered!" the auctioneer shouted triumphantly. "Eleven—eleven—eleven—eleven. . . ."

George couldn't have been much more surprised if the other bidder had slapped him in the face. For an instant he was dazed and astonished. Then a surge of madness swept over him and he struck back blindly, but with plenty of power.

"Twenty!" he shouted.

There was a craning of necks. George knew that people were staring at him, and he also knew that his face was pretty red. In all that crowd the auctioneer was the only one who was not looking at him. That gentleman was leaning over and pointing with the handle of his hammer at somebody on the other side of the crowd for whose benefit he was shouting with fiendish glee a rhythmic repetition of the word "Twen-tee—twen-tee—twen-tee. . . . !"

As George turned and looked in the direction towards which the auctioneer was pointing he saw a hand with the index finger extended, coming slowly up out of the crowd. Then he heard a nasal voice bawl out, "Make it the one!"

Now all the crowd turned and peered the other way, and George got a look at his competitor, a shaggy little fellow with a walrus mustache, who without his glasses would have resembled a Scottish terrier. Undoubtedly a native. And with him was another native, a cadaverous-looking fellow with a long nose in front of which he was holding a pencil and paper.

Suddenly George became aware that the handle of the auctioneer's hammer was now aimed at him and the auctioneer was delivering for his sole benefit a salvo of twenty-ones. So that was it. Another one dollar bid. The thriftiness of it, the stinginess, the timidity angered George, and, without waiting for the auctioneer to show what he could really do in the way of a twenty-one chant, George hurled back a bid meant to show up his penurious competitor—he jumped to thirty. George could see the shaggy little man and his associate with their heads together over the bit of paper. Then the index finger went up again. Another bid of one dollar.

By this time George had lost all sense of values. He was like a boxer who had dropped his guard and begun to slug at an opponent who was easy to hit, but who refused to go down. He would have liked to reduce his bids, but he could not quite see his way clear to do it. The crowd, he felt sure, were expecting him to leap to the even tens and he found himself unable to disappoint them.

By this time George was sweating profusely. He began to look around for Herbert, hoping to catch his eye and get some sign. But Herbert was nowhere to be seen. George was well aware of the reasons impelling Herbert to retrieve the old dugout, but, after all, forty dollars was a lot of money. And the auctioneer was screaming at him and pointing with the handle of his hammer.

"Make it the forty? Make it the forty? Do I hear any more?"

George nodded. And the snowball rolled on. George could feel himself swaying a little when he heard the forty-one and felt the eyes of the assemblage swinging back to him. They all seemed to be asking if he was going to let that shaggy little vagabond get the better of him with a puny one-dollar bid. Had he been bidding for himself, George would have bellowed out a belligerent raise that would have staggered his competitor. But he felt that his hands were tied—he was only the agent, the substitute for another on whose behalf he had already made commitments far in excess of anything that could possibly have been anticipated. His pride in being chosen for the job had by this time completely vanished, and if he thought of family solidarity at all it was as a vain regret for something that had been forfeited and thrown away. He still entertained a feeble hope that Barbara at least would understand how he had been entrapped to his ruin by circumstances over which he had no control. His instructions had been to make the last bid and bring home the dugout, and he must carry on with that program even if it ruined his life and cost him the woman he loved.

"I am bid forty-one—do I hear any more?" shouted the auctioneer hoarsely.

George wiped the sweat from his brow and gave one last look around to see if he could possibly get a glimpse of Herbert.

"Are you all done—all through—do I hear any more?"

Herbert was nowhere to be seen. There was no place for George to go but forward. At an auction one couldn't go back. Inside the patch pockets of his knock-about jacket George clenched his fists. Then he met the auctioneer's eye and nodded. "Fifty," he said.

The tension of the crowd broke. People breathed again. Chairs squeaked as everyone turned to see what the shaggy little man would do. The fact was that he was beaten; but he did not stand there like a dolt and let the curtain slowly descend on the last act. He was too good a showman for that. For his punch line he held up the slip of paper and tore it twice across, and as he walked away he threw the fragments high into the air.

With relief and admiration George watched him go. He had won the victory, but the little fellow had stolen the show, and George was not any too sure that his victory would not turn out to be like that of Pyrrhus at Asculum. But Herbert took his beating as a gentleman should and freely admitted that the antique dealer was a better man than he was. This puzzled Barbara. She didn't see what the antique dealer had to do with it, and finally she asked her father.

Herbert smiled painfully. "The old Shylock must have found out what was going on and he simply sent in a stooge to bid against me."

"Impossible," said Barbara. "He never would have sent in a deaf man to do competitive bidding at an auction."

"A deaf man?" Herbert demanded. "How do you know he was deaf?"

"Didn't you see him?"

"No, I was purposely keeping out of sight."

"Then you don't know who was bidding against you?"

"Haven't the slightest idea."

Barbara let out a ripple of laughter. "It was that old deaf man they call Uncle Walter."

It was later the same afternoon when Uncle Walter stopped in to see Jonathan. "Well, sir," he said, "I could've built you a better one with five dollars' worth of lumber. But when I seen that one goin' under the hammer I thought I might as well put in a couple of bids just to see that it fetched you a good price. I thought it was bein' sold for you—I didn't know you was buyin' it. Well, sir, I had Ezra Miller with me and I got him to do the listenin' and put the bid down on a paper. And when I found out that every time I bid a dollar the other feller would jump nine just to make it even money, I thought I better work it for all it was worth. I was gettin' pretty scairt when we got up to forty. I almost didn't put in my dollar. But Ezra, he egged me on and I took a chance—and when that feller raised it to fifty, I started for home."

Jonathan grabbed Uncle Walter's ear and pulled it towards him like a telephone. "Are you tellin' me he paid fifty dollars for it?" he shouted.

Uncle Walter grinned triumphantly. "That's right."

"What'll you give *me* for it?"

Uncle Walter drew out his speaking tube and handed the mouthpiece to Jonathan. "Are you tellin' me you want to sell it?"

"Why not? I can't use it. When I tried to set it in place it wouldn't go. Too big for the room. What'll you gimme for it?"

"Give you a dollar, same as I offered the auctioneer."

"But you raised his bid of forty, and now you offer me one! What kind of business is that?"

"A dollar's all it's worth to me. I could plug up the hole and use it for a trough in my hogpen. Hogs oughta like that smell."

Jonathan gave a tug at the tube. "Listen—you said you could make me one for five dollars. Now I'll tell you what I'll do. You make me a new one to fit into the place and I'll give you the old one, even. And let me tell you some'pm, that dugout's over a hunderd years old!"

Uncle Walter considered the proposition. "You don't think my hogs'll be gettin' ideas, eatin' out of a fifty-dollar hog trough?"

Jonathan shook his head. "Hogs don't get idees. Only people."

"Where's your yardstick?" muttered Uncle Walter. "We might as well go in and measure."

↟↟

S PICY emanations from the study were filling the house. Even in the kitchen of the new wing the delectable fragrance was driving Mrs. Flint to distraction. Spices were no longer in the market and the small supplies on her shelves had been exhausted months ago, and still, it seemed to her, there was no condiment the essence of which had not been wafted out of that front room since Matilda had started her canning program. Herbert had hinted darkly that there must be a black market somewhere among the natives. But that was not the answer; the fact was that Jonathan knew about the old-fashioned herbs and flavorings, where they grew and what to do with them.

Herbert had seen the old man fussing over a mortar and pestle in the barn but did not realize that he was grinding mustard and pepper. He had looked with curiosity at the clusters of sage, summer savory, and marjoram Jonathan kept hanging from the beams and cross timbers, but did not know what they were. All summer long he had been trampling caraway underfoot without recognizing it, and had hoed quantities of dill out of his garden thinking it was a weed—which it was.

Jonathan, on the other hand, overlooked none of the bounties of nature. He brought in sassafras for a delicious pudding and elderberries for pies. He knew where black currants were to be found, and gooseberries, and during the season he brought in wild strawberries by the pailful. His sharp eyes had discovered in the woods an escaped plum tree gone native, and during the early morning hours while the Gage family were still in bed he picked half a bushel of the sour little damsons for preserving. Spices from the Indies were scarce and expensive, but such as grew anywhere in the neighborhood Matilda had in abundance. Jar rubbers and sugar were hard to come by, and though Uncle Walter was resourceful in trading around among his friends for supplies of both, the preserving of fruits and jellies was not as abundant as in other years.

The Gages had seldom seen the inside of the cellar under the old part of the house, which they considered damp and chilly as well as dark and dismal. But one day after Margie had gone there in search of some missing jelly glasses she came upstairs with her eyes popping.

"It's well worth a visit," she told Mrs. Flint. "The most perfect-looking canned things you ever saw."

Mrs. Flint, though not visibly impressed, was politely inquisitive. "What's there?" she asked.

"Fruits, jellies, vegetables, preserves—just about everything you ever heard of," Margie exclaimed, "and enough for an army."

"Huh—how does it look?"

"Simply beautiful! There are some jars of tomatoes that are red and yellow in layers—and do they look good!"

"I never thought much of yellow tomatoes," Mrs. Flint said. "No flavor."

"But they look so beautiful," Margie insisted.

"How can they with all the dust and cobwebs in that old dirt-floor cellar?"

Margie shook her head. "No dust there now and no cobwebs. Shelves clean enough to eat from. And what do you think—remember that old crock where we used to put the dogwoods?"

Mrs. Flint nodded microscopically. She never cared much for that crock.

"Well, it's full of butter."

"Homemade butter's not so good." Mrs. Flint wrinkled up

[240]

her nose disdainfully. "Depends on who makes it, but you can give me creamery butter every time."

"But," said Margie slowly, "we haven't had any kind of butter in weeks. You don't suppose they'd sell us a pound or two?"

Mrs. Flint compressed her lips for a moment, then said, "Wouldn't dare touch it. Be afraid of poison."

For some time Herbert had heard the sound of a woodcutter's ax reechoing through the woods and had correctly guessed that Jonathan was getting up his winter's supply of firewood. Then one day he came upon the woodpile itself and was surprised at the hugeness of it. It struck him that either the old man was expecting a hard winter or he was intending to be around for some time to come. Not long after this Herbert saw, from a window of his new workroom above the garage, a good-sized load of the wood being hauled towards the house on a stoneboat drawn by Shadrach. At first it was the primitive motive power that attracted his attention. Not even the principle of the wheel was involved. The stoneboat was as aboriginal as the two poles the Indians dragged along when they wanted to move their belongings. It was not until the second or third load had gone past that he began to wonder where all that wood was being taken.

He suddenly remembered the rain barrel, a perfect eyesore if there ever was one. And he thought of the clothesline the old man had stretched from the front corner of the house across to a tree—one of the most prominent sectors of the entire place—where drying dish towels and gingham aprons were fluttering most of the time and where each Monday morning the passing world could see a motley collection of long underwear, outing flannel nightgowns with a ruffle around the bottom, and numerous other articles of apparel that even with Margie's help Herbert had never been able to identify with any considerable degree of accuracy.

If those old folks would decorate the front yard with a rain barrel and a clothesline, what would they not accomplish in the way of disfigurement with all the possibilities of a pile of wood? Herbert rushed down from his workroom fully expecting to find a woodpile extending all the way across the front of the house, but he found no wood in sight. It had apparently all been carried indoors; but how the old folks had disposed of it after getting it into that front room was an engaging mystery.

Herbert slipped into the cellar to see if by any chance they were carrying it down there. He should have known that a practical man like Jonathan would never have carried firewood into the cellar when he could have accomplished the same purpose with only half the work by chucking it in through a cellar window. For a day or two he and Margie puzzled their heads over the matter, and then they made discreet inquiries from Sarah, who, though she was strictly forbidden ever to go into the room now being used as a kitchen by the old folks, was suspected of occasional lapses. But Sarah was too smart to be taken in by what she considered a clumsy and obvious attempt to entrap her, and they got nothing out of her except a honeyed statement that since they had told her not to go in there she had never so much as looked in through the open door.

"Then you have no idea where they keep their firewood?" Herbert asked.

"Not any at all," Sarah replied. "Not any. I just never paid any attention to it, that's all."

"But, Sarah," her father reminded her, "I distinctly saw you walking along beside the stoneboat loaded with wood that was being drawn to the house."

"Oh, but I was watching Shadrach," she said with a laugh. "Do you suppose that with a horse in sight I'd even look at a load of wood? And Grampa Rock—I mean Mr. Rockwood—told me a wonderful true story about a ghost horse. Did you know that this house has a ghost horse? It actually has—actually!"

Herbert and Margie exchanged surreptitious glances. "It

wasn't a horse of another color, by any chance?" Herbert asked, smiling.

"What other color?" Sarah gave him a puzzled look. "You mean a different color from Shadrach?"

"Never mind about the color," said Margie, "but do tell us about the ghost horse."

"Well," said Sarah with an air of importance, "it began back in the days when this house was a tavern. Once upon a time a handsome young soldier of the Revolutionary War rode up in front on a coal-black charger—a charger is a large fiery horse, in case you don't know. This soldier didn't ride his horse right through the door the way one man did. He was very polite and tied his charger to a tree in front of the door and went inside, and while he was in the taproom he got in a quarrel with a Tory and challenged him to a duel. The landlord wouldn't let them fight in there, so everybody went over to the dueling tree down the road to see the fight. The signal was given to draw their swords, but, before the handsome young soldier could get his out, the cowardly Tory stabbed him through the heart and the soldier fell dead on the ground. At the exact moment when he was stabbed, the landlord, who was standing in the door of the tavern, saw the big black charger rear up on his hind legs pawing the air ferociously. And before anyone could stop him he broke loose and went charging down the hill with a noise like thunder—and was never seen alive again."

"You mean he was found dead?" asked Herbert.

"Oh, no! His body was never found. But every once in a while the ghost of that coal-black charger—a charger is a large fiery horse, in case you don't remember—goes thundering down that hill in the night and off into the distance. And whenever that charger thunders down the hill it's a warning and a sure sign that something terrible is going to happen—somebody's going to die or be born or something—maybe a murder or a disaster. Grampa Rock—Mr. Rockwood heard the horse once in the night. It woke him right out of a sound sleep and he ran over to the window. He couldn't exactly see the horse, but he could see the sparks from its hoofs, and he said the sound they made was a terrifying noise that he would never forget. And the charger went tearing down the hill, but it didn't cross the bridge. There wasn't any bridge there at the time of the murder, so it must have vanished into thin air."

"Don't call it a murder," Margie admonished. "That sounds too awful. But tell Mother one thing—was it an omen? Did something terrible happen afterwards?"

"I should say it did," Sarah replied impressively. "That's when Gramma Rockwood fell down the stairs and hurt her hip."

"I wish you wouldn't call that woman Grandma," Margie spoke sternly. "She is most distinctly not your grandma."

"Well, anyway," Sarah said defensively, "that's when she hurt her hip, and it's been bothering her ever since, all that time."

"But it wasn't so long ago, dear," Margie corrected.

Sarah was becoming bored with grown-up company. They made too many corrections to suit her, and she had already started for the door, but she paused long enough to set her mother right. "I don't know what you call long, but it happened before they went out west, and that was a long time ago, and it was still bothering her when she rode in the wagon coming back. She told me so herself."

For some time after Sarah had gone Margie sat looking curiously at Herbert. "Now what did she mean by that?" she finally asked.

"I can't imagine," Herbert said, looking sheepish. "The old lady must have fallen a second time." The more he thought of it the better the explanation looked, and he proceeded to embellish it. "That's it exactly. She had an earlier tumble there—perhaps years ago, and then this recent fall must have aggravated the old injury, don't you see?"

Margie was unconvinced. She was decidedly unconvinced. "I'm not sure that I do," she said slowly. "I wonder."

"Well, you needn't wonder any more," Sarah said, suddenly appearing in the doorway. "Gramma Rockwood fell just that one time. She told me so herself. It made her careful about stairways, and she never fell again." This was a good exit line and she went out, slamming the door behind her as loudly as she dared.

Herbert was waiting for the slam, and the moment he heard it he leaped to his feet. "By God! That settles it!" he declared angrily. "We're going to have a new lawyer."

"Now don't do anything hasty," Margie said, trying to calm him.

"It isn't hasty—I've been thinking about it for weeks."

"But you know as well as I do that the Loomis firm is one of the most prominent in the state."

Herbert glowered. "I don't want a prominent lawyer. I want action!"

"Perhaps this isn't the right time for action," Margie said gently.

"But I hate a lawyer who's so damn' timid. It was nothing but his fear that created this imaginary damage suit. He shivered it up out of his frightened little soul."

"I guess you'll find that he was just being careful. After all, timidity is better than rashness."

"It will be a real pleasure to throw this thing in his teeth and say, 'There, you little fraid-cat! That's what your timidity did.'"

Margie smiled. "But you can't do that."

"Why not?"

"Because you've always said he was *my* lawyer, and I won't let anyone say such things to my lawyer."

Herbert walked across to the window and stood for some moments looking out. "Well, that joke finally caught up with me. I don't suppose it would be wise to fire the little shrimp, not yet anyway, but I'd like to."

When he turned around he saw Margie making a note in her little book. "What are you writing?" he asked.

"Just a reminder to keep an eye open for that firewood."

They both kept a sharp lookout, but when they learned the answer it came by accident. Herbert discovered, to begin with, that all his books had been surreptitiously carried to the attic, and this so aroused his curiosity that he abandoned his scruples against spying to the extent of going out at night and peering into the study window. He found, as he had expected to find, that the shelfroom had been taken over entirely by the firewood, but he was surprised to learn that the neatly cut sticks piled to the ceiling could make such an effective background.

Margie smiled when he told her about it, and Herbert did not like that smile. It seemed to him like a reflection on his good taste, something in which he took quite a pride. "Be careful how you toss around the disdainful smiles," he said, "unless you want the wind taken out of all your talk about decoration being functional."

She blinked at him. "I'm afraid I don't understand," she said.

"Well, what could be more functional for a room with an open fire than a background that you could burn up to keep you warm?" he demanded.

"But, Herbert," she said with great earnestness, "how does it make you feel to have the world's great literature replaced by a lot of sticks of firewood?"

Herbert shook his head, for he knew that he couldn't win. "I don't mind," he said. "I didn't want the books left there anyway. Too much cooking is bad for even great literature."

ʔʔ

J ONATHAN was far from being a poet. And yet as he walked in his garden on the first day of October he felt in his soul a kind of exultation.

Usually he counted on a frost the first week in October. On more than one occasion this early nip had caught him unprepared. This time he was ready for it. He and Matilda had in their jars everything they had intended to put up. In fact, every bit of glass they owned, every jar, every crock, was filled to the top. They could not have put up anything more if they had wanted to.

A few reddening tomatoes were still dangling on the vines, but he intended to let them dangle until the frost was actually threatening; then he would pull the vines and hang them in the barn, where tomatoes would still continue to ripen until well into November.

Only the potatoes remained unharvested. The vines had dried up long ago, but he liked to let his potatoes remain in the ground as late as he could, for, even though they had probably stopped growing, he had a theory that a good seasoning in the ground not only made them keep better, but added to their flavor. Another thing that contributed to Jonathan's sense of well-being that morning was that the postman had just told him of the fall of Naples to the Allies. Jonathan couldn't quite see why we should be fighting Hitler first in Africa, and now in Italy, when all we had to do was go right into Germany and fight him on his home ground if we wanted to put him out of business. The postman agreed that this was a good idea, but he was of the opinion that if the Allies had to wait until they beat Hitler at home it would be a long war because he was so seldom there. But at any rate, said Jonathan, we were halfway up the leg of Italy and soon we'd have it by the bootstraps.

From the potato patch Jonathan rambled over to the barn, which no longer looked like a place for studio parties and cocktail gatherings. One end was stacked to the rafters with the hay that was intended to keep Shadrach and Bonnie Belle, the cow, through the winter, and in the other end was an ample supply of firewood evenly cut and neatly stacked. There was enough here, Jonathan figured, to last until the following June, and it wasn't as if he could not take his ax and go out in the woods and cut as much more whenever he happened to feel like it.

He sniffed at the hay and found it good and sweet. Every spear had been cut with the scythe, and he recalled that there wasn't a forkful that had been caught in the rain after it was down. Jonathan knew that Shadrach was going to enjoy eating it, and he wasn't so sure he wouldn't have enjoyed eating a little himself. Digging with his fingers, he burrowed back into the mow and extracted a single spear, which he broke in two and put in his mouth. It was sweet and savory, and he was still chewing on it as he walked slowly over to the smokehouse that he had put up in a corner of the old orchard lot.

This was one place that he kept under lock and key. He fished the key out of his pocket and inserted it in the old brass padlock that had been around the barn for years. As he swung open the door the fragrant though penetrating fumes of hickory and black birch came billowing out. He stepped aside to let in a little fresh air, then stood in the doorway and took stock. Hams, sides of bacon, shoulders, and all the rest of two fat hogs which had not been eaten fresh, salted down, or preserved in crocks between layers of homemade lard.

He prodded the sides of bacon, slapped the hams, hefted the shoulders, started a new smudge in the blackened embers on the floor, and went away leaving the little house well filled with fragrant smoke.

He stopped at the henhouse long enough to gather up a basket of eggs and put fresh water in the drinking pans. At the pasture fence he paused to examine the scratched udder of Bonnie Belle, found it healing nicely, and went on into the house.

Matilda looked up from an old patchwork project rescued from the attic. "Where you been?"

Jonathan reached for his pipe. "Lookin' around a mite."

"Everything all right?"

"Tol'able."

"Pew—you been in the smokehouse. I can smell it."

"Have to freshen up the smudge once in a while." He filled his pipe.

"Hams all right?"

"Look so."

"Bacon all right?"

"Didn't notice nuthin' wrong with it."

"How's the apples?"

"Middlin', but still sweatin' on the ground."

"How many'll we have?"

"Enough, I reckon."

"How's Bonnie Belle's tit?"

He struck a match. "Which one?"

She glanced up from her work to see what was going on, but found him calmly lighting his pipe. "The one that got scratched on a bramble."

"No worse."

She knew he was feeling good. He always gave short answers when he was feeling particularly good. "How's the potatoes?" she asked.

"Tol'able—right tol'able."

"Are we goin' to have enough to last?"

"Better'n thirty bushel, I should guess."

"Think it's enough?"

"Reckon so."

"Think they'll keep?"

"Ought to. I'll put half in the pit and half in the cellar."

"When'll you dig?"

"Oh, at the end of the week if the weather's all right. Joe and Uncle Walter's comin' to help. I don't bend as good as I used to."

She sniffed approvingly. "I'm glad to hear you admit it. This ain't no time to get your back out of kilter, just at the start of cold weather."

"Don't you worry about my back—it's as good as it ever was. All it needs is a little limberin' on the front."

"Diggin' potatoes by hand ain't too good for nobody's back."

"Uncle Walter's fetchin' his shovel plow."

The weather turned out to be good, and they dug the potatoes at the end of the week. All the thrift of his saving ancestors and the pride of generations of husbandmen arose within Jonathan as he swung along behind the lurching shovel plow and watched the firm solid potatoes come bursting up out of their dark prison, shaking off the loose soil, and decorating the surface of the ground. Here was food for the winter months. Here was something to sustain and cheer when the searching blasts from the north were sweeping over the stone fences, howling under the eaves, and prying between the shingles. What was a meal on a farm without plenty of tasty potatoes?

A satisfying sense of achievement swept over Jonathan. He planted those potatoes and tended them. They were his. The result of something he himself had done. Without his efforts they would not be there—to come rolling up out of the ground as the broad snout of the shovel plow went burrowing underneath. He swung along in his pride, spotting the big fellows, turning them over with his foot, admiring them, glorying in them—and forgetting that the veriest novice, the greenest city hand, could have planted the eyes as well as he, and that without the great sprouting upthrust of nature they would have stayed where they were put.

At the end of a row Jonathan turned and looked back to see the ground literally paved with potatoes. "What do you think of that, Joe?" he called to the cowman.

Joe grinned with a more than ordinarily wide display of the yellow teeth. "Plenty much!" shouted Joe. He was tempted to repeat the phrase, but, feeling that this might sound loquacious, he restrained himself and began to pick up the potatoes and toss them into a bushel crate.

Jonathan, lacking the cowman's control, could not refrain from adding, "Look like cobbles on a country road." Then feeling that he was being too boastful, he hastily geed Shadrach around and started along the next row.

As soon as the potatoes were dug, which couldn't have taken over half an hour, Jonathan hitched Shadrach to the stoneboat, now loaded with empty crates, and started along the rows of newly dug potatoes. He drove slowly, stopping often, with Joe filling the crates on one side and Uncle Walter on the other, and when a crate was full Jonathan hauled it from the stoneboat and left it behind, dropping an empty one in its place.

All three were excited over the prodigality of the harvest. Uncle Walter said there hadn't been such a crop since 1916, when he took so-and-so many bushels to the acre off from such-and-such land. It was quite a story, took him several rows to tell, and nobody listened to a word of it, both Joe and Jonathan giving their undivided attention to the bumper crop immediately at hand. It seemed that 1916 was too far back for anybody to be remembering about potatoes, with all those beauties lying on the ground right in front of them.

And as might have been expected, the potatoes that went into the cellar went in through the window. It was just as they were finishing the job that Uncle Walter saw Herbert coming in from his garden spot with a bushel basket nearly full of puny-looking potatoes.

"What's he got there?" Uncle Walter asked.

Jonathan smiled but made no reply, and Uncle Walter repeated the question even more loudly than before. Then Jonathan pulled him around the corner of the house and with cupped hands shouted into his ear, "That's his potato crop!"

When Jonathan went in to supper Matilda could see that he was flustered and feeling good, though he had said nothing that would indicate the reason for such a state.

"Get your potatoes took care of?" she asked without looking at him.

"Sure. Got 'em all under cover."

"Git as many as you expected?"

"Got my fifteen bushel in the cellar right enough."

"How about the pit?"

"Uh-huh, filled it up."

"How many?"

"Fifteen more."

"Pretty good crop," she said without any marked enthusiasm. "About what you expected, wasn't it?"

"I didn't expect no less. But you ain't asked me how many Uncle Walter hauled away in his wagon."

She flopped over a slice of ham in the frying pan, and when the sizzling had subsided she asked without turning her head, "How many?"

"Twelve bushels. Half for Walter and half for Joe."

Then she did turn and look. She looked at him sternly, and at the same time with surprise. "You mean you give them twelve bushels?"

"Why not? I didn't have no place to put 'em."

"They'd have been satisfied with four—and you could've sold the rest."

"They'd have been satisfied, but I wouldn't. They've done a lot of neighborin' for me, and neighborin' is somethin' that can't be one-sided."

"But twelve bushels!" She gestured with the steel fork. "They can't use that many in a whole winter."

[252]

"It wasn't too much. They had 'em comin', and besides, Gage was right around there, and I didn't mind havin' him see that I was givin' away a hull wagonload right out of hand, as if it didn't amount to nuthin'. Know what his potato crop come to?"

"Couldn't have come to much—they only planted two rows."

"Didn't! He brung the whole crop in a single bushel basket —and it wasn't full at that." Jonathan went over and poured out the water to wash. "If you want to know what I think— those folks ain't goin' to have much to eat this winter, not if they stay here."

"Mebbe they put up more'n you think."

Jonathan doused the water over his face. "Oh, no, they didn't. I know what they took out of that garden of theirs. I used to look at it every mornin' long before they got out of bed. And I'll tell you another thing, they ain't goin' to be too warm this winter neither, not if they stay around here."

Matilda turned and gave him another look. "Now what makes you say that?"

"They ain't got a stove in the house—nuthin' but that oil furnace in the cellar, and the postman told me this mornin' the fuel oil famine is gettin' pretty bad. The folks down in Washington is goin' to punish New England for votin' Republican."

"Do you believe that?" Matilda shook her head dubiously.

"Well, I wouldn't put it beyond that gang down there. All they think about is politics. This country never had so many politics as we got right now."

"Don't sound very Christian to me."

"What's bein' Christian got to do with politics?"

"Well, they open the Congress with a prayer, don't they?"

"Yes, and they open a prizefight by singin' the national anthem, but that don't mean they won't put in some dirty punches when the referee ain't lookin'."

Matilda expertly ran a knife blade under the hash-brown potatoes in an iron skillet. "I don't believe even the Democrats would let folks freeze to death if they could help it."

"That shows how much you know about Democrats. They'd let anybody freeze to death who votes against 'em," Jonathan mumbled through the roller towel they had now hung on the door.

"But how can anyone freeze when there's plenty of wood around here?"

Jonathan extended both hands. "That's the trouble with a oil furnace—you can't burn nuthin' but oil in it."

Matilda transferred the ham to a cracked platter. "But they still got the fireplace."

"That only makes it take a little longer—you freeze to death one side at a time. And you can't keep a steady fire goin' in that big fireplace unless you got one man cuttin' wood and one haulin' it. And even at that there wouldn't be enough heat to keep their water pipes from freezin' up solid. That's another thing about this indoor plumbin'—if it freezes up, it's a goner!"

"Can't use it?"

"Can't stay in the same house without a rowboat—it floods."

Jonathan sat down at the table and speared a piece of ham with his fork. "Ayuh," he said slowly, "looks to me like we're settin' pretty. We got a good roof over our heads; we got a good stove and plenty of wood for it; there's food in the cellar, and a cow for milk; then there's chickens for eggs and a Sunday dinner, and there's meat in the smokehouse. When we hafta go to town, we got Shadrach and no gas to worry about." He cut off a piece of meat and was starting to put it in his mouth when Matilda stopped him.

"Just a minute," she said. "You got all these provisions of the Lord's bounty, and yet you set down to a meal of vittles and start to eat without askin' a blessin'." She bowed her head, took a few moments to compose herself, and then began, "Our Heavenly Father. . . ."

It was a rather lengthy blessing, but all through it Jonathan sat with bowed head and eyed the piece of ham on his fork.

At the conclusion he said a quick amen and popped the meat into his mouth.

"Matilda," he said, chewing appreciatively at the ham, "I shouldn't wonder if you and I are goin' to have this place all to ourselves sooner than you might think."

"Don't look likely to me," she said.

"Well, if it does happen there's one thing I ain't likely to forget."

She looked up from her plate. "What is it?"

"That thing about possession bein' nine points in the law."

Matilda resumed her eating. "It ain't helped you much so far."

"But wait till the other feller tries to come back again!"

She made a derisive sound in her throat. "He ain't gone yet."

"Not yet," Jonathan admitted, "but you wait till the real winter weather comes along."

↑↑

THE winter weather came along much sooner than Jonathan or anybody else had reason to expect. The killing frosts had been a little late in arriving, but when they came they clamped down on the earth with a vengeance. A thin film of ice had formed on the cow pond by early November. Before Thanksgiving the frost had gone so far into the ground that Herbert was unable to set out the fruit trees he had ordered for fall planting. By mid-December the children were skating on the cow pond. The temperature had several times been below zero, and for more than a week did not manage to get as high as fifteen above.

Herbert's supply of fuel oil dwindled rapidly away, especially as he and Margie had persisted in heating the entire house until after the holidays; they felt they owed that much to the children. They still had coupons enough, they thought, if they should be extremely careful through the rest of the winter. But with the unprecedented cold and the short supply the dealers' stocks were approaching the vanishing point before January was half gone.

The family were by this time crowded into the new wing, which was well built, with adequate insulation, and was much easier to heat than the old part. With the aid of an electric blanket Herbert and Margie had continued to sleep in the vaunted master's bedroom, though it was only a question of time before they, too, would be added to the congestion in the new wing.

Being a regular customer, Herbert felt very comfortable

about the oil situation. His dealer had furnished him with conveniently printed order cards on which the postage was paid in advance. Somehow that paid postage gave him the feeling that, come what may, he would be taken care of, and though he saw in the papers frequent references to the oil famine he read between the lines that it applied to improvident people who had been careless with their coupons. He was therefore treated to a rude surprise the first time one of his order cards failed to produce the desired result.

When three days had passed and the big green truck had failed to come rolling into the driveway, he sat down and wrote his dealer a polite letter explaining the urgency of his need. This, however, produced nothing but a printed folder asking all customers to be patient and reminding them that a war was on. Then he tried the telephone, getting a wonderful run-around from one department to another, but achieving no more success than a promise that they would do the best they could.

Up to this time Herbert had kept on a small amount of heat in his workroom over the garage. Just enough to keep his fingers in working order, though it was often so cold there that he had to sit with a blanket across his knees. But he realized that the time had come when the garage could have no heat at all. Finding a new place to work was something he would have to discuss with Margie. He found her in the master's bedroom making the bed—with her fur coat on.

"That electric blanket is a lifesaver," he said.

Margie smiled rather mirthlessly. "Yes, isn't it, though." Her hands looked blue to him, and he could see the vapor from her breath as she spoke.

"Master's bedroom," he growled. "Master's icebox would be a better name for it. Why 'master's' anyway? It's always sounded silly to me."

She went on with her bedmaking. "Was there something you wanted?"

"Yes—a little more heat around here."

"Oh!" Margie relaxed in a cloud of vapor and went on smoothing the bedclothes.

"And please keep your shirt on," he admonished, "while I explain that it has a distinct bearing on our bread and butter."

"Don't mention butter to me." Margie gave one of the pillows a spiteful punch. "I don't even remember what it looks like."

Herbert smiled regretfully. "I'm speaking of it only in the poetic sense. But if I am going to continue as the breadwinner for this family I've got to find another place to work. The loft over the garage is out—takes too much oil to heat it."

Faced with a definite problem, Margie stopped taking out her spite on inanimate objects and went to work on the solution. "I should have known that this was coming," she said. "Probably in the back of my mind I did know it."

"If you had tried to do any writing up there without heat you'd have known it."

"But isn't it rather early for such cold weather to come on?" she asked.

"Probably," he said. "Isn't the weather always unseasonable?"

Margie wrinkled her brow thoughtfully. "Well, one thing is certain, wherever you work it's got to be in the new part."

"Elemental," Herbert said. "There's just enough steam in the old part to keep the water pipes from freezing—say forty or such a matter."

"I know," Margie said reflectively. "But even in the new part the upstairs rooms won't do. I'm keeping them down to sixty, and that's too cold. And anyway, they're too crowded with the extra beds and all the children's things. There's really only one place left, my dear, and that's the dining room."

Rubbing his hands together to warm them, Herbert thought over the possibilities. "Well, I could put my typewriter table over by the east window, and then I'd have the dining table where I could spread out my papers and books and things. But if I use the dining room, where are we going to eat?"

"Right where we always do," Margie replied with a wry

smile. "The idea is that you can use the dining room when we're not using it for something else."

"What else do we use it for?" Herbert growled. "We certainly haven't done much eating there lately."

Margie finished with her bedmaking and put her hands inside the sleeves of her coat, where the fur would warm them. "Well, my dear," she said, "as you know quite well, we've been using it as a living room, and after all you must remember. . . ."

With upraised hands he stopped her. "Don't say it! Don't tell me there's a war on!"

She smiled. "Why, that's exactly what I was going to say; and I was going to suggest that if the dining room doesn't work out you could take an office in town. Those office buildings are almost too warm. I had to take off my coat at the dentist's last week while Sarah was having her teeth cleaned."

The corners of Herbert's mouth drew down into an inverted smile. "An office in town would suit me to a dot, but what would I use for gasoline to get back and forth?"

"I don't suppose you could take the school bus?"

He shook his head. "There isn't enough room in the bus for the school children, and besides, it's against the law for adults to ride in school busses."

"The problem seems to have settled itself," Margie said, determined to be cheerful. "There's no place but the dining room—and what do you say to leaving this icebox and going down there to thaw out a bit?"

He stood aside to let her pass. "Not such a bad idea."

In the dining room they looked around and talked over the new arrangements. The typewriter table could stand here when he was using it, and when it was not in use it could be pushed over there. His papers could be spread out on the end of the long trestle table, and his pen, pencils, blotters, paste, and other useful though unbeautiful desk equipment could be kept in the drawer of the side table, where they would be invisible but handy.

"And my desk chair. . . ."

Margie stopped him before he could go farther. "Your desk chair is going to stay right where it is. That's one thing I simply can't have in the dining room."

"But where do you think I'm going to sit?"

"On one of the rush-bottomed ladder-backs."

"What a thing for a writer to sit on—a rush-bottomed ladder-back!"

"We won't quarrel about it." Margie had read that the war had made people kindly, more considerate, and she did not wish to be lacking in patriotism. Quarreling, she felt, was something that she could do without, and she spared Herbert's feelings by putting an immediate end to the argument. "Of course," she said, "if you really want your old desk chair, if you want to enjoy the feel of it, you can go up and work in the relaxation room for a while on warm days."

Herbert stole a look at her to be sure that she was not joking, and having satisfied himself on that point, he made an unconditional surrender. "I'll try the ladder-backs," he said. "They may not be as bad as they look, and at least I'll be working in a place where there's some heat."

"By the way," said Margie, "the oil hasn't come—or has it?"

He shook his head. "I only wish it had."

"What time did the man say he'd be here?"

"He didn't say. All I could get out of him was that he'd do the best he could."

A troubled look came quickly over Margie's face. "But, Herbert! That doesn't mean anything at all—it's what I always tell the children when I'm getting ready to let them down."

"That's as far as he would go." Herbert walked over and felt the radiator. "He seemed to think he was doing me quite a favor to promise as much as he did."

"Don't you think you ought to call him up and insist upon something more definite?"

Herbert glowered. "You might try that yourself."

"All right, I will!" Margie set her jaw defiantly, threw her fur coat around her shoulders to keep her warm, and started for the telephone in the taproom.

"While you're telephoning I'll go down cellar and measure the oil in the tank."

Margie stopped with her hand on the door latch. "Perhaps I'd better wait until you get back," she suggested. "Then I can tell him how little we have."

"Not a bad idea," said Herbert. "You wait right here; I won't be gone long."

He went down cellar and with a monkey wrench removed the gauge from the top of the tank. "You can't trust the damn' things," the drivers had told him, "especially when a tank gets low, and that's when you don't want any guesswork."

From the nail on which he kept it—the driver from whom he had obtained it insisted that it must always be kept on a nail—he took down a black measuring stick marked off in numbered inches, carefully wiped it with a cloth, and inserted it in the hole where the gauge had been. Very slowly he lowered it until the end rested on the bottom of the tank. When he heard it touch bottom he tapped it a few times, as he had seen the drivers do. Then he drew it quickly out and held it horizontal, numbered side up, to read the result. Holding it this way, he was told, kept the oil from running down and giving an inaccurate reading.

A strong oleaginous fragrance assailed his nostrils as he bent over the measuring rod, but he held his breath until he had carefully noted the depth of the oil. *Four inches.* He whispered the measurement to himself and kept repeating it until he had consulted the table tacked on the back of the door leading into the front cellar.

Inches	Gals.
1	2
2	5
3	9
4	14

He wiped off the rod, put it back on the nail, and smelling to high heaven, went upstairs. In the dining room he found Margie waiting.

"How much?" she asked as he came in the door.

"Four inches."

A blank look came over her face. "Do you measure oil in inches?"

"You do when it's in a tank, but if you prefer it in gallons—it's fourteen—and that means the tank is practically empty."

"That's what I'll tell him," she said, and she went out and closed the door behind her.

She was gone only a very short time, and when she came back Herbert noticed that she was flustered.

"I don't like our oil man," she said. "I think we'd better get another."

"We can't get another," Herbert declared. "Oil companies aren't taking on new customers at a time like this—but what did he say?"

"Well, it wasn't what he said, exactly; it was the way he said it."

"But what did he say?"

"There wasn't much conversation," Margie explained reluctantly. "When I told him who I was and said we were not at all satisfied with his service, what do you suppose that impertinent fellow said to me? He said, 'So what?'

"Of course I was upset by such rudeness, but after all what we want is oil, and instead of slamming the receiver in his face I explained to him very courteously what a desperate plight we are in and asked him to give me some idea when he would be able to fill our tank. This seemed to enrage him, for he shouted back angrily, 'Lady, I wish I could—but you'll have to take that up with Harold Ickes! My tanks are as empty as yours!' And with that he slammed the receiver in my face."

A blast from the telephone summoned Herbert for a long distance call. It was Archie Pyne, but this time Archie wasn't just checking. The story had to make the dead line or Ludlow wouldn't take it.

"Ludlow has gone temperamental again," Herbert said as he came back into the dining room. "Won't take my story unless it's in on time. He's getting to be a regular prima donna."

"When does he want it?" asked Margie.

"It will have to be in Archie's hands tomorrow night so he can take it in with him the next morning."

"Can you do it?"

"I can if I have a warm place to work—and no interruptions."

"But how long will our oil last?"

"You never can tell about the dregs of a tank—probably until tomorrow afternoon or evening."

Margie smiled reassuringly. "Move yourself right in here and go to work," she said. "I'll see that you aren't disturbed."

Herbert moved into the dining room, spread his papers over the end of the big table, seated himself at the typewriter, and began work. When the children came home from school they were shunted into the kitchen, and given a blue plate dinner, after which they were sent off to their room for homework or quiet recreation. For once they were given permission to read in bed.

Far into the night the typewriter clacked in the dining room with very commendable industry. There were times, of course, when it was silent, while Herbert was trying to think of the right word, or struggled to frame or reframe a sentence, or wrestled with the windings of his plot. The noise of the machine did not bother Margie at all, but the periods of silence lacerated her nerves. She kept wondering what made him stop —why he did not go on, when time was running against him and the oil might give out at any moment.

It was almost midnight when he pulled a sheet of paper from the machine and said he was through for the day. He was at it again immediately after breakfast in the morning, but this time the conditions were not quite so perfect. To begin with, the children were not in school, which had been compelled to close by the lack of fuel, and though they had been warned to keep away from the dining room, Sarah was inclined to forget the warning.

Herbert had not been at work for half an hour before she went galloping through at full speed. He called her back and informed her sternly that if she galloped through the room again he would send her to bed for the rest of the day. So the next time she passed through the room on all fours she kept within the letter of the law by trotting, and escaped punishment only by the skin of her teeth.

Around noon the typewriter ribbon began to give trouble. It was one of the wartime ribbons with little stamina and less ink, and when it started to cut up Herbert knew from experience that only a new ribbon would save the day. With their budgeted gasoline an extra trip into town was not to be thought of; but Margie proposed a solution—moving their week-end shopping two days ahead. She felt sure that by getting food that would keep she could manage.

They made a hurried trip into town, and while Herbert was buying his typewriter ribbon Margie exhausted the possibilities of the food market. She had never before done her food shopping in so little time. Much against her will, she shoved in ahead of people who had long been standing in line. She stepped on their toes, and snatched out of their hands articles which they were quite obviously intending to buy. She was ready to start for home as soon as Herbert was. But they knew when they entered the house, that they were too late. The oil was gone, and a chill was settling over the house.

Herbert hurried into the cellar and hastily plunged the measuring rod into the tank. He heard a melancholy ring as the end of the rod touched bottom. It had never rung like that before. And when he drew out the rod he found it dry to the very end.

Margie was waiting for him at the head of the stairs. "What about it?" she asked.

"Gone," he said. "This oil situation could lick us," he said in a low tone. "After all, I make my living by writing, and I've got to be in a place where it's warm enough to write."

She followed him to their bedroom, where he began to change to his rough working clothes. "What are we going to do now?" she asked.

"I'm going out and cut some wood," he said. "We want to keep our pipes from freezing if we can."

"You worry more about your pipes than you do about your family."

"The family aren't likely to freeze up and open a seam—and besides I must have enough heat to finish my story."

"Do you realize how it's going to be without hot water?" Margie asked. "What'll we do for baths?"

"We'll do just what they did around here before they had any plumbing." Herbert pulled on a windbreaker and went tramping out of the house.

While in the barn hunting for his ax, he looked with interest at the neatly piled tiers of firewood Jonathan had stored there. He could easily have appropriated a few pieces, but he scorned the thought of touching anything belonging to the old devil. There was plenty of fallen timber in the woods that could be used for fireplace fuel, or so he assured himself as he lowered the tailpiece of the station wagon. He put in the ax and his one-man crosscut saw, and drove slowly over the rough driveway leading towards the wood lot. Barbara in a scarlet ski suit followed on foot.

With all that was going on, nobody had remembered to look in the box for the mail, and it was not until Herbert had gone out to bring in the evening paper that he found the letter from Richard. To their astonishment it had come from Italy. Richard's only explanation was that his outfit had been transferred a little nearer home. The letter, which covered less than a single sheet of V-mail, was passed around that night as they sat in front of the fire, though it usually came to rest in Margie's hands. She was contented just to sit there and hold it.

"I'm so happy to have him in Europe," Margie kept saying.

"I hated the thought of the jungle with those terrible snakes, to say nothing of the hula dancers."

"The going in Italy is tough enough without the hula dancers," Herbert said dismally. "The Germans are backing up, but they're fighting for every inch of ground."

"Oh, but Italy is so much more civilized—at least he isn't fighting savages."

"No—Germans. Think they're any more civilized than the Japs?"

"But at least he's in civilized surroundings—with all those beautiful monuments and buildings."

"Defaced and defiled, and probably mined with time bombs."

"This letter doesn't tell a thing about the war," Barbara protested. "It might as well have been written in our back yard. It's all about home anyway."

Margie smiled. "That shows he's thinking about us. Let the radio tell about the war."

Herbert glanced at the old pine clock. "I'll do that," he said. "It's just time for the news."

He turned on the radio, but the newscaster had spoken no more than a few sentences before the organ began to peal forth with Matilda's favorite missionary hymn, into which she always seemed able to put a little extra fervor. In an attempt to drown out the organ music Herbert turned up the radio until the volume was approaching that of the public address system of an auditorium, and still the organ music kept seeping through.

The total effect of the broadcast was to leave an impression that the principal centers of news, in addition to Greenland's icy mountains, were India's coral strand, the spicy breezes of Ceylon's isle, the earth's remotest nation (they did not catch the name), Africa's sunny fountains, which might mean any place from Dakar to Algiers, and an unnamed ancient river.

"Do you have to have it so loud?" Margie demanded.

"I do if I'm going to hear anything!" he shouted back.

"Haven't you noticed the way they start up that infernal organ every time we turn on our radio?"

Margie nodded. "Perhaps they don't like the radio."

Herbert scowled. "It's much more likely they know we can't move it out to another room the way we used to—not unless we want to freeze to death." He pointed at her knitting. "What are you making?" he asked.

"A sweater for Richard. I'm so glad he's no longer in the steaming jungles."

"Listen!" Barbara held up a cautionary hand. "Isn't that the telephone?"

"Don't bother to answer," Herbert groaned. "It's probably Archie Pyne."

Barbara smiled. "But I've got to answer—I'm expecting a call."

She hurried out of the room. When she returned her eyes were troubled. "It was Archie Pyne," she said, "and when I told him what had happened, he said, 'That's too bad. We've lost a good sale.' And then he hung up."

Herbert looked knowingly at Margie. "There you are," he said. "What did I tell you?"

ʅʅ

JONATHAN had known all along that the weather could not hold. But such a long spell of such extreme cold so early in the winter was something to look out for. When the break came they might have a pretty nasty time of it.

The aches in his joints rarely played him false, and when Uncle Walter had begun to complain that his ears were feeling as if he could almost hear himself yell, Jonathan knew the January thaw could not be very far off. Joe, passing on the road, pointed to the sky and shook his head. Jonathan nodded and looked up. Only a glance was needed to tell him that the upper air was in a good deal of a turmoil, with clouds scurrying every which way. That might mean one thing and it might mean another, but the rapid rise in temperature could mean only one thing—that the clouds were getting ready to let go.

"How's the weather?" Matilda asked him as he came in the door.

"Not too promisin'. Guess the thaw's a-comin'. Some'pm is."

"Think we'll get rain or snow?"

"Couldn't tell you that. But some'pm's comin'. My bones ain't ached like this since the blizzard of eighty-eight."

"My hip's been grumblin' for a couple a days, too."

"Couldn't be rheumatiz?"

"Nope. 'Tain't that kind of a ache."

"Mine ain't neither."

"Hope it's rain. That's what we need. The barrel's froze solid, and I can't do a decent washin' with this drinkin' water they got in the house pipes. What's he haulin' wood for all of a sudden?"

"Fetchin' it for the fireplace, I guess. Little Sarah says they ain't got no oil for their heatin' furnace."

"No oil!" Matilda turned on him, gaping with astonishment not unmixed with delight. "Will they stay?"

"They got to stay a while. They can't just walk out and leave them indoor pipes to freeze. That's the trouble with indoor plumbin'—you got to take care of it like a baby. You can't just shut it off and leave it. I've heared tell it takes a reg'lar plumber about a day to drain off the tanks and boilers."

"You think a fire in the fireplace will save it?"

Jonathan shook his head. " 'Tain't likely—not with the kind of wood he's gettin' in, most of it rotten and none of it well dried."

Suddenly Matilda gave an angry snort. "And you knew this when you come in the house, and you never told me?"

"I would've," Jonathan insisted, "but you didn't give me no chance. You kept talkin' about the weather and fetchin' in wood, and all like that. There ain't nothin' sure about it, you know. They might get more oil."

"I don't like this keepin' things to yourself."

"The weather might make a difference, too."

"Keepin' things to yourself ain't my idee of bein' aboveboard."

"Folks lived in this house a hunderd years before oil was discovered."

"Just keepin' your mouth shut can be dishonest, you know."

"Sturdy old pioneer stock—that's what's always lived here; not the soft city-bred kind that can't live without indoor plumbin', and got to have a 'lectric heater in between their bedclothes."

Matilda looked at him over the tops of her spectacles. "What do you know about their bedclothes?"

"Sarah was tellin' me," he replied imperturbably.

"Well, what of it?"

"Not a great deal. Just shows you how folks is gettin' softer and softer. Can't even keep the inside of their beds warm without 'lectricity. How long do you think that kind of folks will put up with fireplace heat, even if it does keep the frost out of their water pipes?"

"Why can't they set up stoves? Then they'd be all right."

"Can't get stoves. Government's put a freezin' order on 'em."

"Well, what won't they be freezin' next?"

"Hope it'll be our neighbors—but mebbe the weather man will take care of them. If they don't get enough of this here fuel oil to keep 'em warm, they'll have to get out."

"I'll believe that when I see 'em goin'," Matilda sniffed. "Not before."

For a time Jonathan sat puffing on his pipe, his lips smacking occasionally as he opened them to let out the smoke. Just before nightfall he put on his hat and went out for another look at the weather. A little warmer, he thought. Then he noticed how calm the air had become. Not a breath was stirring. The stillness itself was threatening and oppressive. He did not pretend to know what was coming, but he was ready for it. In the dusk he walked over and laid his hand on the tree.

Smoke from the chimney came floating downward, almost enveloping him. Heavy smoke, damp and musty. Another sign and a sure one. He returned to the house feeling that it wouldn't be long now.

The organ was still wailing when Sarah was sent off to bed. Sarah liked the organ. She would have enjoyed playing it herself. Herbert's feelings about it were in quite another vein. He started to write a letter to Archie Pyne, but was finally forced to abandon his efforts until the organ recital should come to an end. Suddenly the lights from a car glowed in the driveway, and Barbara went to see who was coming.

"It's George," she called back over her shoulder.

"What in heaven's name is he doing out here on a night like this?" muttered Herbert.

"Perhaps he's come to leave the car again," Margie suggested. "Barbara has agreed to take care of it for him, and he may have been taken this time."

Herbert smiled. "I see what you mean," he said.

A gust of cold air swept through the room as Barbara opened the door, and George came slipping and sliding up the steps and steadied himself by clutching the doorjamb.

"Hello, everybody!" he called. "This is the most beautiful and the most treacherous night you ever saw." He came cautiously in and scuffed his feet on the rug. "There's a fine mist in the air that freezes to everything it touches. The road is so slippery you can't even look at it without falling. My car felt as if it had skates on."

"How did you ever get up the hill?" asked Barbara as she took his hat.

"Didn't," he replied. "I tried twice, but couldn't make it, so I went around the other way."

Herbert strolled over and peered through the window. "With the floodlights on it looks like a Christmas card out there."

George nodded. "But even old Santa's reindeer couldn't stand up unless they were sharpshod. I passed literally dozens of cars in the ditch. More than once I thought I was on my way to join them, but I always managed to pull out of it. However, it wasn't the part underfoot that scared me the most— it was the trees overhead. They're getting so heavily iced that the limbs can't bear the weight. They keep breaking off and falling into the road like a ton of bricks. If one of those big fellows should land on a car, it would be curtains for everybody in it."

"So it's really an ice storm?" said Herbert.

"You'll never see a better one," George replied. "And if a good brisk wind should come up . . ." he waved his hands, "people would be talking about the ice storm of forty-three for the next fifty years."

Herbert switched on the outside light for another look. "You're making it sound pretty serious."

"It is serious," George assured him. "All travel is or should

[271]

be suspended, and I am giving you a solemn warning that I am here for the night—even though nobody has asked me to take off my overcoat."

George was mystified by the laughter which greeted his announcement. "Does this levity mean that Lazy Corners is full and I'll have to sleep in the manger with the horse and the cow?"

"Oh, no," said Barbara, "there's plenty of room, and we'll love to have you stay—only you'd better not take off your overcoat, because you may want to sleep in it."

"It's the oil," said Margie, never one to go along with a joke. "Our tank is empty, and this is the only fire in the house."

George turned and stared at the fireplace. "Is that a fire?" he asked.

Margie nodded. "Primitive, isn't it?"

"Did you start it by rubbing two sticks together?"

Herbert was instantly on the defensive. "I built that fire; what's the matter with it?"

"Practically everything," said George. "To begin with, you've built it upside down. If I want a fire to burn I put the small pieces underneath, not on top." He went to work on it with the tongs and in a short time had a fire that was roaring and crackling and throwing out so much heat that they had to move back.

Herbert sank deeper in his easy chair. "First time I've been warm all day."

George glanced at him, then cocked an ear at the not too distant moaning of the organ. He could actually recognize the tune, "What a Friend We Have in Jesus."

"Never ran out of oil before," Herbert said. (All *our sins and griefs to bear*)

"How big is your tank?" asked George. (*All because we do not carry*)

"Two seventy-five." (*Ev-ry-thing to God in prayer*)

"And your reserve tank?" (*tri-als and temptations*)

"I haven't any reserve." (*We should never be dis-cour-aged*)

[272]

George shook his head dubiously. "So you thought the government was fooling when it told you to get ready for emergencies?" (*to the Lord in prayer*)

"We never had any trouble until the government took over the fuel business." (*cum-bered with a load of care*)

"They tried hard enough to get people to convert to coal."

"People didn't want to convert; they didn't want to shovel coal and carry out ashes every day. They wouldn't let themselves believe there was an oil shortage—and a lot of them don't believe it yet. Besides, I couldn't convert; my firebox door is so close to the cellar wall there's no space for a stoker."

"Well," George reached for a cigarette, "I'll tell you one thing you could have done—you could have bought a removable grate, one that you could put in whenever it was needed. Then you could have burned coal, wood, or even some of your rejected manuscripts if you wanted to."

"You think I was negligent about it," Herbert said, "but that isn't so. It was just that I wasn't going to have a lot of politicians in Washington telling me how to run my own household. They already run my finances—they tell me what food I can put on the table, and how many pairs of shoes I can put on my feet; they charge me five dollars a year for the use of my car, but they won't give me enough gasoline to go anywhere in it."

"And your oil is entirely gone?" asked George.

"Completely."

"But you can't stay in this house without heat."

Herbert nodded. "I'm beginning to understand that."

"What are you going to do about it?" George insisted.

"God knows," Herbert answered. "I keep hoping for more oil."

"Well," said George, "you're certainly on the spot."

Herbert stretched his feet towards the fire. "Don't I know it!"

The organ music, which had softened until it had become almost inaudible, suddenly blared out with renewed force,

[273]

and at the same time a disagreeable cloud of smoke and soot was blown down the chimney and out into the room. They all averted their faces and began fanning with their hands, and George, who was nearest the fireplace, jumped up and walked away snorting and blowing.

"There you are!" he exclaimed. "That's what I was afraid of. Wind's coming up, and a nasty squally wind at that." He pulled out his handkerchief and began to make passes at his face. "If it keeps coming we'll be in for a lot of damage."

Herbert smiled. "What's a limb or two between friends? I don't care a hoot about a few broken branches, but I'm going nuts if I have to sit here and listen to those doleful hymn tunes."

"Do you get this all the time?" asked George.

"Not quite," said Barbara; "only when we especially don't want it."

George tried to suppress a smile. "Why don't you see your lawyer?"

"See him?" Herbert exclaimed. "I've hounded him to death, and that's all the good it does."

"And does the law say this noise is unpreventable?" George asked skeptically.

Barbara smiled. "Comes under life, liberty, and the pursuit of happiness."

Herbert gave his glasses a hitch. "It's the second of the Four Freedoms—the right to worship in your own way."

George walked over and stood with his back to the fire. He could see a nice little emergency in the making. Perhaps this was the chance he had been waiting for. His pride had been sadly humbled by his fiasco at the auction. The Gages had been nice about it. They had all assured him and reassured him that he was in no way to blame and had handled the situation with great acumen and presence of mind, but George had his doubts. In his heart of hearts he felt that he had bungled. It wasn't entirely his fault, and still he was pretty sure they would never have the same confidence in him until he had somehow rehabilitated himself. He had been watching for a chance ever since the day of the auction. This might be it, if he could only turn it to his advantage. There was an idea here somewhere if he could just find it. He began groping.

"Well now let's see," he said, "if he's got a right, why—he's got a right. If the law says it's legal, that makes it legal. So then he can play his organ. That's what the law says. Of course we all know he can't, but the law says he can."

"Now you're right back where you began," Herbert said.

"But wait!" Suddenly George had it. "If he can play an organ in *his* room, you can play a piano in *yours!*"

Another puff of wind came down the chimney. "Certainly we can," Herbert said, "but who wants to? Wow! Listen to that wind!"

George stood up. He had for the time being lost all interest in the wind. He walked over to the piano and opened it. He sat down on the bench and loosened the knees of his trousers. Leaning back he looked down at the pedals and tried them with his feet. Then he ran his fingers up and down the keyboard to limber them and to find the proper pitch. Suddenly he found it—he lingered over it a moment feeling it out, softly, searchingly, glancing at the others and nodding to show them that he had found what he was looking for—the key in which the organ selection was being played. For a phrase or two he ran along lightly with the organ. Then he struck out on his own, playing the same hymn tune, but ragging it, jazzing it, swinging it until even Herbert, who did not know one note from another, was swaying back and forth and keeping time by tapping his foot in unison.

It was something that George had learned from a Negro street beggar, a blind man he had seen one day playing an accordion while being led along the sidewalks of New York by a woman companion bearing the inevitable tin cup. As George had paused to listen to the delightful syncopation of familiar hymn tunes, he had been amazed by the steady tattoo

[275]

of coins in the cup, one of which he discovered to his surprise had come from his own hand.

The rhythm had lingered in George's memory long after the blind musician had passed out of sight. George had always been good at the piano and especially good at syncopation, and he wondered why it had never before occurred to him to put the syncopating beat into some of the simple melodies of the hymn tunes. He had found it easy to do and amusing to the boys in his fraternity house, until some of the pious neighbors had complained to the college authorities of the "sacrilege."

It was a fleeting memory of this little episode which sent him over to the piano the night of the storm. Primarily he was after rehabilitation, but at the same time he welcomed an opportunity to get back at the overly pious folk of the world. Three times he played through the hymn tune with all the embroidery he could possibly put into it, and when he raised his hands from the keyboard after the final crash he found the organ silent.

George slid off the bench. "There! See what I mean?"

Herbert was still tapping appreciatively with his foot. "If they'd do it like that in church I'd go there myself—once in a while."

"Thanks for the compliment," George said with a smile, "but I'm afraid you don't see my point."

Herbert reached up with both hands and gave his glasses a hitch. "What point?"

"The organ—I've silenced their guns."

They all listened. "So you have," Herbert said.

"Don't be too sure," Barbara cautioned. "They have to stop once in a while to find another tune."

George was smiling confidently. "Oh, they may try it again, but if they do I'll give them another treatment. I'll pick up anything they play, and I'll embroider it with a syncopation that will make their heads swim. How long do you think they'll go on with it if I throw their sacred music back at them all jazzed up like a Harlem night club?"

"Sit down, George," Herbert invited. "Have a cigarette, and we'll soon find out."

George added wood to the fire, drew up a chair and sat down. Nobody spoke. All were listening intently for sounds from the other part of the house. For a time they could hear nothing but the whining of the wind in the chimney, and an occasional hiss as a drop of moisture found the hot coals on the hearth.

Barbara stood up and started for the door. "I'm going outside and look around. Anybody want to go along?"

"Oh, I wouldn't go out, dear," Margie said quickly. "It's a terrible night."

But George was already on his feet. "I'll go along with her. It's slippery, but she'll be all right."

With Margie still protesting, they switched on the floodlight and went out. Herbert and Margie could hear them slipping and squealing as they skated along the rough stone walk. An occasional peal of laughter came floating back from the yard in front of the house. Then for a time Herbert and Margie did not hear anything more from them.

"I hope they haven't gone far," Margie said nervously. "It's a dreadful night to be out, and Barbara didn't put a thing around her. I think I ought to call her in."

Margie had risen and was starting for the door when a terrific detonation rocked the house like a thunderbolt. The windows rattled. The floors shook. Then with a staggering crash the lights went out. That was when Margie began to scream.

Herbert knew instantly that a limb from the big tree had fallen on the house and had gone crashing on to the ground, taking the utility wires along with it. He sprang to Margie's assistance and tried to reassure her by explaining what it was, but she was entirely out of control and kept up a screaming and groaning until he had dragged her over to the couch and forced her to lie down. He knew that she was not hurt, that

[277]

she was screaming solely from fright—and he let her scream while he went in search of Barbara, for whose safety he had grave fears.

He had, however, not reached the outside door when it flew open and George came bursting in, half carrying Barbara in his arms.

"We were almost under the damned thing when it came down," George panted. "Something hit her and knocked her silly. But it was so dark after the lights went out that I couldn't tell whether it was a chunk of ice, or a branch, or what."

Barbara shook herself loose and began to laugh. "Nothing hit me but the solid ground. I knew what was happening the minute I heard the first crack. It was when I was trying to get out of the way that I fell down."

Margie jumped up from the couch and ran over to her. "Are you all right, dear? Are you sure you're all right? You aren't hurt?"

Barbara patted her mother's cheek. "I'm hurt in just one place, and that's where I sat down on the ground. Try it some time and you'll see."

Soon they were all laughing and chatting, as people will who have just missed being exterminated, but George brought them back to the serious aspects of the situation. "Your service wires are a complete wreck," he said. "That limb came down right over the corner of the house where the wires lead in." He put another stick on the fire. "And we're lucky to have this fireplace. Your oil burner would be of no use even if you had a full tank."

"Good heavens and all the little angels!" cried Herbert. "Do you people realize that every electric installation in this house is out of business?"

"Oh, gracious!" cried Margie. "I hadn't thought of that. No refrigeration, no current for cooking. . . ." She went on and enumerated other installations.

"And no water supply except what is in the tank," Herbert

interrupted. "Thank Heaven I had a large-sized tank put in—five hundred gallons."

"But, Herbert," she wailed, "what would we do without water?"

"We'd nail up the bathrooms, and when we wanted a drink we'd have to go down to the brook."

"Why, Herbert," Margie was a little short of breath. "You make it sound like a disaster. It isn't as if the current had never been off before."

"For an hour or two," Herbert admitted, "but there's no telling how long it may be off. That's the trouble with being dependent on these utility companies. They're too far away, and when they break down they leave you high and dry. If you're going to live in the country you ought to make your place self-sustaining."

"Could be," said George. "At the time of the hurricane the current was off for five days."

"How ghastly," Margie said. "But of course the hurricane was exceptional; there won't be another storm like that for seventy-five years."

"This storm may be worse than the hurricane," George said cheerfully. "There's nothing like the weight of ice to bring down trees and electric wires. Just listen—did you ever hear anything like it?"

As they listened it seemed to them that the world was in the grip of a weird visitation of cosmic forces. The heavy coating of ice creaked like a fusillade as branches were bent by the wind. The tortured limbs creaked and groaned as if in mortal agony. And particles of ice rained down with a noise not unlike the continuous tinkle of broken glass, creating the impression of total loss that goes with the shattering of a window pane.

"Pile on the wood," said Herbert. "Let's be as comfortable as we can."

CHAPTER - - - - - - - - TWENTY-EIGHT

↑↑

THE wind died down as suddenly as it had sprung up, and then came the rain. It was a deluge, but it was, in a way, a relief. After the eerie attack of the ice storm, so understandable a sound as the simple falling of rain was reassuring. Perhaps the end of the world was not so near as it had seemed. Though heavy rainfall is ordinarily of short duration, this time it kept coming. Occasionally it would slacken off somewhat, and then would start again with renewed torrential impetuosity. However, rain is rain, and, even though it falls with the ample abundance of a cloudburst, the sound of its falling becomes monotonous, and in time a little soothing.

Margie, the first to become sleepy, bunked down on the big davenport in the living room, covering herself with blankets. Herbert put on his old raccoon coat and stretched out on a studio couch in the taproom. George with his overcoat and Barbara with her mother's fur wrap close at hand had been detailed as volunteers to keep the fire burning throughout the night. George had offered to take the night watch alone, but Barbara would not have it that way. She said that with two each could keep the other awake.

From the depths of the davenport Margie had assured George and Barbara that they could talk all they wanted to, in fact, she had insisted that they must talk in order to keep each other awake. They did talk, though they really said little until Margie's heavy breathing gave assurance that she really was asleep. After that, so as not to disturb her, they spoke only in whispers—and from the depths of the same easy chair.

[280]

It was Barbara who started the whispering. She came softly over and seated herself on the arm of George's chair. George had been trying, ever since he was sure that Margie had gone to sleep, to figure out some way to get over into Barbara's chair. But he had learned from experience that Barbara was peculiar about such things and that it was best to let her show the way.

"Now don't slip," George whispered, steadying her firmly in his encircling arm. "We don't want to make a noise and wake up your mother."

Barbara laughed softly, her lips almost touching his ear. "Poor Mother," she whispered. "She's conked—she actually is."

George had never put into words the thought that nothing is more effective in bringing loving hearts together than some great convulsion of nature. He was strangely moved on this night when all outdoors seemed to have gone on the rampage, but he felt no inclination to put his feelings into words. In matters pertaining to love, as in the more prosaic affairs of life, he felt a strong urge to do things first and to find the words to account for them afterward. He was much better at explaining why he had, than at convincing why he should.

Barbara, though delightfully uninhibited, did not, so far as George's experience went, go in for petting. There was, of course, the little episode in the chimney passage. But she had never permitted a kiss that was either incendiary or protracted. Nor could one of her infrequent kisses be allowed any affirmative implication—it had to be just in fun. She had on one or two occasions gone so far as to kiss George—if you could call it that. She had touched her lips to his cheek with a laugh, but only out in the open where everybody could see. He had never seriously had his arm around her before, and dark as it was, he had never been so blissfully aware of the beauty and grace of her contours.

What Barbara may have been thinking at that moment he of course did not know, though he felt reasonably sure that she did not object. She was making no protest over his alleged protective embrace, and was showing no indication of going elsewhere. Quite the contrary, for presently she came the rest of the way, leaving her mother's fur wrap dangling over the back of the chair. But George was not one to argue with good fortune. He took what the gods provided and made the most of it. He expressed no surprise and took no unwarranted liberties, though he did ease her arrival on his lap by enfolding her in his arms and drawing her rapturously down until he had all of her resting gently in his embrace.

For a time they said nothing. Then he whispered, "Are you comfortable, dear?"

"Deliriously."

"Why didn't you ever do this before?"

"I didn't want to give you any wrong ideas—you get enough of those for yourself."

"Is it because your mother is here to preserve the proprieties?" he asked.

He could feel her laughing as she shook her head.

"The perfect chaperone," he said. "Are we going to take her with us on our honeymoon?"

She drew a long breath. "My dear," she whispered very tenderly but not without a certain firmness, "we aren't ever going on a honeymoon."

Now he was the one to laugh softly. "Suits me exactly. Spending our honeymoon at home is a terrific idea—so convenient and so economical."

She slowly turned her head to look at him, but in the dim light from the long-neglected fire she could see little more than a blur. "I'm not spoofing," she said. "Marriage is not for me. Every girl I know has gone into the service. I've tried to be satisfied with the Motor Corps, but with all the fighting and doing and dying it has worn pretty thin. If the war keeps on I'm going in. I want to be part of it—I want to do something worth while. Can't you understand—I don't want to be left out of the biggest thing the world has seen?"

"I see what you mean," said George. "You don't want our

children asking what you did in the war—boy, it's coming down!"

"You've been a dear, George."

"You'll have to explain that one."

"Offering me your heart and hand every time I glanced your way."

"But you always repudiated me."

"Of course, but I would have been a raving psychopath if you hadn't done it."

"Now it's coming in bucketfuls!"

She nodded and went on. "But don't you see, my dear, that it is misfortune, not love, that has drawn us together?" She stroked his cheek with her long fingers.

"It's pouring cats and dogs!" he said.

"I'm determined to make something of myself," she went on. "Nothing can stop me."

"Except the little drops of water—just listen to them!"

For a time she did listen, but her thoughts were on George and his own abortive attempts to get into the service. "It's all in knowing how to land when you get kicked out," he had told her. And he had kept on trying until he had been refused by every branch of the combat service and was now angling hopefully for a place in the Merchant Marine. Again she found his ear in the uncertain light.

"I'm positive they're going to take you," she said.

"What makes you think so?"

"Just a hunch."

"They'd better—it's the last chance."

"And the most rugged. You'll have plenty to tell your children."

"But how am I going to have any children if you don't marry me?"

She very slowly shook her head. "I'm never going to marry—not you, and not anybody."

"It's a deluge—a complete washout—listen to it!"

"You've meant a lot to me, George. I never knew how much

until I was—close in your arms like this. I thought it might be easier to say good-by this way."

"But it isn't?"

"It's harder—much harder." She drew his head close and pressed upon his lips a kiss that was neither hurried nor playful. But George knew that it was meant to be final.

With the coming of the dawn, George and Barbara bestirred themselves and piled wood on the fire, slipping a few pieces of kindling underneath to make a quick flame. They made no attempt to be quiet about it, not caring now if their moving around should wake Margie. But Margie slept peacefully on. Herbert, however, came out of the taproom yawning and combing his hair with his fingers. George held up a hand and pointed at the slumbering form on the davenport.

Herbert nodded, and without waking Margie he joined George and Barbara and went outside to see what the ravages of the storm had been.

The rain was no longer falling, though the low-hanging clouds gave warning that more was to come. Limbs, made brittle by their coating of ice and broken like straws, littered the dooryard and the neighborhood. Larger limbs, not entirely detached, swung precariously, as if about to come crashing down at any moment. Century-old trees lay sprawled across the highway, reminding Herbert of old lithographs he had seen of soldiers fallen during a charge. Part way down the hill he saw the prostrate form of his favorite pine, its foliage ruffled like the feathers of a dead bird.

At the front of the house they stopped to see what damage the big maple might have sustained. They found the ground beneath it carpeted with twigs and small branches. A few sizable limbs were dangling here and there or were wedged in a crotch. The only serious casualty was the one which had struck the roof. It had torn a jagged hole in the shingles, and in falling to the ground had, as George had reported, brought down with it every service wire entering the house.

Herbert pointed to it. "That's what knocked out the lights and telephone," he said.

George shook his head. "That's only part of it. I don't believe there's a mile of serviceable wire in the whole county."

Barbara gave his arm a squeeze. "Don't be a kill-joy," she said, looking up in his face.

It seemed to him that she had never looked at him quite that way before, and he wondered what had come over her—or perhaps over himself.

Barbara gave his arm another friendly pressure. "It couldn't be wishful thinking?"

"Do you think I want all this destruction and damage?"

She smiled tormentingly. "Then you don't like being marooned."

As he looked at her he could almost feel her in his arms again. "Being marooned can be wonderful," he said. "But rescue is always staring you in the face."

He wondered how much of this Herbert was taking in, but Herbert was apparently preoccupied with the tangle of wires beneath the fallen limb.

"Do you think it's safe to touch these wires?" Herbert said.

"Why would anybody want to touch them?" George asked. "They're as dead as a smelt."

"I was just thinking that with a little current—enough for the radio—we might get some news and find out how bad the situation really is."

"Good idea," George admitted. "But why don't we try the radio in my car, that is, if the storm hasn't knocked it out?"

They heard a reassuring hum as he turned it on, and soon afterwards the hoarse sputtering of static. They tried first for the local station, but were unable to pick it up. The big metropolitan stations were continuing their programs as if nothing out of the ordinary had happened, though they did interject occasional storm and flood bulletins from White River Junction, Hartford, and other trouble spots. Connecticut, the newscaster said, was hard hit, with vast wire damage, rivers out of their banks, and half the highways of the state either blocked by fallen timber or under water.

It was from a New Haven station that they eventually learned of conditions in their immediate neighborhood. And not only were the wires down and the roads impassable, but their electric power plant had been completely flooded, every generator submerged, and transmission lines so paralyzed and disrupted that restoration of service within a week would be highly unlikely. Flood waters were still rising. More rain was predicted.

Herbert's hand shook as he reached for the knob to shut off the radio. "Looks bad," he said. "We can't stay here a week."

Barbara looped her arm through his. "Don't be downhearted," she said affectionately. Even in the face of disaster she had on this particular morning an affectionate feeling for all the world. "It may not be as bad as you think. You know how those news broadcasters are: every flood is a deluge, every fire a holocaust. They don't want the truth—they want a good story."

"She's right," George said. "They do exaggerate, but they've got me a little scared this time. No telling how long these flooded conditions will last; and when you have a date with the Merchant Marine you keep it, or else. But that guy over in New Haven doesn't know everything, and I have a yen to run down the road a few miles and see for myself."

"Not a bad idea." Herbert clambered out of the car. "No use in trying to make plans until we know how bad things really are. You two have a look, and meanwhile I'll go in and see what Mrs. Flint can scare up for a fireplace breakfast."

They were back in a surprisingly short time with the news that the old house was completely isolated. To the east the road was under water, and to the west the bridge was out. George was uneasy, but his problem was not pressing. Not yet at any rate. He could wait another day for the water to go down; if the roads were still impassable he'd go out on foot, taking to the fields and the high land. That way, he told Barbara, he was sure he could get through.

"I'll get there if I have to swim for it," he said earnestly.

Barbara smiled. "That's the rugged old Merchant Marine spirit—go through even if it gets your feet wet all the way up to your neck."

"By the way," George said, suddenly remembering, "how did you make out with your plan for mellowing the old man and getting a working agreement?"

She shook her head.

"You never got any farther than the initial attempt?" he persisted.

"I knew you'd bring that up before you left."

He felt sure she was not really cross, and leaned around to look into her eyes. "No go?" he asked.

"The perfect flop."

"And you didn't try again?"

"How could I after I found out what he was building?"

Herbert couldn't see any other way. They had no light, no adequate heat, and only a limited supply of water. There was little food in the house and no opportunity of getting anything more except milk from the dairy. He felt humiliated when he realized how well prepared old Jonathan was for coping with the situation. He had a cellar full of food and a stove on which to cook it, to say nothing of keeping the room warm, and a winter's supply of fuel in the barn; he was entirely independent of the utility companies, living exactly as he had lived before electricity had been domesticated and introduced into the American household. It was a shrewd piece of planning. And to Herbert it was the last straw.

"We're licked!" Herbert announced to the family as they sat huddled around the fireplace. "We'll go—when we can get away."

"Go?" Margie cried. "But what will become of the house?"

"God knows."

"But won't we lose all our—our rights and legal advantages?"

"Very probably, but we can't stay here."

"Why not?"

"To begin with, what'll we eat? And we can't stay in this cold house indefinitely. Even after the current comes back on we may not get any heating oil for two or three weeks."

"There's always the fireplace," Margie said cheerfully. "And as for the food—I think that could be arranged if we should go about it the right way."

"How would you suggest?"

"The Rockwoods have more food than they can possibly use —we could buy some from them."

"My God!" Herbert exploded. He jumped to his feet and went tramping angrily around the room. "Do you think that after battling them for all this time I could go whining to them for mercy the moment they get a little advantage!"

"Dad's absolutely right," Barbara said, bristling. "If we go down we'll go with our colors flying—we won't be on our knees begging for a crust of bread."

Margie was puzzled and somewhat incensed. "I don't see what's so terrible about asking them to sell us some of their surplus food. I wouldn't hesitate for a minute if I thought the children needed it."

"Listen. . . ." Herbert was getting his glasses settled and himself braced to resume the argument when George interrupted.

"Aren't we getting a little ahead of ourselves?" he asked. "We've still got wood, and we've still got water—and we can't get away anyhow. So why don't we improve our present situation as much as we can?"

Herbert blinked. "In what way?" he asked.

"Bring in all the wood we can before it begins to rain again."

ↄↄↄ

JONATHAN was no eavesdropper. He would no sooner have listened at the keyhole than he would have stuck his finger in a buzz saw. Anybody who would listen at a keyhole was in his opinion the lowest of the low. However, if Jonathan overheard, fair and square, something not intended for his ears, that was all right. Folks who were careless about being overheard had nobody but themselves to blame.

He didn't like a keyhole, and he didn't like a key. He much preferred a good plain out-in-the-open bolt if you wanted to lock a door. He especially disliked the keyhole of the door leading into the big living room, where, as he knew, the Gage family were hovering around the fireplace trying to keep warm. He had been tempted to stuff up that keyhole, not because he had any fear of being spied upon, but to keep out the sound of the voices which came to him from the other side of the door. He did not like those voices. They irritated him.

How much came through the keyhole was problematical, for the door was old and sagging, and with the passing of some two centuries had shrunk until the frame no longer fitted closely; or perhaps, hung by a handyman instead of a carpenter, it never had been a close fit. Jonathan, however, laid most of the blame to the keyhole. He used to sit and scowl at it as snatches of conversation came through to him, and occasionally he found himself mentally refuting their arguments, denying their statements, and shaking his head over their ignorance of some of the simplest facts of common farmyard knowledge.

Only once was the conversation coming to him through the

keyhole of any particular use or satisfaction to him, and that was the night of the ice storm. That night he laughed.

It was when he heard Herbert explaining how completely the storm had paralyzed the household utilities on which the Gages depended to make livable the part of the house they were occupying. Matilda's hearing wasn't quite so good, and though she had often listened inquisitively at the door when Jonathan wasn't around, she was on this occasion so occupied in finding a candle in the dark that she had paid no attention to the talk in the other room. Indeed, she did not realize that anything worth listening to had been said until she heard the sound of Jonathan's laughter. Coming to her out of the darkness, this laughter from Jonathan startled her almost as much as the crash of the limb which had broken the wires.

She had heard Margie's cry and had despised her for it. Since there was nothing in particular to be scared about, she felt sure that Margie had made it only to attract attention to herself. But Jonathan's laughter was quite another matter. In all the years she had known him she had never heard the like of it, and she delayed her quest of the candle to take him to task for it.

"Was that you?" she demanded.

Jonathan quickly abandoned the levity. "Guess it must have been."

"You guess? Don't you know?"

"Come to think of it I guess I do."

"Still guessin'! What was it for?"

"Some'pm I heared comin' through the door, I guess."

"You mean you don't know what it was?"

"I know what it was all right—and if you'll keep still long enough I'll tell you about it. The storm has busted all their wires and knocked them out completely."

Matilda sniffed. "Well, ain't we in the dark, too?"

"Yes, but it ain't serious with us. We don't depend on it. Light up a candle and we're all ready for business again. But you take the 'lectricity away from them folks and they're all through. They can push the buttons, but there won't nuthin' happen. Can't cook. Can't wash their dishes. Their egg beater won't work, flatiron won't work, toaster won't work. Doorbell, radio, washin' machine, won't nuthin' work. She can't go to bed without her 'lectric blanket, but he's worse off than that—he can't even shave."

"I'd almost have laughed myself if I'd heared all that," Matilda conceded.

"But listen, that ain't all—you know how they ain't had no hot water in the house since the furnace quit? Well, without 'lectricity the water pump has quit, and all the water they got is what's left in the tank. When that's gone all their indoor plumbin' will be useless."

"Useless?"

"Sure. That's the trouble with indoor plumbin'—won't run without water."

"Lift a lid off the stove," said Matilda. "I need a little light to find me a candle in a hurry."

"What's the hurry?" asked Jonathan as he groped for the stove lifter.

"I want to go upstairs before the water in that tank is all gone."

Jonathan was up several times in the night peering out of the window and listening to what was going on, and he had already looked over the damage before George and Barbara had stirred from their comfortable seat in front of the neglected fire. He was at the barn doing the chores when he saw George and Herbert starting out with the station wagon on their first trip to the woods for additional fuel.

There would be plenty of it on the ground. That he knew. And with all the rain that had fallen during the night he knew what kind of firewood it would make. It was while they were in the woods that he happened to remember the water tap. He stepped over and tried it, and finding that the water would still run, he drew a pailful for Shadrach and one for the cow, though both animals could have gone to water by merely walking down to the brook.

Having filled the pails he stood and watched the water run. It formed a little pool on the ground, but it soon ran over the sides of this and made a rivulet. He watched it with fascination as it ran on and on. Other rivulets had been formed in the night, and though most of the rain water had run away the tiny watercourses remained. The stream from the tap found one of these—and ran back into the earth whence it had come. And after a while it didn't run any more and he knew the tank was empty.

He did not tell Matilda what he had done. He did not tell anybody. Not because he was ashamed of it, but because it was nobody's business. When he returned to the house he found Matilda waiting for him just inside the door.

"Got news for you," she said, drawing down the corners of her mouth and nodding in a way to signify its importance.

"What now?" he asked.

"He's been upstairs nailin' the bathroom door shut."

Jonathan pushed back his hat and wiped his forehead with his hand. "What's that for?"

"No water! The tank's run dry."

"Fine," he said. "If that don't get 'em out of here in a hurry, nothin' will."

"But what about us?" Matilda reminded him. "We got to have water, too."

He put his hat back on. "We got the finest barrel of rain water out there that ever fell from the sky."

"But do you want to drink it?" she demanded.

"I don't know why not—it come down off a good clean roof."

Matilda shook her head. "I don't know how clean the roof was, but I know I don't like the taste of rain water."

"Oh, well, if it's just the drinkin' that's ailin' you, I can fetch a couple of pails up from the brook for us to drink."

She went through the motions of looking off out the window.

"Drinkin' ain't the only thing," she said. "I'm goin' to miss that plumbin'."

Jonathan glowered at her. "You mean to tell me right to my face that you've got so you like this plush-lined plumbin'?"

"Well," Matilda began to hedge, "I don't say I like it so much, but it is convenient, and you know I can't get around like I used to."

"I'll take care of that all right. Joe and Uncle Walter's comin' to help me move the outdoor plumbin' up closer to the house."

An hour later the three were in conference outside the window, with Jonathan's plumbing lying prone on the stoneboat, by means of which Shadrach had drawn it from its obscure location behind the barn. Shadrach, always a patient horse, stood with the utmost unconcern as the conference proceeded. Now and then he flicked an ear back and forth as Uncle Walter proceeded to air his views in the loud tone of voice he habitually used in addressing persons of sound hearing.

"You needn't shout," Jonathan kept telling him every little while. "I can hear you even if you can't hear yourself, and I don't want to get everyone in the county mixed up in this argyment."

"Well, sir," shouted Uncle Walter, "I happen to know what I'm talkin' about. I've prob'ly built more of these here things than any man in the township. Prob'ly the nicest one I ever built was for Ezra Miller. Now that one was elegant, I'm tellin' you. Ezra cut down a walnut tree back there on the hill, and when they come to saw that up they saved him a few slabs of the nicest black walnut you ever put your eyes on."

Jonathan caught him by the arm and gave him a shake. "I know—I've heared all about it," he shouted. "They was all corner pieces!" He held up his hands to form a right angle. "I've heared you tell it a hunderd times. We ain't got time for it today. It's fixin' to rain again, and we want to get this thing set up."

"Well, sir," Uncle Walter was off again, "as I was sayin', these was all corner pieces. . . ."

But Jonathan was going to have no nonsense. He caught Uncle Walter by the arm and dragged him over beside the stoneboat, where he indicated by a sweeping circular motion of the arm that the outside plumbing was to be turned around and placed so that the front elevation was facing the street.

Uncle Walter protested noisily. He insisted that there was no privacy to such an arrangement. "Do you want the whole town to see you every time you come and go?" he declaimed.

"The town's got nothin' to do with it," Jonathan insisted. "It's just a question of looks. Nobody puts the back of a buildin' towards the front of a lot. You wouldn't even do that with a hog pen."

But Uncle Walter was adamant. "Well, sir, now let me tell you about that Ezra Miller job. . . ."

Jonathan also was adamant. He gave Uncle Walter's arm an emphatic poke and placed a finger in each of his own ears, shaking his head with a very decided negative. Then he stalked over and took Shadrach by the head. Shadrach, caught napping, threw up his muzzle and lowered his ears, but he was almost instantly ashamed of himself and began to nibble at Jonathan's shoulder.

"Quit that, you old fool," Jonathan scolded, "and get around there." He clucked a few times, yanked at Shadrach's head, maneuvered the stoneboat halfway around and shouted, "Whoa—hold it!"

Shadrach, determined to be accommodating if nothing else, slumped back into his harness and stood at ease. Jonathan motioned with his hands to both Joe and Walter as if both were deaf, indicating the spot where he wanted the structure to stand. Uncle Walter was still inclined to continue the argument, but when he saw both Joe and Jonathan preparing to lift, he moved in beside them and took his share of the load.

"Heave ho! Heave ho! Heave ho!" It was Uncle Walter who

did the calling. Unless he did it, he never could be sure when it was "heave" and when "ho."

Slowly the little structure swung into an upright position and came to rest on its own sills. Jonathan plumbed it with a spirit level, chocked it with flat stones, tilted it slightly so that the door would remain open when it was unoccupied, and pronounced the job finished.

After Shadrach had been led back to his stall and Jonathan's two helpers had left, the rain began again. Jonathan returned to the house well satisfied with himself.

"Did I tell you the big limb that come down is the one where the oriole used to build?" he said as he dropped into his chair and reached for his pipe.

"Never you mind about the oriole," Matilda said sharply. "What I want to know is why you put that thing in the front yard instead of out back?"

"We can move it out back as soon as they've gone," he said.

She turned and looked at him. "Did you think of that afore, or after you put it there?"

He struck a match and held it to his pipe. "Does it matter, so long as it helps to get 'em off the place?"

That night George slept with his clothes on in front of the fire. The rest of them went to their own beds, carrying hot bricks and an ancient soapstone, which was one of Margie's most prized antiques. George's plan was to sleep until he was wakened by the cold, and then to get up and put wood on the fire. If the wood had been dry, the plan would probably have worked all right; but the wood was so wet that George had great difficulty in making it burn even while he was awake, and he found that every time he dozed off the fire would go out.

Nor did the occupants of the beds have too comfortable a night. They managed to get along very well so long as the bricks and soapstone remained hot. But as these cooled the beds developed a clammy dampness which made sleep impossible. Barbara was the only one with sense enough to take her brick back to the fireplace for reheating, and she was accordingly the only one who woke up in the morning at all refreshed.

The food shortage began to be felt at breakfast. By this time the bacon was gone and there weren't enough eggs to go around. The mainstay of the meal turned out to be a dry cereal, with the pleasant aroma of frying ham floating in from Herbert's ex-study. Sarah in her boots and raincoat was sent over to the dairy for milk and cream. She came home bursting with news. The cows were being milked right on the ground without any pails because all the cans were full and they could not take them anywhere on account of the flood.

"Then we're still marooned!" Barbara said.

"That's the very same word the man over there used," said Sarah. "What does it mean?"

"It means," said George, "that I'd better go and look at it myself." He dropped his napkin and moved away from the card table on which they were eating. "I hope you'll excuse me for dashing off."

"But you haven't had your breakfast," Barbara protested.

"Oh, yes, I have," said George. "I've had plenty."

"Perhaps you don't like dry cereal," she suggested.

"I love it," George insisted. "It's the breakfast of champions, one of the seven basic foods that Uncle Sam urges us all to eat every day. But when the Merchant Marine orders a man to report—he reports. He doesn't let anything stop him, not even the breakfast of champions."

"How about hell or high water?" asked Herbert.

George smiled. "Well, certainly not the high water."

Barbara got up and began to pull on her raincoat.

"Where do you think you're going?" asked George.

"With you, of course."

Margie leaned over and whispered to Herbert. "You aren't going to let Barbara go running off into danger like this?"

Herbert smiled. "They won't get far enough to run into any danger. If the dairy trucks couldn't go through, neither can the blue roadster. And anyway, how can I stop her if she wants to go?"

He was right about it. They did not get more than two miles before they were turned back by state troopers, who said the roads ahead were impassable. They had orders to let nobody pass. George tried to find out how bad conditions really were, but they were a surly lot who gave out no information—or perhaps they did not know.

"Tomorrow," George said to Barbara as they were on the way home, "I'll have you take me as far as the car can navigate, and then I'll get out and go the rest of the way on foot."

That night Jonathan made another trial at the hymn tunes. Since the other experience Matilda had been somewhat reluctant; she did not want to be the cause of any sacrilege. But after some urging from Jonathan, who kept saying that he felt lost without lettin' the Lord hear a little music now and then, she opened the Biglow & Main collection called *The Glad Refrain*.

"Play old Number Thirty-three," said Jonathan.

"'Bringing in the Sheaves'?"

"That's what I want," Jonathan said with a nod of the head.

Matilda began turning the pages. "Ain't we a little early with our rejoicin'?"

Jonathan slowly shook his head. "It's my guess that we ain't. They can't hang on much longer. They'll get out of here just as soon as the roads are open and they can get away."

She struck her opening chord, and swung into the hymn.

> Bringing in the sheaves,
> Bringing in the sheaves,
> We shall come rejoicing,
> Bringing in the sheaves.

This was meat for George. He quickly caught the key and was ragging, jazzing, swinging it all over the piano. He played it as a foxtrot and as a waltz. Then, as a gesture to the Good

Neighbor policy, he rendered it as a *rumba,* and for a finale he combined it with "The Daring Young Man on the Flying Trapeze."

With many cluckings and head-shakings Matilda sadly closed the organ, resolving not to open it again until somehow the danger of inciting sacrilege had passed.

"Oh, well," said Jonathan with an attempt at cheerfulness, "the only way to find out is by tryin'. Funny they never done that until just lately. Wonder why."

He heard a car coming down the road and stepped over to the window to watch it go past. He could see the lights shining on the naked limbs of the big tree, and on the white pickets of the fence. He wondered who would be stirring on a night like this. Where had the car come from? Where was it going? It came closer, but it did not pass. Instead it swung slowly into the driveway and came to a stop before the side door.

Jonathan slipped out and peered round the corner of the house. Matilda noticed when he came back that he was breathing hard.

"What was it?" she asked.

"It was a Army jeep."

"Mebbe they're after that George. You reckon he could be a deserter or a draft dodger?"

"A soldier was drivin' it, but it wasn't no Army men who got out and come in, flashin' a light all around."

"Who was it?"

"It was that little hoot owl of a lawyer from Fairfield—and he's got the sheriff with him."

↑↑

GEORGE had just returned from the piano and was standing before the fireplace warming his hands when he saw the flash of lights through the window. "Look!" he said. "A car is coming."

Barbara started towards the window. "Who can it be?" she wondered. "A car can't go anywhere tonight."

George followed along. "Probably somebody from the dairy. Their delivery trucks are around at all hours of the night and day—but hold everything—it's turning in!"

Barbara, shading her eyes to peer out, suddenly called out, "Jeepers-creepers, it's an Army car! Probably it's the MPs after George."

"I have nothing to fear from the Army," said George. "If I'm in, I'm in the Merchant Marine—and all that time I spent at Officers' Training will come in handy."

"Well, see who it is!" Barbara said with a laugh. "You needn't hide in the closet after all, George—it's Winnie Loomis!"

This brought Herbert up out of his chair. "Loomis—at this time of night?"

"Yes, I could see him plainly in the lights of the car," Barbara assured him. "There's another man with him, a large man who stoops like a trained bear."

Hunched in his overcoat with the collar turned up and looking like a bird coming out of a hole in a tree, Mr. Loomis made clucking sounds as he entered the door. "Well, well," he said, "this was hardly what I expected to find." He introduced his companion as the sheriff.

Margie caught the lawyer by the arm and backed him up before the fire. "I hope you've brought food with you," she said, "for we're running out of practically everything."

Mr. Loomis blinked. "Well, the truth of the matter is that we didn't bring any food at all. We didn't know you were short. There seems to be plenty of water around."

"But," said Margie, "our pump is not working and we have to bring it from the brook."

"In gin bottles," Barbara added.

"Well, well!" said the lawyer. "But listen—I have news for you."

"You don't mean the war's over?" George demanded.

"No, no, not that. This news is from the home front." Mr. Loomis darted a pleased look all around. "It may startle you." He indulged in another brief pause, then said, as if addressing the court, "I have found the flaw in the flaw!"

Herbert was puzzled. "What does that mean?" he asked.

Mr. Loomis smiled. "It means that your neighbors are here merely as intruders—trespassers, if you will."

"But does it mean that we can throw them out?"

"Why not?" said the lawyer. "They are without so much as color of title. Why else would I have brought the sheriff out here on a night like this?"

"Then we win!" shouted Herbert. He grasped the lawyer by the hand and shook it until the little fellow was quivering all the way down to his boot tops. "Margie! We win!"

"Oh, but you can't drive them out in the storm!" Margie protested.

Herbert dropped the lawyer's hand. "What about that?"

The lawyer turned his other side to the fire. "Naturally not. They'll have three days to get out after the sheriff serves his writ." He drew a bundle of papers from his pocket and handed them to Herbert. "Read these over," he said, "and you'll find a notice for you to sign."

Herbert took the papers, but did not immediately open them. "You say you've discovered the flaw in the flaw. All right, what is it?"

Mr. Loomis laughed softly. "Well, Herbert, it's so hopelessly simple that I'm afraid you'll wonder why we didn't discover it before. This farm, like a good many others, was composed of several parcels of land. Somebody started off with one parcel and kept adding to it, a field on this side and a field on the other, whenever an adjoining owner was in the mood to sell. Perhaps you'll remember that in the deed from Jonathan Rockwood to the Power Company there were four separate parcels described?"

"Yes, yes—I understand that," Herbert replied impatiently.

"Very well," said Mr. Loomis. "Now in making his deed to the Power Company it was the probable intention of Jonathan Rockwood to reserve for the life use of himself and his wife, the parcel containing this house and the other buildings. You understand that?"

Herbert nodded, still a little impatient.

Mr. Loomis raised both hands with an eloquent gesture. "Right there is where he made his mistake—he reserved the *wrong parcel!*"

Herbert swallowed hastily. "What parcel did he reserve?"

"That pasture lot halfway down the hill," said the lawyer.

"But how could he make such a mistake as that?" asked Herbert.

"Very easily," said the lawyer. "There were few surveys in those old days. Most of the descriptions were ad lib.—made up on the spot. Bounded on the east by lands now or formerly owned by this one, on the north by lands belonging to the estate of so and so. They all sounded very much alike and were copied from one deed to another regardless of the adjoining owners. It was easy enough to mistake one for another. I did myself—and so did you."

"But—but, listen," said Herbert. "I thought if both parties made a mistake it could always be corrected."

"As between the parties, yes; but not to the prejudice of a third person who has purchased for value, which is your status in the case."

"Now just a minute," said Margie slowly. "I want to ask you something—does that mean the old people won't have anything at all, no place to go?"

"Oh, no." The lawyer smiled and rubbed his hands together. "They'll have the use of that pasture land as long as they live."

"But," Margie protested, "there are no buildings on it."

"Not yet, at any rate," said Mr. Loomis, "but they still have their remedy at law against the Power Company. All they have to prove is that the Company was responsible for the mistake, and the law will take care of them."

Herbert fingered the legal papers he was holding in his hand. "Do you think the old folks have any chance of beating the Company?"

"Every chance in the world," the lawyer said emphatically. "Prettiest cause of action you ever saw. The papers were drawn right there in the offices of the Company by persons in their employ. Due care required that those descriptions should be accurately checked. Had they done so, this mistake could not have been made. The principle goes back to that old case of dropping a brick from a tall building into a crowded street. *Res ipsa loquitur*—the thing speaks for itself. If it happens, negligence is presumed. The Company cannot escape."

"But somehow—I still feel sorry for these old people," Margie murmured.

"Don't be namby-pamby," said Loomis. "Those old folks have come in here without any legal right whatever; they've practically ruined your home for you. They've harbored animals in your beautiful studio barn, they've plowed up your lawn, and hung their funny underwear in your front yard; they've set up a cookstove in your study and made your library bookshelves into a woodpile—and now you're feeling sorry for them."

Mr. Loomis was now pacing up and down the rug in front

[302]

of the fireplace. "You don't seem to understand that they won't have any remedy against the Power Company unless you throw them out. Their case depends on their ability to show that they have suffered injury from the error made in the papers.

"This summary method of proceeding may seem tough on the old folks, but it's the only way you can preserve their right of action against the Power Company. And," the lawyer shook a clawlike finger before Herbert's face, "it's the only way you can clear your own title so that you can live here in peaceable possession—you and your family after you." He uncapped his fountain pen and handed it to Herbert.

While Herbert and the lawyer were bending over the papers, the sheriff was walking around looking over the place.

"Candles look nice in here," he said. "Kinda natural. That's all the light the old-timers had."

Margie nodded. "Tallow dips. We found the old molds in the attic. There they are on the mantel, with ivy growing in them."

"Uh-huh. Look nice up there. These old beams would tell some great stories if they could talk."

Why was it, Margie wondered, that the natives were always wanting the old beams to talk? The sheriff smirked wisely.

"This must have been the old kitchen—that's where things used to happen, all right."

Mr. Loomis gathered up the papers as Herbert signed them. "Everything seems to be regular," he said as he shook out the pages and folded them back into their original creases. "All right, Sheriff," he said. "You might as well perform your disagreeable duty."

"I hope you don't want us to go along with you," Margie said.

The lawyer shook his head. "Much better for you not to. With you there, it's a personal matter—without you, the law is in charge, and he'll get the feeling that what he is up against is the state of Connecticut and county of Fairfield. We'll go around to his door—that will make our visit more official."

Herbert nodded with satisfaction. He was glad he didn't have to go. A good position at the keyhole would have suited him much better, but by the time he had let Mr. Loomis and the sheriff out the side door and had closed it behind them, Barbara and George and even Margie had the complete area of the keyhole well covered with their ears.

Then came a loud knock on Jonathan's door. The sheriff scorned a doorbell. They could hear Jonathan going to answer.

"Who is it?" he called.

"The sheriff of the county of Fairfield—open up!"

They heard the bolt go back and the click of the iron latch.

"What do you want here at this time of night?" Jonathan demanded in a tone which sounded more annoyed than either scared or impressed.

"I've come to serve the mandate of the court."

"Well," Jonathan snarled, "can't you come in and serve it just as well with that door shut? Or do you need the nasty weather to help you?"

The listeners at the keyhole heard the visitors come in and slam the door behind them.

"This your wife?" the sheriff's voice boomed out.

"Certainly is."

"Are you Matilda Rockwood?"

"That's my name."

"Well, here's a paper for you. And here's one for you, Jonathan Rockwood—is that your name?"

"'Tain't nuthin' else. Gimme your paper. I ain't afraid to take it. Now what's it all about?"

It was Mr. Loomis who answered. "That paper is an order of the court requiring you to quit and surrender these premises on the ground that you are a trespasser, a squatter without color of title."

"How do you make that out?" Jonathan demanded. "When

I deeded to the Power Company I reserved the right to live here the rest of my life."

"That's what you told us when you came in here, but it isn't so," the lawyer declared. "We've just discovered that what you reserved is the second piece or parcel of land described in your deed—and that's the pasture lot partway down the hill."

"Now, just a minute," said Jonathan. "I got a copy of that deed right over there in the draw. We'll have a look at it." The eavesdroppers could hear him opening the drawer. "What in tarnation would I want of that pasture lot? Ain't no buildin's on it, and the biggest part of it is boggy most of the year."

"That's for you to say," replied Mr. Loomis. "You're the one who made the reservation."

"Here you are," said Jonathan. "This paper will show you what I reserved." They could hear the pages crackling as he turned them. Then followed a long pause which was terminated by an angry outburst from Jonathan. "This here's a mistake! 'Tain't what we agreed—and, by thunderation, I'll never get out!"

"It ain't healthy to resist an officer of the law," the sheriff said quietly. "A lot of people have got in trouble trying it."

"And you'll find it ain't any too healthy for a officer of the law to come bustin' into a man's home in the middle of the night," Jonathan fired back.

"What do you mean 'bustin''?" the sheriff inquired. "We knocked on the door and you let us in yourself. You ain't got to go tonight. The law gives you a full three days to vacate."

Jonathan was full of fight. "Three days or three minutes is all the same to me," he sputtered. "I tell you I won't get out!"

Mr. Loomis sought to pour oil on the troubled waters. "No use quarreling about it," he said in a conciliatory tone. "You don't have to decide now—you've got three days to think it over. I'd advise you to consult counsel, and it's my opinion that a settlement with the Power Company out of court is not at all unlikely. And with a nice bill of damages. . . ."

"Damages!" Jonathan snorted. "Who said anything about damages! What I want is my own home!"

"Of course," said the lawyer agreeably. "That's what I'm talking about. The Power Company got you into this and they can get you out. You've got plenty of land reserved—just take your damages from the Company and build yourself a house. Then you'll have it exactly the way you want it, and there'll be nobody to suit but yourself, no more bickering, no more quarreling. Nice little place for you and your wife to spend your declining years."

"It ain't just a house I want," Jonathan said slowly. "It's this house. I wasn't borned here, but I've lived here all my life. I was married here, and I've growed old here—and I'm stayin' right here until I'm carried out in a wooden box."

"I know what you mean," said Mr. Loomis. "Folks get notional about houses, but it really doesn't make much sense. One roof over your head is as good as another as long as it keeps the rain off. That's what I always say."

"This roof's good enough for me," said Jonathan, "and whenever you want to find me, I'll be right here."

"No use in being hasty about it." Mr. Loomis sounded very amiable. "You have plenty of time to think it over. I know as well as you do that you're a good citizen, and I have every reason to believe that, when you sit down and read over these papers and study the situation, your Yankee common sense is going to tell you the right answer."

"You can save your palaver, Loomis; I know the answer already."

"But are you sure you know the question?" the lawyer asked patiently. "It isn't the same question you faced when you came in here. The new question is, how can a man honorably defend his title to a house and lot when his papers call for nothing more than a cow pasture? And now, Sheriff, we'd better be on our way and give Mr. Rockwood a chance to think over this new question."

The listeners at the keyhole heard the front door of the

house open and close, and then Herbert went to the side door for a final word with his lawyer.

"Do you think he'll go?" Herbert asked in a low tone.

Mr. Loomis blinked doubtfully. "Heaven knows. He may—and again he may not. He's mad right now, and he's doing some stubborn talking. But after he's had time to digest those papers, he may be in a very different mood. However, he hasn't a leg to stand on, and either he'll get out within three days, or the sheriff will put him out."

Herbert shook his head dubiously. "I hope he goes peacefully—I'd hate to have the sheriff use force."

"Where do you suppose they'll go?" asked Margie.

Mr. Loomis shook his head. "That's their lookout, not yours." He turned to Herbert. "You'll stay and see this thing through, of course? It'll all be over in three days."

"What!" cried Margie. "Three days more in this ice house, with no heat, no light, and no water—and only your promise of food?"

The lawyer smiled. "It's all over but the shouting. Somebody's got to stay here and see that there's no sabotage. I'm afraid I can't do anything about your heat or light, but I'll get some food out to you."

"I don't care for myself," Margie said. "It's the children I'm thinking of."

"You couldn't crowd them into the jeep?" Herbert suggested. "I wouldn't mind staying here alone for a few days."

"You can't crowd me in," said Barbara promptly. "I'll stick with Daddy. If there's any trouble I want to be in on it."

"You want to go along with us, Margie?" asked Loomis. "We can take one all right."

"Oh, I suppose I ought to stay and see it through," she replied, "though I don't like roughing it. But don't forget the food. Mrs. Flint is half crazy trying to find something to feed us."

Mr. Loomis turned up his coat collar. "I won't forget," he said. "Well, Sheriff, are you ready?"

The sheriff, who had been talking to George, looked around. "All ready," he said. "But this gentleman thinks he'd like to ride back with us. How about it?"

"By all means do," said Loomis. "We'd be delighted with your company. I hope you've got a heavy overcoat and galoshes. It's pretty cold riding in these Army jeeps. They'll get you through if anything will, but they don't go in for comfort." He held out a limp hand to Herbert. "The sheriff'll be back in three days all ready for business."

Herbert nodded rather glumly for a man who had just been told he had won a law suit. "I'll be here," he said. "I suppose eventually we'll get oil and electricity. Either that or I'll have to get hold of a plumber and drain the system so that we can go away until the utilities are restored—and in the meantime somebody's got to keep the plumbing from freezing. What we really need around here is a good caretaker."

George put out his hand. "Sorry to leave you in such a spot," he said. "But I'm afraid there's no other way. If I make the grade and they give me a leave I'll come back."

The jeep swung out of the drive, and the last they saw of it was when the taillight disappeared over the top of the hill to the east. As Herbert turned away from the window he had a feeling that the entire responsibility was now resting on him. And he wondered if the old man would make any trouble.

ʸʸ

GRADUALLY Jonathan's wrath burned itself out. The fling of defiance he had taken in the presence of the functionaries of the law had blown off some of the initial pressure, but he still had to reckon with the unavoidable fact that he had nobody but himself to blame. He was incensed at the Power Company for making the mistake; he was aggravated at Loomis for discovering it; he was provoked at the Gages for taking advantage of it; but all this was as nothing compared with his exasperation at himself whenever he remembered that a little more care on his own part would have averted all the trouble.

Long after he was in bed this self-recrimination kept coming back to torture him and disturb his rest. For hours on end the spool bed creaked with his rolling and turning. Matilda, too, was unable to sleep, and though neither one spoke for fear of keeping the other awake, the old couple lay side by side long into the night, Jonathan fuming over things that were past, and Matilda worrying over the future.

By morning Jonathan had arrived at the point where he could accept the fact that his side of the case would no longer hold water. He knew that by hiring a lawyer he could delay matters. But he had no money to spend on lawyers. The most they could give you about anything was an opinion, and he had plenty of opinions of his own. Indeed, he already had one lawyer's opinion, that of the little hoot owl, Loomis. Probably not his own opinion all by himself. Must have come from his father, who really knew what was what, and knew how to charge for knowing it. At least Jonathan had the satisfaction of getting a legal opinion from the most expensive firm in Fairfield County, without paying a red cent for it.

Of course that opinion had come from the other side, and, while Jonathan didn't think there was much hope for him, he felt that he ought to take counsel from somebody. Uncle Walter—and Joe—were of course the inevitable choice.

How much of this, or any situation, Joe had taken in, Jonathan could not be sure. How much English he could understand was problematical. How much he could speak was equally so. The only part that Jonathan could be sure of was that he never did speak more than a dozen words. And yet Joe always seemed to have a very good idea of what was going on. More than once Jonathan had pondered over the possibility that Joe might absorb knowledge through his pores, or even draw it up out of the earth.

With Uncle Walter the case was quite different. He wasn't exactly a lawyer, but he had in his earlier days been a justice of the peace and a mighty good one. He would probably still be holding the office had not a severe attack of influenza resulted in his deafness. Like so many deaf persons, Uncle Walter was inclined to do a great deal of talking, taking it for granted that since he could not hear he continuously held the floor. And since he himself was unaware how his talk sounded, quite a little of it was somewhat silly. However, Uncle Walter was, to Jonathan's way of thinking, as smart as a steel trap, he was honest, and he wasn't afraid to give a bitter pill or take one.

Unfortunately, Uncle Walter could not absorb information through his pores, and, though he still rather fancied himself as a lip reader, Jonathan preferred to regard him as just another deaf man, and if he wanted Uncle Walter to be dead sure of his facts he insisted on using the speaking tube, or in the absence of the tube he took the hard way—by shouting.

Moving his lips as he read, Uncle Walter went carefully through all the papers in the case after Jonathan had given him a verbal account of the visit of the sheriff and the attorney. When he had finished his reading, Uncle Walter spread the papers out on the top of the oat bin and pulled out his speaking tube.

"You got to get out—no two ways about it. But who drawed these papers?"

"Power Company!" Jonathan replied into the tube.

"Did they ask you if it was correct?"

"No!" Jonathan shook his head emphatically. "Didn't ask me nuthin'. Just handed me a pen and told me to sign. They'd been all around the place and they thought they knew all about it. Think they'd condescend to ask me what was what?"

"Well, you're licked. All the life use you've got is down in the cow pasture."

"How you think we're gonna live in a cow pasture? No buildin' on it!"

"I handled a case against this same Power Company once," said Uncle Walter. "Made 'em pay through the nose. That was the time they come over onto Ezra's place by mistake and cut some timber. Triple damages, by thunder! I must have told you about that. It happened seven years back or such a matter. . . ."

Jonathan bawled into the mouthpiece. "I know all about that timber! Now you listen to me—I got some'pm to tell you. You say we got to get out. How can we get out? We got no place to go."

"Sure you have—you'll come down to my house till you get this all straightened up. I wouldn't mind havin' a woman around there for a while. I'm gettin' sick of my own cookin'."

Jonathan shook his head. "Have you got room for Shadrach?"

"Sure I have, I'll turn him in with Jerry. Did I ever tell you how they cheated me on Jerry?"

Jonathan pushed Jerry out of the conversation with the back of his hand. "Got room for the cow? She belongs to you anyway—I never paid for her."

"Plenty of room, but you'll need her when you get your place fixed up." Uncle Walter looked up with a smile. "You can keep her in that pasture lot you reserved."

"What do you think about my case against the Company?"

"Can't tell."

"Loomis says it's a sure thing."

"No law suit is a sure thing. But you let me handle it and I'll get some'pm out of 'em—they're afraid of me."

"And you say we got to move?"

"You ain't got a leg to stand on."

"What'll I do with my hay?"

"Stack it in your pasture lot. You can move it with my hay-rack."

"You sure I got to go?"

"Positive."

"But I told 'em I wouldn't."

"You will. If you don't the sheriff'll throw you out. I got plenty room for you folks down there. I'll clean it up and get it ready."

It was about what Jonathan had expected. It was what his own common sense had told him the answer would be. The law was so busy followin' a lot of rules that it kinda lost track of justice. It made no difference in the eyes of the law that he had been done out of his home by a plain ordinary mistake that might have been made by almost anybody. The law didn't correct a mistake, no matter how plain it was, if a third party had come in afterwards; and it didn't give the loser any more than a fightin' chance to get back some part of his loss from the one who made the mistake.

But when the law wouldn't help a man, there was only one thing left to do—and that was for a man to help himself the best way he could.

Much as it went against the grain, Jonathan forced himself to accept the fact that he had lost forever all his rights in the old house, and that the best he could expect from the law was

[312]

the life use of a cow pasture. It had always been Jonathan's belief that a man's home was his castle, something to be defended to the death; and he had vaguely pictured himself as firing through the crack of the door at the sheriff and his deputies, with the old Civil War musket. Then suddenly he thought of something better, something surer, something that would give him a measure of justice the law had denied. If he could not live there himself—why should he let anybody else?

The thought came to him without any particular shock— just as other vengeful thoughts had come to him. It was one of those things a man would have liked to do but did not think he ever would—not at that time.

At first he only toyed with the idea, thinking of how and where he could best set fire to the place in case he should make up his mind to burn it. He thought of the attic filled to overflowing with dry as tinder material. The flames would go quickly up through the roof, but he wondered if they wouldn't be a little slow about burning downward. Then he remembered the closet under the front stairs in which he had been storing old newspapers and dry kindling. A fire started there could burn upward, and would have the whole house enveloped in flames in no time. The closet, he felt sure, would be the ideal place for the match—though he had no idea even then that he could really bring himself to apply it. But he went so far as to open the door and look over the ground. He could see at a glance that all he would need to do would be to shift a few sticks to the top of the pile of newspapers and strike a single match. He even looked at the matches, a large box of the bird's-eyes used to light the fire every morning.

He picked up a match and fingered it. That single match, he was thinking, would do the deed. But he did not use it. He dropped it back in the box and closed the cover. No man with any sense, he reasoned, would use that match before movin' out his own things—leavin' mebbe just enough to avoid suspicion. Jonathan began to make a mental inventory of the articles he wanted to save, and those he was not so particular about. Heading the list of property to be left behind was Matilda's spool bed, for which he had come to have little regard after sleeping for a time on one of Margie's beds with a custom-made innerspring mattress—even though it was a little too short for him. Then, too, the way Matilda would moan over the loss of that bed would dispel any doubt that the fire had been accidental. Jonathan took the precaution of following his mental inventory as he was moving his things down to Uncle Walter's house. He had not definitely made up his mind to use the match, but he kept telling himself that he might as well be ready just in case. If he did decide to do the job, he'd have everything in order.

Once the idea of destroying the house had come to him, he could not seem to get rid of it. It was gnawing at him like a toothache, keeping him awake at night and preying on his mind by day, although he tried to make himself think of other things. It was the physical act of applying the match that he could not face. But instead of banishing the idea and forgetting it, he kept skirting around the edges of it, looking for a new opening, and at last he found one. It was while he was speculating over the question of where a fire of accidental origin would be most likely to start. His first supposition was that it would be in the oil furnace or the electric wiring. Perhaps this was because he distrusted both these improvements, for he must have known that the most frequent cause of fire in old houses was from some defect or failure developing in the chimney. But when once he got around to the chimney the solution to his problem came to him like a flash from the blue.

All he had to do was to find some way of getting the Gages to build a fire in the Dutch oven—and they'd burn down the house for him without his even striking a match.

He went over the familiar ground in his mind a dozen times. How well he remembered the bolt of lightning. They had all been sitting in the kitchen when the blinding crash had come. At first they were too dazed and too startled to move, and then they had begun to run up stairs and down to see if the house was on fire. He was the one who had eventually discovered the damage. Nobody else had thought of looking into the old oven, which had not been used in some years, having been superseded by a range. He remembered the peculiar satisfaction with which he had made his discovery. Being at that time little more than a boy, he felt very important about it. If he shut his eyes he could still see the jagged hole in the inner end of the oven. Looked funny with the daylight coming through there where no daylight belonged.

The cave-in was a long time in getting itself repaired. Probably never would have been patched had the break not gone through the wall right onto the front stairs, where you couldn't miss it whenever you went up or down. He remembered how Matilda used to nag about that hole whenever she saw it. But old Pete was busy and was a long time coming. When he did come he had fixed it in a hurry. No use of brickin' it up, he said. Brickwork cost money, and nobody would ever want to use that Dutch oven again. A little patchin' plaster would fix it up, and nobody'd ever know the difference from the outside.

Jonathan enjoyed bantering with old Pete. "But what if somebody should build a fire in it?" he had asked.

Old Pete had cackled with laughter. "Don't reckon nobody will. But if they do . . ." he shook his trowel at Jonathan, "they'll burn the house down for sure."

Later, when they were in the cellar having a glass of cider, the mason had repeated the warning. "No use of wastin' your money puttin' in brickwork you ain't never goin' to use; but if you ever do get a hankerin' to build a fire in there, don't forget that I warned you."

It came to Jonathan, as it had come to him before, that the flimsy patch had long outlasted the man who had put it there. The mason had been dead for years and years, but the plaster was as good as ever.

That night Jonathan picked up the Bible and began thumbing the pages. He had just found what he was looking for when Matilda asked him to read aloud.

"What do you want I should read?" he asked.

"Just what you're readin' there—it's all good."

So he read: "And thine eye shall not pity; but life shall go for life, eye for eye, tooth for tooth, hand for hand, foot for foot." He glanced around the room, letting his eyes come to rest on the walls, the ceiling, the wide oaken floor boards. Since boyhood he had known this room. Once it had belonged to him—but not any more.

"Eye for eye, and tooth for tooth," he repeated slowly. "Nuthin' chicken-hearted about that, but you got to admit it's as fair for one as the other."

Matilda turned from the dishpan and scowled at him. "Don't be cavilin' at what you find in that book. If it's there, it's right. You got to believe it."

"Oh, I believe it all right," Jonathan replied. "Always did believe it; but that's no reason why I can't say it's pretty strong medicine."

"Just read and believe. There's no call for you to interpret."

He leaned back in his chair still looking around the room. "Eye for eye, tooth for tooth."

"Is that the only verse you can think of?"

"It's the only one I am thinkin' of, right now." He closed the book and put it on the table. Then he reached for his pipe and tobacco.

Jonathan watched his chance and intercepted Margie in the yard, where he spoke to her with the utmost civility. It was the first time he had spoken to any member of the household since the sheriff's visit two evenings before.

"I reckon I won't be able to get all my firewood out of the barn right away," he said. "Be all right with you if I leave it there a while?"

"Quite all right," said Margie, relieved that it was nothing worse.

"It's extry good or I wouldn't be troublin' you with it. Seasoned wood, you know, dried under cover."

"No trouble at all," she said. "Leave it there as long as you wish."

He started to go on, then stopped. "How you makin' out with your fireplace cookin'?"

Margie shook her head disparagingly. "We don't like it too well. It's all pots and frying pans. We can't bake anything."

"You can't?" He feigned surprise. "Why, I've always said the finest bread on earth was baked in a Dutch oven."

"But how does anybody bake in a Dutch oven? How can you get one hot enough to bake?"

"There ain't no trick to it," Jonathan assured her. "You just build a roarin' big fire in the inside and keep it goin' a few hours, and you'll have the finest bakin' oven there is."

A troubled look came over Margie's face. "There's a little more to it than that," she said. "I'm afraid we couldn't build a roaring fire with our wet wood. We can hardly make it burn in the open fireplace."

"Well," Jonathan rubbed the back of his head and looked thoughtful. "I got some elegant firewood piled there in the barn. Seasoned just right for a Dutch oven. I was goin' to say I'd sell you a few wheelbarrow loads of it, but you been so decent about storin' it for me I'll give you some of that wood. You can just help yourself to what you need for the oven. Lucky you spoke about that wood—I might have took it away tomorrow. Now I'll leave it there a few days."

Margie brightened up at once. "That's very generous of you," she said. "I'll be glad to accept. I've always wanted to try Dutch oven cookery—I have a book about it—but the book doesn't tell how to heat the oven."

She was delighted at the turn affairs had taken. She had expected nothing but bitterness and anger, and was very much relieved to find that the old man could take defeat with such good grace, that he was really a good sport. And, wishing to do her part, she offered him storage space in the barn for any-

[317]

thing that he was finding inconvenient to move. Jonathan thanked her and said that he might have liked to put the organ down there, but he'd already moved it to Uncle Walter's.

It was the next morning when Jonathan saw Herbert bringing in armfuls of the dry wood from the barn. So this was the day. He returned to the house and told Matilda she might as well be getting ready to go.

"What's the hurry?" she asked. "We got all the rest of the day, ain't we?"

He could not tell her that he did not want to be anywhere around when the disaster actually occurred, so he made an excuse of wanting her to get things settled right away at Uncle Walter's. By this time Jonathan had removed from the house everything he intended to take and was leaving behind only the items destined for the burnt offering. His plan was to say he would come back for the final load with Uncle Walter's lumber wagon. But not to come until he was quite certain there was nothing to come for.

Matilda, however, seemed to be in no hurry to go. She dawdled over one thing or another as if she had all the time there was. Jonathan hurried her as much as he could without making a point of it, and as he went back and forth with the articles he was loading into the democrat wagon he would pass his hand along the wall where the repair of the Dutch oven had been made. He could tell the place because the plaster was a little rough even though it had been covered over with wallpaper.

The wall was warm the first time he felt it, and before they were ready to go it had become so hot he could not bear his hand on it. He tried his best to keep calm and to cover his anxiety to be gone, but Matilda sensed his excitement.

"Seems to me you're in a terrible hurry to get out of this place, but I can't say I blame you. It's got so full of hatred and malice that all the happiness has gone out of it. I won't be sorry to be done with it myself, and still there's things to be finished before we can go."

[318]

At last he got her out and up on the seat of the wagon, with her patent rocker tied on the top of the load, which wasn't very large, mostly odds and ends. When he came back to take a final look around, he could see that the paper was curling over the patch on the wall, and smoke was beginning to come through the boards of the floor. It wouldn't be long now.

On the way out he went to the rain barrel at the corner of the house, filled to the brim by the recent downpour, and with a powerful shove tipped it over and allowed the water to go to waste. Then he spun the empty barrel through the gate and hoisted it to the tailpiece of the wagon, where he secured it with a piece of rope, western style.

"We ain't obliged to furnish them with water," he muttered as he climbed up on the seat. "Besides, the barrel belongs to me. Giddap, Shadrach!"

It was just as they were driving away that the car of a state trooper caught up with them, from the door of which the sheriff leaned out.

"Hold on there a minute," he ordered. "Are you vacatin' the premises peaceable-like?"

Jonathan glowered at him. "I'm gettin' out, ain't I?"

The sheriff half smiled. "You're showin' some horse sense, old man. It don't pay to tamper with the law." He dropped back into his seat. "All right, Trooper," he said. "I guess we won't be needed today, and we might as well turn around and go back."

"Just a minute, sir!" called another voice from inside the car. "Let me dock my cargo of stores and provisions right here. Then you won't have to stop again, sir."

As Jonathan started along he glanced back and saw a tall young fellow in a dark blue uniform getting out of the trooper's car. He was laden with paper bags and cartons, which he carried into the house. The old man kept looking back over his shoulder to watch what was going on, and was relieved to see the trooper's car turn and drive away in the direction from which it had come. Jonathan felt that it would be just as well not to have police officers around when the fire broke out. The fellow in the blue uniform was no policeman. Looked more like a service man, though he could not quite make out the branch of the service to which he belonged.

No more did Barbara as she peered from a window of the taproom and saw him entering the gate. "It was a State Police car that stopped," she called back to the others. "But it turned around and went away again—and you ought to see the snorting blue uniform that's coming in the gate!"

Herbert started for the door to see who it was, but before he could get there George Husted swung it wide open and stepped inside.

"Why, George!" Herbert shouted enthusiastically. "What does all this mean?"

George put down the bundles and saluted smartly. "It means, sir, that I've been taken into the Merchant Marine, sir."

The next moment Barbara was in his arms. "You darling, sir!" she breathed.

After that time stood still. The first that George could remember about it was when he heard her saying, "But that uniform! It's supercolossal—it's out of this world!"

George looked down at himself. "Like it?"

"I love it; but, George, that uniform looks as if it might have been made for an admiral. Actually."

"Was." He beamed all over his face.

"You're not trying to tell me. . . ."

"Nope. Not that. What I mean, I got a gleam of this when I went in to tell the tailor I'd changed my plans and wouldn't be bothering with the Marines."

"And he let you change? Just like that?"

"Used to it. He'd gone along with me from one service to another all down the line. First uniform I ordered was for the Air Arm. Remember? And when old Tape-measure saw me looking with favor on the navy blue—he knew what was coming. He said blue would look well on me, but I'd have to be an admiral to wear this one *unless*—I should go into the Merchant Marine, where they allow a fellow a bit of latitude as to dress."

"But do they have admirals in the Merchant Marine?" Barbara asked, bantering though still breathless from the sudden upsurge of emotion.

George smiled down at her. "Don't forget I've had Officers Training, and in the Merchant Marine every man above deck is virtually an admiral. This is my idea how the well-dressed seafaring man should look."

"You're just in time, George," Margie said. "We'll bake the wedding cake in the Dutch oven. There's a roaring fire in it right now."

This was the first that George had realized Margie was there, though for some time she had been poking into the packages. "Yes," he said. "I can smell it. The thing must be smoking like a volcano."

As he stepped over to take a look at it all were startled by a wild clatter of horse's hoofs on the roadway, followed by a thunderous pounding which shook the house to its foundations.

A T THE crest of the hill Jonathan drew up and turned for a final look at the old house. There it stood, just as he had known it. He stared at it hard, trying to fix a lasting image of it in his memory. Slowly he became conscious of the tree standing stark and motionless before the door, its giant trunk anchored to earth by a thousand roots, its naked limbs towering above the rooftop.

It seemed to him as he peered back into the years that it wasn't more than half its present size when he had first seen it. No sapling at that. Must have been a couple of feet through even then. He remembered how he used to tap it for sap when he was a boy. Got a few quarts of syrup out of it every year. . . . At one time or another he had climbed all over that tree. Been on every limb of any considerable size. Looking all around the country and peering into birds' nests. Great old tree for birds' nests. Same pair of orioles had built there year after year. Same robins and blackbirds, too. And during the migrating season the birds had acted as if they owned it. . . . And there was that big hornets' nest he knocked down. Must have been the size of a full-grown watermelon, and even though he had waited until after dark to tackle the job he had somehow managed to get a few stings. . . . Then there was that fight over widening the road. If the scheme had gone through it would have killed the tree for sure. That rascally Dixon had been planning the thing for years, but he never could get anywhere with it until he had managed to squeeze in as selectman—and then he started to railroad his project through just because it would benefit his own property. Jonathan had to put up a stiff fight to save the old tree, but in the end he won. Saved the tree and lost the friendship of a neighbor. Dixon had never spoken to him from that day to this. . . . Another big battle was when the Power Company ran its lines down the road to get to the dairy. They wanted their wires to go spang through the tree—took some patrolling with a shotgun to keep them off, but once more Jonathan's loyalty had saved his old friend from defacement and perhaps destruction.

There they were—the house and the tree—rugged and magnificent. He had been proud to be associated with them, and it made him sad to think that the three old pilgrims would never again be together. As he continued to look he could feel himself dwindling in size and significance in the presence of the other two. He began to wonder if he had not been a little presumptuous to assume an equality with them. His own days, as he well knew, were numbered; but there was no reason why the house and the tree—without his interference—might not have gone on for another century or even longer.

Exasperated at the thought, he slapped the reins bitterly on Shadrach's rump and ordered him on. Shadrach snapped back his ears and with an indignant switch of his tail moved resentfully forward; he could be just as cantankerous as the driver, and though he kept going he took his time.

Jonathan, trying to reason himself out of his exasperation and into a state where he could justify himself by saying that he was glad of it, paid no attention to Shadrach's bad humor, but only to his own. He had intended to drive out of sight without another backward look, but he could not quite make it. Just before he reached the bend in the road he stopped the horse and stood up in the wagon. This really would be the last look.

Smoke had all this time been rising from the chimney, but now he could see it leaking out between the shingles on the roof and curling up among the overhanging branches of the tree. The chimney, as he very well knew, had nothing to do with the smoke in the shingles, and in his mind's eye he could see the ancient timbers smoldering within the walls. Soon the flames would break into the open—and the house would become a roaring furnace. Suddenly it came to him that the tree would also burn, its giant limbs writhing and crackling among the tongues of flame. This was something that he had not thought of, and the startling comprehension of the great injury he was doing stunned and almost overwhelmed him. It was not so much the house—he had argued himself into a state where he felt that he could see another person destroy it, if by doing so he was letting a cheat rob himself of his ill-gotten gain. But the tree—that was quite another matter.

All his life Jonathan had been a fighter. He had never been afraid to do battle for his rights, and he had gloried in a well-won victory. But somehow this time was different. It wasn't like any victory he had ever won. There was no glory—no satisfaction—no triumph. He felt more like a loser than a winner. He kept assuring himself that he was not actually committing a misdeed, and still his conscience kept gnawing at him. He fought it off as long as he could, but in the end it downed him, and he saw his carefully concocted revenge as a cowardly injury to his friends rather than as a blow at an enemy. His friends would be destroyed, but his enemy would come back as soon as the embers were cold, and would begin a new house on the ashes of the old.

A wave of self-condemnation swept over him. Why had he done this shameful thing? This was no eye for eye or tooth for tooth. It was the wanton destruction of something he loved, for the sake of a revenge that could never be realized. Was he too late to undo the damage even now?

Matilda had turned in her seat and was staring back. "Why, Jonathan, look at all that smoke!" she cried. "Ain't the house on fire?"

"Come down outa that wagon in a hurry!" he shouted.

"Mebbe I can save it yet—if I can only get there quick enough with some water!"

He had leaped to the ground and was hauling her patent rocker from the top of the load. With unbelievable agility he placed it on the ground by the side of the road and swung up into the wagon as part of the same motion. "Set right there till I get back!" he ordered. "Giddap, Shadrach!"

Jonathan lashed the astonished horse down the road to the brook, where he drove into the stream and hastily dipped water in a bucket and poured it into the open top of the rain barrel. Though he was working with feverish haste the water level in the barrel rose so slowly that by the time it was only halfway up he was so wild to be on his way to the fire that he dropped the bucket in the wagon and caught up the reins.

"Giddap there, Shadrach!" he shouted, slapping the reins violently on the horse's rump. "Go long! Git a move on you!"

Taken completely by surprise Shadrach lunged and leaped, splashing the water in all directions and almost upsetting the wagon as he hurriedly pulled out of the stream and scrambled up the driveway leading to the road. Once he was on the road Jonathan lashed him unmercifully, striking him repeatedly with the buckled end of the reins. Now that he had resolved to go to the rescue, Jonathan's one fear was that he would not be able to get there in time. In his imagination he could see the flames getting away from him. He could hear them roaring in the wall and snapping and crackling in the tinder-dry accumulation of rubbish in the attic. A terrifying vision of the old house kept passing through his mind, a vision in which smoke was pouring out of the shattered windows and flames were bursting through the ancient shingles of the roof.

As he was approaching the turn in the road from which he would catch his first glimpse of the house, he could hardly bear the thought of actually seeing it. A strong temptation to close his eyes almost overcame him, but he drove it off and told himself that he must face the music.

It was, however, not as bad as he had feared. Smoke was

still pouring out around the chimney and leaking through the shingles on the roof, but the windows were still intact and no sign of a flame was anywhere to be seen. The hope that he might yet be in time brought him to his feet and he redoubled his efforts to get more speed out of the horse.

But the hill was tough, and Shadrach's wind was old and wheezy. Willingness was not lacking, but the aged steed was already giving his utmost. Matilda rose with a shout of encouragement as the fire brigade went thundering past, but neither horse nor driver was even conscious of her presence. At the top of the hill Shadrach leveled for his final burst of speed. Into it went all the strength and all the gameness left in his mustang soul. But he was beginning to falter by the time that he felt himself being pulled up. Never a horse who needed any encouragement to whoa, Shadrach sprawled out his legs and skidded to a stop so suddenly that he almost spilled Jonathan off the seat. But the old man quickly recovered himself and rushed into the house, his long-handled ax in one hand and a bucket of water in the other, leaving Shadrach panting and heaving, and swaying back and forth with every breath.

Jonathan still did not know how far the fire actually had advanced, and the uncertainty of what he was going to find inside the house almost unnerved him.

What he first noticed on shoving open the door was that the hall was rapidly filling with smoke, but he was relieved to see that no actual flame was in sight. He might yet be in time. He quickly set down the bucket and went at once to the seat of the trouble. A few frenzied blows with the ax laid open the wall enough to see the flames within, but the tough oaken planks, hardened by centuries of seasoning, turned the strokes of the ax and made cutting most difficult. And now it was Jonathan who was giving his all.

As he struggled on, the smoke became stifling. It impeded his breathing and caused him to choke and cough. And after a lifetime of expert axmanship, his blows seemed to have lost their accustomed force. To be so near to success and then to fail was maddening. The fear of failure gave him renewed strength for one final effort, and the ax went crashing through, hacking out an opening into which he was able to empty the water from the bucket.

A cloud of steam came hissing out and the flames subsided, but as soon as the water was gone they sprang up again and were soon roaring as before. If Jonathan had only had more water within reach he was sure he could have put out the fire. But the water was gone, and his strength was gone. He was gasping for breath as he felt himself sinking down on the stairs. He could hear distant voices, and people coming on a run, but he was too far gone to tell them what to do. He was, in fact, unconscious by the time they had reached him.

The next thing Jonathan knew, he could feel himself being carried outside and laid gently on the ground. The fresh air quickly revived him, and as his eyelids fluttered open he could see Herbert Gage bending over him. Jonathan struggled to sit up.

"Get in there and chop open the wall!" he cried feebly.

Gage pushed him gently down. "Take it easy, neighbor," he said soothingly. "You'll be all right."

"But it's climbing up inside the wall!" Jonathan screamed in a frenzy.

"Hold it, brother, hold it. Everything's all right."

"Do as I tell you!" Jonathan raged. "Chop it open upstairs!"

"Quiet, Jonathan," Gage said gently. "We did chop it open upstairs. We got an extinguisher on it and the fire is under control. Another bucket of water and it will be out entirely. Just keep quiet a little while and you'll be all right."

Jonathan stopped struggling. "You say the fire's out? And the house is safe?"

"I'm telling you it's safe! Turn around there and take a look at it—you are the one who saved it for us. If it hadn't been for you we wouldn't have known where to fight the fire—and we wouldn't have had the water to finish the job."

Jonathan raised his head and looked around. The house was there all right—same as ever. He turned his head and looked the other way. On the wagon stood Barbara in the act of handing down a bucket of water to the tall fellow in brass buttons. At Shadrach's head was Sarah, patting him and telling him he was a wonderful charger. To one side stood Margie, looking a little sheepish, with her notebook and an armful of priceless antiques she had saved when she thought the house was going up in flames.

With a long breath of satisfaction Jonathan dropped back.

Matilda sat placidly in her rocker by the roadside when at last Jonathan returned with Shadrach ambling slowly along. "Well, what about that fire?" she asked.

Jonathan was still feeling a little wobbly as he replied, "We got it out."

"Couldn't have been much of a fire—I didn't see nuthin' but smoke."

"There was plenty of that." Jonathan passed his hand across his forehead. "It liked to knocked me out."

Matilda stood up. "What kep' you so long? You took time enough to put out half a dozen fires."

"I was talkin' to that feller they call George, the one in the uniform, and what do you s'pose he told me?"

"I ain't doin' no s'posin'. You might as well go ahead and tell me."

"He says our Matt's a sailor in the war. Been submarined twice and got his picture in the paper!"

Matilda blinked. "Our Matt in the war . . . ?" she gasped.

"That's what George says. Matt was floatin' around on a rubber raft for sixteen days before he was rescued."

Matilda's eyes filled. "Why, that boy musta been starved. I'd like to cooked him a good meal of hot vittles—I know just what he likes."

"The whole story was in the newspaper. George says he's got a copy at home. Says he'll send it to us when he gets back."

Matilda wiped away an escaped tear. "I knew that boy had the stuff in him, if there was only some way to bring it out."

Jonathan nodded. "I guess it must be the old Pilgrim blood. You can't beat that breed. Well, we might as well be gettin' on down to Uncle Walter's. He'll be expectin' us. There's some'pm I want to ask him anyway—what does a caretaker do?"